FALCON'S QUEST

KATHLEEN GARNSEY

Publishing Coordinator – Sharon Kizziah-Holmes

Paperback-Press
an imprint of A & S Publishing
A & S Holmes, Inc.

ISBN -13: 978-1-951772-14-7

CHAPTER ONE

Falcon cringed when another wave of pain ripped through his battered body. Scorching twin suns baked his burnt skin a darker shade of red than it had last sun-cycle. At least he thought he'd been lying in the sharp crystal sands for only two sun-cycles, or had it been three?

By the stars, he had no idea where he was, why he was here, or how he'd arrived in such a place. From the ache in his head, and inability to move any part of his body, he assumed he was severely injured. What little he could see from his prone position gave little hope of rescue. About the only thing he knew was the name embroidered on the left shoulder of the uniform he wore, Falcon Rovarn. That must be who he was, unless he was wearing someone else's clothes.

At the rate his skin was burning nothing would matter. He'd be dead before the moon-cycle appeared. His throat was so dry it felt grittier than the desolate sand beneath his body. His eyes closed and his eyelids stung from the intense heat of the twin-suns. At this point pain was a good thing, it meant he was still alive and conscious. Dizziness and nausea washed through him with an intense vengeance. He summoned every ounce of energy still available in his body in an effort to move one hand, yet his fingers refused and lay in the sand still as death.

It seemed as if his entire body belonged to another entity. All he had control of was his mind, and he feared even that was rapidly slipping from his grasp. His stomach rebelled violently, yet there was nothing inside to purge. Without food, water and shelter there was no hope.

Sadly, he doubted anyone, anywhere would mourn him. Would anyone even know he was missing? Gone from where? A silent curse was all he could manage as even the power of speech had been taken from him. How? So many questions raced through his mind, but he was too bone tired and drained to care what the answers were.

Death would be welcome under the circumstances, yet something deep inside begged him to live. Survival instinct? Possibly. Whatever his feelings might be, a dire urgency gnawed him to solve the mystery and be on his way to. Right now he could not remember what the mystery was, where he was headed or why. It seemed all he had were questions without answers.

Everything abruptly went black. He tried to lift his lids, but they would no longer open at his will. This was it. The end. For some reason he regretted dying alone.

CHAPTER TWO

Arella held up her hand to halt the scouting party she led. She wiped her forehead with her forearm. The heat of this blasted desert was more than irritating, it was unbearable. Living beings should not have to endure such conditions. There were other locations on Nacrem with far better climates.

"What is it, Counselor?"

She glanced at Gorcey, her military chief. "There's something down there in the sand."

"I'll see to it."

While Gorcey and three of her men rode their esroths down the slope into the gulley, she hoped that whatever lay in the crystal sands was not another threat to her people. She had only held a seat on Nacrem's council for one annual-cycle, and in that time she'd already dealt with far too many threats to want to face yet another.

Gorcey waved his arm in the air then pointed down. "Councilor, it's a human, not of our planet. His heart still beats, but not for long."

This was a major complication. She'd been sent to the farthest corner of Nacrem where life was simple and as low-tech as she'd ever seen. There was no med-unit and no med-tec in attendance. She had no choice in this assignment, especially since she was the first woman to ever hold a council seat. She had very little authority, but it was a start for the women of Nacrem. A pathetic start, but she was determined to be a success in her position, and a shining example for other women to follow.

Gorcey crested the hill and pulled his mount to a stop next to Arella. "What is your wish, Councilor?"

"Take the men back to Mardin, bring supplies and a liter to carry him back. I'll stay with him until you return."

"I'll leave a guard for you."

"Fine." She watched her military chief slap a hand on his chest in the traditional salute before he and his two warriors turned their esroths and rode toward home. Home was where one's family and friends were, and the sad truth was, she had no home in that sense. A place to sleep and work, yes, but she could not use the word she longed to use to describe where she stayed.

Arella walked her esroth over to where the remaining guard waited. "Keep watch here." With a nudge of her heels her esroth carefully made his way down the slope toward the black clad man. When she reached the flat, sandy bottom, she quickly dismounted, grabbed her water flask and knelt next to the intruder.

The man was rather handsome. He was fair of face even though he had several sun-cycles' growth of facial hair and a severe sunburn. His strong features indicated strength and diligence, while long dark lashes lay on red, exposed cheeks. From his muscled build she assumed he was a warrior of some sort.

There was a name embroidered on his shoulder, Falcon Rovarn, if it was indeed his garment. At least his uniform covered most of him so only his face, neck and hands would pain him. She removed the stopper from the flask, slipped a hand behind his head, held him up a bit and trickled water over his lips.

"Open your mouth. Drink, stranger. You don't want to die." His skin was so hot she felt the burn on her hand. Her stomach fluttered. Just his presence unsettled her, but then, she was not accustomed to tenderly touching men, only fighting them. It was plain this man had no fight left in him. If he lived out the sun-cycle it would surprise her.

Many humans had been found in the Crystal Desert, but none had survived. The sun's rays over Nacrem's desert areas mixed with the minerals in the sand, and that formed a toxic chemical blend which was fatal if absorbed for more than one sun-cycle without telmet cream to protect the skin. Normally when they found someone they would be mumbling incoherently, but since he was unconscious he was even closer to expiring. He might be gone before her men returned.

A lump rose in the sand close to the man's feet. Arella released the man, pulled the small sword from the scabbard on her belt and raised it over the growing mound. A moment later a sardnake reared its ugly head, salivating teeth moving straight for the man's leg. Without further thought she swung her weapon down and decapitated the desert scavenger. She hated those nasty creatures. She hated this entire place with a passion. However, she'd do her duty as required and pray for a better assignment.

The man still had not moved a muscle. She placed two fingers on the side of his burnt neck and sighed when she found his nearly imperceptible pulse. It would be a shame to see such a powerfully built, handsome man die. What color were his eyes? He had a look of importance about him she could not fully define. Maybe it was his hair, dark, silky and quite long, a sight not often seen on Nacrem. Her men all shaved their heads and wore the traditional revoc cloth tied turban style.

There was nothing ordinary about this man, including the way he made her feel. She had no words to describe what stirred within her when she gazed upon his perfect face. She doubted he was a warrior since he bore not one scar. She lightly touched his cheek and hoped he would stir. Once again, she lifted his head and trickled water over his lips. She smiled when he opened his mouth slightly and allowed some of the water to slide down his parched throat.

The sound of hooves alerted her of her men's approach. After allowing him a couple more swallows, she released him and stood to greet the rescue party. No orders were necessary. This group had rescued many travelers from the death grip of the Crystal Desert. None ever lived to thank them for their efforts, yet she held a high hope that this striking man with a foreign look might be the first.

That was like wishing for a true moon-cycle on Nacrem, a planet that enjoyed perpetual light due to twin suns during the sun-cycle, and one sun during what should be the moon-cycle. When the twin suns set the other sun rose, which kept darkness away from the entire planet.

With little effort Gorcey and the others secured the visitor to the liter and began their journey back to Mardin. It was little more than a refugee outpost, but the League wanted to increase the population, plus they needed the crystal. It seemed that those who took the miserable jobs here were a rough and tumble lot who loved to drink after work which turned into fights. It was about all there was to do in this isolated, desolate location.

They trudged slowly through the hot desert sands and she thought they would never reach Mardin. The man on the liter did not look alive. He bounced along behind Gorcey's esroth until finally they reached the settlement and stopped in front of the healer's establishment, the only place where medicines and care were available.

Relief washed over Arella when the healer, Marca, opened the door and stepped outside to greet them, concern in her aged eyes. "We've brought a man in dire need of your care." Arella dismounted, handed her reins to Gorcey's assistant and walked to the end of the liter. "He's near death."

Marca opened one of the man's eyelids. "Has he opened his eyes? Groaned? Made any sound at all?"

"He tried to swallow some water I poured in his mouth, but that's it."

"Not good. That's just a natural reflex to keep from choking." Marca walked back to the entrance. "Bring him in."

Gorcey and his assistant picked the man up, carried him inside and placed him on the examining table in the med-room. Without ceremony, Marca cut the man's clothes from his body so quickly Arella did not even have time to look away. Or was it she did not wish to look away? The sight of a rippled stomach and bulging biceps took her breath away. He was magnificent. Every inch of him perfection, including the parts of him she should not have noticed. Ashamed for her curiosity she turned her back on the activity and went to the sink to wash her hands.

In the mirror over the sink she noted Marca had draped a small blanket over his manhood. She dried her hands then returned to the examining table to watch and to pray, for it was all she could do for the man. "What do you think?"

Marca scowled. "He's a fine looker, that's for sure. Too bad he won't be with us long." She smiled. "Then again, if he's half as strong as he looks, he just might have a bit of a chance."

Arella sighed. "A bit is not much."

"True, but I fear a bit of a chance is all he has." Marca scanned him with the violet light wand that fed information into the computer. "Oh my," she said, staring at the diagnosis screen.

"What?" Arella held her breath, fearful the man had already passed from this life. She waited while Marca continued to scan the man, thankful the League had at least allowed her to bring some high-tec med equipment to this God-forsaken place.

"It's been four sun-cycles since he has last eaten." Marca looked at Arella. "Did you give him water?"

"Only a swallow."

"It's a start." She gave him an injection of some kind, inserted a needle connected to a tube and a bag of gold liquid that she hung on a holder over his head. "I'm afraid he has absorbed a high amount of the toxic minerals from the sand."

"Will that kill him?"

"Not sure. As you know, everyone had died from exposure, so I cannot say." Marca looked into Arella's eyes. "'Tis all I can do for now, however, he must not be left alone." She checked her timepiece. "I cannot stay, I'm needed at the mine. An accident I'm told. Would have already been gone if Gorcey hadn't caught me locking the door earlier."

Arella smiled at Marca. "I'll stay with him. +I'll certainly be in no danger."

"True enough. If he survives the starvation, dehydration, and the burns, we'll see if the toxins have an adverse effect. All in all, he might make it." Marca patted Arella's hand. "Do what you can for him. If he wakes at all, give him all he wants to drink. Hold food from him for a bit. We need to start him back to the living slow and easy if he. . ."

"I understand. You go. I'll be fine."

"He may burn with fever from the sun toxins. Sponge his skin with cold water. Apply telmet cream and keep him as comfortable as possible."

Arella nodded her agreement to Marca who then quickly strode out of the med unit.

Gorcey snapped to attention. "Will there be anything else, Councilor?"

"No. Dismissed."

Gorcey slapped a hand on his chest then left the room with his two other men. Here she was, alone again with this man she found herself strangely attracted to. She must be sick to have such a thought about a man she'd never met and who was on the verge of death. By the stars! She could not keep her gaze from him, especially with all that bare bronze skin that lay before her.

She pulled a chair from the corner of the room and sat next to the table where he remained still as a stone. Her fingers found his forearm of their own volition and she traced a path to his fingertips. He was extremely hot. She walked to the sink, filled a basin with cold water, picked up the sponge and returned to her patient. With care, she started her ministrations on his arms, moving higher to his powerful shoulders. The hair on his forearms and chest seemed odd since the men of Nacrem had no hair on their bodies. He also had hair on his muscled toned legs and she could not resist running her hand lightly over his skin, the feel of the hairs on her palm excited and enticed her. She dipped the sponge in the water because it was safer than touching him with her bare hands. She soaked down his hair and gently wiped his forehead.

Who was this mystery man? Did he have a family? How did he come to be in the Crystal Desert? She remembered Gorcey saying he was not of their planet, which sent a whole new series of questions floating through her mind. They would have to wait, or go unanswered. Fate was a funny thing, and she tried not to question it, but this sun-cycle only substantiated the many turns fate could take. As a woman she had much to prove to the League, as a Councilor she had several decisions to make. The first being, what to do with this man? Should she report his appearance, or wait to see if he recovered first?

At the moment she was too tired to think. She pulled a deep breath into her lungs and finished sponging his body, all except the parts under the cloth. He did feel cooler. His neck, hands and face were turning a bright shade of red, as expected. She found the telmet cream Marca used for burns and generously applied it to all the red areas, her fingertips ablaze once again from the feel of his bare skin. Marca was right, the man was certainly a looker, and it would indeed be a pity not to learn more about him. She sat in the chair to regain her composure, ashamed for even having such a reaction to the unconscious man. Closing her eyes felt good, something she had not done in far too long.

CHAPTER THREE

A deep groan rumbled through Falcon's burning body when he tried to move. His face was on fire, as were his hands and neck. His stomach was empty and his throat dryer than the very sand itself. Beneath his fingers he felt something hard. Not desert! His eyelids opened and a sterile white ceiling slowly came into focus. He blinked several times, aware that at least his eyes were responding to the request of his brain. Where in the universe was he?

When he turned his head, his mouth fell open at the sight before him. A woman sat curled in an overstuffed chair at the side of his bed, sleeping. Sunlight streamed through the window behind her and kissed the strands of her honey-colored hair. It was not exactly blond, and yet not brown, but the luxurious strands were as beautiful as the face they framed. Long lashes lay on flawless tan cheeks. Her kissable lips were slightly parted, and he thought if she smiled, she might have a dimple on the left side since he saw one tiny indentation where one should be.

As loud as he could, he cleared his throat. He did want to meet this lovely lady, but more than that, he desperately needed a drink. The gesture worked. She opened her eyes and jumped to her feet so fast it would have made him dizzy had he not be lying down. "Hello," he managed to croak. "Could I please have a drink?" The lovely creature stared at him as if he were from another planet and spoke a foreign language. Both might be true, but how would he know since he didn't even know his own name.

"You're. . .You're. . ."

"Thirsty?" He smiled at her astonishment. "I'm either alive, or you're a heavenly being beyond human life."

She picked up a glass of water and held it close to his lips. "Heavenly being I am no. Alive makes you."

Falcon repressed a chuckle. She spoke the Universal language of The Protectorate, but very badly, yet coming from her it sounded musical. Was that a memory? No, since he had no idea what function The Protectorate served. Knowledge was a funny thing, like a computer. Computers stored information but gave no real thoughts of concern where the information came from as long as they were functional and correct.

Falcon lifted his head and drank greedily, water running down the sides of his mouth. He finished off the first glass and she refilled it and helped him down the contents. "Thank you." He pushed himself to a sitting position. "I moved! I actually moved my arms and legs!" The woman stared at him as if he had lost his mind. Okay, he had, but she did not know that small fact yet.

For the first time, Falcon realized his lack of garments. His nakedness, even in front of this lovely woman, did not bother him. What kind of a man did that make him? Did he have a reputation with women? Did he have one woman he remained faithful to? Right nowhe was more concerned about quenching his thirst and filling his empty stomach. "I believe I owe you many thanks for saving my life."

"Welcome, you are. Name do you have?"

When he finished his second glass of water he replied, "Falcon, I think."

"Know not? Only think?"

"Actually, I have lost my memory." He studied her quizzical expression until she started to blush. "I was hoping you might have some idea of who I am, and how I got to this location." He gave her a grin that always turned a woman's head. Whether that thought was instinct or memory he didn't know. The woman's blush deepened, so he must be having some effect on her. "By the way, where am I?"

"Mardin, town of."

"What planet?" The look on her face was priceless. It would appear this young, innocent woman had never left the confines of her home let alone her planet. She was a beauty. He had no memory of other women so there was no one to compare her to, but he knew what he liked, and he liked her.

"Of course, Nacrem. Where think you?"

"That seems to be the problem. I have no idea." Falcon grinned. This slip of a woman dressed more like a male soldier, spoke so quaintly he was enthralled. However unflattering the leather garb was, he had to admit that every feminine curve she had was displayed quite well, and he deemed her to be in fine order. "Maybe you should bring whoever is in charge here so I might have a few words with him. Would that be possible?"

The scathing look she gave him said in no uncertain terms that he had made a grievous error. Her extraordinary lavender eyes turned dark and dangerous. "I'm sorry if I have offended you in any way, my lady. That was not my intent. I just. . ."

"Women no in charge, assume you? Ignorant in bed too much to be out?"

This time he had to laugh, which only made her angrier. He knew she meant he thought women were only good for one thing, warming a man's bed. Her glare pierced his burning skin and he wiped the smile from his face. "Never would I think such an archaic thing, and I apologize if I gave you the wrong idea." Falcon wrapped the small blanket around him to cover his backside that felt a bit drafty. "By the galaxy!" He held up his hands, twisted them, raised his arm, then kicked his legs. "It feels so good to move. I thought for sure I was paralyzed for life."

"Why think you paralyzed?" She stepped closer and stared into his eyes. "Sun of ours poisons, but paralyze no."

"That is good news, but it doesn't explain what happened to me." Her eyes roved his chest and he wondered if he was unlike the men of this planet. He suddenly felt like a science project. "Did you find a ship?" She just stared. "You know, a spacecraft?" Her gaze did not waver and her expression remained blank. "Did you see any kind of conveyance I might have traveled in?"

"Con. .con. . .veeeey ounce?"

"A means of travel." This was not going well. He eased his feet to the floor and stood. Dizziness and nausea assailed him and he sat back down. Not a good sign. The woman still stared at him. Had he grown horns? "We seem to have a bit of a language barrier here."

"Bad I speak Universal, learned just. Long have way back."

"Long way to go." Falcon chuckled to himself. "You're doing fine."

"No fine."

"Yes fine." He pushed himself back up to his feet and this time he managed to remain upright.Slowly he made his way to the foot of the examining table. He let out the breath he'd held during those very important steps. At least his legs worked again, even if he were weak as a newborn. He sat in the chair by the bed and stared at his burning, red hands.

"Help you, I will."

Falcon watched as she walked to a cabinet, removed a jar of something and returned to him. She removed the lid, scooped out some green cream and began to massage it into his hands. Instantly the burning quieted. When she finished with his hands she began to smooth more of the soothing stuff on his cheeks. Her tentative touch told him she was not used to men.

"I thank you for your help." He thought he detected the beginning of a smile and decided he wanted to know how she'd look if she were to laugh. Her hands found his forehead, nose and ears.

"Welcome you are." She stopped her movements. "Close eyes, you must."

He closed his eyes, her feather light touch spread cream over his eyelids. It was a relief to the burning, and he knew without her, he would be dead. "Who is in charge here?"

"Councilor Arella."

"May I see Councilor Arella?"

"Looking at her, you are."

It was his turn to stare. Angel, turned med-tec, turned ruler. "So happy I am to greet you, Arella."

"Mock me, you do?"

With a smile he shook his head. "Never."

"Backwards might I say things, forwards I know right to be."

"You're a very intelligent woman, Arella." Her name sounded like musical notes, her voice soothing, her beauty more than pleasing. Just the thought of her as a woman stirred parts of him that were best left at rest for the moment. "Where are my clothes?"

"Marca off cut them."

He was afraid to ask what that meant. "May I have them, please?"

"Most certainly."

She bent down and retrieved a pile of rags from the floor that were the same color as the uniform he'd been wearing. Just his luck. Stuck in an unknown place, half starved, weak as a babe and naked as one could be. He took the paltry offering and examined the fabric. Not much left, but he felt something in the pocket of the pants. He removed three items and laid them in his lap.

Arella stepped to his side. "Have you what there?"

"I wish I knew." He glanced up at her questioning gaze and desperately wished he had the answers they both wanted to know. Never had he felt this helpless or stupid. Unfortunately he knew of nothing to return a lost memory except time, and he was not sure how much of that he might have. Something inside him screamed an urgency to move on, to find something or someone, yet he had no idea of who or why.

"Hungry are you?"

"I could eat a gastrodomos."

"Sorry. Have no gastro. . .dooo. . ."

"Just a joke."

"Joke?"

Falcon sighed. He knew he shouldn't joke with a person who did not understand his language well enough, but he couldn't help himself. "It means saying something to make another person laugh." Again, she just stared.

"I have not done a very good job of. . ." He stopped in mid-sentence not even sure of what he was saying or doing. Maybe the sun had done more damage than he thought. If his memory did not return he'd be doomed to an existence he could not tolerate. Whoever he was, he knew he'd never accept failure.

"Eat you must." Arella walked to the door. "Be back, I will."

The door shut behind her. "And a nice backside you have, my little saving angel." Since he was in this position he had to look for the positive, and Arella was the only good thing so far. Food would be most welcome, but he grew impatient, angry and overly frustrated. He felt as if he were born an hour ago and had no knowledge of anything except pain and speech. Yet how could he remember to speak and nothing else?

"Damn the fates!" Falcon stood, laid the three mysterious items from his pants' pocket on the chair, secured the sheet around himself and started to walk. At least his legs worked better even if he were still weak. This situation was impossible. How did one even go about remembering?

He studied the room while he meandered in a circle around the examining table. There were jars filled with meds and bandages. Various charts of the human body hung on the wall with labels next to things in a foreign language. Nothing made sense. He had an overpowering urge to escape, yet he had no idea why, or where he'd go even if he could. When he returned to his chair he stared at the items from his pocket. Surely there was some clue here if he studied them long enough.

The first item was a small, metal cylinder that looked to contain something he felt would be used for self-defense. Of course, there was no actual reasoning behind any of his assumptions, simply gut reactions which made him wonder if he were even close to right. Next, he picked up a small green opaque stone that seemed to light up the room. When he reached for the flat, round metal disk the image of a spacecraft flashed through his mind. He placed it in his hand, its weight barely noticeable even though it covered his palm. With one finger he traced the outer edge of the object stopping at a recessed button on the side. When he pressed down on it a lid a popped open and a small vid-screen came into view. For the first time, a ray of hope surged through him.

The door opened and his lovely rescuer stepped in carrying a tray laden with various dishes of food and pieces of fruit. He closed the object and slipped it under his leg when he sat back down. "I thank you for your kindness, Councilor Arella."

"Welcome, you are, Sir Master Falcon."

He didn't have the heart to correct her speech. "Will you join me?"

"In what?"

"Share this meal with me." He smiled. "I could use the company, and conversation."

"Conveeersaa. . ."

"It simply means talking between two or more people."

"Talk, yes. Is fine." Arella laid the tray across his lap. "Eat you. Strength you need."

"You're right." He picked up a spoon and ate some of the soup that steamed in the glass bowl. "Very good. What kind of soup is this?"

"Ask you the cook, you must. My department this is not."

"Then tell me about your department." He continued to eat while Arella stared. "What is your job?"

"These people backwards, they are. I needs bring them into tec world."

Falcon took a bite of fresh bread. "Is that another place from here?"

"Funny you are. Technology they have not much. Bring it to them, I must."

"How will you do that?"

"Time is little."

He laughed. "A little at a time?" She nodded.

"Laugh at me again, do you?"

"As I said, I would never laugh at you, only with you." Falcon polished off every last bite of soup and bread while she simply watched him. Arella had a seriousness about her that made her appear sad and lonely. That assumption could be as wrong as the others he'd made this sun-cycle, but her expression did not lie. No woman who was beautiful and smart should be lonely.

"Clothes I will get you. Naked you cannot be."

"My thanks." His gaze followed the sway of her hips when she walked out of the room which caused his burns to grow hotter. That woman could prove to be quite a handful, and he had no desire to make her angry. If he were honest with himself, he wanted to hear her moan in passion and see the look on her face when he brought her to fulfillment. More delusions from the sun. He really had lost his mind in the desert, or he was indeed the worst kind of scoundrel who only used women. If he was not a scoundrel, then Arella had a most dangerous effect on him, one he would have to work hard to control.

It was that tight-fitting warrior garb she wore that turned him on hotter than a lazer light. Still, he doubted she was as tough as she pretended. There was far more to Arella than the way she dressed and the brave face she put on to reassure him. She hid something deep in her soul, and he must be hiding his own demons to recognize hers.

CHAPTER FOUR

Arella assessed the clothing in supply, not sure any of it would fit this stranger's muscular frame. He was broader in the chest and arms than any of the other men, and when her mind wandered to all the parts of him that were larger she felt her skin flush with the same heat that assailed her every time she got too close to him. It was disconcerting to say the least, and she hated not being in control of her mind and body at all times, but the sight of his massive chest and muscular arms did cause her heart to flutter, and her lungs to malfunction. Clothes, she must find clothes.

On the top shelf, labeled extra-large, she found a cloth tunic and leather pants that would have to work since there was nothing bigger. She grabbed the largest pair of socks and boots supply held and headed back down the hall to the med-room. When she opened the door she could not help the smile that tugged at the corners of her mouth. Falcon's head was tipped to the side, one leg draped over the arm of the chair causing quite a gap in the sheet. She shook her head and willed her gaze not to look at the blatant display of manhood she was sure to find open to her view. He had no idea what he did to her—or did he?

If he thought he could waltz in here and get information from her by seduction he was sadly mistaken. She tossed the clothes into his lap and dropped the boots to the floor one bouncing badly, landing on his left foot. He nearly jumped out of his skin. He was on his feet so fast it startled her, his hands wrapped around her throat. "Sorry," she croaked.

"Arella, I. ." Falcon immediately released her. "Never sneak up on a warrior when he's sleeping unless you want to be harmed."

"Warrior? This is what you are?"

"I must be or I would never have grabbed you the way I did. My apologies." He returned to his chair.

Warrior. Of course he was a warrior. He certainly had the build for it with muscles bulging in places most men only dreamed of, yet he took it all for granted. Possibly all men were built the same as he where he came from. Her heart still raced so fast she had trouble catching her breath. "Scared me, you did, but afraid I was not." Of course she lied, but she would not have this man think her a coward. She was half warrior herself and proud of her abilities. If she had not trained so well and passed all the tests given to men she never would have earned this post.

"Thank you for the clothing. I am deeply indebted to you, my fair Councilor."

"First dress you, then we conveeersss. .talk."

"You have a deal."

"Deal? I wish not to play with you."

Falcon laughed. "It does not always indicate what one does in a card game, it also means an agreement. I will dress and be more than happy to speak with you."

"Eagerly I await down hall in office. Door is my name. When ready, you are." She could not wait to shut the door behind her and take a deep, fortifying breath. Why it was so difficult to breathe with Falcon in the room she couldn't guess, but he robbed her of her ability to fill her lungs. She quickly made her way to her office, opened the door and stepped inside. Behind her desk she all but fell into the soft Ekove leather chair.

What would she do with this man? That thought was dangerous if she considered her options too long. He was perfectly built and glowed with strength, charm and intelligence. Falcon was a difficult man to ignore, but for her own good, she would handle him professionally. She had no interest in men—could not afford to be interested. To date, men had only caused her pain and suffering, so why would any woman consider taking a man as a mate and be possessed? No. She refused to be owned, mind or body, by a man who only cared about his own interests. Rarely had she seen a woman on her planet make a love match that was truly happy.

A knock on the door interrupted her musings. "Enter." And he did, looking like a Nacrem God of legend, sculpted to perfection in all the right places. The leather pants hugged his legs, reminding her just how muscled he was, and the white fabric of the tunic strained across his chest, barely hiding leashed power.

She'd forgotten to give him a sash, so at least she did not have to look at his trim waist. She could only imagine his true strength, and a part of her wished for a demonstration. "Please, Falcon, seated be you." She gestured to the pair of hand polished Brackenwood chairs in front of her desk. Dear stars, she hoped her speech would not embarrass her further. She felt plain stupid trying to hold a conversation with this monster of a man.

"What did you wish to speak to me about, Councilor Arella?"

"Attention you have created in me."

"Excuse me?"

"For something you do?"

"No, I'm afraid I don't understand you."

"Forgive me, you will. Wrong I speak, this know us both. By the morrow, better I will be, this is word to you give."

"You speak fine. I just didn't understand what you meant by attention."

"Yes. Explain I will. You have need to go somewhere, yes?" She watched him nod. "Where be this place?" Her heart ached for him when he shook his head with such a lost look in his dark eyes. "Then we find you a place. Agree?"

"Agree. And how do you purpose to find this place I'm to go to?"

"Know I do not. However he, head of Nacrem League, can decision make. Together we attend League."

"Sounds like a plan. Where is this League?"

"In Votrella. Nacrem Capitol."

"When do we leave?"

"Immediate, if your health okays trip." He looked tired, and she knew he had to be in pain from the burns on his skin. In fact, it was a miracle the man was even alive let alone moving around. She certainly did not need him collapsing on her while they traveled. There was no rush, except for the fact his presence bothered her in ways she couldn't explain. "On thought second, we wait one sun-cycle. Then, decide I will." He nodded his consent. Now she had to find him a place to stay.

"I am well enough to travel now, Councilor. It would not be a problem. I'm afraid staying here would create more inconvenience for you."

"Inconveeeen. . . eance you are." He stared at her strangely and she wondered what she'd just said. This moon-cycle she'd wear the headpiece, and by the morrow the Universal tongue would roll off her lips. The only reason she had not worked harder at learning the Protectorate's Universal Language was the lack of necessity. Only a few ambassadors from The Protectorate had ever even visited here, and she was not high enough in rank to speak with them. The twelve High Councilors and a select few of the sixty regular Councilors in the League were allowed to deal in off-world affairs, and all of them were fluent in Universal, and soon she would be also.

Arella stood. "Stay here, you will. Back I will be." She left her office and walked down the hall to the guard's headquarters where she found several men gathered around a small table playing Arkatar. Why men liked to waste their credits on a dice game she'd never understand. As soon as the men realized she was there they all rose and saluted. "Please be seated."

"What can we do for you Councilor?" Gorcey asked.

"Our survivor will live. He will need quarters for the moon-cycle."

"We will take care of it. How does he fare?"

"He'll recover." Arella saw questions all over Gorcey's face, and she sensed he held animosity for the stranger. "He only speaks Universal. He has no memory of who he is. Next sun-cycle I'll take him to the League. They can decide what to do with him."

"I'll ready a team to escort you, Councilor."

"That will not be necessary. I want all of you to stay here. What if there are others like him? See if you can determine how he arrived here. Patrol the area with diligence, Gorcey. You're in charge while I'm away."

"Of course, however, I must insist you take guards with you.

Your safety must be insured."

"This man is no threat. We'll travel faster alone. I also don't want to call attention to ourselves. Two travelers will not be noticed."

"I still must officially protest this, Councilor. And I. . ."

"You think me a foolish woman, Gorcey?" It was written in his eyes, as it had been since her arrival. Half her reason for going alone with Falcon was to get away from these overly biased men. She knew he'd never admit how he resented her being in charge. "Are we clear?"

"We are." Gorcey saluted.

Arella turned and left the men to their game. She almost hated to turn an unsuspecting stranger over to those bullies to taunt, yet she had no choice. He could not share her small, simple quarters. It was not accepted to sleep with a man before life-mating. Sure, many women did such things regularly, but she was a Councilor, and her position dictated she keep her reputation beyond reproach. Granted, it was a bit of a risk traveling alone with the man, but if all went well, the trip would be over in one sun-cycle.

CHAPTER FIVE

Falcon lay on the rough cot and listened to the men chatter away at his expense. Damn. He may not know what they were really saying about him, but he knew he was the butt of their jokes. Nacrem. Who had ever even heard of this planet? That thought cemented the idea that he was definitely an off-worlder.

He stared at the flat, white ceiling and listened to footsteps heading toward his bed. Without looking he knew it was Gorcey, the one Arella indicated was in charge. Gorcey had it in for him and did not even try to hide his aggression. He wished his hands didn't burn so badly because before this moon-cycle was over he'd more than likely have to pass some kind of warrior's test. If these men were like his, then it would definitely happen. Warriors he knew.

His men? Was that a memory? Was he in charge of a crew, or simply one of the men? That he couldn't remember, but fighting and a warrior's way of thinking were foremost in his mind. It was a very strong feeling, so it had to be part of his recent past. He'd learned long ago never to ignore his inner voices because they were always right.

Gorcey stood at the side of his bed, babbling something that sounded derogatory. Why couldn't the man just go to sleep and leave him alone? Temptation was too great. Falcon rose to a sitting position and placed his feet on the floor. The boots Arella provided fit reasonably well, but they were not as hard as the ones he was used to wearing. Was that a memory flash? Hopefully. He was obviously a warrior who wore tough boots. He shook his head and rose to his feet and stared at Gorcey. The man kept babbling, then shoved a fist into his shoulder in an effort to knock him off balance.

"What is it you want, soldier? Your endless chatter bores me."

Gorcey shoved him again. That was it. In a flash he grabbed Gorcey's wrist and wrenched it behind the man's back. "You are an idiot. Too bad you don't understand me. I'd love to clean the floor with your face, but for Arella's sake, I won't." He released the man. Gorcey took a step back while several of his men moved closer. This could get ugly and he was not in the physical condition to take on the lot of them. He sat back down on his bunk and held up his hands. "I do not mean any of you harm. All I want is some rest."

At that statement he lay back down, turned toward the wall and hoped they'd tire of this useless game. There was a lot of grumbling, some shouting and name calling, or so he thought, but they finally returned to their silly gambling game, and for that, he was grateful. His entire body felt like it had been badly beaten. Even though he'd eaten, his stomach cramped and his head throbbed. The burnt skin cried for relief. The soothing effects of whatever cream Arella used had faded, but he'd sure like to have her apply more.

Arella's touch had been like heaven. He wondered if there was a woman in his life, someone he shared his bed with? Certainly that memory would be strong enough to return, if he did indeed have such experiences. Time was his only friend, and he feared it was also his worst enemy. He pulled the blanket over himself and with as little motion as possible removed the flat, round disk from his pocket. There was enough light in the room he could study it, and from the sounds the guards made, they were engrossed in wasting their credits.

When he popped the lid he stared at the insignia on the small vid-screen. There were fourteen planets in a circle with two crossed swords in the center, which must mean something. With his index finger he touched the center of the screen. It immediately changed and he heard a feminine voice say, "Welcome, Falcon Rovarn. Enter password."

Okay, he must be Falcon, but with no memory he had no password. It was possible to make a few guesses. "Warrior," he whispered to the disk. "Password in error. All information will be destroyed if incorrect password is given again." With a curse he slammed the lid down and shoved it back into his pocket. He sensed he needed whatever information was in the mini computer. He closed his eyes with a feeling of failure the likes of which he assumed he'd never experienced.

~ ~ ~ ~

"Falcon?" Arella put her hand on his shoulder and shook him. Before she could take another breath he was on his feet, his arm around her throat, his other hand on the side of her head as if he were about to snap her neck. Before she could utter a protest he released her.

"My apologies, Councilor Arella." He stepped back.

"You did warn me not to surprise a warrior. It's my own fault." He squinted at her and gazed with a strange look on his face. The man did truly seem lost and disoriented. "Is something wrong?"

"Your speech, it's perfect. What happened?"

"I told you this sun-cycle you'd see an improvement."

Falcon shook his head. "You're good. Very good."

"My thanks." Arella pointed to the table. "I've brought you some food before we begin our journey. Please." She watched him rise and walk to the table where he took a seat. He ate with a ferocious appetite and quickly finished everything she brought. "Would you like more?"

"No. I'm fine." He stood. "Let's go."

"Hold on there." She smiled and nodded for him to resume his seat, which he did rather unwillingly. He was a handful and she knew he would never be easily convinced of anything. "Our mounts are being readied as we speak, but it will be a little bit. So why don't you enjoy your juice and coffa since we won't be stopping for quite a while once we do leave.

He nodded and took a few sips of his quadra juice, which he did seem to like. Maybe he had the same fruit where he was from.

"Has any part of your memory returned yet?"

"Not really. Wish it had." He looked up from the glass in his hand. "I really mean that. I hate not knowing who I am, or what I'm doing here."

"Or how you got here?" She laughed at his quizzical expression. "What I mean by that is we are at a very remote location most people stay away from. There isn't much here except the crystal mines and a lot of sand and rocks."

"I didn't know about the mines, but I have noticed the sand."

"I'm well aware of that." She looked at his red hands and face. "How are you feeling this sun-cycle?"

"Better. My sun-exposed skin is on fire, but other than that, not too bad."

"Good. Our ride will be difficult and I wanted to be sure you were up to it. "Not if you want to get out of here. As I said. We are remote. Not even public transportation caters to us."

"Then I have no choice?"

She chuckled. "You catch on fast, and you're smart. I like that. I hate stupid people." Instantly she looked around the room. "For a moment I was afraid we weren't alone."

Falcon laughed. "I know exactly what you mean. I may not remember much, but stupidity has no place in my book."

"You're a writer?"

"No, it's just an expression, or at least I think it is. Somehow it just spilled out of my mouth."

Arella shrugged her shoulders. "I suppose that's good. Your memory is spilling out."

Falcon nodded and smiled. "How much longer will it be?" He looked at his wrist-piece.

"You act like you have an appointment to get to yet you cannot remember anything. You are a very confusing man."

"I apologize. I am in a hurry for everything, and my memory is at the top of the list. I just have this overwhelming feeling that I have a life and death mission resting on my shoulders. I can't shake the feeling that I'm letting someone very important down."

"Oh my. That sounds critical." She stood. "Shall we go?" He was on his feet before she could take her first step toward the door. "Follow me." She led him out of the men's quarters, into the hall, then quickly through the door that opened to the outside. When

Falcon stepped onto the porch and saw their mounts he stopped so fast he nearly fell over, taking her with him.

CHAPTER SIX

Y**ou want me to ride that?"** Falcon raised an eyebrow and stared at Arella.

"Unless you plan to walk." She smiled. "It is quite a distance on foot. I would not recommend walking."

"That is the sorriest looking beast I've ever seen. He's even too lazy to stand! Look at him."

"He is a she. And if she stood you could not mount her."

"What is she?"

"A Cameora. She will serve you well. Now mount up. My patience grows thin."

"Indeed." With a grumble Falcon mounted the sorry, hairy creature. The moment the animal felt his weight she rose to her feet and nearly unseated him. He held on to the strange looking saddle horn and went with the flow. Cameora? What next? "Does she have a name?"

"Hateu."

He would hate her all right, but he kept his remarks to himself. How could he criticize her world when he did not know what to compare it to? Hateu followed Arella's mount, if that's what one called these creatures. They slowly left the small, remote, little village behind. "I'm surprised Gorgon did not insist on coming with us."

"Gorcey. And he did."

"Thank the universe I don't see him."

"You may thank me. I insisted he stay behind and rule in my absence."

Falcon could not get over the change in her speech. Her Universal was now perfect. At least he wouldn't have to spend the day deciphering her words. He studied the scenery, such as it was. Tall rocks, flat rocks, and sand—tons of sand. Twin suns beat down on him and his hands burned even worse than yesterday. He should have asked Arella for more of that cream. He tucked his hands in his armpits to shade them from the suns' direct rays. The stupid animal he rode did not need to be directed since she had her head up the backside of Arella's mount every step of the way. How he hated deserts and Cremoras!

At that moment Arella turned in her saddle and gave him a good looking over. Her gaze made his heart pound in his chest. She was appealing in every sense of the word. Seductively beautiful might sum it up better. He'd love to create a tender memory with Arella. Why did that thought enter his mind so easily when everything else had   fled?

At least his natural instincts were still with him. He smiled back at her. She had no idea what watching her shapely backside did to him. If she realized, she would certainly ride behind him so he would not be able to enjoy the view.

Arella's hand raised and his mount stopped so fast he nearly flew over the ridiculous hump in front of him. He caught himself by grabbing a handful of the long hair that hung down the center of Hateu's lengthy neck. "Why are we stopping?" Without warning his animal went down on her front knees and threw him forward, then down on her back legs until she settled onto the hot sand.

He let out the breath he'd been holding. This animal made him nervous and he hated the feeling. He swung his leg over the top and rose to his feet. When he turned he was shocked to find Arella right in front of him.

"Hold out your hands."

Arella opened the small jar she held in her hand. "Bless you. I was hoping you'd remember."

"It is my job to remember such things."

"Too bad you can't remember things for me."

"I do not understand."

"My past. Who I am. That kind of remembering."

"I see."

Arella spread salve on the front and back of his hands. The feel of her soft touch awakened a demon inside him. He had an overpowering urge to pull her into his embrace and kiss her senseless. How inappropriate could he be? Well, there were other things he could think to do with this lovely woman, but nothing she would permit. "Thank you for your help."

"It is nothing." She moved her hands to his face.

"Damn!"

"I did not mean to hurt you."

"Hurt me?" She had no idea. "You did not hurt me. I just do not like injuries. They frustrate me. That's all." Her fingers massaged the ointment into his cheeks, over his nose, across his forehead and around to his ears. He would let her do that all day if she would. When her hand moved to the back of his neck he leaned toward her, moving so close her breath tickled his face. Damnation. He wanted this woman in his arms, her lips pressed to his, her tongue doing battle with. . ."

"Is something wrong?" Arella stepped back and replaced the lid on the jar.

"No. I thank you for your care." Falcon took a deep breath to get a grip on his runaway urges. "How far do we travel?"

"Be there before change of sun-cycle, we will."

For some reason she seemed a bit nervous and her speech slipped with her mood. Had their closeness affected her in the same manner? He could only hope he had aroused her feminine curiosity.

"Up to it, are you?"

"I'll be fine." Her nervous language slip was still in place, which only made him want to move closer. The thought made him smile, which had the opposite effect. Arella. all but ran back to her Cameora, jumped onto the saddle and spurred her animal into a run before the wretched thing even had steady footing. Then his mount lunged to her feet and ran after Arella. "I do hate you!" At that admonishment Hateu picked up speed with a strange sounding groan.

His stupid mount finally caught up with Arella and she stopped, grabbed Hateu's reigns and turned around. She looked amazing while she rode toward him on the large lumpy animal. Of course, a woman with her features could never look bad. She quickly made it back to him and gave Hateu a signal and she went down on her knees for him to mount. He swung his leg over the hump and barely had his balance when the cameora rose to her feet. He did not have to tell Hateu to move since she was on auto-pilot.

They rode for hours across scorching hot sands, past countless rocks, but no water, no people, no cities, nothing. What a foreboding place. If he had to be stranded why had he picked such a desolate planet? Like he had a choice. Why was he here? That question hovered above all others in his mind. Hopefully this League of hers would help him find the answers he so desperately needed.

Long shadows appeared across the desert sands and grew longer at a rapid rate. Great. Stuck in a vast desert in the dark. Not his idea of a vacation. They traveled on, yet darkness never fell even though it was past time for the moon-cycle to have taken over. He searched the sky for a moon, but instead found another sun rising on the opposite horizon. No wonder they had so much desert. In the distance he spotted the glow of lights. Thank the fates. Civilization at last!

CHAPTER SEVEN

A rella was not sure she was happy to be back in civilization after being away nearly an annual-cycle. Her supplies were brought to her, and the League requested her communications be kept to a minimum, so she had little contact with her fellow Councilors and none with the outside world. Out of the sixty members, she was the most junior in age and time on job. It was no secret the majority of the voting body had not wanted her on the council. If it had not been for her mentor, Eldron Passer, she would not be in this position at all.

The city of Drearn was far more advanced than Marden, but nothing like Votrella. They had to leave their Cameoras at the boarding stable, then jump a flight to the capitol. It was late and most commercial flights stopped about this time. She turned her gaze to Falcon. The moment Hateu parked herself he slid from the saddle like a man in a hurry. Her stomach lurched when she remembered the closeness they shared. She could not erase the feel of his skin, or the look in his extraordinary blue eyes when he gazed at her.

She walked both Cameoras up to the stable booth where a man sat with his feet up on the desk. He looked over at the window where she stood.

"Can I help you?"

"I'm Councilor Arella and I need to stable two Cameoras for

several days. I'm not sure how long they will be here."

"That will cost you, Councilor.

"You need not be so gruff. I will pay you."

"Show me the color of your coin and I'll change my attitude."

Nasty little man, she thought while she handed him two kwaffa coins, which was outrageous for the short time the two Cameoras would be stabled here. When she turned to face Falcon he had a gruff expression, like he wanted to pounce on the stable master. "What's wrong?"

"I do not know your language, but that man was giving you trouble, and I have a strong urge to make him take back his words."

Arella laughed. "You don't even know what his words were."

"I don't need to know, only that he was rude and disrespectful to you, Councilor Arella."

"I appreciate your chivalry, Falcon, but it's best we do not draw undue attention to ourselves. You are a stranger here, and most of Nacrem is not in favor of a woman Councilor, so you see, we are a most unpopular couple."

"Point well made. Where to?"

His expression softened and a chill coursed through her. No man had ever come to her defense before and it gave her an intoxicating rush, especially from one so boldly qualified to complete the job. "We need a ship to take us to Votrella, and I'm afraid we have missed the last public flight."

"So, we'll charter one."

"That will cost more credits than I have." She watched a gambit of emotions flitter across his masculine features. Was this an insight to the man? Was he accustomed to buying anything he wanted with credits not being a problem? He did have the air of the rich, yet carried the attitude of a determined warrior, but it was his tempting looks that stopped her dead in her tracks.

He reached out, took her hand in his and smiled seductively. The simple gesture made her feel so weak she thought she might faint, but she was willing to follow him anywhere. The man made her lose her good sense. She reluctantly pulled her hand free of his. She could not afford such contact if she were to make coherent decisions.

"Well, where to, my lady?"

"I am not your lady." That was the truth even though the very thought sent a delicious tingle down to her very toes.

"Maybe you should be?" Falcon laughed. "Are you quite sure?" He shook his head. "As you know, I don't remember, but you certainly feel like my lady."

"You are a shameless flirt." She turned and began to walk away. She heard his chuckle behind her since he followed so closely his male aura nearly consumed her. It would be a relief to turn Falcon over to the High Council so they could deal with him. Then she could return to her mundane existence where no one cared if she lived or died.

Arella glanced over her shoulder and noted the arrogant man still grinning while he followed her down street after street. He was certainly an improvement over the men at her station, but if she were to advance in her government career there was no time for men, no matter how tempting they may be.

She turned the corner and sighed in relief. The shuttle station lay directly ahead, lights burning brightly in the waning sun-cycle, which was as close to dark as Nacrem ever came. Drearn and Votrella were both cities that never slept, and for once she was glad since she wanted to get there and free herself of Falcon.

Falcon slipped in front of her and opened the tall, tinted glass door for her, a smug look on his face. She groaned when she stepped inside and walked up to the ticket maker. "Do you have a flight available to Votrella?"

"How many?"

The ticket maker was a bit abrupt, but she was not here to make friends. "Two."

"If there's a problem, just ask about a charter, I'll pay for it," Falcon said.

"Sure you will. Show me your credits and identification." He gave her a blank stare. "You are not sure of your name, you cannot prove who you are even if you knew, and you have no credits. Now, how exactly were you going to arrange this?" He still stared. "Well?"

"Sorry." Falcon turned and walked to a nearby bench and sat.

"Identification please?"

Arella turned back toward the woman. "Oh, here," she said taking her ID out of her pocket and handing it to the woman behind the counter.

"That looker over there is with you?"

"Yes, he is." The woman could not take her eyes off Falcon, and for some reason that irritated her. "Is there a problem?" The clerk's eyes widened when she entered the ID information into the computer.

"No, Councilor Arella. My apologies." The woman looked back toward the man on the bench. "And your companion's name?"

"Falcon Rovarn."

"I will need his ID in order to allow passage."

"That is not possible. He is in my custody and I am taking him to the High Council, and as a councilor, that is within my authority. So. . ."

"Very well, Councilor. I will make the notation."

"Thank you.

"All is in order, and your shuttle is ready to leave now, so I suggest you board immediately."

"I thought the last shuttle had already left. I'm glad to catch it."

"Normally so, but there was a technical delay. You're lucky indeed."

"Thank you." Arella walked toward Falcon who sat remorsefully on the bench watching the locals come and go through the terminal. "We must hurry." He simply nodded and fell into step behind her. Her words must have bothered him more than she thought.

"I'm sorry if I upset you earlier."

"No harm. You're right."

"Really?" She could visibly see by the look on his face that he was bothered. Obviously a man used to being in control would become agitated when put in his place by a woman, especially when he had no memory to pull from. "I'm glad you finally see it that way."

"It's a matter of fact, nothing more."

"Fine. Let's go. We're about to miss our shuttle." He nodded and followed her up the ramp to dock nineteen where they boarded the twenty-person craft and took the last two remaining seats in the very back. No sooner had they strapped in when the craft hovered out of the docking bay and jetted off into space.

"How long?"

"Only a quarter of a time-unit." The question seemed odd since everyone knew travel times, but he was not from this planet, a fact she seemed too willing to forget. If he were from Nacrem she might consider him life-mate worthy, but he would return to whatever world he came from and she'd be alone again. Better to put him out of her mind now than be left behind like yesterday's luggage.

CHAPTER EIGHT

Falcon surveyed the tightly packed transport feeling extremely claustrophobic. They crammed extra seats in the small quarters for profits, which made comfort non-existent. This was not a ship. He shook his head. Vague memories of large vessels staffed with uniformed men played at the fringes of his memory. Had he been in charge, or just one of the crew members? With a sigh he looked out the port view next to him. Never had he been so frustrated in his life—at least he thought it to be the case. Everything he said or did made him second-guess himself, and he hated not knowing.

The only thing that made this experience bearable was the beautiful, seductive woman sitting next to him. She'd crossed her shapely legs in an attempt to keep from touching him, yet she was so close her body heat set him on fire. He couldn't make a play for her because he could be life-mated or promised to someone. The sooner he regained his memory the better. Even if he learned he was wanted for rape and murder it would be an improvement from being a non-entity.

The craft suddenly descended, glided to a stop. The hatch slowly opened from the center and the bottom formed steps for disembarking. Gladly he stood and followed Arella out of the ship, his eyes focused on the cute little sway of her shapely backside. All he knew at the moment was he was definitely a man who adored women. Was that another memory? More frustration. Would it never end?

Arella swiftly descended to the pad's surface and walked into the building behind. He followed, as usual, like a pet Atew. Pet Atew? Whatever an Atew was, it must be a pet, and it must follow mutely the same as he was doing. They proceeded down a long, brightly lit hall, the white polished marbastone floor gleaming, and the light green walls with portraits placed at measured intervals seemed to go on forever.

This must be the capitol building where Arella would introduce him to the Council, who just might know his identity. He glanced up at the ceiling where strips of light glowed from behind carved crown molding along both sides. Suddenly he ran into the back of Arella. "I'm sorry. I didn't see you stop." He smiled. "I was admiring your architecture."

She laughed. "Here?"

"Yes, what's so funny about that? Are you not proud of your capitol building?"

"Of course we are, it's just that this old building is being replaced by a much finer, larger, better equipped facility. So, you see why your comment made me laugh."

Falcon stared at his surroundings. It was difficult not having memories or a sense of being. People took knowledge for granted and he vowed never to make that mistake again when he recovered.

Arella opened the doors to their right and stepped inside a reception area and spoke with the attendant behind the tall counter-type desk that stood sentinel in front of huge double doors. She motioned for him to take a seat while she and the rather boorish looking man spoke.

He watched the interplay between Arella and the uniformed man. Whatever the man's position, he felt superior to Councilor Arella. The feeling that women were not equal to men here was pervasive, because in his heart he knew that was not the case in his homeland.

A quick study of the room confirmed his earlier assumption. All the buildings he had been in or seen so far were round in shape and connected with covered halls. Most interesting. He'd ask Arella why, if they ever had a quiet moment.

Arella finally finished speaking to the strange little man behind the counter and returned to sit next to him on the long, richly upholstered bench against the wall. One glance at the determined look in her eye and he knew she was not happy. He had no understanding of her language, but from the tone of speech and heated looks that passed between her and that pinched looking man, he knew matters did not bode well for their audience with the council.

"Is everything all right, Councilor Arella?" He hoped he could soften her mood.

"As always, things are fine. We must wait for an audience."

"Of course. We did not have an appointment, so a wait is to be expected." His compliance did nothing to put her at ease. Was she afraid of the High Council? Possibly, but he doubted this determined woman backed down from anyone. "Are there many women Councilors?"

"I'm the only one so far."

That explained many of his questions, and accounted for much of her attitude. "And I suppose you're hoping that will change?"

"Yes."

Short and sweet. He rather liked women with little to say, since too many had far too much to add. That could be another possible memory, one best left alone. Finally the doors opened and two ushers held them open in a quiet invitation. Arella stood, tipped her chin up and walked forward more boldly than he'd seen her do since they met. Falcon followed her lead and hoped this slip of a woman knew her job well because he had a sinking feeling that the council would be a very difficult audience.

They walked into the huge, high ceilinged room and stopped a respectful distance in front of the council. All the rather elderly men before them were seated in high-backed chairs with large carved arms that bumped up against the polished, U-shaped dais was the twelve members of the High Council.

"Councilor Arella, step forward and be heard."

Arella moved closer to her peers and bowed her head in respect. Her stiff posture said she was not at ease, and the slight quiver of her lip revealed her true feelings. He felt sorry for her, yet somehow he knew she'd do her job with pride.

"Honored Councilors. I have brought before you a man I found near death, lying in the Crystal Desert. He has no memory of who he is, or where he is from. I thought it prudent to present him to you."

"You did well. Please, bring him forward."

Falcon listened while they shared remarks to each other in their language. Arella motioned for him to stand next to her. He moved to her side and studied the serious group and wondered how he'd gotten himself into this mess.

"May I present the man I believe to be Falcon Rovarn."

Arella announced him in the universal language so he could understand. The total silence in the room played on his nerves. It appeared it was his turn to speak. "Honorable Councilors." Falcon bowed to them the same as Arella had to show his respect. "Thank you for this audience." Several members whispered between themselves and pointed in his direction. He now understood how Arella felt under their scrutiny.

"I am Head Councilor, Whitten. We are honored to greet you, Falcon Rovarn." Whitten held his hand up to silence the murmurs. "How is it you are here?"

"I have no memory of my arrival, only that Councilor Arella found me in the desert and saved my life." He glanced at Arella and caught a slight blush on her cheeks. "Thanks to her good judgment, she brought me here for your possible assistance." Their nods of approval to Arella were a bit of comfort. "There was a name on the uniform I wore when I crashed." He pointed to the area over the left pocket of the shirt he wore.

"I thank you with all sincerity for your hospitality." Falcon hoped he'd said all the right things, and that his manners were politically correct enough for the formal council that sat stiff in their chairs on the curved dais before him.

"You do indeed resemble your brother, Dacton, who was here only one duo-cycle ago, working to gain our trust and allegiance to join The Protectorate." Whitten stroked his long white beard. "We will notify him at once. In the meantime, please, accept our hospitality. You will be made comfortable."

"I thank you, Councilor Whitten." His heart raced at the thought of having a brother. He had no conscious memory of family or friends so it was good to hear anything he could use.

"You are most welcome. Now, please excuse us while we speak

further with Councilor Arella."

"As you wish." Falcon bowed to the council, turned on his heel and strode from the room. The two men he passed in the open doorway quickly closed the doors behind him. It seemed they were in a big hurry to close him out. He walked back to the bench he waited on before and made himself comfortable. This could be a short or a long wait and he wasn't sure which would be better. Either way he felt trapped with no place to run.

CHAPTER NINE

Councilor Arella, please explain your actions to the council immediately.

"Yes sir." Arella held her head high. She took a deep, calming breath. It remained imperative she remain cool and calm since she knew she was on trial herself. "If this man is who he says he is, I thought it best you meet him. If he is not he could still be a spy who could harm Nacrem."

"As the man said, you exercised good judgment." Whitten stood and walked around the table to stand in front of Arella. "I believe he is Dacton Rovarn's brother, but you will not let him out of your sight, even when Dacton arrives, we want you with him, until we release you of this duty. Do you understand?"

"Yes, sir."

"Good. Make no mistake about your assignment. The Protectorate desperately wants us to join them, and we fear they may use treachery to convince us of such a decision. Somehow Dacton knew his brother's ship and the escort ships all disappeared in our air space, which is the main reason he was here, but he also pushed us to decide in their behalf by quoting several instances of justice. The Council suspects Dacton's visit and you finding Falcon are connected somehow. We will not be forced into anything."

"I understand completely." Arella took a deep breath.

"I hope you do because the man you brought to us could well be part of a bigger plan to convince us. He could cause trouble and you will be held responsible if he does. Do you still understand?"

"Completely." The council was up to their usual ways of putting her down and controlling her. Now if anything happened on Nacrem before she got rid of Falcon it would be her demise. It wasn't fair, but she was used to being treated in that manner." How long do you think it will be until Dacton arrives?"

"Our intelligence tells us his ship is approximately two sun-cycles from us and he will be contacted immediately."

"I see."

"I hope you do, Councilor Arella. You job is most important, so do not let us down."

"I will not let you down."

"Good." Whitten returned to his seat at the head of the table. "You may go execute your duties."

"I thank the High Council for their time." Arella bowed, turned and marched toward the exit. When she reached the door the guards opened it for her and she stepped into the reception area. Falcon was nowhere in sight and she wondered how far he may have wandered. This would not be a good time for him to get into trouble.

She entered the long hall on her right and found him standing close to the wall, arms crossed over his massive chest, feet slightly apart. The man looked ready for battle. especially with that scowl on his face When she walked closer he turned that scowl on her but he didn't scare her. He was intimidating to be sure, but she understood his current mood.

"What did the Council say?"

"Not much of anything. You heard everything that applied to you." He looked at her like a poor, little, lost pet Atew.

"At least tell me what we're going to do now."

"Well we could. . .uhhhh. . ." She searched her mind for what to tell him, but it wasn't easy while he looked straight at her and began to smile. The man enjoyed her loss of words way too much. She refused to let him ruffle her composure. "I will show you to my quarters."

"Your quarters?"

"All Councilors have private quarters since we come from all over the planet when the main body is in session."

Falcon bowed slightly. "Lead the way, Councilor."

Arella led the way through the maze of hallways which led from one building to another. It was a long walk to the farthest housing facility, then again, she was still a junior member and felt lucky just to have quarters.

"Do all your buildings look alike?" Falcon asked.

"On the outside they do." The look on his face was difficult to explain as he surveyed his surroundings. He paused in the clear hall between buildings to admire the famous peace gardens tucked between the tall, white walls of the capitol. Falcon appeared in awe, but that was an assumption. He may simply be confused.

"Why are all your buildings round?"

"They weather sand storms better than buildings with flat sides and corners."

"Good point." Falcon looked out through the window. "The gardens are beautiful."

"That is our peace garden. I often sit in the back area out there to refresh my spirit."

Falcon nodded at her, but kept walking. Of course he'd have questions about places and things she took for granted. This was her home, not his.

At the end of the last long hall Arella stopped, stared into the identifier pad while the beam scanned her iris, then the door quietly slid open. "This is it." She stepped inside and waited while Falcon examined the door, the frame around it and the lock mechanism. He was a curious sort.

"It looks secure."

"I assure you, it is very secure." He walked past her and checked both bedrooms, the sitting area and the galley. "Looking for something in particular?"

"I'm not sure. I just feel I'm supposed to check things out. Call it an instinct."

"Does anything here look familiar?" He took a seat on the pale green sofa that separated the sitting area from the dining area. He leaned his head against the back and sighed.

"I'm afraid nothing looks familiar, yet it does not look foreign either." He lifted his head and turned to look at her. "Does that make sense to you?"

"Yes and no. I can understand your dilemma, but have never experienced myself."

"Trust me, you never want to."

Trust him? How could she trust someone she did not know? Why did the High Council want her to watch him so closely? As far as joining The Protectorate, she had next to zero influence. A final vote was pending, however, most of the Councilors she spoke to wanted to join since it would offer them the protection they currently lacked. It would also greatly expand Nacrem's trade and commerce, which put credits in everyone's pockets. There were still some on the High Council that were vehemently against the alliance, but those members were usually against everything.

She poured them both a mineral water and carried it to the couch. She handed Falcon his cold drink then sat on the opposite end from him. "I can't imagine not having a past, not knowing even my family if I saw them." She watched Falcon shake his head in despair and he looked so helpless she wanted to pull him into her arms and tell him everything would be all right. At the same time, she wanted to get as far away from him as she could since his nearness caused thoughts she should not consider doing with any man—especially this one.

"The council said my brother, Dacton, will arrive soon." He stared into Arella's eyes. "How will I even recognize him? I feel powerless!" He shook his head. "I don't know much about myself, but powerless is a feeling I do not relish." Falcon raked his fingers through his hair. "I need to change the subject, so tell me, Arella, how did you become a councilor?"

"My mentor, Eldron Passer, used his influence with the council to finally accept a woman to the position. It was as simple as that."

"Simple? I'm sure your planet has a long history, as most do, and yet you are the first? I'd say you've been very honored, and carry a great responsibility. You're breaking new ground here, and I offer my congratulations."

Arella saw genuine admiration in the depths of his blue eyes. "Thank you, but I do not exactly feel honored. I. . ."

"Feel like you're being used?"

How could he possibly have guessed that? It had always been her secret suspicion, yet Falcon, a man foreign to her and everything she knew saw through her as if she were made of glass.

"No, that's not what I meant." She stood and walked into the galley to get more mineral water.

While she poured another drink she nearly jumped out of her skin when a large hand grasped her shoulder and gently turned her around. Dear stars, just looking into his sensual blue gaze made her melt. What would she do if he actually touched her in a personal way, or kissed her the way she wanted him to? It was best she never find out. She could do no less than her duty, and right now he was her responsibility, not a lover.

"I didn't mean to startle you, I only thought to. . ."

She smiled when he stopped speaking. Could she be responsible for his loss of words? She certainly hoped so. Every woman wanted to think she could render a man speechless, especially one as dauntingly handsome as Falcon Rovarn. She tried to discern what the look on his face meant. What was he up to? Right now her stomach tingled so much her legs felt weak.

Then he did what she most feared yet wanted. He leaned close and placed his lips on hers, lightly skimming, then he settled in to deepen the kiss, his tongue pressing for entry. Her hands found his chest, but they refused to push him away. She could not resist this man! She never wanted him to stop.

His lips were like velvet and steel, soft, yet demanding. Her body trembled with excitement from the top of her head to the tips of her toes, her stomach fluttered wildly, and her heart raced so fast she could barely catch her breath. If he did not stop soon she might faint for the first time in her life. His strong arms had wound around her. He made her feel protected and cared for, a feeling she was not acquainted with. Slowly, erotically, he ended the kiss. She was now breathless and speechless, among many other things she dare not think about.

"I just wanted to say thank you for all you have done for me."

With his arms still holding her tightly against him she took several deep breaths in an effort to regain her composure. "You welcome quite." The words no sooner left her mouth and she knew her nervousness showed in her grammar slip. She finally had enough courage to push him back far enough to breathe easier. She should be outraged at his forward behavior, instead she was so flattered she wanted to ask him why he found her attractive enough to kiss.

"I make you feel uneasy, don't I?"

"No, it's just that," she paused, trying to think of something intelligent to say, and at the moment nothing came to mind.

"I understand. I should not have kissed you, but I fear I could not help myself. I have wanted to do that since I first laid eyes on you."

"Was your curiosity satisfied?"

"Only for the moment."

He gave her a wicked smile, the kind that said he intended to kiss her again and he knew she wouldn't stop him. She opened her mouth to reply, but the chime of the wall-com saved her. She hurried to the unit set into the wall close to the entryway and pressed the hidden button to answer. "Yes?"

"Councilor Arella, the Ora delegation will arrived in two time-units. They will wait for Falcon in the main reception area."

"Very well. Thank you." Falcon suddenly turned from seducer to lost soul, it was clearly written in his expression. How could she blame him? His moment of truth just arrived faster than they planned. "Would you like to refresh yourself before we meet your brother?"

"That would be nice."

"The lav is between the bedrooms. Everything you need should be there. If not, just ask."

"Thanks."

He disappeared from sight and she let out the breath she'd been holding. What a man he was. Tough, yet tender, strong and vulnerable. That was an intoxicating combination. He must have at least one flaw or he might be considered the perfect man, and all women knew no such thing existed.

CHAPTER TEN

Falcon paced relentlessly across the lush burgundy carpet in the elegantly appointed reception room while he waited for a brother he did not know. On each pass of the sofa he glanced at Arella, whom he barely recognized now that she wore a long, flowing gown in the most delicious shade of pink he'd ever seen. Yet even her presence could not quiet the anxiety that roiled deep within his soul.

Surely he was a man of honor and his brother and he were close. Or were they? Having no memory was truly the worst curse in the universe—it had to be. He passed Arella again and couldn't hold back a smile. Her lips appeared a bit swollen from their earlier kiss, and if they weren't he would certainly remedy that, which could take many time-units. The woman caused the strangest effects, and he wished he had many more sun-cycles to understand what it was all about.

The large, double doors opened and in strode six people, five of which he'd never seen, the sixth was Whitten, head of the Nacrem High Council. He turned to face them and brought himself to attention, not sure whether he should salute or bow.

The tall, dark haired man who looked much like himself, extended his hand in greeting. After they grasped wrists in greeting the man hugged him like a long lost brother.

"Brother, it's so good to see you alive! We feared the worst."

"I apologize for causing any undue anxiety."

"Anxiety?" Dacton ran his fingers through his hair. "Is not the word for what you caused." He laughed. "Don't look at me like that, little brother. I know that look. Seen it a thousand times."

"What look?"

"The look that says we're about to have a friendly battle." Dacton shook his head. "They told me you had no memory, but until I saw for myself I couldn't believe it." He slapped his brother on the back. "Never fear. I've brought a solution to your problems." Dacton turned and motioned to one of the men behind him. "Falcon, this is Doctor Karlin Dryko, and he has brought the antidote for the drug Zotar gave you."

"Zotar?" Falcon inquired, wondering why Dacton's voice changed when he said the name Zotar. It was as if the man were evil and Dacton's worst enemy.

"There is a very long story attached to that name, and I think it best if the good doctor here simply restored your memory. The experience may not be pleasant, but more thorough than any explanation I can offer. Agreed?"

"I'd agree to almost anything to get my memory back. I'm ready for Dr. Dryko." Falcon studied his brother closely. "We do look alike, brother."

"It is well known that I am by far the better looking one." Dacton laughed. "I hope your sense of humor returns with your memory, or I shall be forced to beat it into you. Now, go with the doctor before I become frustrated with you."

Falcon nodded then followed the doctor out of the room, past people he had not met, or had he? Maybe when he returned he'd know everyone and everything. "Doctor," he began while they walked toward the central med building, "will I still retain recent events after my memory of the past returns?"

"Yes. Nothing will be erased, only enhanced."

That was a relief since he didn't want to forget Arella, his lovely rescuer who tasted like fruit nectar and looked like a warrior goddess. Definitely a memory to cherish. "Good. Do you know why I lost my memory?"

"Not until I examine you fully. However, Dacton suspects you were drugged, as he was once, except he didn't lose his memory, only the ability to move. We believe Zotar has perfected the drug further since he first used it on your brother."

"That sounds like an interesting story." They rounded the last corner and entered the large med unit where they were directed to a private room where a nurse waited to assist them.

"Lie down on that table and we'll get started."

Falcon sat on the table, then laid down as the doctor requested. This procedure created a lot of anxiety. He had the distinct impression, memory or no, that he was not fond of doctors and drugs, but he'd do whatever was necessary to put an end to this exasperating situation.

The doctor scanned him with the blue light that assessed the body's vital information, a process that took only seconds. The handheld vid-viewer in the doctor's hand lit up and he watched Doctor Dryko's eyebrows move up and down while he read the stats. "Well? Don't keep me in suspense here, Doctor."

"It's as we suspected. You were drugged with a very potent, illegal concoction which given to anyone in poor health would either kill them, or render them less than human for the rest of their life."

"I see. So you're saying I'm lucky?"

"Far more than lucky." The doctor rolled the med-mix unit to the side of the bed.

"Haven't seen one of these used in a long time."

"True, we have far more sophisticated methods of medicating, however, what you are about to receive must be taken into the body very slowly or the effects could be fatal."

"Great. Slow it is then."

"I'll be starting an IV drip which contains a drug to counteract the one you were given. You may experience some discomfort, at least in the beginning. This process will take hours. You might think you are hallucinating at times, so expect the unexpected."

"Has this drug been used before?"

"No, and I'm not sure if there will be side effects." Dr. Dryko shook his head and looked into his patient's eyes. "I'd like to say this will completely cure you, but I'm not sure since it is a new drub. You will be our test subject, unless you do not wish to continue. It is your choice."

"Do it. I don't believe I'm the kind to run from a challenge." Falcon smiled. "By the way, do we know each other?"

"We certainly do! I delivered you. I've been your family's physician since your parents life-mated."

"Then you know me better than I do. In your humble opinion, do I want this?"

"Very much. And I have one message for you that I promised to relay before I start this procedure."

"And that is?" Falcon wondered who would think to send a message with the doctor? A life-mate maybe?

"Your mother wants you to know that she loves you and eagerly awaits your return. She was unable to come, but insisted you know her heart is with you."

"That is reassuring." Falcon took a deep breath. "Doctor Dryko, I have to ask, am I life-mated, or promised to anyone?" He almost fell off the table when the doctor started to laugh. "Did I miss the joke here?"

"I suppose you have." The doctor worked to control his laughter. "You are too well known with the ladies, if you get my meaning, to settle down with just one."

"Oh." What else could he say to that news? At least it put his mind at ease. He did not want to think he was cheating on a life-mate, mentally or physically when he had those tempting thoughts about Arella. At least when he regained his memory he'd be able to thank her one last time properly without wondering if he should kiss her.

The doctor inserted a rather large needle into his forearm, taped it to his skin and adjusted some settings on the med-dispenser. Immediately warmth crept up his arm and into his body. The effect intensified, he grew very warm as the medicine moved gradually through his veins until his whole body was on fire. His sun burnt skin pained him unmercifully due to the added heat, and increased to the point he thought he might actually melt.

Then images formed in his mind, gruesome, evil and bloody. Was this part of the hallucinations the doctor spoke of, or were they returning memories? If it was a memory it was one he could have lived without. At the moment he welcomed any information that would free his mind from the current state of bondage that held him trapped within its grasp. He watched the play before his eyes and could not believe anyone could be as cruel as the men he saw. Innocent people were tortured and murdered, their mangled bodies left where they fell, lying in pools of their own blood.

In contrast the picture of a woman, elderly and kind flooded his consciousness. His mother. An image of his father formed, then another brother. One by one his memories came back, first as places and things strange to him, then realization cemented them in his mind and he knew what he was seeing belonged to him and everything began to make perfect sense.

Bright colors flashed and he was consumed with emotion. Love and hate, rejection and acceptance. Just when he thought all was well he felt himself losing his grip on reality. No! He would not give in to madness. It was as if his mind were a computer and he was on information overload. Confusion took over, and the beautiful colors turned dark and menacing. Evil pervaded and swirled around him and he felt it was looking for a way to invade his soul.

He would survive this. Lives depended on him. His family cried for vengeance and he would not let them down. Zotar. That name belonged to the one man in the universe he vowed to destroy for the evil he had brought to countless families, including his own. Zotar would take nothing more from him, and that was a promise he would keep. No obstacle would stop him, even if it meant his death!

~ ~ ~ ~

Arella paced nervously. She wished she could be by Falcon's side so she could reassure him and help him. All she could do was wonder how he fared. He was a strong man, but she overheard Dr. Dryko tell Dacton how dangerous this could be, and that Falcon's mind could become worse instead of better. Why then had he agreed to such experimental treatment? It was simple. Falcon was a determined, stubborn man who had too much pride to live his life without knowing who and what drove him.

It felt odd to worry about a virtual stranger, but he certainly did not feel like a stranger. Actually, he felt too good. The way he'd held her in his arms and made her want more consumed her every thought. The taste and feel of his lips lingered, as did the strength of his arms and the feel of his chest tight against her. The man was a dream, and she only hoped she would have the opportunity to know him better.

She glanced at the group of chairs in the far corner where Dacton sat alone. Several people had tried to speak to him, but he'd waved them all away. He loved his brother, that was obvious, but he was in pain and she wanted to help. Cautiously she approached Dacton, unsure if she should reach out to him, or leave him to suffer the wait alone. "Excuse me, Ambassador Rovarn. May I have a word with you?" He looked up and assessed her with eyes that reminded her so much of Falcon's.

"Of course, Councilor Arella."

"Just Arella, please." She lowered her eyes and took a seat next to Dacton. "I can only imagine how you feel. I have a sister, Nodia, and I know how I'd feel if she no longer knew who I was, and how worried I'd be considering the treatment necessary."

Dacton nodded. "I want to thank you for saving my brother's life. We both owe you. If ever you need a favor I'd be honored to repay you."

"Thank you, but I ask no repayment." Dacton stared at her in silence and she knew he wanted to ask more questions about Falcon. "Is something wrong?"

"No, I was just thinking of my wife, Talina. She's beautiful and caring like you. Falcon is fortunate indeed to have been found by you."

"I did what anyone would do, no more, no less." Except kiss him and want him as a man. She had to stop these thoughts, but the way she felt about Falcon would forever be locked inside her. There had been so little love in her life that she was sure she read more into Falcon's words and actions than he meant.

"Modesty becomes you." Dacton checked the timepiece on his wrist. "It's taking too long." He stood and began to pace.

Arella had counted every moment since the doctor had taken Falcon away, and she too was worried. Had he lost his mind in the process as the doctor feared might happen? Or had his memories been to overpowering for him to accept? She had one other fear, one she should not even consider—that he had a woman in his life and she meant nothing to him and would forever remain the stranger who saved him, the stranger he once shared a kiss with and nothing more.

The door at the end of the room opened with a swish and the

doctor approached, his expression grim, his body showing signs of exhaustion. Her heart raced and the palms of her hands suddenly became damp. She wiped her hands on the skirt of her gown, then stood to face the doctor.

Dacton rushed to the doctor. "How is he?"

"As I explained, this drug is experimental just like the combination of drugs he was given." The doctor shook his head. "Some of his memory has returned, but. . ." He continued to shake his head.

"I've lost one brother and I will *not* lose another! Do you hear me?"

The demand Dacton made of the doctor was unfair but said by a very desperate man. He loved his brother, of that she was positive, but he was about to lose his composure. Arella noticed him rub the amulet fixed in the center of his wide belt. It was beautiful and exotic, and she sensed the stone held some sort of magic, or at least she hoped it did by the way he stroked it repeatedly.

"Dacton," the doctor began, "you know I'd never let anything happen to Falcon, or any of your family." Dr. Dryko cleared his throat. "I've always felt a part of the Rovarn family. Your father and I were. . .were the best of friends. I delivered you Rovarn boys. It pains me that you'd consider, even for a moment, that I wouldn't do my best."

Dacton rubbed the back of his neck with his hand. "I know where your heart is, Karlin. Forgive me for any insult. I'm just worried." He glanced at Arella. "And I feel so helpless."

Karlin Dryko nodded. "Now, if you can stay calm, I'll allow you and the lady to sit with him."

"Let's go." Dacton grabbed Arella's hand and started toward the door.

"Hold, Dacton."

He stopped and turned. "What?"

Arella watched the interplay between the two men, who obviously cared deeply for each other, and shared a mutual pain she could not identify. Dacton held her hand firmly like a brother protecting his younger sister. She liked Dacton, his aura said he was honorable, truthful, and devoted to those he cared about, yet strong and willful, which could cause him to take risks. Yes, the Rovarn brothers were very much alike.

"Falcon is delirious." Dr. Dryko moved to stand closer to Dacton and Arella. "He's hallucinating, as well as reliving everything in his life through visions, and some of those visions are disturbing, as you well know. He's fighting every demon he's ever known, and yet, he calls for both of you."

"Then we'll go to him."

"Keep him calm." Karlin lowered his head. "I had to restrain him, so he's bound to the table. Do not, under any circumstances, free him." He lifted his gaze. "It's for everyone's safety. No matter what he asks, remember your job is only to calm him, reassure him, agree with him, even if he is wrong. Can you do that?"

Arella nodded, unable to speak. This was all too much, and she truly did not know how she felt about any of this. Her assignment came before personal feelings, and it was her job to stay with Falcon. In her heart she felt compelled to learn more, and to be by his side where she felt protected. In all her twenty-six annual-cycles she had never felt protected by anyone. In fact, she was the only protector of what little family she had.

"We can." Dacton squeezed Arella's hand. "Right?"

She nodded, stunned by the way her mind had wandered. "Of course. We'll do everything we can to speed his recovery."

"Fine. Just remember to always agree. I will not have him upset any further. Even if what he says is a complete lie and makes you angry, you must agree." Karlin watched the couple nod in agreement. "It will be difficult. I'd like to tell you the outcome, but I'd be lying if I did."

"Let's just go. We'll be fine, right, Councilor Arella?"

"Yes, please, let's hurry. I doubt it's wise to leave him alone for very long."

Finally they walked the long hall to the end room. Dr. Dryko opened the door and her heart nearly stopped beating. Falcon lay strapped to a hard table, naked from the waist up, his muscles straining against the straps that held him firmly in place. His chest heaved, his breathing became rapid and sweat ran down his brow. His hair was damp as if he were fighting a war.

"I will not!" Falcon screamed. "Let me go!"

Arella watched in horror while Falcon strained against his bindings so hard that even the padding was not enough to stop the straps from digging into his skin and drawing blood. How she wanted to free him, but knew he'd hurt himself, or someone else if she did.

"Falcon, it's Dacton, I'm here to help you."

"No one can help. I'll kill him, I swear I will. He'll die for what he did to Beliko. He's a monster, he does not deserve to live."

"We'll stop him together," Dacton said.

"No. You have a family and a life-mate. I have no one. I'll do it. Only me!"

"You're not alone, Falcon. I'm here." Dacton looked at the woman across from him. "Arella is here."

"Arella?"

She was amazed at the calm that came over Falcon at the mention of her name. "Falcon, I'm here. Tell me what to do." His eyes were shut tightly, yet he turned his head toward the sound of her voice.

"There's nothing you can do. Nothing I'll allow you to do." Falcon violently pulled against his bindings again.

His declaration made her bristle, but she remembered the doctor's instructions, simply agree. "I will do nothing." That was the truth since she had no idea what he was even talking about. At her statement he relaxed slightly, but not enough to stop his wrists from bleeding.

Falcon lifted his head from the table. "You should leave. I don't need a woman. I'll not have one in my life."

Arella drew in a deep, calming breath and reminded herself he was delirious. "I'm just a friend, nothing more."

"Nothing. That's right, you're nothing!"

How could his words hurt when she knew the circumstances under which they were said? Because they'd been said to her before by other men in other circumstances she'dspent a lifetime trying to forget.

"Falcon, tell me what you remember?" Dacton grasped his brother hand.

"All. I remember it all, but it won't stop, the blood, death everywhere!"

"What do you see?"

"Protectorate escort ships, blown out of the sky, all six of them! Gone! There's nothing left. Then my ship is hit. We lost power. Then we're boarded, I don't know who they are. I'm attacked from behind. As I fall to the floor six of my men are cut down in front of me. Then everything goes black. The next thing I know I'm lying in scorching desert sand, unable to move, taking my last breaths."

Dacton sat back in his chair next to the examination table. "You don't know who these men were?"

"No." A smile played on Falcon's face. "I was saved by an angel. I would have died, but she came. She saved me. She tasted good."

Arella felt a blush cross her cheeks even before Dacton's gaze found her. What was the Ora Ambassador thinking? This was no time to explain even if she could. Nothing made sense. Falcon turned his head toward her.

"Kiss me, Arella. Kiss me now, before I die."

She stared at Dacton who nodded his consent, so she took a deep breath, then pressed her lips to Falcon's. For some reason it did not feel right, kissing a man who was for all intents and purposes, unconscious. Without his arms to hold her it seemed shallow and unimportant. She pulled back from the chaste kiss.

"No!" Falcon roared. "That was not a kiss. Do it right!"

Dacton stood. "I'll be right back."

Dacton quickly left the room to give her the privacy she needed to comply with Falcon's request. She leaned down and kissed him, allowing him to explore her mouth at will, their tongues dueling and searching. Even though Falcon was not himself, his kiss stirred her emotions and her lust. Her hands found the strength of his shoulders and moved slowly down the taught muscles of his arms.

When she tried to end the kiss, he groaned and deepened the kiss as if his mouth alone could hold her to him. What was going on between them? Her body sang with need for this man, yet he just said he didn't want a commitment. Had that been a lie, or was he simply out of his mind? Lust. He felt lust for her, and she for him, that explained it.

He kissed her senseless. She shivered, her knees felt weak, and the flutter in her abdomen made her giddy. If only this were real, but she reminded herself it was not. The doctor said to agree, and the council assigned her to him, yet this did not feel like duty. Her hands found the hard ripples of his chest and explored the wide expanse inch by inch. He felt so good, the dusting of hair in the center of his chest tickled the palms of her hands. Again he groaned and she took the opportunity to gently end the kiss.

When she pulled her hands away Falcon opened his eyes and looked at her as if looking through her. "How do you feel?"

"Better when your hands are on me."

"I don't think. . ."

"No, don't think. Just put your hands back where they were."

Arella did as he asked, the warmth of his skin a firm reminder he was flesh and bone man, full of strength with a high degree of lust more than evident under the covering below his waist.

"I would so like to return the favor," Falcon whispered.

"And what favor would that be?"

"To heal you."

"It is not I who needs healing."

"No? I sense that deep in your soul you are wounded, and need someone to drive away the loneliness."

"And that would be you?" Arella laughed at the idea and inwardly cried at the truth of his words, a truth she could not let him learn. "You were delirious, but I do believe you're back." She pulled her hands away from his most tempting body.

"Untie me and I will show you. . ."

The door opened and Dacton and Dr. Dryko entered.

"I think he has recovered sufficiently. If you don't mind, I'll take a moment for myself." Arella turned and left the room.

"What did you do to her brother?" Dacton laughed. "And with your hands tied. This trick I would like to learn."

"Just one of many I could teach you, but for Talina's sake, I'd better not."

Dacton laughed. "It's good to have you back, little brother."

"I'd like to say it's good to be back, but I fear I've failed The Protectorate. Zotar has escaped, my fleet is destroyed and my mission is a failure."

"It may seem like that now, but. . ."

"No buts about it." Falcon tried to raise off the table. "Untie me before I hurt you."

"That's persuasive." Dacton smiled. "But it sounds so much like you, I'll take a chance.

Dr. Dryko cleared his throat. "Am I not to be consulted first?"

Dacton and Falcon both glared at the doctor. "Fine, untie him. I believe the worst is over."

Once freed, Falcon stood, rubbed his wrists and stretched. "No. The worst has just begun."

CHAPTER ELEVEN

Dacton sat in the chair next to Falcon. "We have so much to discuss, but not here. Arrangements are being made to leave immediately."

"Good. I have no love for this planet."

"I wouldn't think so. You nearly died here. Damn Zotar to Diabolus! He's caused enough trouble. But enough said here. We must proceed with caution. I've been working with the Council here to join The Protectorate, and diplomacy is crucial."

"What more could go wrong" Falcon chuckled. "I think we've done about all the damage here we can."

"You might be surprised. The High Council convened, and will speak with us before we leave."

"Great. I just want off this dustbowl."

Dacton smiled. "And here I thought you might be reluctant to leave that lovely lady behind. You know, the one you insisted kiss you while you pretended to be unconscious?"

"I may have been a little conscious." Dacton slapped him on the back and grinned widely. "Okay, maybe it was pretense, but it worked very well, wouldn't you say?"

"I believe you enjoyed it too much for a sick man, or a healthy man for that matter. But tread softly or you'll ruin all the diplomatic progress I've made on Nacrem."

"You were ever the diplomat. However, I remember you as

Chief Protector shocking everyone when you threw caution to the wind and violated every rule The Protectorate had to capture Zotar and keep the woman *you* loved."

"Be that as it may. Learn from my experience."

"Say no more. I've always been more level-headed than you, or so I've been told by everyone who knows us."

"They're wrong, brother."

Falcon laughed. "No, Dacton, you've just matured and now think you know everything. Do you forget, my memory is back? Or would you like to test it?"

"Where is our mother right now?"

"I believe she's still on her life-mating excursion with your father-in-law. It took them long enough to pledge themselves, if I remember correctly."

"Mother felt she was betraying our father's memory. They loved each other deeply."

"That they did, but I'm delighted she's found love again."

Dacton laughed. "You only say that so she'll be too occupied to play match-maker for you."

"It's your fault. Until you broke the rules, Protectors couldn't life-mate."

"I did not wed as Chief Protector."

"A technicality." Falcon glanced around the room. "We need to go."

"We don't have clearance yet. I can't imagine what is holding up our departure."

~ ~ ~ ~

"Councilor Arella," Whitten began, "your assignment is not over."

"But I thought the Rovarns were leaving Nacrem."

"Not without you."

Arella's mouth nearly dropped open. "I don't understand."

"You will, Councilor. You see, Falcon and Dacton are on a mission to destroy Zotar Alucard, and we do *not* want this to happen. We, The High Council, consider him a friend." Whitten cleared his throat. "He has supplied the funding for rebuilding the capitol, and several other projects we're doing. This information is top secret. Zotar does not want his name mentioned in connection with our affairs. He's very modest."

"I see." Arella didn't see at all. Why was this the first she'd heard of Zotar being a benefactor to Nacrem? Why all the secrecy? The Council's reluctance to inform her of important government issues was just another problem in a long list she had with the council.

"Good. You will report to the med-tec immediately to receive a track-chip implant. We want to know of your whereabouts at all times, and Ora's ship has equipment to render our tracking devices useless without the special track-chip in you."

"What is it that you expect me to do?"

"You're a woman, and in this case that works to our advantage. Falcon is a man who enjoys women well, and we want you to be that woman for a while. What better way to learn their secrets and thwart their assassination of Zotar?"

"By what crimes is Zotar wanted?"

"The Protectorate has accused him of murder; however, we do not agree with their verdict." Whitten stepped closer to Arella in the small meeting chamber. "There's one more thing you need to know, and one more reason for your compliance."

Arella stood, too stunned to offer a reply. For the first time she was being trusted and offered an assignment worthy of a Councilor.

"Zotar has many identities. He came to us a changed man from his past and started a new life here. In fact you know him well, he is Modark, your brother-in-law."

"How can that be?"

"We gave Zotar his new identity here as Modark. In return, he's given us much." Whitten turned and walked to the chair a few feet away. "So, you see why we've chosen you?"

"Of course." They knew she'd protect what little family she had left. Nodia, the sister she loved, and her two annual-cycle old nephew, Ducard. She never had a great fondness for Modark, but Nodia loved him, and for that alone she'd be happy to do the High Council's bidding, even if they were using her.

"We do not care to what extremes you must go to stop Zotar's capture and destruction. Just be sure you accomplish the mission."

"I understand.

"We've supplied you with enough credits for any eventuality. Dacton has been informed that you will accompany them to watch The Protectorate in action. We also told Dacton that after Zotar's successful capture we will join The Protectorate."

"A most convincing story."

"Yes, we thought so. Now, if there is nothing further, report to the lab to receive your implant. You leave immediately. Their ship will not leave without you, but please hurry so they will not become more suspicious due to further delay."

"Of course." Arella bowed. "I thank the High Council for their confidence."

"And we trust you will uphold your duties with honor, Councilor Arella."

"I will." She bowed again, turned on her heel and left the room. Once in the hallway she took a deep breath and wondered what had just happened? She knew the council well and they were using her in the worst way, but the assignment did not displease her—not completely anyway. The council would be happy if she never returned, then there would be no women Councilors again. This was far from a routine mission. Only time would tell the results and who was right, if there was such a thing.

She entered the med-unit and was quickly ushered into a small room. With haste she disrobed, put on the exam gown and lay down on the table. The door opened and the doctor entered.

"Councilor Arella. I am Doctor Rosheine. I will run my tests, then insert the implant in your left arm. It should not be painful."

Arella nodded at the middle-aged, stocky man who ran the blue light over her from head to foot, a stoic expression on his face. He was all business, and gave no hint of what he was thinking, while her mind whirled with every emotion known to humans. What bothered her most was the lust she felt every time she thought of the handsome, virile Falcon Rovarn, whom she'd be spending all her time watching.

"All is in order," the doctor announced.

Reality slammed into Arella with great force and she shivered. She could not become attached to Falcon, and nothing he said or did could change that. Circumstances has pitted them as enemies, and she'd do well to remember her place. Traitors were executed. If she did not stop Zotar's capture she'd be tried for treason, and that was not acceptable. Her family name would forever be ruined, and even though her sister was mated, she'd be forced to leave Nacrem with her son and husband.

Life-mated. Nodia loved Modark, also known as Zotar. Arella knew the High Council played on her emotions for her sister and her child. They knew that was the extent of her family and she cared deeply about their happiness and well-being. They did not really trust her as a government servant, but they were sure she'd do nothing to ruin her sister's life.

Nodia's life was a dream, and she was happy for her. A handsome man who loved her, a beautiful baby boy, and all the credits she ever dreamed of having were at her disposal, not to mention a fantastic home in the city, and a country get-away that made most family's dwellings pale in comparison. No. She could not ruin Nodia's perfect life. Some said she was jealous of her sister, not true. Sure, what woman wouldn't want a life like that? However, jealousy was an ugly emotion, and the only emotion she held for her sister was love.

Pain shot through her left arm and she nearly jumped off the table. Doctor Rosheine did not so much as blink at what he was doing, but she wanted to scream at the top of her lungs! Wow, so much for, "this won't hurt"! Slowly the pain receded and she gritted her teeth and a silent curse rolled off her tongue.

The doctor wiped Arella's arm with antiseptic and applied a bandage. "Done. Your arm may be sore for a few days. After that you'll forget the implant is there. You need do nothing. It's safely inside you and operates by itself. Even if you died, it would continue to send its signal."

What a reassuring thought! She cleared her throat. "Thank you."

"Success to you, Councilor."

Arella nodded then sat up. The doctor left as abruptly as he entered. She slid off the table and began to dress. What should she should take with her on a trip she knew nothing about? She quickly left to pack for destinations unknown.

Chapter Twelve

Falcon paced the confines of the Commander's quarters while his brother sat in the chair with the same confidence and calm he always had. Why could he not be more like Dacton? Dacton had successfully captured Zotar at great personal danger. Falcon Rovarn, the new Chief Protector managed to ruin everything! His men and ships were gone and he'd nearly died in the process! He was a failure!

"Little brother." Dacton stood and stopped his brother's pacing. He placed his hands on his shoulders and looked him in the eye. "I know what you're thinking, so just stop right there. You did *not* fail me or the mission."

"I lost six ships, nearly seven hundred men, and Zotar, enemy number one of The Protectorate! And you have the audacity to say I did not fail?" Falcon laughed. "You've lost your mind! Being life-mated has softened your brain."

Dacton chuckled. "You may be right about my mind, but not about yours. The Council understands you were overtaken. Of course, they wonder why Zotar allowed you alone to live, but they also know what a demented mind he has, and how he hates the Rovarns."

"All the more reason he should have killed me with the others."

"He wants you to torment yourself exactly like you're doing now. He'd be happy if you did it for the rest of your life, or for as long as he decides you should live. I know the man better than most."

"I can't argue with your reasoning, but it doesn't make me feel better. I lost good officers, Protectors and friends, and will never forgive myself."

"That's exactly what Zotar wants. Mind torture. He's good at it."

"Well, it's working."

"I understand, but if you're to get through this mission you'd better come to terms with those feelings."

"Don't worry, I hate the man enough to kill him several times over."

"Good. Hang on to that hatred." Dacton put his hand on Falcon's shoulder. "You get to do what I was forbidden to do. Your orders are to eliminate Zotar."

Falcon's head snapped up and he studied his brother's expression to be sure he was serious. "Those are my orders? You're sure?"

"Quite sure. This I would never joke about. I've wanted that man dead since he murdered our brother, not to mention the other reasons too numerous to list. I'm just glad that it will be a Rovarn who sends him to his grave."

"And I will. In this I will not fail."

"No, brother. You will not." Dacton gave Falcon a quick hug then stepped back. "You'll make us all proud. I have no doubt."

"I'll kill him or die trying."

~ ~ ~ ~

Arella unpacked what little she brought with her and placed her things in the drawers built into the wall of the Oran space craft. It was a massive ship, larger and better equipped than the finest Nacrem craft. The interior was lit with hidden lights that circled the room just below the ceiling. She sat on the small bed against the wall and thanked her lucky stars she had a private lav so she would not have to meet Falcon and the crew at every turn.

Falcon. He was a mysterious man. There were times he looked like the fiercest warrior she'd ever seen, then he'd appear to be a lost little boy, and she had no idea which of these traits represented the real Falcon. Both identities suited him, and she was attracted to both. Strength and vulnerability—very seductive.

A chime rang and she assumed someone was at the door. Arella pressed her palm against the lock pad and a panel slid to the side and she found herself face to face with her assignment. "Commander Rovarn," she greeted.

"You do not need to call me Commander, Councilor."

"I'm here on official business, and you're the Commander of this vessel, are you not?"

"As you wish." Falcon entered the cabin and took a seat at the small table. "I just thought to be less formal."

Arella's breath caught in her throat when the handsome Commander flashed her a devilish broad smile that made his deep blue eyes sparkle with mischief. Did he know what effect he had on her? Of course he did, and she would not be fooled by his frivolous flirting. She was here to stop him from capturing Zotar and she'd heard enough about Protectors to know they'd do anything to accomplish their goal, even seduction. "I think formal would be best."

"I was hoping that the woman who saved my life would allow me to use her name." He winked. "You have a beautiful name. I like the way it sounds."

"You flatter me, Commander, but I will not be swayed in my opinion by games."

"I assure you, Councilor, I'm not playing games."

She felt her cheeks warm and feared he'd see her blush, so she rose and walked to the in-wall galley. "Can I offer you a drink?"

"Actually, I came to offer you a tour of the ship so you can learn your way around."

"Thank you." Arella walked to the door, opened it and stepped into the hall. "Shall we?" Falcon swept past her, his scent heavy on the air she so desperately tried to breathe. What was that wonderful scent? It reminded her of the outdoors, of pinus trees, of flowers, of leather, but most of all, everything male.

Falcon pointed to his left. "This hall will take you to the med-unit and supply room. And if you'll follow me, and this hall," he pointed to his right, "will take you to the main galley and entertainment room. But right now, I'd like to show you the control center."

She kept pace with his long strides and wondered if he was in a hurry since he walked so fast. There had been a change in him the moment he stepped inside the ship—his ship. Falcon was a powerful man, and she doubted anyone questioned his authority. His command was total. He consumed everything around him with ease, including her. He could easily control her heart, something she could neverallow. The council told her to do everything in her power to fulfill her mission, including going to bed with the man, but *only* for information. Anything more would devastate everything in her life.

They stepped through an opening into the most awesome room she'd ever seen. Every square inch of wall space held a view screen of some sort, and the entire nose of the craft opened into space where distant stars twinkled their white lights against the dark expanse that stretched out before her eyes.

"Crew," Falcon announced, "I'd like to introduce you to Councilor Arella from Nacrem. She's here to observe and is to be given every courtesy. Please make her welcome and answer any questions she may have. We'll make the rounds so she can meet each of you individually."

Arella counted twelve men sitting at their stations, all with their eyes on her. She smiled and gave the group a courtesy nod. "I look forward to meeting all of you." Her gaze turned to Falcon, who gazed at his men with pride. There was a fine line between arrogance and confidence, and she did not know Falcon well enough to discern which of the two emotions were written all over his face. Whichever it was, he looked too ruggedly appealing in his black uniform, arms crossed over his broad chest, legs slightly apart, his physically fit body ready for anything.

At the moment she had no words. Why the man overwhelmed her so was a mystery, yet she couldn't deny the strong magnetism that radiated from every pore in Falcon's magnificent body. Did he feel the same pull of attraction between them? She remembered the kiss he'd given her in her quarters before he met his brother and her lips began to burn. Where had *that* man gone? Before his memory returned he'd seemed happy, carefree, and attracted to her as a woman. Now he stood with military stiffness and indifference. It would be easier for her if she took a lesson from Falcon instead of falling all over him like a besotted fool.

Falcon uncrossed his arms and walked to the first station on his left. "Councilor Arella, I'd like you to meet First Officer Marco. He is second in command on the ship."

"I'm honored." Arella extended her hand. Marco did not grasp her wrist in the traditional greeting, instead he stood, raised her hand to his lips and placed a light kiss on her fingers.

"It is I who am honored, Councilor Arella." Marco released her hand. "If I can be of service to you in any way, you have just to ask."

Falcon groaned. "I fear Officer Marco is a bit of a romantic. He studies ancient history far too much and believes himself to be a mighty warrior of times past."

"I see nothing wrong with history," Arella smiled and tilted her head a bit to look up at Marco's tall, elegant form, "or romantics."

"Thank you, my lady. Our Commander has lost his sense of humor recently." Marco grinned at Falcon. "And I do hope he finds it soon."

"Carry on." Falcon placed his hand in the center of Arella's back and guided her to the next station."

"Second Officer Margon is in charge of navigation."

Arella noticed the strangest look on Falcon's face when he glanced over his shoulder at Marco. Just as quickly he turned his attention back to her and Margon and the look was gone. They exchanged a few words, then moved on to each of the other ten men hard at work in the control room.

"I'm most impressed, Commander. You run quite a ship here."

"Thank you." Falcon escorted her out and down two halls to the galley. He ordered two cups of coffa and carried them to a table in the corner of the near deserted dining area. He held a chair for Arella while she seated herself. "I hope you enjoy this coffa. It's a special blend only available on Ora. I became fond of it while visiting my brother and his wife."

"I am anxious to meet Talina."

"She's quite a woman. My brother is most fortunate."

Arella took a sip of the steaming liquid. It was a great flavored coffa with a slightly sweet, nutty taste. "I can see why you favor this blend." He smiled at her and she was glad she was sitting, fearful her legs would not hold her. If she were to make it through this mission she could not let the man turn her to jelly every time he smiled at her. "How did Dacton and Talina meet?"

Falcon chuckled. "He kidnapped her, took her on quite the adventure, nearly got himself killed by a pengore." He looked deeply into Arella's eyes. "Together they successfully captured Zotar and brought him to trial. They both paid a high price. However, it brought them together and I've never seen a happier couple."

"I see." Falcon looked like a haunted man, running from demons only he knew about. He could change moods faster than anyone she'd ever known.

"Do you?" Falcon pushed his cup aside. "Zotar Alucard is the most heinous human ever to walk the universe, and I intend to destroy him. His crimes are too numerous to list, and to ugly to tell." He leaned closer to Arella. "You've heard about him, haven't you?"

"Some, but not like you describe." Arella had to be careful not to reveal too much about herself, the High Council's mission, or how Nacrem felt about the very man Falcon wanted to destroy. She'd save Zotar, it was her job. Besides, he could never have done the things Falcon alluded to, not the man she knew. Modark, or Zotar, was married to her sister, he fathered a child he loved. No man could care about a child if he was as evil as Falcon believed him to be. Nor could he love a life-mate the way she'd seen him love Nodia. No. Falcon was wrong.

"I could show you vids if you like."

"Vids? What would that prove?" Arella did not like the direction of this conversation. She had to hide her feelings about Zotar or Falcon would learn more about her than he should.

"It would show you the truth. The truth you seem reluctant to admit. The truth your High Council refuses to believe." Falcon shook his head. "My memory is back. I know Dacton has been before your High Council many times to convince them to join The Protectorate, and I know Nacrem is reluctant." Falcon stood and walked to the doorway. "I'll arrange for the vids to be available on the view-screen in your cabin should you wish to view them." He stepped into the hall then turned. "And I suggest you view them carefully."

Falcon disappeared down the hall just as a roiling sense of nausea rolled through her. Confusion settled heavily in her mind, her chest tight. She wanted to believe Falcon was the kind of man who spoke the truth, yet she could not trust what he said. The man was a representative of The Protectorate, and they desperately wanted Nacrem to join them so they could gain more support for their causes. The Nacrem High Council said they'd viewed the vids Falcon spoke of, and considered them clever fakes to show Zotar in a bad light when the man was actually a great supporter of Nacrem's people.

There was only one way for her to learn the truth. She stood and quickly retreated to her cabin, the door closing behind her with a whoosh. She sat in the chair and stared at the vid-screen on the wall. What would she see? What could she believe? Truth could be elusive and hard to discern, especially when one of the parties involved wanted it hidden.

With a sigh she pressed the power button and the screen lit up in swirling shades of purple and soft feminine voice crooned, "Speak your instructions, Councilor Arella and I will comply." So, Falcon worked fast. "Show me the vids of Zotar Alucard."

"Do you wish to view them all in succession?"

"No, show the last vid first."

"As you wish."

Before she could take another breath, Arella watched a vicious sword fight between Dacton Rovarn and Zotar. She did not recognize the location, but Zotar's voice was angry, and he clearly wanted to kill Dacton. Then he spoke of doing vile sexual things to Talina. This could not be! She watched intently as the two men fought for their lives, unable to comprehend why Zotar, or Modark as she knew him, would say, or do such things to any woman.

Thoughts ran through her mind, yet nothing made sense. Finally it was over, Dacton the victor, Zotar in custody. "Show two vids before this one." In a beautifully wild, country setting Zotar questioned a prisoner he had strung between two trees. The man wore primitive clothing, nothing like she'd ever seen. Zotar kept asking him where Dacton and Talina were. The man refused to answer, then he told Zotar they were dead. Zotar didn't believe the man so he pulled a cutter from his belt and cut the man's throat from ear to ear.

Hot tears streamed down her cheeks. No! This could not be. Zotar acted like a brutal, cold-blooded murderer! That could not possibly be the truth. There was that word again –truth. "Enough. Vid-screen off!" The screen went black. She could not watch any more lies. It was well known how vids were made and changed to suit one's purpose. Why Falcon thought this would be proof was beyond her. Did he think her that gullible? If so, he just made a fatal mistake, because she'd easily thwart his request, and he'd be destroyed in his position with The Protectorate. She knew the rule; never underestimate the enemy, and that was a mistake she would not make.

There was an outside possibility that Zotar really had done those horrid acts, but she simply could not, would not, believe him capable of such behavior. Not the brother-in-law she knew. She'd stop this insanity. She walked to the door and stepped into the hall when it slid open. The red lights in the dark, windowless hall of the ship gave her an eerie feeling.

Arella walked the structure up and down not sure what to do, or where to start. How much sabotage could she complete without notice? Falcon was a smart Commander, and his crew most competent which made matters difficult. She couldn't open doors she wasn't authorized to, and the control room always had a complete crew working.

For now she'd content herself with learning all she could about the ship, it's workings, and the elusive Commander who controlled it all. She had no idea of where or how Falcon would search for Zotar, which meant she still had time to formulate a plan to stop him.

"Are you lost?"

Her heart leapt into her throat when she heard Falcon's voice behind her. After a deep breath she turned to face him. "I suppose I am."

"Maybe I can help." Falcon leaned against the wall with one shoulder effectively blocking Arella's path. "What were you looking for?"

He had her there. "I was restless and thought perhaps you had a workout facility on board." The grin he gave her was devilish, flirtatious, and disbelieving. She took another breath to steady herself. Regardless of what the man was thinking, his potent masculine power sent chills of excitement down her spine and flutters in her abdomen. Damn the man. She reminded herself she had to keep her enemy close.

"Actually, we have such a facility." He pushed away from the wall and started down the hall. He turned his head back toward Arella. "Follow me."

Great, now she'd have to exercise to prove her story. At least physical exertion calmed her nerves, and she was in sore need of calming. Between the vids, the High Council's orders, and her unwanted attraction to the dazzling Commander Rovarn, she might need to stay in the gym for the entire voyage.

Falcon's long stride made her nearly jog down several different halls to keep up with him. The sight of his backside in those well-tailored black pants was enough to make her want to follow him anywhere, orders or not. He was overly self-assured, with a commanding presence that oozed virile, warrior-like power and pride. It would not be easy putting anything over on Falcon. He'd be a true test of her abilities.

Finally, he stopped in front of a wide door at the end of the hall and it slid opened. He waited for her to enter the well-appointed workout room, so she walked inside. There were several exercise machines, various apparatuses, and lots of open space to practice whatever one wanted. "I'm impressed, Commander." She should have guessed they'd be well equipped since Falcon's physique was perfect, muscles everywhere with not a pinch of excess flesh.

"I'll leave you now, unless you have further need of me."

"I was wondering when we'll reach our destination?"

Falcon sat on the seat of a weight bench. "We'll reach Ora in," he glanced at the timepiece on his wrist, "exactly forty-seven space hours."

"Then what?"

"We'll go before the Council, make our report and receive further orders."

"We? You mean they'll permit me to be with you?"

"Of course." He stood and crossed his arms over his chest. "The Protectorate understands Nacrem's distrust, which is exactly why they'll permit you to be a part of this mission from beginning to end. They want to prove to Nacrem, once and for all, that we only have Nacrem's best interest at heart."

"Your words are persuasive, Commander, but as you well know, it's your actions I'm here to observe."

"Then I shall endeavor to impress you, Councilor Arella."
Falcon bowed at the waist, then left the room.

The man had transformed before her eyes from a lost, desperate
soul in the desert to a commanding, authoritative, cold
Commander. Her body was attracted to both men, but her heart
preferred the lost soul who needed her help. He seemed happier,
freer, and far more flirtatious when he had no clue to his identity.

Arella picked up a pair of hand weights and began her workout
routine. She wanted to rid her mind of all stray thoughts of Falcon.
He was nothing more than an assignment, and she was a fool to
make more if their relationship than that. They may have shared a
brief kiss that teased and tantalized her down to her toes, but that
Falcon was gone. In fact, that part of his personality probably
never existed. His mind and personality had been altered by the
drug induced amnesia, so he was not responsible for any actions
toward her.

From the look on his face a moment ago, Commander Falcon
was not attracted to her. He was all business, conducting himself
with the proper decorum expected of an officer. That should serve
as lesson one. It was far too dangerous to venture over the line
between personal and professional, and she was determined to
keep her distance. Granted, the High Council expected her to do
whatever was necessary to stop Falcon from capturing Zotar, and
she prayed she could stay true to her convictions.

CHAPTER THIRTEEN

"**S**it down, Brother." Dacton grabbed Falcon's arm and shoved him down on the chair behind the desk. "That's better. How can I talk to you when you're constantly moving around the room?"

"Sorry."

"What's bothering you?"

"It's nothing."

"I'm your brother, remember? Now, tell me before you explode."

"It's Arella. The woman drives me to distraction." He would not admit to Dacton that he had been watching Arella workout on the security vid-screen. She looked so damned tempting, her body glistening with sweat, her clothes clinging to her magnificent body, her breasts outlined against the pale pink tunic she wore. He wanted her in the worst way, there was no denying it, he had been in some stage of arousal since the moment he laid eyes on her.

"You're attracted to her."

"I wouldn't say that."

Dacton cleared his throat. "You're in lust with her then."

Falcon simply glared at his overly astute brother. "Tell me how it was with you and Talina." Dacton's laughter filled the office.

"Some things are better experienced."

"And what is that supposed to mean?"

"Let me just say I see some similarities between you and Arella and the way I reacted to Talina."

"Great." Falcon stood and started to pace once again. "Any advice then?"

"Follow your heart, not your mind."

"I will simply stay away from the woman." His brother roared in laughter once again. "What I mean is. . ."

"You owe me no explanations, Falcon. You are a wise man, capable of making your own decisions. As a leader, there are none better. You are loyal to The Protectorate, they trust you."

"Do you?" Falcon stared at his brother. "I failed The Protectorate and the family when Zotar escaped. By the Gods, he was in my custody! It was my fault."

"You judge yourself too harshly. Why not let the High Council have their say before you condemn yourself."

"I still don't believe The Protectorate's High Council agreed to meet us on Ora. They never leave Bronic."

"This is a special case, and Ora is closer. Every sun-cycle counts as you well know."

Falcon checked his wrist-piece, then glanced at the screen in front of him. "You're right, as always. We are in descent and will dock in minutes."

~ ~ ~ ~

Arella stared at the beautiful Princess Talina of Ora sitting across from her in the private waiting room of Ora's Royal Palace. She had not seen Falcon since he left her in the workout room. He was not supposed to be out of her sight, but circumstances had a way of deciding their togetherness.

"I understand you are to observe Commander Falcon in his pursuit of Zotar."

When Talina said Zotar's name a tear glistened in her eyes. She obviously had no use for the man. "Did Zotar hurt you, Princess?"

"He hurt many of my people, and people of other worlds as well. He is evil." Talina dried a tear from her cheek. "I do not wish to influence your decisions or opinions, but the best thing that ever happened to Ora is The Protectorate."

"I believe, on that issue, you may be just a bit prejudiced?"

Arella noticed a blush take form on Talina's face. "I mean no disrespect. I've met Dacton, and he is a fine man, my reservations are for The Protectorate itself."

"I understand more than you think, Arella. And in case you don't know, Falcon is just as honorable, proud and capable as his brother." Talina leaned closer to Arella's ear. "And *almost* as handsome as Dacton."

"Falcon's appearance has nothing to do with my assignment, I assure you."

Talina smiled. "Of course. Being with a handsome warrior had no effect on me either." She laughed.

"This is no laughing matter, Princess."

"Forgive me. I do know the seriousness of finding Zotar before he destroys more lives. Believe me, I want him captured." Talina took a deep breath. "Don't you?"

"I want what is best." That was not a lie. Arella could not bring herself to lie. Besides, if she did everyone would know since she was not very good at verbal deception.

"I see."

A harmonic chime filled the room and Talina stood and walked to the door. "It is time. Follow me."

Arella rose, straightened her long blue gown, and followed Talina into the hall. She much preferred her military apparel, but she would show proper respect while she was here. The last thing she wanted to do was draw undue attention to herself.

"Ladies," Dacton greeted. "The High Council is ready for us." He offered his arm to Talina. "Shall we, Princess?"

The loving looks that played between Dacton and Talina were so charged Arella thought the air might sparkle and crack around them. It must be nice to have so much trust and love for one man. Such a rarity in her world.

Falcon stepped into the hall, walked to her side and offered his arm. "Shall we, Councilor Arella?"

Her heart beat faster the moment her gaze fell on Falcon's devastatingly handsome face. She saw tenderness in the depths of his deep blue eyes and felt her heart melt yet another degree. She entwined her arm with his, her hand resting on the steel strength of his forearm. Even through the long sleeves of his black uniform, she felt power pulse through every toned muscle. Her stomach began to flutter and she cursed the effect this man created whenever he touched her.

They entered a large, formal room and walked to the front where thirteen men were seated behind a marbelus table. The man in the center stood. His robe was different from the other twelve men, and he looked a few sun-cycles older than all the others. Dacton, Talina and Falcon bowed, so she followed their lead. They all straightened and waited for the man to speak.

"Greetings Ambassador Rovarn and Princess Talina, Commander Rovarn, and to you, Councilor Arella, our honored guest." The doyen glanced up and down the table at the other High Council members, then back at the four people before him. "We are all gathered here under very dire circumstances, as Dacton, Talina and Falcon are aware. My hope is that Nacrem realizes the gravity of the situation. So, if I may ask, Councilor, what is Nacrem's position toward the convicted criminal, Zotar?"

Arella swallowed in an attempt to ease her suddenly dry throat. She had to choose her words carefully. The enormity of this assignment settled over her like cosmic storm. "At the moment Nacrem is taking a neutral stand against the criminal you call Zotar. We shall reserve judgment until we see the outcome."

"Those words might serve to comfort this council. However, we are well aware of the personal relationship you maintain with the galaxy's most notorious criminal. What say you to that, Councilor Arella?"

Sweat beaded on her brow and her hands felt clammy cold. They had her on that one, and she knew her answer to that question could make or break the entire assignment. With a silent prayer for help she answered, "You know well my relationship to Modark. He is my brother-in-law and has been a good husband to my sister, Nodia, and a good father to his son. Of course, my opinion of the man has been challenged by The Protectorate. I learned of Modark's other identity so recently all the ramifications have not yet taken root. I answer you as honestly as I can. I am here as an observer, and I intend to perform my duties as such."

The doyen nodded his head. "Well said, Councilor. Should you have answered any other way, we would have known you to be lying. We appreciate your honesty."

Arella's legs began to shake. She may have won the first round in this little battle, but there was far more to come. How did one prepare herself for such a confrontation? She was totally alone in her stand before the council, especially with the Rovarns at her side. The doyen walked around the table and came to stand in front of her. He was relatively short, yet his total authority and command of the room made him seem like a giant.

"We wonder if you are truly here to observe, or if your council sent you to sabotage our mission?"

Her shaky legs went rigid with fear. She took several calming breaths. They could not possibly know her instructions. They were merely probing her for information. If she were to be believable she had to remain calm and collected. Out the corner of her eye she noted a frown on Falcon's face. Did that look mean he believed the doyen, or was he reacting as a woman's protector? What a foolish thought. Falcon was a Protectorate man through and through with no feelings for her, and she'd do well to remember where his loyalties remained. "With all due respect to you and the council, I doubt there is much I can say to convince you that I am but a mere observer, for the truth of my words will only be proven when this mission is over with the results you desire."

The doyen smiled at her, and that made her more uneasy than the questioning frown he'd maintained from the start. Beside her Falcon stood at rigid attention, his gaze straight ahead. How she wished she had his strength. Mustering what little courage she had she lifted her chin and gazed straight into the doyen's eyes, eyes that held uncanny intelligence, like wisdom of the ages.

"You are quite right, Councilor. We will all await the outcome, but please be warned, we will succeed, no matter what you do. You will be with the best Protector we have. As you know, Commander Falcon Rovarn is also our Chief Protector, as Dacton was when he pursued Zotar to a successful capture. It was only through treason and treachery that Zotar escaped as he did, taking many lives in the process, an occurrence that will never happen again."

Silence descended and all Arella heard was the heavy beat of her own heart. She'd always wanted an important mission to prove women could handle anything a man could, yet somehow she felt she was in way over her head. Failure was not an option. "I understand completely."

"I hope you do, for anyone who stands in the way of complete success will be destroyed. Those are Commander Rovarn's orders, and he will follow his orders to the letter." The doyen turned his gaze to Falcon. "Make no mistake about my words, Councilor, for it would pain this council to see any harm befall a representative of Nacrem, for we truly seek a peaceful alliance that will benefit all of The Protectorate's planets. We still hold high hopes that Nacrem will join with us."

"If all goes well, that will undoubtedly be the outcome. As I stated before, I am here to observe The Protectorate's procedures of justice. Only when we are satisfied that The Protectorate acts in the best interest of all will we vote to join."

"Very well then. We will insure that you have first-hand knowledge of everything concerning this mission. You will be personally involved so there will be no questions later that we did something without your knowledge."

"I thank you for the opportunity, and your trust."

"Trust must be won. You are welcome for the opportunity." The doyen returned to his place at the head of the table and took his seat. "Now, Princess Talina, if you would escort Councilor Arella to her quarters, make her at home, and prepare her for her journey, we would be most grateful."

"As you wish." Talina bowed, then turned and walked to the door.

Arella bowed to the High Council then followed Talina out of the room, the big door closing behind them.

"Commander Rovarn," the doyen began, "now that we have met Councilor Arella, we realize how difficult your mission has become. You may have to make some sensitive decisions, decisions that may not agree with your better judgment where women are concerned, but you will do what is required of you, of that we have no doubt. But hear me well, nothing will prevent you from eliminating your target."

Falcon's eyes widened at the word *eliminate*. That meant he just received official orders to kill Zotar. It would be sweet, something he'd wanted to do since the man killed his brother all those annual-cycles ago. Dacton had wanted the pleasure, but was denied, with orders to return Zotar to The Protectorate for trial. Now, the High Council was telling him to. . ."

"Yes, Falcon, you heard me correctly. You are to kill Zotar Alucard. You will watch him take his last breath." The doyen turned his attention to Dacton. "I am sorry we denied you the pleasure, but Zotar had to be publicly tried so all would see crimes like his are not to be tolerated. You learned much in the process, and gained a devoted wife. We are very proud of your accomplishments, Ambassador Rovarn. Now your brother will take up the fight for justice. Give him whatever parting advice you think will help, for he leaves on the morrow."

"I will endeavor to impart my limited wisdom to my brother." Dacton glanced at Falcon. "He's a most able warrior, with a true heart. He will not fail The Protectorate."

The doyen nodded. "Now, Falcon, we must reveal to you that your mission may take on some similarities to Dacton's. We've learned that Zotar is making one last attempt to raise an army and amass a fortune. He is said to be on Millia. We will provide a briefing chip for you to view in flight. Study it well and follow all instructions. You know we ask only what is necessary."

"I will follow orders, as always."

"The remainder of this sun-cycle will be for you to relax and say your farewells. Your fleet is being readied. Dismissed."

Falcon and his brother bowed, straightened, then turned on their heels and left the council chamber. Once in the hall Falcon sighed deeply. At least that part was over and he'd soon be on his way to rid the galaxy of a man consumed with evil. Death was too easy for Zotar. He wished he could make Zotar suffer the way all his victims had, and even that would not be enough.

"Brother," Dacton said, placing an arm around Falcon's shoulder. "Our mother is making arrangements for a family dinner before you leave. She had to cut her honeymoon short, which was quite a sacrifice."

"She's that happy?"

"Yes. Who would ever have thought that our mother and Talina's father would fall head over heels for each other?" Dacton laughed and slapped Falcon on the back. "I suppose it will be your turn next, right little brother?"

"Not on your life. I enjoy flying solo. Besides, I couldn't possibly choose only one woman when there are so many out there. No, I'll leave life-mating to the rest of you."

"Shall we place a wager on that?"

Falcon grinned. This would be an easy wager to win because he never wanted to life-mate. The military life was exciting, and the women plentiful, what more could a man want? Though Arella was a tempting morsel, he had no wish to be tied to domestic responsibilities. "Okay, I'll put up my sword collection." Dacton would back away now since he knew how much that sword collection meant to him and that he would not wager something that valuable if he was not assured of victory.

"I have always admired that collection, as you well know, and I shall so hate taking it from you."

"So, brother of mine, what will you sacrifice?"

"I suppose it only fair I put up my cutter collection you have always admired."

"Done." They grasped wrists in the traditional warrior's greeting to seal the wager. "Now, let us find our mother and her new husband. I have yet to speak to her."

CHAPTER FOURTEEN

Arella glanced around the opulent room that Talina said would be hers for the duration of her stay. The glossy rose colored fabric on the windows and bed shone with an ethereal brightness that did little to lift her spirits. Her time before the Protectorate's High Council had been brief, but the doyen had managed to effectively warn her with his carefully chosen words. He believed her to be exactly what she was, a spy working against them. Had the man really been able to see inside her, or was it merely a guess? Whatever his reason she needed to proceed with extreme caution.

"Arella?" Talina stepped closer. "Are you well?"

"Of course." Arella turned toward the beautiful blond woman. "Why do you ask?"

"Your face has lost all color and you look as if you might faint. I, forgive me, please. It's just that I've been in similar circumstances to yours, and if I can be of help you only need to ask."

Arella pulled the crystal triangle from beneath her gown to let it rest on the outside. There was no reason to hide such a beautiful gift from her sister, even if Modark had given it to Nodia first. Nodia said it would protect her, and right now just the thought calmed her.

"That's beautiful!" Talina reached out and touched the crystal pendant.

A moment after Talina touched the clear stone she quickly pulled her hand back as if the pendant has burned her. "Is something wrong?" Arella watched the woman shake her head no, but she sensed a fear in Talina that was not present before. "It's a gift from my sister. She said it would protect me."

"And so it shall," Talina replied.

Arella opened the burris wood armoire and found it full of not only beautiful gowns but traveling clothes as well. Tunics, pants and boots in various fabrics and leathers, all of the finest quality caught her eye.

"They are all for you, Arella. I hope you approve?"

"Approve?" Arella turned her gaze to Talina. "You are most generous. You have my approval and my sincere thanks."

"I hope I have chosen well. It is always difficult to know what to pack for an adventure such as you are about to have."

A smile curved Arella's lips as she thought of the many stories she'd heard about Dacton and Talina's adventures. She had no idea if they were true or not, but they did sound romantic. Kidnapped from her home by a handsome warrior who took her into the forbidden hills, facing perils no one else had ever been known to survive? That was an adventure worth taking.

"I'm no mind reader," Talina began, "but I suspect you're wondering about my quest with Dacton?"

Arella swallowed hard. Had she been so transparent? Damn. So far she was failing miserably at being an undercover agent. It seemed everyone knew what she was doing and thinking at every turn. "Do you have any stories you can tell?"

"Well, I gained a wonderful pet Atew, I met the Burly people and really liked them. I nursed Dacton back to life after he fought a Pengore. He is the only person to live to tell about what it was like." Talina smiled. "We don't have time for such stories now. Maybe someday when we have the luxury of time."

"I must say, I certainly would like to hear all the details. Your adventures sound quite interesting. However, I agree I must pack and get ready for my journey." She looked at Talina. "I don't even know where I'm going."

"Neither do I, but that's the fun of it, right?"

"Fun? How can you even say such a thing?

"My sweet Arella, how can I not when you'll be with Falcon?" Talina laughed. "You'll see what I mean, I'm sure of that."

"Well I do not plan to have fun. I am an observer, that's all." The look Talina gave her said far more that she wanted it to. She really did think that Falcon would fall in love with her, and that she would not resist him. Well, the princess was very wrong, but she did not want to argue and cause trouble. "Maybe you should tell me more about your adventures."

Talina smiled. "All I will say is that we accomplished our goal, and in the process found an enduring love neither of us expected."

If that were to be her fate, she'd gladly welcome this trip with Falcon. However, since she was here to stop him, there could be no successful outcome for them together. One of them would go down in defeat, and she was determined it would not be her. "I'm happy for you, Princess Talina. You're a lucky woman."

"That I do know, but I will tell you, it wasn't easy falling in love with a man I thought to be my enemy."

There was the difference between them, Arella did not think Falcon her enemy, she knew. "I don't suppose it was, but the outcome is astounding. You and Dacton have rewritten history."

"No, we created history. My only regret is that Falcon must now risk his life to put that despicable man down for good."

Arella's only regret was being on Ora. Talina seemed like a genuinely wonderful person, but she hated Zotar with a passion. Talina knew Zotar was her brother-in-law, Modark, but she could not possibly know how much the man loved her sister. They had no idea who Modark was, or what the man was capable of doing. He was not a killer! She refused to believe that of him.

Modark loved his wife and son, prided himself on being a huge benefactor to the people of Nacrem, and he'd always been nothing but kind to her. No, that vid she'd seen on Falcon's ship had not been real. She suspected, even then, that The Protectorate would do anything within their power to influence her to their will.

"I see you're a bit distracted. You might want to rest before dinner." Talina walked to the door. "I'll send someone to escort you around seven."

"Thank you," was all Arella could mutter. Her emotions were confused. How could she feel so at home with these people when they wanted to kill Modark, and in the process, destroy her family?

Something was terribly amiss, and before the night was over, she'd discover exactly what was wrong.

~ ~ ~ ~

Falcon whistled while he walked the long hall to Arella's suite. Talina was going to send a messenger to fetch Arella, so of course, he had to volunteer. He did not want the Councilor to think ill of the Rovarns for not showing proper hospitality to a guest. Truth be told, he was too anxious to see her again to wait for someone else to bring her to the family dinner.

Stopping at the last door on the left, he pressed the call button and listened to the harmonic chimes that would bring the fair lady before his gaze once again. At last the door opened and there stood Councilor Arella in the sexiest lavender gown he'd ever seen. He opened his mouth to speak, but words failed him, and that was a rare occurrence.

"Falcon? I thought to find a messenger."

"I. .wanted to extend a warm Rovarn welcome, and so, you see, a stranger would not do as your escort. So, shall we go?" Falcon extended an elbow toward her and she slipped her hand around his offered arm, her touch warm and inviting. He straightened to his full height and led the way down the long hall. "May I say how lovely you look this evening, Councilor Arella."

"Thank you, Commander Rovarn."

"You needn't be so formal." She gazed up at him, her eyes nearly the same color as her gown. If he dropped his guard for one moment around her she'd shatter the wall around his heart and pierce him to his soul. Every fiber of his being responded to her in a most unfamiliar manner. He was well acquainted with lust, but not the caring part. He cared. It made no sense, other than he owed her his life, but something stirred deep inside him every time he was near her. The urge to pull her into his arms and kiss her senseless was always there, and that thought shocked him since lip contact was not the first thing that crossed his mind when he looked at a desirable woman.

"Falcon, I understand this is a family dinner, are you sure I should attend? I do not wish to intrude on your private life. My duty only requires I observe your work."

"It will be my pleasure to have you at my side this evening, and introduce to my family the woman who saved my life." He watched the expression on her face and caught the blush she tried to hide by looking away. His heart beat a little faster at the realization she was not unaffected by him.

If ever two people were opposites it would be them, yet he felt the undeniable pull between them. He wished he could claim no memory again and kiss her like he had before he knew who he was, and before she became his watchdog. He swallowed hard to avoid that entire line of thinking.

"If you're sure. I don't want to make anyone uncomfortable. I'm a stranger, Falcon, and this is a family dinner." Arella stopped walking. "Take me back. This is not right. I feel like an intruder."

Falcon pulled her to him and satisfied his burning need to feel her lips against his once again. It may be folly, and Dacton would say he was out of control, and he may well be, but it felt right to have this woman in his arms. Her lips tasted sweet, so soft and welcoming. His tongue pressed for entry and ever so slowly she opened for him, meeting his invasion with one of her own.

Oh, what this woman did to him! If he followed his desires she'd be naked beneath him on the hallway floor. He deepened the kiss even though it was a mistake. Of all people on the face of the planet, he, Commander of The Protectorate, trained to be cautious, patient, and above all, to use his intelligence, was making an utter fool of himself in a public hallway. Reluctantly he pulled back from Arella, his heart racing like a green lad having his first experience with a woman.

She looked at him with a slight smile on her lips, and the glassy, dazed appearance of her beautiful eyes sent a bolt of relief through him. It was obvious she enjoyed the kiss as much as he had, but now they both stood in stunned silence. "I thought to make you feel like part of the family." By the fleet, he doubted he could sound more stupid if he tried. He had difficulty thinking when he was so close to her.

"I do hope the rest of your family does not greet me quite so intimately."

Falcon chuckled, took her arm and began the trek down the hall once again. "They'd never be so bold, nor would I allow such a greeting." He kept his gaze straight ahead, not wanting her to see that little spark of jealousy that shot through him at the thought of another man kissing her. He had no reason for such feelings, yet they were real. Maybe he'd spent too much time in space with his fellow men, because he certainly was not acting properly around this woman.

Out the corner of his eye he detected her smile. At least she found him amusing, that was a start. A start to what? He was surely losing his mind! They were to share a professional relationship for the duration of this mission, and here he was thinking and hoping for a romantic interlude. It would be career suicide at the very least, and total destruction at the worst. He knew better than to become involved with a woman, and he would have to erect an even thicker wall around his emotions than he already maintained.

~ ~ ~ ~

Arella shut the door to her room, mentally and physically exhausted from the Rovarn family dinner. Falcon's family was extraordinary. They were open, passionate, and willing to accept a stranger into their midst. They made her feel welcome, and for that she was glad, but something had changed in Falcon. One moment he was kissing her with all the passion a man could have, and the next he seemed cold and aloof, just like every other Protectorate officer she'd met.

Falcon's mother, fresh from her honeymoon with Talina's father, was now the first lady of Ora. The couple was so much in love they created a warm glow everywhere they went. It was reassuring to see that some life-matings were made for the right reason, although she knew such a blessing would never happen to her. If she ever took a mate it would have to be for political gain, and the chances of that being a love match was about one in a million, if that.

No. It would be better to live her life alone than to spend it with someone she did not love. Her only fear was being forced into such a union because of her political responsibilities. It would be difficult to know what the League would demand of her since she was the first woman Councilor. She'd seen many men forced to life-mate women they did not love for credits and social connections deemed politically correct.

Nodia and Modark came to mind. Theirs was a union the League wanted because of Modark's unlimited wealth, yet it turned out to be a love match, so it was possible. She knew, deep within her soul, she'd never be that lucky. Any thoughts she had about Falcon were sure to break her heart. The league would never allow a union between them since they had no intention of joining The Protectorate.

Her future may be bleak in the romance department, but she felt her success in the political arena would be great. She could open the door for other women, but only if she succeeded in this mission. If she failed, she'd be the last woman to serve the government. That was a huge responsibility, one she could only pray she was worthy to hold.

Arella quickly donned her sleeping gown and lay down on the soft bed. She pulled the silky covers over her and her mind immediately focused on Falcon's kiss. He was a man of great passion when he allowed his barrier to slip and his emotions to rule. He made her feel sexy, wanted, and. . . No! Falcon was her assignment, nothing more. She rolled over, beat her pillow into submission and willed herself to sleep. She forced all thoughts of Falcon from her mind and prayed he would not invade her dreams.

~ ~ ~ ~

Falcon tossed and turned, then bolted upright from a dead sleep with sweat beaded on his forehead and his heart racing. Images of Arella still clouded his mind. She was too beautiful to be touched by Zotar in any way. In his dream Zotar held her captive, a cutter at her throat. Then he held her over a precipice and threatened to toss her to her death.

A powerless feeling gripped him tightly, and not for the first time. Falcon had not been able to stop Zotar from murdering Baleko, nor had he been able to help Dacton in his quest to capture him. This time it would be different. He'd be in control, but caution remained paramount. This dream was a warning. He knew in his soul Zotar would destroy Arella without a thought to get what he wanted. Zotar savored his new found freedom. Plus Zotar still wanted the two surviving Rovarn brothers dead.

Zotar still held Dacton responsible for his only sister's accidental death. If Dacton had not found Zotar trying to change his grades at the academy that fateful night, everything would be different. Dacton turned him in, which forced a court martial and Zotar's expulsion from the academy. If Zotar had met his sister that night as planned, Julya would not have crashed into that mountain in an emotional moment—she would be alive, and Zotar would not be their enemy. Life did not always go as planned.

Nothing seemed to go as planned. He'd been taking Zotar to Obitus for his appointed execution until fate turned the tables on him and he found himself baking in the desert with no control over his mind or body. Now he had to chase the murdering bastard across the galaxy again, this time with a woman to worry about. Arella. He sighed. When had he become soft and addle-brained?

He was Commander Rovarn, Chief Protector, celebrated for his heroic exploits. He held the highest position in The Protectorate, with total command of every man and ship The Protectorate owned. Certainly, he could keep one woman safe and apprehend one criminal. Then again, Zotar was no ordinary criminal, and Arella was one extraordinary woman.

CHAPTER FIFTEEN

Arella hugged the wall in an effort to become invisible while Falcon said goodbye to his family. Her heart ached to know what it was like to have people love you and care so much they had tears in their eyes knowing they would be separated from each other. She'd decided in her youth not to long for what never could be. She had her career, and that was enough.

Wherever they were headed she had to devise a plan to stop all progress. Zotar must remain free. As if her thought had been read, Talina Rovarn walked over and stopped in front of her. Talina smiled at her as if everything were beautiful and they were best friends.

"Arella, I just wanted to say how glad I am that we met." Talina reached out and took Arella's hand in hers. "I wish you luck in your journey, and I have one request."

"What might that be?" She wanted to like Talina. The woman was warm, kind and caring, but this mission prohibited personal feelings.

"Only that you keep Falcon safe. He's quite stubborn at times, and he takes too many risks. I hope you can persuade him to be cautious. Dacton and I want him to return in one piece. And it would kill Galina if anything happened to him."

"I will do my best." Arella was pleased with her carefully chosen words, which could be interpreted many ways, so she did not have to worry about breaking a promise.

"I know you will. You have my thanks."

"It's time to depart," Dacton announced. He slapped Falcon on the back and leaned closer to whisper in his ear. "Good luck, brother, you'll need it."

"I will succeed in finding Zotar."

"I don't doubt that. I meant good luck with Arella."

"There's nothing to. . ."

"Save it. Been there." Dacton chuckled. "As I said, good luck, brother."

~ ~ ~ ~

Falcon could not believe how long his family had taken to say goodbye. The way they acted he would never return. He refused to even consider that possibility. It was Zotar's demise that kept his mind occupied. Arella stood by his side while he gave flight orders to his crew. Space was the one place he found peace, but he feared this mission would afford him no time for relaxation with Arella aboard. He had a hunch she was here to stop him, and the Nacrem League picked the right person for the job.

She would not succeed. His family dubbed him the most practical of the Rovarn boys, a title he'd earned the hard way, and one woman would not cause him to lose his head. He'd keep her with him as much as possible so she would not have the opportunity to sabotage the mission. It was time to put his plan into action. He strode to where she stood. "We have much to discuss."

"Do we?"

"Yes, if you intend to stay informed. I wouldn't want to do anything behind your back. I was told to include you in everything I do, so, shall we get started?"

"Very well."

"Good. Follow me." He made his way through the large craft to his private quarters where he looked into the retina-scan and the door slid open. He motioned her in, then followed. "Welcome to my cabin." Her discomfort was obvious, and that was good. He certainly did not want her getting too comfortable. "Please, have a seat on the couch. There's a vid we need to watch together."

"I don't think. . ."

"Please, indulge me." Falcon watched her take a seat on the sofa that faced the large screen. "Start vid." The moment he spoke the instruction the High Council's usual boring instructions began, so the sooner it was over, the better.

He sat a respectable distance from Arella on the couch, careful not to touch her, but close enough to sense the warmth of her body. She was a distracting morsel, and he knew better that to give in to lust. For a moment the couch vibrated and he saw Arella turn to stone. "Relax, we're just getting underway. As soon as we leave port you'll not feel or hear the engines." Judging from her color, the woman was terrified of flying, but she settled back and pretended all was well.

The doyen's face filled the screen, his soft, but authoritative voice filled the room as they listened.

"Commander Rovarn, Councilor Arella, greetings. The instructions I'm about to give may sound a bit unorthodox, but I assure you, they are necessary and are to be carried out to the letter. First, Arella, we know all about Modark being Zotar, and that he is your brother-in-law. Our sources tell us he appears to be devoted to your sister, Nodia and their son, Ducard. Do not let appearances fool you, he is evil. Believe it, whether or not you have witnessed such behavior does not make it less true. For your safety, assume the worst.

"We understand how difficult this will be for you, but if you value your life, and the lives of your family, you will take precautions. Falcon is most capable. Trust him with your life, for if you don't, you will surely die on this quest."

"Stop the vid!" Arella jumped to her feet and slammed her fists on her hips.

"What's wrong?"

"That man just called me a spy and threatened my life, and you have the audacity to ask me what's wrong?"

"Calm yourself. Why don't you wait till the end, then we'll discuss any matters you like." He could see anger clearly written in her every feature, and she gave him a glimpse of the warrior woman that lived within her. Her once kissable lips were pursed tight, her usual creamy complexion nearly glowed red. "Deal?" He repressed a laugh, knowing good and well it would infuriate her should he show his amusement.

"Laugh at me, not. Furious I am!"

Now he knew just how close to breaking she was. Every time she was upset her mastery of Universal slipped to a primitive level. "I won't laugh, and I don't blame you for being upset, but please, just sit down and let's finish the vid." She threw herself back onto the couch and folded her arms over her chest and he had to look at the floor to keep from a belly laugh. She was quite a sight when angered, and even more appealing, if that were possible. "Begin vid."

"Falcon, we trust you to keep the Councilor safe, and to do whatever is necessary—this we have discussed before. Our surveillance indicates Zotar has landed on Syramis after a brief stop on Millia. This planet is steeped in legend and ruled by the lawless, which is why it is a perfect hiding place for Zotar. It is also rumored to hold great hidden wealth. The planet is mostly primitive, but never equate primitive with stupid.

"There are escaped convicts of all rankings running wild, making their own laws and enforcing them. They do not take kindly to shows of force, and everyone who has tried to apprehend or remove a criminal has met defeat. Again, the perfect place for Zotar. However, we have faith that the two of you will succeed where many have failed." Falcon felt her gaze bore into him. What the doyen said struck terror in his heart, and it had nothing to do with criminals and everything to do with *the two of them*.

"You will meet an old religious man there who will guide you on your journey. I can say no more at this time as even I do not know all he will confide. Trust is of the utmost importance, not to mention faith. Dacton and Talina's experience will be a comparison for you, Falcon. Take heed of all that has transpired before you, and you will have a head start on what to expect yourself. There are dangers unique to this planet, all of which we are not aware, but the basics will be spelled out for you on a second vid. It is imperative to your success to follow all instructions, and with that thought, I will sign off. Go with the Gods."

"Indeed." Arella shook her head and sighed.

That was an understatement. "So, my lady, what questions do you have for me?" He could barely stop the grin that tugged at the corners of his mouth while she squinted at him. Her look was meant to cower him into submission.

"What gives this doyen of yours the authority to say I'm a spy? He knows me not. Here am I to. . ."

"Observe. I know."

"And for him to say die I will if told exactly to do? Insult my abilities he has. Competent am I. Commander, forget that you won't!"

"I'll remember." She was angrier than he'd ever seen or heard her, and he had no idea how to calm her down right now.

"As should you well. Now, to quarters mine I must. Permission I have?"

"Permission granted. I will summon an escort for you." Before he could press the com pad she was at the door, glaring at him with all her warrior prowess. He ignored her and summoned Guardsman Larkin on the com, then walked to the door. Her honey gold hair lay on her shoulders and enticed him to run his fingers through the silky strands. Even her violet eyes softened and he couldn't help notice the rise and fall of her chest with each hurried breath she took. The thin fabric of her pale green gown covered her completely, but enhanced all too well the firm, lush fullness of her breasts.

His gaze caught on the triangular crystal that snuggled between her lush cleavage, right where he wanted to sample the taste of her skin. When his gaze dropped to the gold chain that served as a belt around her trim waist, he could not avoid the temptation the curve of her hips presented. She was all woman. Spy or friend mattered not when every inch of his body tightened in response to her blatant sexuality.

"I hope you get some rest. Once we reach Syramis it will become difficult."

"Fear never. Commander. Keep pace with you I will. Worry not."

She'd yet to regain her fluent speech. He wanted to believe it was his closeness, but she was both angry and nervous. "I'm not worried about your abilities, just your health." He thought he saw her bottom lip tremble. "Are you sure you don't want to watch the second vid with me? It could be most informative."

"You tell what know I must."

"Of course." The faint chime sounded and he opened the door.

"Guardsman Larkin," he greeted, "please escort Councilor Arella to her quarters and see to her needs."

"Yes sir." Larkin saluted and walked down the hall with Arella.

Falcon studied her as she walked away, the tantalizing sway of hips under pale green fabric making him grow hard, verifying his attraction to her, no matter how foolish it was. He mentally shook himself. Misplaced emotions led a person to impetuous deeds, and that was dangerous.

With a shrug he returned to his quarters and the now empty couch. He inserted the second disk and settled down to watch. A narrator explained the vegetation, terrain, and a wide variety of animals and insects sure to cause the most stalwart warrior hordes of pain. Great. All he needed was more problems. As if Arella and Zotar didn't challenge him enough.

When the tour of Syramis came to the only religious encampment on the planet, he knew it would be his first stop. Just as the vid was about to end the doyen appeared once again. "Falcon. I will assume that by now you are alone, and these instructions are only for your ears."

The doyen paused in case he had to usher a pretty little someone out, but as usual, the council had anticipated her reaction and made the correct assumption. "As I indicated in the first vid, you and Arella will travel alone. Your ship will not be far away, and you will be under complete surveillance at all times. If we feel you're in any danger men will immediately be dispatched. We also have several watchers on Syramis who can aid you. If needed, they will find you. Everything is in place. Travel light and travel well."

With those last words the vid ended, and he knew their meaning well. He was to take every weapon at his disposal, survival gear and little else. This would indeed be a mission to remember. He would survive Zotar, but could he survive Arella?

CHAPTER SIXTEEN

Arella fastened the belt around her leather tunic, happy to be back in more familiar garb. Gowns were fine on occasion, but she was most at home in pants and tunics. Falcon had sent instructions for her to pack light and meet him at the shuttle port. She shoved her comb into her bag and zipped it, finally ready to begin the mission. Everything up to this moment had simply been a warm-up exercise. Now she could perform her tasks as ordered. Or so she hoped, for failure was not an option she cared to consider.

With bag in hand she left her cabin and traveled the three different hallways to the shuttle bay. When she entered the large chamber several pairs of eyes looked in her direction, yet she felt one pair above all sear into her. Falcon stood in the open hatch of a two man shuttle looking fit, overly masculine, and impatient.

"Morning, sir." He gestured for her to enter and she complied. The last thing she wanted to do was give him cause to doubt her intentions. One step at a time, she reminded herself. There must be some simple yet effective way to stop Falcon from finding Modark, and she was determined to find it, but she had to be patient and learn his habits and routines first. His overwhelming presence behind her caused her heart to beat faster than normal. Damn the man.

"Please, take the seat on the right and we'll be on our way."

"Are you sure we should be going alone to this outlaw planet? Seems to me you might require help."

"You're very astute. However, I have my orders, as do you, and I intend to execute them properly."

Execute. She didn't like the sound of that word. Would he execute Modark? Of course he would if she didn't stop this insanity. Emotions raced inside her and she fought hard to maintain a calm and confident façade. "I have no intention of doing any less." She strapped herself into the seat then folded her hands in her lap, not quite sure what he expected of her.

Falcon strapped himself in then flicked several switches, pushed a few buttons, then grabbed the stick while engines roared to life. The craft slowly floated off the floor of the large craft and headed out an open portal. The moment they cleared the main craft their small shuttle sped off into dark space at a speed she'd never before experienced.

"How can this little planet hopper go so fast?" She gripped the arm rests of her seat and watched her knuckles turn white. She glanced at Falcon. He had the audacity to smile at her, and a devastating smile it was—too handsome and warm to belong to an enemy.

"This is a special craft designed by The Protectorate for speed and endurance. It's a new design with state of the art propulsion."

"I see." Actually she didn't see at all. She'd spent so much of her time in the low-tec sectors of Nacrem that she was embarrassed to admit her lack of knowledge where spacecraft were concerned. Until this mission, she never had the need to know how or why they flew. Now she might have to disable the craft without endangering their lives. No easy task when she understood so little.

"How long can it go without refueling?"

Falcon chuckled. "Let's just say we will not have to worry about fuel on this trip."

"What should we worry about then?" Arella concentrated on relaxing her grip on the armrest before her hands cramped. She had to get over her fear of flying and claustrophobia. Her fears were a well-kept secret, but if she had to spend too much time cooped up in this little craft, with a man whose presence unnerved her she was liable to have a breakdown.

"My only worry is keeping you safe so you can make your

report to the Nacrem League, along with your accurate appraisal of how The Protectorate maintains peace in the galaxy for all their members."

Falcon's arrogant, overly male statement proved his confidence level was off the charts, but he had earned the honor of being the best-looking Protector. "I count on your expertise." He gave her a satisfied grin then turned his attention to the control console.

"Then I can count on your cooperation in all matters?"

"Of course." She'd cooperate with him and with her council's orders, so that was not a lie. "How long will our flight be?" Her hand found the chain around her neck and followed it down to the crystal lying between her breasts. Nodia had been right, she did feel safer wearing something that belonged to her sister.

"That is a lovely pendant."

Startled he noticed her, Arella returned her hand to the armrest. "It's a good luck piece from my sister."

"I take it you two are close?"

"Very."

"Are you also close to Modark?"

Arella shifted in her seat. "Don't make this a personal issue between us. What my thoughts and feelings are for Modark will not alter my duty, and I do not wish to discuss him with you."

"Sorry if I offended you. Just making conversation."

"Then tell me how long our flight will be."

"Thirty-nine space hours to Syramis."

"That long?"

"You do not enjoy flying?"

If he only knew. She swallowed the lump in her throat and gathered what reserve patience she had left. "I love flying. I just wondered, that's all." Lying was becoming easier, and she might as well practice with the small ones since far bigger lies were on the close horizon.

~ ~ ~ ~

Zotar paced the cramped confines of his room at the Bartose Inn. He was used to far better than this, but it would all be his soon. So far everything was proceeding as planned, but he knew that fool, Falcon Rovarn, would not be far behind. With a little luck his equally stupid brother, Dacton would join the hunt and they could both meet their end in his trap. Uhh, now that would be gratifying.

Nothing excited him more than destroying the Rovarns. He even had a backup plan ready in case anything went wrong. He would not stop until he held the treasure in his hands, as well as putting Falcon and Dacton's heads on a pike. Yes, he did like the primitive ways of displaying an enemy's downfall to all who would see, and there would be a crowd to gaze upon two of The Protectorate's finest.

A knock on the door pulled him from his very bloody and most pleasant daydream. "Speak!" he yelled through the door.

"Trydon, sir."

Zotar opened the door and yanked the man inside, shoving him half-way across the room. "You're such an irresponsible moron I should end your miserable life right now, but, you do have your uses. Next time use the password we agreed upon, you idiot. Unless you want everyone to know who you are and what you're up to."

"Sorry sir. It won't happen again."

There was no use warning the idiotic fool. If he disobeyed again it would be his last mistake. He did enjoy having simpletons cower before him, but it was difficult to hold patience when dealing with such ineptitude. "Give me your report."

"Everything is in place to welcome Falcon, and whoever comes with him. All landing ports are covered, and the trap is laid at the monastery exactly as you asked."

"Good. Now out of my sight and let no one see you. Do you understand? All of you are to stay out of the public eye."

"Okay. We'll just have our drinks at the bar and."

Zotar struck the man so hard across his face he fell to the floor. "Is there a brain in that empty head of yours? I doubt it. Think you fool!"

"Yes sir. Sorry sir. I suppose a bar is a public place." Trydon scrambled to his feet.

"Not only that, but you men are stupid enough without liquor clouding what few thoughts cross the empty space between your shoulders. Any man who does not follow orders will be killed. Can you comprehend that?"

"Yes sir."

"That also means you will not earn the credits you were promised."

"We want those credits, sir."

"I'm sure you do. Now go, and don't come back here again. Any future meetings will be at the designated place. I'll send word when I need you."

"Yes sir."

Zotar laughed deeply while Trydon cowered out of the room, closing the door quietly behind him. Credits indeed. Not one of his lackys would live long enough to be paid. When each of their jobs came to an end, so would they, and not a one of them ever gave that eventuality a thought. Oh, that's right, they had no thoughts. He laughed long and hard.

He was more than anxious to greet Falcon Rovarn. Unfortunately he could not deem the man a moron, but he could call him a competitor. He'd nearly killed Dacton more than once before, unfortunately the bastard always lived. Falcon was a bit too young to be in the same class at the Academy, but brothers were usually alike. And he well knew Falcon wanted him dead as did Dacton. Just because he butchered their brother Baleko—okay they had reason to hate him.

They never mentioned his sister, or why she died. Three brothers for his one and only sister was fair payment and he wouldn't stop until he was paid in full!

No loose ends—ever!

Chapter Seventeen

Arella had contemplated exactly which wires she should cut for the past several hours. Maybe she should disable one of the buttons or switches. The truth was she did not want to die. Surely there would be plenty of opportunities to stop Falcon once they were on the ground.

Did her High Council realize that if she didn't stop Falcon from killing ZotarThe Protectorate would just send another and another until they met with success? The Protectorate had unending resources far superior and an ample supply of able-bodied Protectors. That thought made her wonder about her mission, but she could only do her duty as ordered.

So, what had her superiors been thinking? How could she possibly insure Zotar's safety with those odds against her? Had they purposely sent her to fail? That thought had crossed her mind on several occasions. It would be one way for them to be rid of her, and never again allow a woman to serve on the League. That was her reason to succeed—no matter what!

She had to get brave. Falcon had been asleep for a couple of hours now, so if she didn't do something fast, it would be too late. Arella released her safety harness and slipped to the floor, closer to the red wire she'd been staring at for half the flight. Should she? What if they crashed, or lost their air supply? No. She could if, and, or but herself to death. It was time to take matters into hand,

and she did just that. Her fingers tightened around the unknown wire and she yanked hard. Success! The fated wire was in her hand and they had not met with disaster. The Gods only knew what she'd just disabled, and she had no idea what trouble they would run into, but at least she'd done something.

Quietly she resumed her seat, shoved the wire in her pocket, refastened the safety harness and closed her eyes. She refused to think about the ramifications of her first covert deed. It was now Falcon's problem. Maybe she could become a famousspy after all?

She glanced at Falcon and could swear she'd seen a hint of a smile on his face a moment ago, yet now he appeared to be in a deep and peaceful sleep. With one hand she reached for her drink that rested safely in its holder at the edge of the console, but before she could get a good hold on the glass the craft began to vibrate and shake. She lost her grasp and the glass shattered on the metal floor.

Her gaze immediately flew to Falcon who stared wide eyed at her as if he knew of her duplicity. "What's happening?" Her voice was so weak she couldn't utter another word. The small craft began to plunge downward, if one could tell where down was in space. Whatever direction they now headed was the wrong way.

Falcon grasped the control stick. "I don't know what's wrong. I have no control over the ship!"

Arella's heart hammered so hard in her chest she thought she might die of a stroke before any tragedy occurred.

"There's a special crash helmet under your seat. Put it on. I have no idea where we'll crash but crash we will."

He had told her not to argue, so she pulled the helmet from under her seat and placed it over her head. It was very heavy, and far too big. She was sure she looked ridiculous, but who cared in the face of death.

"Aren't you going to put one on?"

Suddenly Falcon burst out laughing and she could take no more. "This is not funny! We're going to die, and all you can do is laugh? Some Protector you are."

"Some observer you are."

She watched Falcon make a few adjustments to the panel and the ship immediately stopped its course of travel, leveled out and cruised the same as it had before. "Damn you Falcon Rovarn!"

Arella pulled the helmet off and threw it over her shoulder into the small open area behind her that served as a galley. It thudded loudly, metal against metal and she didn't care how much noise it made. "You knew!"

"Of course I knew." Falcon reset the controls then turned his seat to face Arella. "It was a simple test."

"And I failed."

"No, you passed."

She grasped his meaning all too well. Humiliation was not an emotion she liked very well, and Falcon was very good at evoking it in big doses. "I suppose I owe you an apology?" Curse the stars, she hated groveling, and an apology was exactly that,

"I suppose you do."

"Fine then, I'm sorry. Does that make it better?"

"No."

Arella gritted her teeth. The man frustrated her past all decent limits. "What do you want?" She gasped when he removed his harness, knelt in front of her, then pressed his lips to hers. He tasted good and smelled even better. She could not liken his scent to anything she'd experienced before, but it suited him—wild and carefree. All man.

An instant ago she wanted to kill him, now she wanted to bed him. How could her body betray her so fast? Her heart beat quickened and she could barely breathe. Her abdomen tingled, and everything else felt like jelly.

He deepened the kiss and she now knew what it was like to be lost in passion. When his tongue met hers she cared not where she was, or who he was, only that he not stop his sensual assault. If she were a better woman she'd push him away, especially after he made a fool out of her, yet how could she stop him when he made her feel so wonderful? She should, she really should, but instead she heard herself purr like a kitten.

Then it ended as quickly as it had begun. He returned to his seat, grinning at her like a child who'd just put one over on his elders. She wanted to reprimand him for his behavior, but words failed to form, only thoughts of carnal pleasure.

"That makes it better."

His deep, husky voice set her insides fluttering wildly. "You shouldn't have done that."

"You're quite right, Councilor, but do not deny you liked it."

"You're too arrogant for you own good, Commander."

"And you're a very good observer."

"You're making fun of me again."

"Never. I find you amusing." He looked her in the eye. "Among other things."

"Other things?"

"Things best left to wonder about. Now, strap yourself in good and tight. It may be a rough landing."

Arella had been so caught up in their little escapade she'd failed to notice a huge planet now visible in front of them. It appeared all green and blue with strange rings around it. "Why a rough landing? Don't they have ports, or terminals, or whatever they call them?"

"Yes, but we're not docking at any of them. I'd like a craft to return in."

"Oh." So much she'd not thought of, too much to learn. Falcon was as she'd been told, very competent, and far more capable than she at everything, or so it seemed.

"Learn to trust me. It will make both of our jobs a lot easier. Now, hang on."

He could have saved his request since her knuckles were already white while they gripped the end of the armrest. Trust him? He gave her little choice. If the truth were known, she did trust him to care for her safety, but that was as far as she'd compromise. Thoughts of her humiliation returned causing new anger to consume her, and it was a relief next to the uncontrolled, heated lust that still sizzled through her veins.

~ ~ ~ ~

Falcon concentrated on the planet that loomed before him, its dangers hidden behind beautiful pastel colors and cloudy rings. He had to get his mind back on the mission after kissing Arella, and that was easy if he focused on the main purpose—killing Zotar.

Arella's feeble attempt to disable the ship had confirmed her true purpose. It mattered not. As a spy she was inept, the worst he'd encountered in many annual-cycles, possibly ever. He'd be wise to keep that secret to himself since she was the most beautiful and tempting he'd ever seen.

Again, The High Council was correct, but how much he'd tell them depended on his progress with Arella. He had to convince her Zotar, or Modark as she knew him, was an evil manipulator who did not deserve to live. If he were successful, she'd no longer fight him, and possibly become a help, and that's what he'd report.

It would be difficult to hide her antics since they'd be under constant surveillance, but he knew ways of finding privacy, he'd done it many times, but never with a woman he wanted so badly. From the moment he opened his eyes and saw her sweet face looking at him he'd been lost, and that was something he could tell no one, especially Dacton, considering their wager.

He glanced at his conspiring co-pilot and wondered exactly what made her tick? She had compassion since she rescued him, and he'd discovered her passion when he kissed her. Then there was the Councilor, bent to thwart his mission. If they kept to kissing it would be far more enjoyable, but just as dangerous.

The shuttle began to shake as they entered Syramis' atmosphere. The capsule became hot, but the heat shields protected them against the unbearable temperatures of entry. The vibrations continued. He glanced at Arella who looked absolutely petrified in her seat. It didn't take a psychic to know she had a fear of flying. Good. A little fear might keep her in line, at least until he'd safely landed.

Little by little the shuddering lessened until the flight once again became smooth. The closer to the surface they came the more he fought excessive winds. He hated wind. It blew things in the eyes, created flying hazards, and slowed progress, and he didn't need anything to slow this mission. Not Arella, nor the difficulties that lay ahead.

Greenery as far as the eye could see loomed before them. Only patches of blue water broke the endless vegetation. Where was one to land with so many trees? He skimmed the tops of trees, the likes of which he'd never seen, fighting the near gale force winds that continued to rock the ship.

There it was, a small stretch of sandy beach along a body of water that appeared to be a lake, or possibly a wide river. He guided the craft lower until he located an open spot. He brought the engine to a hover then carefully edged it closer to the dense jungle foliage, then ever so slowly down to the ground. He shut off the engines and took a deep breath.

Silence fell over him like a blanket. Every time quite hit him he usually ended up ambushed, fighting for his life. Just when the lack of sound nearly sent him for his weapons the loud screech of a bird put his nerves at ease. If animals talked humans were not about. He turned toward Arella who sat like a statue, eyes closed tightly, her white knuckles still in a death grip on the arms of her seat.

"You're safe. We've landed." Still she didn't move. He unfastened his harness then moved across the small space to free Arella. The moment his hand reached to release Arella's buckle her eyes opened and he lost himself in the intriguing violet depths. Her lips parted as if she wanted to speak but couldn't. To him it was an invitation to kiss away her fear, instead he moved a safe distance from her and began to gather their supplies.

"Falcon?"

He turned at the sound of her tentative voice. Her normally confident look had been replaced by a lost child searching for something precious she just realized she would never find again.

"What are we doing here?" Arella knelt on the floor next to Falcon. "I mean, where are we going? Shouldn't we have landed somewhere else?"

Arella seemed off balance and he liked it. Gone was the confident Councilor and before him stood a woman in distress and saving women in distress was what he excelled at, or so he'd been told. "We're here to find Zotar. And we landed exactly where I planned." That might be a bit of a lie, but it was the best he could do to keep her calm.

"Where do we look first?"

Here's where it became tricky. How much to tell her when he knew she'd work against him every chance she could, yet they had to work together. If they didn't trust each other they'd be doomed. "First we go to the monastery."

"Are you a religious man?"

"We're to speak with someone there." Falcon put the largest backpack on himself then turned to Arella. "Let me help you with this." She complied while he secured the smaller pack on her. His hands worked to adjust the straps over her shoulders, but the warmth of her body and the tempting curves made him want to adjust more. How could every simple task take on such a sexual overtone? Even now he was becoming aroused and all he was doing was his job. Curse it all! Women should not be on missions.

At least his hands did not tremble and he was grateful for small favors. How could an experienced warrior, veteran of more skirmishes and battles than he could count, fall prey to one woman who made him want to pull her into his arms and show her the finer points of love?No, not love, simple lust. That is all this was, nothing more. Now that he acknowledged the pull for what it was he could ignore those feelings in the future.

"Strap on your weapons. All of them." Falcon secured a leather belt that housed his sword and various knives, along with other little weapons tucked here and there. Both high-tec and low-tec weapons had their place, only the situation dictated which to use. He loved his sword above all, so reminiscent of times past, yet still a very effective weapon in the right circumstances. He glanced at Arella who now looked exactly like the warrior she claimed to be. Could he depend on her to watch his back? Too early to tell, but he hoped eventually he could.

"Let's hurry. We have far to go before the moon-cycle."

"I've never experienced a true moon-cycle."

Falcon grabbed her hand, opened the hatch and pulled her outside. "You're about to." She stared at him with a quizzical look on her face, then he realized he was still holding her hand for no reason. He let go and stepped back. Okay, so ignoring her would not be possible, but he could control his lust.

He twisted his wrist several times to wake up the small computer he always wore. Fourteen planets formed on the tiny screen, then crossed swords formed in the center. He moved the device close to his lips so Arella couldn't hear. He turned his back on her and whispered "Egnever." He waited a moment. "Password accepted, Falcon Rovarn," the soft feminine computer voice replied.

"Hide and secure ship. Remember coordinates." Falcon watched the ship literally disappear before his eyes.

"How did you do that?"

At the sound of Arella's question he turned. "It is a technique developed by our scientists. All I can say is they developed a way of changing molecular structure so an object appears transparent, yet still occupies its current space."

"I've been away too long."

"What do you mean, away?" Arella gave him a half smile and sighed. He assumed she wasn't comfortable talking to him, especially about her work, but if they were to combine forces on this mission, they had to reach some common ground. Understanding her might never be easy, but the process could prove interesting.

"At one time I worked in the capitol center where everything is high-tec. When I became Councilor, they sent me to Marden to supervise the crystal mines. Everything there is primitive, including the people and their thinking."

"I take it you hate your assignment?"

"Hate is a strong word. Let's say I'd prefer to work where I'd be more useful."

Falcon nodded. There were times in his past he'd felt the same, but he knew everything happened for a reason, and all experiences became a part of who he was. "Let's go." He pulled a machete from its scabbard and began hacking a path through the thick jungle vegetation. They had to reach the monastery before night fall. The last thing he wanted was to test his abilities against the dangers of an unknown planet in the dark.

CHAPTER EIGHTEEN

Arella followed Falcon, mesmerized by his ability to use the machete. The shiny weapon flew back and forth while he cleared a narrow path. He hacked plants and small trees that dared to be in his way as if they were nothing, and made every movement seem like child's play. She could only guess the effort it took to wield the heavy curved blade with such commanding power.

Sounds of insects squeaking and buzzing grew louder the darker it became, adding to the eerie foreboding that swarmed her senses. She did not want to think about what had been on the second vid she refused to watch. Maybe if she had she would not be so afraid, then again, maybe she would have refused to come.

Falcon suddenly froze in his steps and reached a hand back to stop her movement. Then she heard it, a slithering noise that sounded like a large creature crushing plants and leaves beneath very large feet. Her heart beat heavy against her chest and she heard the rhythm in her ears so loudly it nearly overtook the creature's movements.

Falcon turned, slipped his left arm around Arella's waist, pulled her to him and pressed his lips to her ear. "Stay behind me. Make no noise."

The warmth of his breath sent a shiver down her spine. The steel strength of his arm around her gave her the courage not to faint or scream. Then his cheek brushed against hers as he slowly straightened his head. He left behind a few beads of sweat and her skin tingled from the stubble of his beard.

He still held her close while the unknown creature methodically crunched its way closer. It was hard to breathe when the power of Falcon's muscled chest was tight against her breast. She had never wanted, or needed a man before, but at this moment she did. His lips moved to her ear once again.

"I will protect you. You have my word."

Before a reply even formed in her mind his hands were on her waist and he lifted her effortlessly to a low tree branch. He did not have to tell her his intentions, she only wished she could be of help. Darkness began to descend like a cold blanket and the reassuring jungle sounds ceased, leaving only the growing sound of giant footsteps. The ground vibrated and a tree limb shook as it absorbed the shock of the creature's weight.

Below her she watched Falcon shed his backpack then take a defensive stance. He transferred the machete to his left hand and drew his sword with his right. With all the high-tec weapons in his bag, why did he not want to use them? Damn her for not viewing the vid, if she had she might have knowledge of what they were facing.

A ghostly green glow approached at the same speed as the footsteps. A deafening growl-like roar rumbled through the jungle moments before one large yellow glowing eye appeared in the middle of a head that seemed nothing but a mass of sharp teeth and fangs. The long, lizard-like body glowed in the dark, its spiny back dotted with razor sharp spines. Falcon's only chance was speed. The creature seemed clumsy and slow, but that did not stop it from moving ever closer.

It opened its mouth to roar again and saliva dripped from the two longest fangs in the top row of teeth. Dear stars, the thing had four rows of teeth! She'd never seen anything like it, and each set rotated separately in different directions which would tear a man limb from limb instantly!Falcon did not stand a chance. She closed her eyes and said a prayer of protection for the man she could not lose.

The creature lunged toward Falcon. He jabbed his machete into its top jaw and she heard a loud snap. When he pulled his hand back the blade was missing and blood dripped from the creature's mouth. A sickening, agitated growl split the air. The being lurched again, and when it did, Falcon jumped and landed on its back. He jabbed his sword between the sharp spines and the thing lurched again, this time throwing its body against the tree trunk that protected her. The force shook the tree so violently she fell to the ground. When she pulled herself to her knees she faced the one-eyed creature. In that one dark eye she witnessed her own death.

Falcon's instructions were not to move or make a sound, but it was total fear that kept her immobile and quiet. She had no idea where Falcon was, or if he was still alive. When it charged the tree she saw him fly through the air, catapulted from the creature's back as if he were an inconsequential insect. Death was the only thought she had when the huge jaw opened and four rows of teeth reached for her.

She refused to look away. She would die with honor if that was her fate. When the angry jaws reached for her a huge tree limb landed in its mouth and she was suddenly pulled backwards, away from certain death.

Falcon instantly released his hold on her and rushed straight at the monster who now bent lower to the ground, both jaws busy trying to get rid of the large piece of wood impaled in its fangs. Sword in hand, Falcon ran straight at the creature and shoved the long blade straight through the single eye. A loud, terrifying shriek resounded through the jungle. She covered her ears to stop the sound.

The ugly monster lay still, black liquid oozing from the hole where its eye once was. The prominent, intimidating green glow of its hide slowly faded and she knew it was dead. Her body began to shake violently and shivers racked every inch of her. She wanted to cry, yet she was paralyzed. A true warrior she was not, but Falcon was the best she'd ever witnessed. He wielded a sword like a champion, and he was fearless, never once losing sight of his goal. He was magnificent in mind and body, and she had a new respect for the warrior and the man.

"Are you injured?"

She turned toward the deep purring voice behind her. "I'm. . ." More shivers raced over her skin. Falcon retrieved his back pack and pulled out some kind of silver blanket and wrapped it around her. Then he helped her stand, wrapped his arms around her and held her close. Instant warmth quelled her violent reactions and she leaned her head against his comforting chest and listened to the rapid beat of his heart. "What you did. . ."

"Was nothing."

She straightened her head to gaze into the depths of his blue eyes. "You saved my life. I am forever grateful. I don't know how to thank you, except to say. . ." His mouth descended on hers and she melted. Tears burned behind her closed lids while she lost herself in his kiss. Tender lips brushed hers, then his tongue traced their outline. How could a fierce warrior be so gentle?

Then he deepened the kiss, his tongue pressed for entry and she opened to him as if it were the most natural thing in the world. They were adversaries, both with a job to do, both wanting a different outcome, yet at this moment they wanted the same thing. She should push him away and feign indignation, but everything inside her screamed for more.

When his hands roamed over her back the silvery blanket rustled. A strange sound formed in her throat, something between a groan and a purr, then she heard a similar sound rumble deep within his chest. His hands roamed lower and he pressed her hips against his and she felt his arousal, sharing his need. He tasted her with a new urgency that made her abdomen flutter in excitement.

Her legs started to fold, but he held her firm. He stopped his deep exploration and gently, lightly nipped the edges of her lips before pulling away. Arella caught her breath, but her senses reeled with new sensations she wanted to know more about.

"That, my fair lady, is all the thanks I need."

"You have my gratitude, Falcon Rovarn."

"You have my respect, Councilor Arella, for keeping your head about you. It could have been far worse if you had started to panic and scream."

"I couldn't imagine worse." She eased out of his arms, unable to think while he held her. "What was that thing?"

"A lacerta."

"Are there many of those?"

"I don't think you really want to know."

"Is that the worst of the creatures here?"

'It's time to move on before his friends come looking for him."

"Say no more." She folded the shiny lightweight blanket and handed it to Falcon. He put it in his backpack then strapped all the equipment back on.

"Let's go."

She'd follow him anywhere. For the first time in her life she felt protected and cared for. When she watched her sister with Modark she'd wondered what it would be like to share her life with a man, but never had a true desire to do so. Falcon stirred those remote longings. He made her realize how nice it might be to have a normal future filled with love and children. However tempting Falcon may be, she could not share a life with him. She was here to destroy him. It wasn't fair, but life was rarely what one wanted it to be.

~ ~ ~ ~

Falcon hacked his way toward the distant glow of lights. If his calculations were correct that would be the monastery where they were to meet their contact. The closer they came the more he sensed something was wrong. Instincts could be wrong, but he'd learned to trust them first and worry about mistakes later. He sliced the low hanging branches of a tall, wide-leafed bush and stopped. He crouched down and turned toward Arella who followed his lead. "There it is." He pointed to the building in the clearing ahead.

Arella stood. "Good, I'm starving."

When she tried to walk past him he grabbed her hand and pulled her down beside him. "Not so fast."

"Why? It's a monastery. What evil could lurk there?"

"You might be surprised."

"Fine. So what do we do?"

"We'll circle around to the back."

"I think you're just looking for trouble. It looks peaceful enough."

"That's the problem." She glared at him with those lavender eyes of hers and he wanted nothing more than to feel her in his arms again, his lips against hers. Instead he stood and led the way along the edge of the clearing, keeping to the shadows, making as little noise as possible.

It was a trap. If he knew one thing about Zotar, he knew the man would be one step ahead of him, anticipating their every move. This was no time for a mistake. The doyen said he was to make contact here, which meant Zotar would have a trap laid for him.

They reached an area where the vegetation came closer to the buildings. A four foot rock wall surrounded the compound, yet he saw no guards, nothing lurking about. No shadows passed in front of the well lit windows. If anyone moved inside he'd see them.

"Wait here. I'm going to see if it's safe. If it is I'll whistle. If I don't return. . ."

"Oh no you don't! I'm not staying in the creature infested jungle alone. Besides, you might need my help." Arella pulled her cutter from her belt and held it up.

He resisted a smile. Did she really think him so inept? She'd yet to see him in battle, and he really didn't want her to. Killing was never pleasant, in fact it was quite messy at times, especially with the barbarians that worked for Zotar. He'd witnessed it too many times. So much blood and carnage. "Stay close, and do exactly as I say. I'd hate for one pretty hair on your head to be harmed."

"I'll be right behind you."

Was this to be the test to see if she would protect his back? He hoped not, because if it came to that, she could be seriously hurt, or worse. The or worse with Zotar and his men was something no woman withstood without permanent damage. He'd seen the abused, raped women left behind who cursed Zotar to the depths of Diabolus for what they'd done to them and their daughters.

Obviously Arella meant to observe everything. "So be it." Why couldn't Nacrem have sent a male observer, someone he wouldn't have to worry about every step of the way. Why had they insisted their observer be Arella? There was some master plan underway here, but he didn't have the time to worry about it. He sheathed his sword then pulled a small cylinder from his pocket. "Put your cutter away and use this instead." He handed her the weapon that was about the size of her thumb.

"What's this?"

"Somna. Push the top down one click and point it at your target's face. You must be within ten feet to use it. Exact aim isn't critical, but take care not to inhale any or you'll wake up on the floor next to your victim."

"Will it kill them"

"A one click dose will render a large man unconscious for over an hour. A two click does and he may not wake up." She looked at him like he'd gone mad, then he realized, she'd never killed anyone before. A warrior she may claim to be, but she'd never been put to the test. "The chemical is very potent. Take care."

"How many doses are in here?"

"Over one hundred. Let's hope we don't need that many." She nodded and he decide there was no better time to make a move. He grabbed her free hand and pulled her across the clearing then crouched by the rock wall. She started to speak and he placed one finger on her lips and she understood.

Slowly he rose and peered over the wall. He did not see anything out of the ordinary, yet his gut told him not to step on the ground. There was no way in without walking across that open stretch of dirt. He pulled a rock off the top of the wall and tossed it half-way into the area in question. An explosion rocked the ground. He threw himself on top of Arella to shield her from falling debris. The moment it stopped raining rock, gravel and wood, he grabbed Arella's arm, pulled her to her feet and ran for the cover of the jungle.

They reached the foliage just as ten men ran out of the closest building, lazer weapons in hand. He heard them yell, "Search for them, you fools!"

Behind them he heard the unmistakable walk of a lacerta. "Up the tree," he whispered, and hoisted Arella off the ground to the lowest branch. Once she was on her way up he began his climb. They no sooner left the ground when the green glow appeared and footsteps rumbled below.

Arella grabbed his arm and held tight, but she remained quiet. He was proud of her, and he'd tell her so when he got the chance. "Higher." She did as he asked. The tree was very large with wide boughs. He pointed to a wide cradle in the center of the tree and they had plenty of room to sit side by side.

He heard Arella's anxious breaths so he leaned close and slipped his arm around her shoulders. "It won't bother us. Hear all the noise those men are making? That's where he's headed, toward the voices. That's why I told you not to make a sound. They have extraordinary hearing to make up for only one eye."

"I didn't realize."

"You should have stayed for the second vid."

"It's a bit late for that."

Falcon kept his eye on the men in the compound as the lacerta moved toward them. As he suspected, they ran. More men poured out of the surrounding buildings and they all jumped into some kind of vehicle and sped away. The lacerta roared loudly at his defeat then ambled back into the dark jungle.

"You said he'd have friends."

"I suspect that was his mate. If it were a male lacerta it would not have left so quickly."

"Now what?"

"We're safe here. We'll wait till the sun rises before we check the monastery."

"Good. I'm very tired, and the dark. . .well, I'm not used to it."

Falcon straddled the tree ledge, leaned his back against the trunk, then cradled her against his chest. "Sleep." Her breathing slowed and he felt her body relax against his. "You are a brave little warrior, my lovely lady." He only said that because he knew she was asleep, but it was true. She showed more bravery this moon-cycle than many male warriors he's seen in battle.

She was fierce, yet so soft and beautiful. He could hold her like this forever, her soft curves molded to him and invited his touch. He'd never violate what little trust she had in him by making unwanted advances, instead he'd simply savor the feel of her as long as he could. They'd have been safe enough going to the monastery, but he wanted to keep her to himself, and spare her the ugly truth, at least until morning, of what happened behind those sacred walls. If his suspicions were correct, she'd soon learn the truth of her brother-in-law's ruthlessness first hand.

CHAPTER NINETEEN

A rella started to stretch, surprised when her arms met hard, warm resistance. With clarity she remembered where she was, and whose strong chest supported her. The total darkness of the previous moon-cycle had terrified her, but Falcon's quiet commanding presence had kept her calm.

"Good sun-cycle."

She felt the deep resonance of his voice vibrate through her. Her cheeks warmed. "This is a first for me." Reluctantly she tried to pull away from his over stimulating intimate closeness.

"You mean experiencing a moon-cycle?"

"I meant spending the night with a man in a tree."

His laughter warmed her to her toes. She made the mistake of looking into his intriguing blue eyes and instantly regretted it. He seemed very relaxed, yet there was a twinkle in his eye she remembered from when he'd kissed her. At lease he wasn't immune to her as a woman. She'd hate to think she was alone in the attraction she felt.

"Laugh if you like, but I have never. . .spent the night in a tree." She wanted to say in a man's arms, but she did not want him to know the scope of her inexperience.

"Trees are a bit hard." Falcon pulled his feet up and managed to stand on the wide tree branch. He held his hand out toward Arella.

"Thanks." She accepted his assistance to stand, no easy task on a tree trunk.

"Follow me down. If you fall, I'll catch you."

There was an interesting thought. It might even be worth the embarrassment to feel his hands on her again. She admired the way he expertly descended to the ground, then she followed the same path. When she reached the last foothold, she slipped. A hand instantly pressed firmly against her bottom and heat surged through her.

"Thanks." She knew her cheeks were as red as the rising sun. She regained her footing and started to drop when his hands were on her waist, setting her down on the jungle floor. Her abdomen fluttered more than the plant leaves in the wind. The man turned her insides to mush every time he touched her, and that was not good under the circumstances.

"Is it safe now?" No sooner had she asked the question when the sounds of loud, angry growls drowned out the insects and birds. "I'm afraid to ask what that was."

"I think our friend from last night just became breakfast for a few large cats."

"Will they. . ."

"No. They're quite busy at the moment, so let's make our escape before they look for seconds."

She followed his lead toward the clearing. When they broke free of the dense vegetation and stepped into the open area her breath caught in her throat. She gasped and her hand moved to cover her mouth.

"It's not pretty. Are you sure you're ready?"

All she could do was nod. Nothing had prepared her for the devastation before her eyes. Animals lay butchered in pens, their blood still pooled on the ground. The closer they walked the more overwhelming the metallic smell became. Who would slaughter animals for sport? She couldn't ask Falcon, she knew he'd say Zotar.

He led her to the open gate and stopped. "Are you sure you want to go inside?"

"Yes." Her replay sounded braver than she felt. Falcon pulled a fazer pistol from his belt with his right hand and held it firmly in front of him while he led the way toward the main chapel. He opened the door, looked inside then turned to face her.

"I think you should wait here."

"No. I'm assigned to observe, and I will not be left behind."

"As you wish, just be warned—it's not pretty."

"I stand warned." He solemnly nodded and led the way inside. When her eyes adjusted to the dim, candle-lit interior she wanted to scream. Instead she held her breath and walked toward the three slain men lying in a sea of blood, their throats slit from ear to ear. "Why would they kill priests like this?"

"Zotar."

She turned and focused all her attention on his eyes. "Do you blame every disaster and crime on Zotar?"

"When he's responsible."

"You don't know he did this."

"Look at them, Arella. Their throats are cut. That's Zotar's trademark. Remember it well because you need to understand what we're dealing with. It you don't," Falcon pointed to the three dead men, "that could very well be you."

"Modark would never hurt me. He's my brother-in-law, not a criminal. You're making all this up just to convince me he's evil. Well, I won't believe it until I see proof."

"Zotar, or if you prefer, Modark, may not have done this with his own hands, but this was ordered by him, of that I'm sure."

Arella's body began to shake. How could she believe him? She'd known Modark far longer, and not once had he shown any demented tendencies capable of deeds such as this. "I'm sorry Falcon. I'll need proof before I believe your accusations."

"I do not accuse. I state facts. And I will show you proof before this is over."

"Fine." Arella tried to stop the eerie shivers that ran up and down her spine and caused her legs to feel like rubber. Her left arm ached and with her right hand she rubbed the place where the implant rested. She should be reassured her people knew exactly where she was, yet at the moment she was not sure who to trust.

She stepped closer to the slain holy men, their eyes open, their death stares evidence of their cruel end. Whoever killed the priests had little regard for life, or respect for religion. Falcon rolled one of the men over and the sight was too much for her stomach to take. She ran from the building and retched on the ground outside. Falcon had been right about it not being pretty. She should have prepared for such a scene.

Failure here was not an option. She straightened, gathered her resolve and returned to where Falcon stood by the bloody bodies. He held something in his hand, but she had no idea what it was and decided it best not to ask unnecessary questions. She looked toward the ceiling and slowly turned, taking in the construction of the chapel. It was by most standards primitive, simple and clean with only a few artifacts and statues.

"What do you notice here?"

Arella turned toward Falcon's deep voice. "I don't know what you mean?"

"Theft was not the motive. If it were, the artifacts would be gone as well as the three silver chalices on the table over there where the priests were conducting their ceremony when Zotar's men invaded."

"I agree. What does it mean then?"

Falcon stepped toward Arella and stopped. "Do not play the fool with me. It does not become you."

He was right. The council told her to do whatever was necessary, including seduction. Her life depended on convincing Falcon she was on his side and that Nacrem would join The Protectorate. She hoped she could be a better actress than a spy. "They were after us?"

"Very good. And who do you suppose *they* are?"

"Zotar's men?"

"Finally."

Arella felt numb at the moment. She almost half-believed what she'd just said. The killers could have been anyone, yet no one had reason to kill her and Flacon except Zotar since he was their target. Damn. "What now?"

"We hit the trail and pray they don't find us."

She wanted to ask who, but her urge to flee the awful scene overwhelmed her curiosity. Falcon led the way out and she dutifully followed. They quickly made their way back into the jungle. She watched with fascination the play of muscle across Falcon's back while he hacked a path through the overly dense foliage. The man was amazing. Strong, intelligent, and far too handsome for his own good.

The League told her to seduce the man since he enjoyed

women. Could she lower herself to the task of bedding a man for duty? That thought was the hardest to decide. She'd vowed to give herself to a man she loved, which made this decision difficult. Attraction to Falcon was not the issue. He drew her like a magnet, his sexual appeal exceeded every vision of the perfect man, but he was the enemy.

The only way she could succeed with a seduction was to keep her feelings buried. She had to convince herself that he meant nothing except a job. He was for information only, never pleasure. If they mated it would be because duty demanded it.

Falcon stopped abruptly, removed his backpack, then pulled off his shirt and tied it around his waist. His sweat-slickened skin rippled with strength and vitality which did little to dampen her urge to run her hands over his hard muscles. When she moved within inches of him she saw a long, well-healed scar across his back. It appeared like a tiny white line across his tan, right in the center from his left shoulder blade down toward his right side. Who had inflicted such a wound? Falcon was a capable warrior, but even the best fighter could not always protect their back.

"Let me carry your backpack so it'll be easier for you to cut your way through this mess."

He handed her the pack. "If it becomes too heavy let me know."

"I will." As she followed him through the jungle her mind reeled with the possibilities of who hurt him and how they did it. Without warning her foot caught on something and she found herself up against the back she had so admired, her hands reaching for his thick arms in an effort not to fall. Before she could regain her balance, he turned and pulled her to him, his chest heaving from physical exertion. "Sorry." Her breath suddenly became as rapid as his, but for entirely different reasons.

"Be careful, my lady, I would not wish to lose you to a," Falcon glanced at the ground, "tree root."

Arella straightened and tried to regain some semblance of dignity. "I shall be more careful."

"Let's find a place to rest."

She followed him another fifty feet to a small stream where he found a few flat rocks that jutted over the water. They both sat and dangled their feet over the side. Falcon laid his sword beside him and Arella placed both backpacks behind her. "If it wasn't for creatures and criminals, this place might be considered beautiful."

"I've seen much better, and much worse."

"So, what makes you happy, Falcon Rovarn?" He turned his penetrating gaze on her and she immediately regretted asking the question. It was none of her business, and she was quite sure he would not give the answer she was hoping for.

Falcon shook his head. "Very little actually."

"So, what would that *very little* be?" She turned her attention to the gurgling water below, her feminine confidence level dropping rapidly. She'd never been good with men, and feared she was really making a mess of things with Falcon. A seductress she was not, something she'd been told many times over by men who should know.

"A secluded location, a good bottle of wine, and a beautiful woman."

"Well, you've got one out of three here."

"No, I have two."

Arella kept her attention on the water. "I didn't know you had a bottle of wine in that backpack."

He leaned into Arella and whispered, "I don't."

Her gaze left the water and focused on the bluest eyes she'd ever seen, eyes that seduced and promised to fulfill every sexual fantasy a woman could have. "There's no need to flatter me anymore. No one is around to see or hear your sweet words but me."

"You're the only one meant to hear."

She smiled. "Oh, you're good Falcon Rovarn. Very good. I've heard tales about all the women you've had, and I can understand how they became trapped. But don't you think for a minute that I'm like them. I will not be trapped by a handsome face and a hard body."

Her heart melted when he grinned from ear to ear, his straight white teeth gleaming in the sunlight. She wasn't sure if she wanted to kiss him or hit him.

"So, you think me handsome?"

Arella had no answer for that. If she could take back her stupid statement she would. Her cheeks felt hot and flushed. She'd made another blunder with a man she was no competition for. He was suave, an accomplished womanizer well versed in the sexual arts, so what had the council been thinking to send a virgin to seduce him? Ludicrous was the only word appropriate to explain this mistake.

"You like my body?"

The purr in his voice only made her want to shove him head first into the water. "That's not what I meant and you know it."

"I know what you said, and I know the way you look at me."

He had her there, but she would not allow him to win this verbal battle of the sexes. "Well, Commander, if I remember correctly, it was you who kissed me, and on several occasions. And it was you who had lust in his eyes, so don't. . ." His lips closed over hers and she lost all will to fight him. Everything about this man told her it was a trap, that he was only here to use her, that he did not care about her in the least, but still she could not stop kissing him.

Everything about his sensual assault sent her stomach fluttering and her heart racing. His hand cupped her chin so she opened her mouth wider to allow him the access he desired. His fingers trailed down her throat, then lower toward her breast. She cursed her weakness for him. His fingers found her nipple through her tunic and she gasped at the sensations he created. His kiss deepened and she knew if she allowed it to go on any longer she would totally give in to his temptations. Reluctantly she pulled her head back and stared at him, his hand still on her breast.

"Don't deny you want me."

"I could say the same to you, Commander."

"I suppose you could."

Slowly he removed his hand and stared at her with eyes that melted her from the inside out. "That kiss meant nothing to you and you know it."

"I know a lot of things, Councilor. Would you like to hear more?"

Arella thought she heard a man clear his throat behind her. The sound pierced the air again. She turned and was shocked to see a man in a priest's robe standing like a statue a few feet behind them. He appeared harmless, but in a place like this, who knew anything for sure.

"I was wondering when you'd find us." Falcon stood and faced the man.

"I am Watcher Ranby."

"Lead on, Ranby." Falcon took Arella's hand and helped her

stand. He untied his shirt from his waist and put it back on, then donned his backpack.

Arella followed Falcon's lead and slipped her arms through the straps of her pack. She followed the two men, not quite sure if Ranby's presence was a blessing or a curse. At least Ranby saved her from humiliating herself further with Falcon, a man she found extremely impossible to resist.

CHAPTER TWENTY

Falcon ushered Arella to walk in front of him and they followed Ranby a short distance north to a small home that actually looked more like a shack. This did not seem like a logical place for anyone to live, but what did he know about the entire situation here?

Ranby opened the door. "Please, be seated. Father Weston will be right with you. And help yourself to some wine."

Falcon watched Ranby leave, then poured two glasses of very red wine into the wooden cups on the tray. He handed one to Arella who eyed him with suspicion. If only he could read her mind. "I suppose I now have all three." She blushed at his statement, and he decided it best not to pursue it any further. If he were to win her confidence he needed to go slowly.

His hand still burned from the feel of her breast, and his ardor had barely cooled. Going slow with a woman was not his style, and he definitely was not used to having any woman pull away from him. Arella offered him a new challenge, one that fascinated him beyond any he'd ever experienced. She'd be a conquest worth the wait. He knew she wanted him and that's all the mattered.

If the passion between them was any stronger the priest would have found them both naked by the stream. He'd known the man was there long before he heard him. Instinct. That was the only reason Arella was still dressed when the man made his presence known.

"What are you thinking?" Arella removed her backpack and set it on the floor next to her chair.

Her voice drew him back to reality. "Just wondering who Father Weston really is." That thought had crossed his mind before the warmth in the palm of his hand had reminded him of lush fullness of Arella's tempting breast. He could only wonder if she were as beautiful without her clothes as she was in them. Of course she'd be more beautiful since nothing compared to the natural beauty of a naked woman.

"I thought that vid of yours explained everything."

"Not quite." The main truth he'd learned from the vid was how difficult it would be to deal with Arella. He doubted the planet's natural dangers would create more problems than the woman in front of him. He shed his pack and waited.

"And I'm supposed to view this as the best The Protectorate has to offer?"

Falcon could not stop the smile that tugged at the corners of his mouth. "We try to please."

"So far you're not very successful."

"I hate to admit when you're right." Before Arella could answer him the door opened and a grey-haired man stood in the entrance. He wore a priest's robe of rough brown fabric and he jagged bottom drug the ground as he stepped inside. The man took a seat at the head of the table. His long, thin hair hung loose, and his beard nearly touched the rough tabletop. Falcon's gaze fixed on the man's black eyes, that held a sparkle of life and a promise of secrets.

"I'm Father Weston. I was told to expect you." He cleared his throat. "I'd hoped to welcome you to the sanctuary. Unfortunately, that's not possible."

"I'm sorry for your loss, Father. If I could have prevented it, I would have."

"Understood." The priest looked at Arella. "And you, my dear, must be Councilor Arella from Nacrem. Welcome to Syramis. I'd hoped to offer you food and shelter, but all I can offer is the information you seek."

"That's why we're here."

"Don't be so quick, my son. You will not like what I'm about to tell you, but *do not* doubt the worth of my words."

"Give us your message, please. I will give your words their proper respect."

"Respect is not what I want. You must become a believer."

"I've never been a very religious man, Father."

"It's not religion I'm talking about."

He watched the father bow his head and sit quietly for several long moments. "I didn't mean to insult you. I was just trying to explain. . ."

"There are powers in the universe far greater than ourselves. Some call it God, others the Creative Force. There are many names for supreme beings, or forces that man alone cannot explain. Whatever your personal beliefs, you must believe that there is a force greater than yourself at work in the universe."

"Go on, Father. I think Falcon and I can both agree on that point."

"Very well."

"Have you heard of the *Pyramid of Power*?"

Falcon shook his head and so did Arella. "The vid The Protectorate made mentioned a pyramid, but they did not explain anything about it."

"This planet was once a grand and glorious place ruled by a queen. Women held all the high offices and men were simply for their pleasure. Queen Phedra adored her life-mate, Thoran. She wanted to show her love for him in a grand way, so she decided to build the Pyramid of Power in his honor, and as a symbol for all lovers.

"It took twenty annual-cycles to complete. You see, this is no ordinary pyramid. Only the top is visible from outside, the rest is underground. The top portion is all glass meant to let in the sun and the stars for protected meditation."

The father rubbed his chin. "It is said that one night when the moon was full and high in the heavens, Phedra went to the temple to surprise Thoran who had gone earlier to meditate. When she arrived, she found another woman in Thoran's arms. Being a potent mystic, she lifted her arms to the heavens. When she did, powerful bolts of green lightning struck the tip of the pyramid electrifying the entire edifice. When this happened, both Thoran and his lover were turned to statues, which still stand inside, an eternal flame burning between them. Some believe it to be the flame of Diabolus, others believe it is Phedra's presence, ready to destroy any who enter."

"Why Phedra's ghost?" Arella asked.

"Because she was never seen again."

"Why is all this important to us?" Falcon poured another glass of wine and took a sip. He glanced at Arella who seemed mesmerized by the priest's story.

"It is said that Phedra stored the wealth of the planet somewhere in the pyramid." The priest helped himself to a glass of wine and took a drink. "Do not judge Syramis by what you see today. In Phedra's time the land was rich, and so were the people. No one went without. There were jewels aplenty, jewels that many come to search for. They are very rare and sought after."

"I understand." Falcon stared at Arella who was about to learn the truth about her beloved brother-in-law.

"Well, I certainly don't."

"Councilor Arella, Phedra's treasure has been sought after since the decline of Syramis. When she disappeared the prosperity quickly failed and chaos reigned. The planet has evolved into nothing but a crime pit, mixed with enough natural dangers to keep the faint-hearted away. But there's enough riches hidden here to encourage the greedy to keep searching."

Arella shifted in her seat. "So why hasn't the treasure been stolen long ago?"

"Many have tried and all have failed. Countless men have entered the pyramid, but none have left. Phedra's treasure is intact and continues to lure evil men, including the worst of the worst. He is so evil I have no words to properly describe him."

"Have you seen him?"

The priest nodded. "He's been sighted in many locations, and has purchased mining equipment and retained the services of many of the most unsavory characters Syramis has to offer."

"Who are you talking about?"

The priest turned his full attention on Arella. "Zotar, of course." He took her hand in his. "I'm sorry. I've been told he's your brother-in-law." He patted the back of her hand. "This will be difficult for you, my child, but you must have faith in your quest. Trust your intuition, do your duty, but be true to yourself first."

Falcon saw the wheels turning in her head while she tried to assimilate this latest tidbit of information. He commended Arella for her devotion to family, but that made the choices before them difficult. His mind had long ago been made up about Zotar, but Arella had never seen the dark side of Zotar. The consequences of this mission would be permanent. For Arella and her sister he could only envision disaster—complete disaster.

Arella looked into Father Weston's eyes. "And why should I believe anything you've told me? No disrespect meant, Father, but how am I to be sure you're even a real priest and not just a man planted to tell me what everyone wants me to believe?"

"Auhh, good question, my child. If I were in your shoes I might feel the same, but I assure you, I'm real and so is the evil that lives in Zotar."

Falcon watched Arella pull her amulet from under her tunic to let it fall free on the outside of her clothing. He knew her sister gave it to her for protection, and by the way she fondled it she was extremely insecure at the moment. Any other woman would be weeping by now. Not Arella. She lifted her chin the way she always did when she wanted to present a brave front.

The Priest eyed the crystal pendant. "That is lovely. May I touch it?"

"Of course." Arella pulled the chain over her head and handed it to Father Weston.

The priest no sooner grasped the crystal in his hand when he shrieked and dropped it on the table, a shocked look on his face. He looked first at Arella, then back at the pendant. Something was very wrong here, and as Commander, he had to know. "What is it, Father?"

"Evil. . .the stone is full of evil. It vibrates evil, and evil owns it."

"Father, surely you cannot mean that Arella is evil?"

"No. She is not the owner. Crystals hold the vibration of their current owners, they have memory, they are alive."

"That explains it. . ." Arella picked up her pendant, slipped the chain over her head and tucked the crystal back inside her tunic.

"Explains what, Arella?" Falcon would never understand the female mind, and he suspected Arella's was more complex than most.

"Talina had the same reaction as Father Weston. She touched it and dropped it as if it had burnt her hand. She didn't say anything, but I saw it in her eyes. She was scared, as if she'd seen her worst enemy. Father, my sister wore this before she gave it to me. Surely her goodness would also be in the crystal."

"I wish it were so, my dear child, but you see, the evil is so strong and overpowering there is no room for light."

"Why does it not burn me? Why do I not feel the evil everyone speaks of?"

"As I said, there are forces at work we do not understand. I don't pretend to have all the answers. Just know that the universe is infinite in its wisdom, and you have been sent here for a purpose."

Arella picked up the crystal pendant and threw it to the dirt floor. "I will not wear anything that is full of evil."

Father Weston turned pale, and Arella's features were strained, the color leaving her beautiful face. Falcon stood, carefully picked up the amulet and handed it to Arella. "There are no accidents. You were meant to have this." He carefully lifted the chain over her head and placed it around her neck. The crystal snuggled between her breasts as if it belonged there. That thought gave him a strange feeling.

"Did it not burn you?"

"I felt its anger."

"But you didn't drop it. Why?"

"Children, please. Don't try to understand. Just believe." Father Weston took Arella's hand in his. "You are not evil, and wearing the pendant will not make you evil. That stone holds an important key so protect it at all costs."

"How could a triangular shaped crystal be a key?"

Father Weston smiled. "That is a very logical human reaction, but I assure you the answers will become clear. You need patience and faith."

Falcon did not like this turn of events. If Zotar gave the pendant to Arella's sister, and she gave it to Arella, there was a reason. Zotar was clever, and would have known Arella would be sent here. That meant Nodia was a part of Zotar's plan, whether willing or not. He didn't believe Nodia was guilty of any wrong doing, but her complicity could not be denied. "Is there anything more you can tell us, Father?"

"I'm afraid not. The rest is up to you. Just remember that light is stronger than darkness, and light is on your side."

"I shall take comfort in that." Actually, the priest's words did nothing to ease the nagging in his gut that danger waited around every turn. His training prepared him for combat, war tactics, space flight and survival, but unseen forces, legends and evil stones had not been included. Comfort indeed.

"You must go to the village of Karatk. There's a witch woman there you must speak to."

"Seriously?" Falcon shook his head and wondered if this mission could turn any more bizarre.

"Very serious." Father Weston nodded his head. "I know what you're thinking, but you're wrong. It goes back to the faith issue. Now." He pushed from the table then stood. "You had best be on your way. It is not safe here."

Falcon watched the old man shuffle toward the door. Dacton and Talina's experiences invaded his logical mind. They'd been given similar advice, forced to believe in a legend, but theirs had involved a crystallinus bracelet and a warrior's belt with an amulet. He'd questioned Dacton in private many times about what had happened, and all his brother said was there were forces at work no one could understand. Since he respected his brother, he had to believe him. Now it was his turn. All he could do was pray he was up to the challenge. "The good Father is right. We cannot stay anywhere for long."

"I agree." Arella walked to the priest and hugged him. "Thank you for your help."

"I wish I could do more."

Falcon patted the man on the back. "My thanks as well. Keep us in your prayers, Father. We'll need all the help we can get."

"I promise." Father Weston opened the door.

"Farewell." Falcon and Arella both donned their packs, then he took her hand and guided her back into the thick, oppressive jungle. He felt reluctance in her grip, her palm was moist with perspiration and her muscles were tight. Once they were well away he found a small opening and decided a short rest would do them both good. He led Arella to a felled tree and guided her to sit.

He stepped away from her and pulled the palm-com from his

pocket, opened the lid and whispered his password. He needed to get his bearings and figure out the location of the village Father Weston mentioned. "Locate Karatk on Syramis." A few seconds passed before a map appeared on the screen. "Set route." A pulsing dot appeared indicating his location, then a wiggly red line appeared showing the route to the tiny village. "Walking ETA." Forty-nine time-units blinked at him. Unacceptable. They needed some form of transportation.

The soft breeze turned into a fierce wind with no warning. Trees swayed and the sound of scurrying creatures filled his senses. Then he caught the sweet scent that only Arella wore. She was right behind him. He should teach her a lesson and scare her to death. No one should sneak up on a warrior, but he'd save that lesson for another day.

"What are you doing?"

"Setting our course." The moment he turned to face her his body immediately reminded him he wanted her. Curse the planets! Their survival should be the only thing on his mind, yet all he could think about was touching her, kissing her, and far more intimate activities. She grasped the crystal in her hand. "You might want to keep that concealed."

"I didn't know it bothered you." She slipped the stone and chain under her leather tunic.

"It doesn't, but it might be tempting to someone else."

"You're right."

For once she agreed with him. Changes of heart were always a clear warning signal. He moved the palm-com closer to his mouth. "Nearest inhabited area." He hoped there was something close because they needed some form of transportation.

"Usted, three time-units by foot."

Falcon studied the suggested route on the screen and glanced around to get his bearings. They needed to travel north which put the waning sun at their back since it set in the south. "If we hurry, we'll arrive before dark."

CHAPTER TWENTY-ONE

A rella gasped for each breath while she followed Falcon up the highest hill she'd ever seen. They'd been climbing this stupid mountain for over two time-cycles –no easy task on the rugged path. She still had no idea where Usted was, and at the moment didn't care. Sleep was all that mattered, and a tent was fine with her. The muscles in her legs felt like rubber and quivered from over-exertion. The cramps were painful. Just what she needed right now.

A glance at Falcon and she wanted to scream. He carried himself erect, every well-toned muscle in his body responded perfectly, and he looked extremely handsome in his snug black uniform. Did the man not tire? She'd been assured Falcon was the best The Protectorate had to offer, and she had to agree. How in the universe could she keep up with the impossible pace he'd set?

The setting sun shone on his black hair and brought out red highlights that were normally hidden. The back pack looked small on Falcon, yet it was the same size as hers that covered her entire back. How could his rest so nicely in the center and offer her a clear view of shoulder blades that moved relentlessly to clear the path? Her gaze slid lower to a trim waist and the nicest backside she'd ever seen. At least her view on this adventure provided entertainment she did not have to report to the League. Nor would she ever think about it.

With sensual thoughts came the League's directive, *seduce Falcon if necessary.* Seduction would be easy, she knew he wanted her. He found every opportunity to touch her, kiss her, and he always kept an eye on her. Falcon Rovarn was a typical man who wanted a woman to satisfy him. She knew without a doubt she could never satisfy a man like Falcon. He'd had too many women, women far more beautiful and desirable than her, yet she knew he'd take what she offered and more. The more could be her heart if she wasn't careful.

How many women had fallen in love with the womanizing warrior? Countless, she was sure. However, she would not be one of his many victims left behind to cry. She was here to stop him from capturing Zotar, and would use every weapon at her disposal, and if that meant her body, then so be it. The thought of prostituting herself for the cause sickened her, yet the man was very tempting. The one thing she refused to think about was the last choice she might have to accomplish her goal, and that would be to kill Falcon.

Darkness fell fast upon them, even Falcon's glistening red highlights had turned blue-black in the rapidly approaching moon-cycle. There was something peaceful about the dark, but she didn't want to be alone when it consumed her. This would only be her second real moon-cycle in her entire life. Perhaps it was too early for a judgment. It didn't matter since she'd soon return to Nacrem and go back to perpetual light.

The terrain turned rocky, the vegetation had substantially thinned and the trees were now taller with needle-like leaves. In the distance she heard a creature scamper away, and wondered what kind of animals lived here. The only light came from the dimming red sunset behind her. She'd been missing a lot since the view nearly took her breath away. She wanted to stop time and just enjoy the moment, but. . .

Her forward motion instantly stopped. She gasped when she realized her breasts were pressed into Falcon's chest. "Sorry. I was admiring the sunset and didn't see you stop."

"That's obvious."

She turned her back on him and watched in amazement while the sun sank lower, the fiery red glow barely visible above the jagged black horizon. Before she could blink again the sun was gone and she instantly missed the light. The truth of the situation made her heart race. It was dark, very dark, and she had a need to be held and comforted.

"We're almost there. Usted will be on the other side of this hill. I must ask you to remain silent, follow my lead and speak only if I ask you to. Can you do that?"

"Not willingly, but I'll follow your instructions. I hope you have good reason for this request."

"I do." Falcon turned, then continued up the hill.

Arella followed, not sure whether to be angry with his arrogance or relieved he was here to protect her. The verdict was still out on Falcon. He didn't exactly inspire trust, yet she couldn't label him the complete enemy her fellow Councilors claimed. Whether he was friend or foe, she had little choice but to do as he instructed. Her chance was coming. This journey was far from over.

The moment they crested the hill she stopped and stared in wonder at the lights below. The settlement was far larger than she'd imagined. "I never knew how lights appeared in the dark."

"I can't imagine living in perpetual daylight."

"Then I suppose we're even." Arella started down toward the enticing glow below. Falcon's comment made her realize just how different they were, yet they also shared so much. They were both warriors fighting for their governments, each believing they were right in their approach, and their undeniable attraction to each other. What set them apart was the outcome of this mission, and they could never get over that unbridgeable gap.

It didn't take long to arrive in front of a rather dubious looking inn. The entire settlement appeared far more welcoming from the hilltop. Falcon took her hand and pulled her over the threshold into the Bartose Inn. The true inhumanity of the place engulfed her. All eyes turned to them and it felt like they were being sized up as the new victims rather than patrons.

Grateful for Falcon's request to remain silent, she allowed him to pull her through the throng of drunken men to a back office where he proceeded to inquire about a room for the night. Luckily, he held her hand tightly, as if to tell her without words that he'd make everything right. She heard him barter with the wretched, greasy-looking man behind the desk, and gave a sigh of relief when he exchanged credits for a key.

Without further discussion Falcon led her up a flight of stairs and down a long hall to a room at the end. He opened the door, placed his hand on her shoulder and escorted her inside, then secured the heavy lock. She sighed in relief at the size of the lock that looked big enough to stop an invasion.

"We'll stay the moon-cycle here. I want you to bathe and rest, but do not unpack. We may have to leave in a hurry, so sleep in your clothes."

"As you say."

Falcon stepped behind her and eased her backpack off, then placed a hand on each of her shoulders and gave a gentle squeeze. Why did his touch reassure her so? And why did he inspire a burning need to feel his arms wrapped around her and be held close to his chest?

"I'm not trying to be arrogant, just practical."

"I fully understand. And I didn't say a word in front of anyone."

"This is a dangerous place, and it's my job to protect you. It's only for your safety that I give you orders."

She stepped away from him before her speech failed yet again. "When do you become human, Commander?"

"I can't afford the luxury." Falcon removed his pack and placed it on the bed.

"Really? That's not what I've heard." She watched him remove several items from his pocket and put them in his pack. He also removed the wide weapons belt and attached a select few to a smaller belt. He grabbed a change of clothes and disappeared into the lav.

After a few moments and a lot of wrestling noise, he returned dressed in light brown leather pants and a vest. Underneath was a rather dirty looking white shirt with ample sleeves that laced up front and hung open at the top, the laces loose so his sexy chest hair showed and enticed her. Was he going out looking for women? Falcon didn't have to look, women would find him in a fast hurry. She'd seen the men around here and he did not compare. In fact, he stood out like a special event prize.

Falcon grinned. "If you're referring to the stories about the numerous women I have supposedly been with, I'd prefer to show you rather than tell you about my talents."

"You know very well that's not what I meant." Or had she? Her cheeks burned. She doubted she could embarrass herself any more than she just had. "I only meant you're always on duty with the protection thing, and I wondered when you relaxed."

"I don't." He secured more weapons on his belt then walked to the door. "I'll be back. I have the key so I don't have to wake you. Lock the door behind me and open it for no one. I don't care who knocks. No one. Understand?"

"Yes, but where are you going?"

"We need information."

"Then let me go with you."

"Didn't you see those men downstairs? Their eyes were popping out of their heads, and if you showed yourself to them again at least one of them is sure to drag you off somewhere and have you flat on your back. I may not be able to stop them because I'd most likely be dead. The odds are not in our favor."

Arella nodded. He was right and she couldn't argue the logic even though she wanted desperately to stay with him. Why did he always have to be the consummate Protector? Damn the man.

"No matter what you think, I have your best welfare at heart. Now please, get some rest. I'll be back."

Without another word he was gone and she dutifully locked the door. She turned and stared at both backpacks on the bed. This may be her chance. The temptation to rifle through his belongings was strong even if it felt wrong. Duty called. She walked to the bed and opened his pack. Inside she found that small, round computer like object he was so fond of. She opened the lid and watched while fourteen planets formed a circle and crossed swords appeared in the center. A sexy female voiced said, "Welcome, Falcon Rovarn. Enter password."

What could his password be? She had no idea, but if this were like most computers she might fumble around long enough to stumble across the proper word. "Protector," she said with as much authority as she could muster.

"Password in error. All information will be destroyed if incorrect password is given again." Slamming the lid shut she clutched it in her hand. Fine, she'd simply destroy the stupid thing. She wandered to the closed lav door to the right of the window and opened it. The inn was not clean, but that didn't matter right now.

She dropped the mini-viewer into the commode and reached for the lever to remove the object forever. The moment she began to put pressure on the bar, second thoughts assailed her. She reached down and fished the thing out, water dripping all over the floor.

Fine, she'd hide it from him, make him think it was gone forever, but if they needed it to save their lives she could produce it. Right now, it was past time to get the trail dust off and the shower called her name.

~ ~ ~ ~

Falcon ordered another round of drinks for himself and the three men he'd plied with liquor for the past four hours. He'd lost his patience since he'd not gained one bit of useful information. "Any jobs around?"

Samson set his tankard down on the table. "There's a man hirin' 'fer excavation work."

"Not many takers." Doyle picked up his mug and took a drink.

He studied Doyle for a moment. The man had not bathed in weeks, his clothes were nothing more than rags, and his teeth were either missing or black. "Why's that?"

"He's wantin' to dig under that cursed pyramid. Men die there."

"I see." Falcon took a swig of the strong ale.

"Don't think ya do, partner." Samson set his mug down on the table.

"Enlighten me." Samson stared at him while he sized him up. Falcon waved the server over and ordered another round for his friends, which brought smiles all around the table.

Samson leaned closer to Falcon. "Like he said, the damned thing's cursed. If ya go there, you'll die just as sure as you're sittin' here."

"And who's going to kill me?"

"Them ghosts!" yelled Fry and Doyle together.

"Ghosts don't scare me." All three men glared at him as if he were the biggest fool on the planet.

"They scare me!" Fry emptied his mug. "You sure ya been here before? Cuz you sure don't act like it."

"It was a long, long time ago."

"Lost year mind, ya have," Doyle added.

"Go work fer Zotar if ya like. He's offerin' good pay, but ya won't live ta' collect it." Fry pushed back from the table. "You're as crazy as Zotar. Ya deserve each other."

"Ya do, and that'd be the truth." Doyle stood and slapped Fry on the back. "Let's go."

The two men stood then staggered toward the door, but Samson remained in his seat. "Aren't you going with your friends?"

"Nah. They're both fools. In fact, I might just work for Zotar."

"You said the pyramid is cursed and that any who went there died. What's changed your mind?"

"Just didn't want those two idiots comin' with me." Samson glanced around the room then back at Falcon. "Been tryin' to rid myself of 'em fer a while." He looked behind him then leaned close to Falcon. "I know you've never been here before, and you're scrounging for information. I'm no fool. Anyone who's been here knows about the pyramid."

"You're right. I'm on the run. Came here till things cool off."

"That I understand. Just remember one thing, no one here's your friend."

"Thanks for the advice. Now, where do I find Zotar? I want that job."

"Meet me here in the morning and I'll take ya to him." Samson rose from his chair, walked to the door and left the tavern.

No one on this planet was trustworthy, but if Samson could take him to his enemy he'd go with him. He shoved his drink aside, sick of the foul-tasting ale. It was time to return to his room. Even a Chief Protector needed sleep; however, he'd get little rest sharing a room with the lovely Arella.

If he were smart he'd spend the night right where he was, but he did not want to leave her alone any longer than he already had. If he were honest, it was not all duty that pulled him back to her.

He rose and walked to the bar. He purchased several packages of jerky and three canteens of wine from the barkeep since a hasty exit might be necessary. He generously over-tipped the man so he'd forget his face and ask no questions.

With room key in hand he bounded up the stairs the down the hall. He slipped the key in the lock and turned. With a click he opened the door and stepped inside, greeted by a faint sleepy moan in the darkness.

The light between the two chairs by the window came on and he was surprised to see Arella standing there seductively in a thin sleeping garment.

"I thought you'd be asleep." He locked the door behind him and set his purchase on the floor beside his bag.

"And I thought you were going to spend the entire night away from me."

When she turned to face him, his mouth opened and every part of his body responded to her. The beguilingly thin sleeping gown revealed hard, taut nipples pressed against the fabric and all her feminine curves were outlined perfectly. "I said I'd be back. Did you doubt me, Councilor Arella?"

"Never, Commander."

He was in deep trouble and had to stop her before she made another move. She was using the oldest trick in the spy book— seduction, and the hardest for a healthy male to resist, especially when there was such a strong attraction.

He took a deep breath. She moved so close her body heat consumed him. She was tempting him and his sanity beyond reason. He clenched his fists at his sides instead of pulling her against him. He sighed and turned away from her with a silent curse. He picked up his backpack from the floor and went into the lav. His only hope for rest this moon-cycle was a cold shower.

CHAPTER TWENTY-TWO

A rella stared at the door long after it slammed shut. As a seductress she was a total failure. Falcon did not even kiss her. Her cheeks burned with embarrassment. Never had she worn such a seductive nightgown. If she could not get the infuriating warrior in bed with this flimsy thing on there was no hope.

Did the League want her to fail? It made no sense, unless they viewed this as the perfect opportunity to be rid of her once and for all. Maybe they thought Falcon would kill her? Of course! They knew Falcon's orders were to let nothing stand in the way of his mission, and they put *her* in his way.

No matter what path she chose, she was doomed. If she stood in Falcon's way he'd destroy her; if she helped him, the League would destroy her. Death by failure, but who would she fail?

What was her life worth? She was merely a pawn in a much larger game, and everyone knew how expendable a pawn was to achieve a greater goal. Her only chance was to become necessary to Falcon so he had to keep her alive. It was a poor plan, but the only one she could think of right now.

An itch on her left arm reminded her that the League knew exactly where she was, and probably thought they knew what she was doing. She was a terrible spy. Maybe women were not cut out for this type of work. Nodia tried to convince her to stay out of government, to life-mate and have a family, but no, she had to lead the way, be an example for every woman on Nacrem. Some example she turned out to be.

The door to the lav opened and Falcon stormed into the room as if he owned every square inch. From the looks of his imposing figure, he did. She stared at his bare chest, mesmerized by every muscle, curve, plane and hair her fingers itched to explore, and not because she had to, but because she wanted to as a woman. The man was a poster for fitness. With iron hard biceps like his, Falcon could rip a man apart, limb from limb, with his bare hands—or a female spy.

Dark, shoulder-length hair, still wet from the shower, clung to him. He never looked better. Her gaze slid lower to the towel that covered the middle of his body, where an unmistakable male bulge stopped her assessment. She should not stare like an innocent, but she was and didn't care. She'd seen men naked before, but none could compete with Falcon.

Shame on her for such wayward thoughts, yet they felt so right. Right? She just failed miserably at seducing him. He made his answer clear when he fled the room so fast she'd barely seen him move. The muscled warrior rifled through his bag then simply stood before her and stared. The silence grew awkward, yet words failed her. She had to do her duty, but it seemed more like she was about to please her own carnal cravings with a man she could never have.

She reached out and her hands found his shoulders then trailed down until they rested in the center of his chest. Her stomach did summersaults. His arms slid around her and pulled her close, then his mouth found hers with an urgency that stole the breath from her lungs. His tongue found hers and they dueled for control, neither of them winning, both of them surrendering to the sweet bliss of the heated kiss.

Falcon groaned deep in his throat which sent shivers of pleasure to her most feminine regions. He excited her like no other man had. Memories of past kisses and feeble attempts at intimacy flooded her memory and panic roiled deep inside her. She could not stand it if Falcon saw her body and then ridiculed her like the others did all those annual-cycles ago. She abruptly pulled back.

"What's wrong? Did I hurt you?"

"Of course not. I just. . .don't think this is wise, we. . .."

"We what, Arella?"

"We shouldn't."

"Kiss?"

There was no way she'd tell him of her past experiences and that men found her unacceptable and unwomanly because of muscles and scars. She'd trained with men and developed a shape that men found distasteful, and was told her breasts were too small, and her hips not full enough. So why did he want to kiss her? She pushed against his chest to free herself, but he held tight.

"Don't turn from me, Arella."

"You suffer from lust, and I'll not be used." This time when she pushed he released her, and she immediately suffered the loss, but if he humiliated her because of her faults she'd be heartbroken. It was best this way.

"You couldn't be more wrong."

"Really. And I suppose you're going to tell me you love me?" She snickered at his silence. "I thought not." She stared at the only bed in the room.

"Is it that you don't find me desirable? Or do you fear being hurt?"

She glared at him, furious he sensed the truth of her feigned outburst. "I fear no man, you obnoxious warrior! Now, can we share this bed without you touching me, or must I sleep on the floor?"

"I've never touched a woman who did not welcome me, so rest assured, we can share the same bed. I give my word. Your virtue is safe."

"Fine." Arella threw back the covers, flopped down on the left side, then pulled the covers up to her chin. She faced away from him to hide the lone tear that rolled down her cheek. She was a coward. She just turned her back on the one man who even pretended to want her. What was wrong with her?

Why was this so difficult? Because she actually cared about the man. There, she admitted it, now maybe she could get some sleep. She snuggled deeper into her pillow and ignored Falcon when he dropped the towel and slipped into bed. How would she ever get a moment's rest with a naked man beside her? What happened to sleeping in clothes?

CHAPTER TWENTY-THREE

Falcon could hardly believe he'd left a beautiful woman in a warm bed to follow Samson through the dirty, deserted streets of Usted. Sleep had been hard to come by with Arella next to him in that thin gown. He violated his own rule of always being ready to run by sleeping naked. He'd hoped to tempt her into submission, but her will was strong.

Someone had obviously hurt Arella in the past which triggers her reluctance to be intimate. The question was who? If he knew he'd go kill the low-life geratass for hurting one of the sweetest women he'd ever met. Maybe in time she'd confide in him. He'd like to be the man to heal her pain and show her the joy of love. Leaving her alone was not a good idea even though it seemed necessary last moon-cycle. To get a lead on Zotar he'd traded her safety, and if anything happened to her he'd never forgive himself. Hopefully she'd sleep until he returned.

All he'd learned on this outing was that Zotar was not here, which didn't surprise him. Right now he needed to get back to the inn to see what trouble Arella might have found in his absence. So far, she'd behaved, but he had a nagging feeling that was about to end. The closer he got to the Bartose Inn the more apprehensive he became.

He entered and all but ran up the stairs to their room. Once inside his suspicions were confirmed. Arella was gone. Where, he could not guess, but he was sure she needed help. A woman like Arella was an easy target for the sex-starved ruffians that inhabited Syramis.

When he reached for his pack he knew she'd tampered with it. He always left a single hair lying on top, and it was not there, same as last night. Only God knew what she'd done. She did not take her backpack so she planned to return, but he knew he couldn't wait. A woman on the street was not a good idea.

He stuffed her belongings into her pack, quickly checked the lav, then returned to the bedchamber to be sure there was no trace of their presence left behind. He slipped his backpack over his right arm and hers over his left and quickly put the room behind him.

"Damn her to perdition!" He took the stairs two at a time. The hall was empty and he slipped out the back door to be sure his exit was unnoticed. Not trusting another living sole is what kept him alive. Betrayal stood at every turn, and he could only hope Arella had not betrayed him.

~ ~ ~ ~

Arella's stomach growled loudly. She'd left the inn to search for food, not willing to eat with the drunken riff-raff that either still drank or slept at the tables in the disgusting Bartose Inn. So, in her foolishness, she'd struck out on her own when she discovered Falcon had deserted her once again. The exasperating man had a habit of disappearing at inopportune times.

Few people were about this early, but those who were scared her to the bone. Across the street in front of the only food establishment she'd seen, stood six men, all staring directly at her. Falcon's warning hit with a vengeance and she wished she could simply disappear.

The tallest of the men waved at her to join them and she shook her head. It would be a mistake to run, so she turned back the way she'd come and walked at a normal pace, which was difficult when her body trembled with fear. In her right hand she carried the somna Falcon gave her.

She quickened her pace when she heard footsteps behind her. The footsteps gained. Too scared to look over her shoulder, she began to run. The faster she went, the faster the footsteps. Hands grabbed her from behind and pulled her into the narrow alleyway right beside her.

Her breath was ragged yet she gasped at the man's face. "Jorken." Since he was from Nacrem, she slid the somna into her pocket.

"I'm glad you recognize me, Councilor Arella."

"What are you doing here?" She knew why he was here. Jorken was the man who did whatever the Councilors did not want to dirty their hands with, and he'd use any means necessary. She'd always turned her head to the whispers of murder, theft, blackmail and sex, but those whispers always involved Jorken.

"Did you think you were alone? Why do you think you have an implant?"

"For your convenience, of course."

"Of course. An update, Councilor."

"We haven't found Zotar, so he's safe."

"Where's The Protector?"

"I don't know."

"You weren't supposed to let him out of your sight!" He shoved her shoulder. "Have you seduced him yet?"

"You tell me, you know everything else."

Jorken slapped her across the left cheek so hard she fell backwards and hit her head against the stone wall of a building that stood tall behind her. She slumped to the ground with a groan a grabbed her face.

"Impertinence will not be tolerated. If you wish to remain alive, Councilor, you'll do as you're told. Understand?"

Pain shot through her head and her vision blurred. It felt like a dream, one she wanted to wake up from.

"If you don't destroy Falcon Rovarn, Nacrem will destroy you. And remember, your every move is being watched."

Jorken kicked her in the ribs then turned and strode away. She let out the breath she'd been holding. She covered her face with her hands and just sat there. Her cheek burned with pain and she felt it swelling beneath her fingers. There would be no hiding this from Falcon, but she needed a believable explanation.

It took several attempts before she managed to rise to her feet. Her head throbbed and her vision was still blurred. She was not cut out to be a spy. Guilt ripped through her. So many times she'd called herself a warrior, yet she could not even defend herself against Jorken. She took pride in her training, her muscles, her ability with a sword and knife, yet Jorken humbled her with a slap and a punch. She was truly a failure, and the price would undoubtedly be her life.

She tried to walk, but her knees folded and she slumped to the ground. She should have listened to Falcon. No matter how capable she thought herself, she was no match for a man. The truth hurt. Then again she had not even tried to make a move against the man since he was supposed to be on the same side. If she had tried to harm him he would have killed her.

She thought she had the somna Falcon gave her, but which pocket was it in? She was such a failure at this spy game. Now she knew for sure it was her government's way of getting rid of her the easy way.

Where was that damned Protector when she needed him? She leaned her back against the cold stone wall, pulled her knees close to her chest with her arms and bent her aching head to rest. If she could just sleep for a while, everything would be fine.

~ ~ ~ ~

Falcon continued his search for Arella. Where had the troublesome woman gone? Why had she disobeyed his directive? He would never understand women. They talked when they shouldn't and listened when they should talk. He was blessed with one who did not listen and who struck out on her own. If he had not sworn to over-see her safety, he might well leave her to her fate. No, he'd never do that, but he would have to teach her a lesson. His stomach knotted tighter and he feared the worst.

Falcon turned in the opposite direction. With every step his anger grew, yet his heart cried for her safety. He cared about the aggravating woman. He questioned The Protectorate's wisdom in sending her on this mission. Thoughts of what Dacton and Talina endured made him worry even more.

The streets were now heavily crowded with women doing their daily shopping, a few kids, and men strolling looking for work, or women. He searched face after face, but none were as lovely as

Arella. Beggars worked their favorite corners and held out filthy hands. Criminals were not generous by nature and he wondered why these pathetic men bothered. One lone beggar that sat, head down in a deserted alleyway caught his attention. He'd know that gorgeous head of honey-blond hair anywhere.

He broke into a run and reached her in seconds. He knelt by her side. "Arella?" She remained lifeless. "Get up!" Nothing. He shook her shoulders and her arm fell lifelessly beside her. Her head bobbed with no control when she moved. With both hands he lifted her chin and found a large bruise on her left cheek.

"Who did this? Arella? Wake up!" He gently let go of her head, slipped his hands under her arms and pulled her to her feet. She groaned then blinked several times before her glassy, lavender gaze tried to focus on him.

"Falcon?"

"What happened?"

"A man, he came out of nowhere. He tried to rob me. I didn't have anything he wanted, so he hit me and ran. I fell against the bricks and hurt my head."

"Let's get you out of here."

"I want to sleep. My head hurts." Arella raised her hand in the air. "Everything's blurry."

With one arm securely around her, Falcon touched her scalp with his fingers where she indicated it hurt, not surprised to find a lump the size of an ostroch egg. "I can't let you sleep." She groaned and gave him an ugly look. "You must walk."

"Can't. Too tired."

Falcon tried to shake her awake, but she'd passed out. He swept her into his arms and headed toward the inn. He had not planned to return to the room, but since Arella was unconscious he had no choice.

They had a few hours until check-out and Arella might be awake by that time. He had to tend to her and it would be easier in a private room. He reached the back entrance and stepped into the hall. Voices stopped him and he moved to the basement entrance for cover. He leaned against the wall in the darkness and waited.

"Who are they?" a man yelled from the top of the stairs.

"Don't know. Kept to themselves, they did," the innkeeper said.

"What names did they use?"

Falcon heard a punch followed by a pained groan.

"Tell me before you take a nasty fall down those stairs."

"Marty Simmons and his sister Lanie. That's what he said, and that's the names on the register."

"Where'd they go?"

"I'm not their keeper. Now get your hands off. . ."

Another punch resounded and Falcon silently cursed. He picked Arella up in his arms and left the way he entered. He fled down the back alley, only this time he turned toward the hills. Carrying an unconscious woman and two backpacks slowed his pace, but at least they were getting away from Usted.

He wanted to kill the man who did this to her. Nothing about this mission had gone well. He still had to find the witch woman, and that journey would take another forty-six hours by foot, longer if he had to carry Arella the entire way. She groaned when he moved her over his shoulder in order to make his way up a steep incline.

What the witch woman would tell him had better be worth the trip. He had serious doubts since everything he'd done so far seemed like an effort in futility. Right now he had to take one mountain at a time. Half-way up the mountainside Falcon paused, checked behind him, then ducked behind a large group of rocks. He laid Arella on a small, grassy patch of ground, shed both backpacks and placed one under her head for a pillow. Smoothing hair from her brow he stared at long lashes that caressed high cheek bones. She was without a doubt a flawless beauty. Her physical features were absolute perfection, but her inner beauty made her irresistible. He thought about their last kiss and hoped he'd soon be able to give her another.

From the first moment he saw her his thoughts had been out of control. He had no business thinking about bedding the woman, no matter how desperately he wanted her. Why he felt so strongly that she should belong to him he could not answer, nor could he deny the sexual pull he felt every time she was near.

The bruise on her cheek had become darker and his temper flared just looking at it. No man should ever hit a woman—ever! Especially one as beautiful as Arella. He wanted to find her attacker, flay him open and remind him with each painful cut what he'd done. If there was one thing that infuriated him, it was a man putting bruises on a woman's face or body. Women were precious and should be treated as such.

She needed him at her side so he could not exact justice. It would not serve either of them if he raised eyebrows and drew attention. Even a lawless planet took notice of vigilante action. In a town like Usted you never knew if you would be fighting one man or an entire band of men. He had to stay low-profile since surprise was always the best weapon.

"Arella?" She lay too quietly. "Arella, wake up. You must not sleep. *DeJorelle Kari*." He had to get her on her feet. He slid an arm under her shoulders and pulled her to a sitting position which elicited a moan. A rustling sound in the bushes behind him drew his attention. He laid Arella back down, drew his sword, turned and waited for the eminent arrival. A man stepped into the clearing and he pointed his sword at the intruder.

"Easy there."

The man walked closer to him and he led three tall, hairy animals. "Who are you?"

"I'm Watcher Landers. Saw you leave the inn and thought you might need help."

"Prove yourself."

"Uhh, a careful one you are. Fair enough. Password Ratoz."

"Who sent you?"

"You're getting tiresome, but I'll play the game. The Protectorate sent me. Said to approach you only if you needed help, and I thought this was the time."

"Give me a name."

"Doyen Whitten and Dacton Rovarn issued the orders."

"How is my fair-haired brother?"

"You test me, Falcon. Your fair-haired brother was murdered by Zotar. Dacton has dark hair like yours."

He had no choice but to trust the middle-aged man before him who looked more like a criminal than the criminals themselves, yet his instincts said the man was safe enough. "Many know Dacton's hair color."

"He said you'd be difficult. Now, if we can get past this interrogation, I have news for you."

Falcon sheathed his sword. "Such as?"

"First I brought transportation, and a map." He handed Falcon two sets of reigns and a folded piece of paper.

"That's a start." Falcon glanced at the saddled Bemothras, thankful they'd no longer have to walk. "What else?"

"Arella's sister and nephew are missing. We suspect. . ."

"Zotar." Falcon expected this news. In fact he was surprised Zotar had not taken them sooner. "Do you have a location on Zotar?"

"A few sun-cycles ago he stayed where you did, but he's returned to the *Pyramid of Power*. The map I gave you should guide you there."

"Thanks."

Landers cleared his throat. "I'm here to remind you of your orders, Commander Rovarn."

"I've never disobeyed orders."

"Good, then you'll do the right thing." Landers slapped Falcon on the back. "I'm off. May the Gods be with you."

"My thanks." Landers mounted his transport animal and rode away. Falcon tied the Bemothras to a tree then turned toward the moan behind him, relieved to see Arella sitting on her own, her left hand over the bruise on her cheek. He walked over and knelt in front of her. "It must hurt."

"No more than my pride."

"Pride causes pain."

"No doubt, but I'm a warrior. I should have protected myself against that thug."

"Maybe this was a lesson in following orders?" Falcon watched her hands slip into her pockets. She had a temper, one he hoped she'd control. He decided to wait to tell her about her sister and nephew, especially when there was nothing either of them could do.

"Why you arrogant, lizorodous-tongued demon!"

"Anger is an emotion a warrior must resist." He watched her then carefully and easily caught her fist before she made impact with his nose. "You're a slow learner, *DeJorelle Kari*."

"What did you just call me?"

My Sweet Warrior did not exactly apply at the moment, but to him that is what she would always be. She looked even more tempting when angry. Stealing a kiss crossed his mind, but he did not want to tempt fate. Timing was everything.

"Answer me."

"I'll tell you later. Right now we need to leave." There was no way he'd tell her it was an endearment, not yet. It was far too much fun watching her fume. He offered her a hand up, but she refused. It was difficult not to laugh at her stubbornness, and her clumsy attempt to rise without assistance. Finally on her feet, she turned and froze.

"What are those things?"

"Revenge for making me ride that Cameora." She straightened, pushed her shoulders back and tilted her chin up high. Her walk resembled a tavern crawl, but she managed to make her way to the hairy beasts.

"So, that's how it's going to be."

"Actually," Falcon said, pulling her into his arms, "this is how it should be." His lips found hers and instant passion flared through his veins with a vengeance. Lust, strong and hard engulfed him. It took every ounce of control he could muster not to lay her down on the ground and take her sweetly, here and now.

The kiss deepened. Her feeble attempt to push him away ceased when her arms threaded around his neck. He tightened his embrace and forced her against him so she could feel his swollen need. She inhaled sharply when he pressed his manhood against her abdomen. He wanted her as he'd never wanted a woman before, and there had been many, yet none touched his heart like Arella.

She tasted tempting, dangerous and sweet. Their tongues fought a duel for supremacy, a battle neither would win, but both could enjoy. Just as he was about to take kissing to the next level, he remembered they were visible to the surveillance ship and decided his lust would have to wait. Slowly, reluctantly he ended the kiss.

Arella's rapid breathing matched his. He took pleasure knowing he excited her, and that her need appeared as great as his. She hid her warmth and vulnerability well under that tough, Councilor's exterior.

"You're a most persuasive man, Falcon Rovarn, but you can let me go now. You have my attention, and for the moment, my cooperation."

"What I have in mind would require your cooperation for more than a moment." She lowered her gaze and her other cheek turned as red as the injured one. He broke the embrace, but his arms still tingled from the warmth of her body against him.

Arella was a tempting enemy. It was common knowledge women were his weakness, but he never let any woman interfere with his work. "We really need to leave now."

"Tell me how you got them, and what I need to know to ride such a monster."

"Never call a Bemothra a monster. They're gentle creatures, but sensitive, and if they suspect you dislike them, you're in for a rough ride."

"Shall I apologize?"

Falcon laughed. "Just treat them kindly and you'll be fine."

"Right." She looked Falcon in the eye. "You still didn't tell me where they came from."

Falcon chuckled. "Well, as some would say, 'Never look a gift Bemothra in the mouth'."

Arella rolled her eyes at him then cautiously approached her mount. She patted the animal's long, shaggy-haired neck. She stroked the animal gently and he noted a faint smile tug at the corners of her mouth. Her question confirmed she'd slept through Lander's visit so she could not have heard their conversation.

"Their hair is deceiving. It looks coarse and dirty, but it's not." The animal turned its long neck toward Arella and licked her hand.

"He likes you."

"He has beautiful brown eyes, and an adorable face. And look at those lashes! I'll call him Baby."

Just like a woman to name an animal before she even rides it. He inwardly chuckled when Arella stared at the stirrup that hung at eye level. She turned a pleading glance at him.

"Need help?" Her eyes narrowed and he stepped to her side and lifted her so she could put her foot in the stirrup and mount. When she swung her leg to straddle the animal, she miscalculated and lost her balance. He steadied her backside with both hands.

"Are they all this tall?" Arella settled herself onto the saddle.

"Some are taller, with even longer necks than *Baby*."

"Great." Arella glanced around. "Where are we going?"

Falcon laughed. "To find a witch."

CHAPTER TWENTY-FOUR

Arella's legs ached and her backside hurt from riding the overly wide Bemothra who had a gait she could not quite master. She'd forgotten about her cheek, but not where Jorken had kicked her ribs. To ride required movement which caused more pain. An endless cycle.

Falcon had been concerned about her injuries, but he did not know about her ribs. At least he believed her story about being mugged in the alley. The last thing she needed was for him to learn about Jorken. They appeared to be as alone as two people could be out in the wilderness, yet both their governments knew exactly where they were. It was a strange feeling.

It was nearly dark and still no signs of civilization. This witch woman must live as far removed from the public as possible. No one welcomed witches, even she had reservations about people who claimed special powers. Fear of the unknown was a curse many people suffered from. She tried to be open-minded, yet she could not shake the uncertainty that grew in the pit of her stomach.

Was it possible Nacrem was wrong about The Protectorate? Could Zotar be the enemy they claimed? These thoughts were traitorous and dangerous, yet she could not deny the underlying truth that screamed to be recognized. She'd never told anyone, especially not her sister, but Zotar's aura had made her uneasy from the moment she met him. Nothing she could put her finger on, but she always suspected he had a hidden agenda that bordered on the dark side.

Evil was a word she tried to ignore, and so was the feeling she had about Zotar, but there was a connection to him. She wanted Nodia to be happy, and on the surface she was, yet there was a secret sadness that lived deep within her sister. Nodia had changed drastically since her life-mating three annual-cycles ago. Their son, Ducard, appeared well-adjusted, but he outwardly feared his father. Children instinctually knew adult's moods and personalities, and young Ducard was only himself around his mother.

Damnation! She was here to save Zotar's neck, please the Nacrem Council, and prove herself worthy as the first woman Councilor. Instead, her thoughts had turned to support the Protectorate, which would destroy her career and her sister. Some Councilor she turned out to be.

Truth. She'd always believed her life was built on truth, or at least the truth she'd been told. Now the truth seemed blurry and uncertain. So far Falcon had been the most convincing force. He seemed to live in truth, and that she could respect. Although the truth was often twisted to gain a particular outcome. The situation around Zotar held many possible outcomes. The question was who would benefit the most from those outcomes?

Love, greed and power had devastating effects on humans, no matter what planet they hailed from, or what galaxy they claimed. All life forms were born with survival instincts, some just carried those instincts too far. Were the High Councilors any different? No. They were just as human as the next man, and many fell prey to greed and power.

Zotar offered Nacrem untold riches for safe sanctuary. The High Council relayed to the assembly that the crimes charged against Zotar were unfounded, and that The Protectorate was unjust, corrupt, and wanted nothing more than to destroy anyone who might expose them. They claimed Zotar's threats against The Protectorate were what prompted the trumped-up charges against him.

Nodia was drawn to the man because he showered her with gifts and compliments, and he gave her the attention she so desperately craved. On the surface he appeared kind, yet the sadness in Nodia's eyes did not lie. Before Nodia life-mated she laughed and sang, now she did neither. What secrets could she be hiding?

How she missed Nodia. If Zotar's death sentence were imposed, it would either free Nodia, or destroy her fragile sister. She no longer had a problem thinking of Modark as Zotar. If she were to believe him guilty of murder she'd need proof. Nodia had no idea who she'd life-mated.

"Arella?"

"Hmmm?" She looked up and saw Falcon looking at her over his shoulder.

"You've been so quiet. Are you okay?"

"My legs could use a reprieve, and I am a bit hungry."

Falcon pulled his Bemothra to a halt, and Arella did the same. He dismounted then walked to her left side to help her down. When she placed her hands on his shoulders, he grasped her waist and guided her smoothly to the ground. With legs that felt like rubber she faltered when she tried to walk. He slipped an arm around her waist and held her tight.

She winced when pain shot through her. Falcon held her gently, but her ribs hurt so bad she wondered if any were broken. Falcon stared at her and she knew she could no longer fool him.

"Show me your ribs."

Reluctantly she lifted her tunic while he inspected her. She felt like a child with their hand caught in the candy jar. His hand caressed her skin then stopped. His fingers pressed hard on her rib bones one at a time. She bent forward, fighting the urge to double over.

"You're lucky, they don't feel broken, but that won't help the pain." Falcon walked back to his Bemothra and removed his pack tied to the back of the saddle.

He returned, dug through his bag and pulled out a medical box. After sorting through the compartments he removed a yellow capsule, put it in the palm of her hand then handed her a flask.

"Take that pill with the wine. It will speed your healing."

She uncorked the flask and took her pill, trusting he knew what he was doing. The way she felt right now she'd take almost anything. She watched him remove her pack and he began to empty both bags. "What are you doing?"

"I think we should rest here for the moon-cycle. You're exhausted."

"And you're not?" Arella knew the moment the words left her lips she was a fool to make that assumption.

"I'm not the one who got mugged in an alley." He smiled. "Don't be so hard on yourself. It could happen to anyone."

"Maybe, but he wouldn't have attacked you."

"I'm not a woman." He pulled the silver blanket out of the pack and handed it to Arella.

"Not all women are helpless and. . ."

"I meant no disrespect to women, but we both know you're an easier target."

She felt a bit dizzy so she walked over to a large, flat rock nearby and sat down. "I'm not in the mood to argue."

She watched him set up camp and decided he was right. Her aches and pains, coupled with the stress of the mission had exhausted her.

Her gaze settled on Falcon. While he erected a small tent, the muscles of his back rippled beneath the snug material of his shirt. He wiped his brow with his hand, then in one fluid motion, stripped off the black garment and continued to work, bare from the waist up.

It was suddenly hard to breathe. The man was beautiful, sensual, and so well built she had to suppress the urge to run her hands over every well-honed curve. His long, dark hair rested on his shoulders and she loved it. Men on Nacrem shaved their heads, so being with a man who proudly wore hair was a fun treat.

She worked out with her men, yet none of them compared physically with Falcon. She remembered the feel of those muscles beneath her fingertips, and the experience left her craving more. He pulsed with power, and she loved how she felt safe with him. His position described him well, Chief Protector, or Commander. How could she betray him?

Falcon was dedicated to The Protectorate, with a desire to do the right thing whether anyone else agreed or not. Her orders to seduce him had become unnecessary because her body cried for his embrace, his lips, his tender touch. Damn him to Diabolus! Why did he have to be so exotically tempting?

Her gaze followed his every movement while he created a rock circle and built a fire inside it. His easy manner said he was used to being watched by women, but having the company of a tempting man was a new experience for her. Falcon tempted her by being in her line of sight. She hated to admit such a weakness.

Falcon picked up a wrapped package and carried it over to her. When he sat down so close they were almost touching, every nerve in her body stood at attention. He handed her several strips of dried meat, his fingers brushing hers while he put them in the palm of her hand.

"It's not much, but it'll keep up your strength."

As long as he sat so close she'd never feel strong. She took a bite of jerky and chewed. Salt invaded her mouth and consumed her taste buds so completely she nearly choked. "I need a drink." The words barely left her lips and Falcon jumped to his feet and sprinted to the pile of supplies. He immediately returned with a canteen.

He handed her a flask. "Wine washes jerky down better than anything."

Arella took a swallow and smiled. "You're right. Sweet wine goes well with salt."

"I'll provide a better meal tomorrow."

"I'm surprised you had this."

"I bought these from the barkeep last moon-cycle."

Her cheeks became hot. He took the canteen from her hands and took a long drink, then handed it back. His shoulder rubbed against hers every time he took a bite. Did he have to sit so close? They were in the freedom of nature with unlimited space, yet he deliberately pressed against her. He knew the effect he had on her, she'd seen that conceited glimmer in his eye.

"So, where's this witch woman?"

"In Karatk, several hours from here." He looked Arella in the eye. I'd give you an exact reading if you'd return my palm-com."

Arella cringed. He knew. Was there anything that escaped him? "I don't know why you'd accuse me of taking that stupid thing."

"You had access." He leaned forward, picked up a stick and pushed logs around in the fire. "I don't lose things, nor do I misplace anything."

"You're too suspicious for you own good, Commander." His outward expression showed stern control, but she sensed her incompetence amused him.

"Instinct keeps me alive, Councilor. I hope you still have it, because we may need it in the near future." Falcon tossed two more pieces of wood on the fire then leaned back on his elbows. "Get some rest, you'll feel better."

"What about you?" Rather than answer, he rose, walked to the small tent and crawled inside. Fine. He could have the tent to himself, she'd sleep under the stars. She lay down on the silver blanket and stared at the star-filled sky. The moon-cycle was upon them and she was amazed by the brilliance and quantity of twinkling dots before her eyes.

The beauty of the heavens alleviated her fear of darkness. Her eyes drifted closed, her body relaxed. Thoughts of Nodia calmed her apprehension. At least there was one person who loved her unconditionally, who cared what happened to her and would offer help anytime she asked.

Nodia. She missed her sister, but at least she was safe on Nacrem with her child. She wished she'd had time to say good-by before she left, but there had been no time. Hopefully, the situation with Zotar would be resolved without destroying her family.

A loud roar crushed the silence. Whatever threat that might be, she refused to die alone. She rose to her feet, grabbed the blanket and ran to the tent.

~ ~ ~ ~

Arella's hard-to-get game intrigued him. It was fun to guess what a woman wanted for a change. Falcon Rovarn, spending all this time alone with a beautiful, single woman and he has yet to bed her? If Dacton knew he'd never let him live it down, and laughter would be heard throughout the galaxy.

He wondered how long she'd last alone in the dark. She tried to hide her fear, but she was not a good actress. He understood her reasons, but he wished she'd be honest with him. She was afraid he'd think her weak. He had no right to judge her, nor would he. The entire human condition was the result of one judgment or another, and the joy or devastation it left behind.

A Lacerta yelled in the distance and he was glad it was too far away to worry about. This place crawled with danger, but even a warrior needed his rest. The tent flap flew open and Arella dove inside, breathing as if she'd run across the entire planet. By the light of his luna stone she looked pale and scared to death lying next to him on the bed he had rolled out for her.

"Where's your sword?" She pulled herself to a kneeling position and grabbed Falcon's arm. "Hurry, it's coming!"

He pulled her to him and held her tight against his chest. Her heart raced and she shook in fear. "We're fine. Don't worry. I assure you, he's too far away to hurt us."

"You're sure?"

"I am." He smoothed stray hairs away from her face. It was soft and silky. He bent his head slightly and inhaled her sweet scent. "Let's go out by the fire. Lacertas hate fire. We'll be safe there."

"After you, warrior."

With a nod he crawled out of the tent. When she emerged he helped her to her feet and escorted her to the flat rock close to the fire. He threw a few more logs on the embers and the flames roared back to life, lighting the night with a warm, orange glow. Arella leaned against him and he put his arm around her. "Are you better now?"

"Much."

Her body no longer shook and her breathing had returned to normal. It felt good to hold her, too good. He'd spent his entire adult life dedicated to duty, never spending leisure time with a woman. This may not exactly be leisure, but it did not feel like duty.

"And what do we have here?"

Falcon jumped to his feet and turned in the direction of an odd, screechy woman's voice. Instinctively he reached for a weapon. "Who's there?" A long cackle came from behind the bushes.

"Wouldn't you like to know, you handsome tease."

"You think you know me?" The foliage to his left rustled and into the firelight stepped a short, squatty old woman wearing the most ghastly combination of clothes he'd ever seen. Purple blouse, orange skirt, green sash belt, and a red plaid scarf tied over scraggly, shoulder-length grey hair.

"Aye, I know you both. Been expecting you." She cackled loudly. "You're the chosen ones."

CHAPTER TWENTY-SIX

Arella stood and stepped closer to the old woman. "Chosen ones? Explain self, you will." The woman looked at her with laughter in her eyes. She certainly looked like a witch, but Falcon said they were not that close, so how had she found them? She felt Falcon's hand grasp her shoulder, and she was very relieved to have him close.

"You two love birds were sent to find me, were you not?"

The hair on the back of Arella's neck bristled. She opened her mouth to object to the implication, but the old woman's hand gestured their silence.

"I know what 'yer both thinkin'. Who am I? How did I find you? What could I possibly have to do with your quest? Well, I cannot give you all the answers you seek, but I do have information, if you're willing to listen."

Falcon tightened his hold on Arella's shoulder. "We'll listen, won't we, Councilor?"

"Speak if you will, listen we are." The old woman cackled again, only this time the sound relayed a knowingness with a light-hearted twist.

"They call me Sadar. Some call me witch. Some fear me, others seek my help." She pulled the scarf from her head, spread it on the ground then sat. "You must forgive me, I'm older than I look, and my legs are tired."

Falcon sat on the ground on the opposite side of the fire from Sadar. "Can I offer you something to eat or drink?"

"You have wine?"

Falcon nodded. "Very little."

"Oh, that will never do."

Sadar waved her arms over her head and mumbled words in an ancient, foreign language. A puff of smoke welled up around Sadar's outstretched hands and when the air cleared, the witch held a tray with a pitcher full of deep burgundy wine and three glasses. Arella stared in shock, unable to believe what she'd just seen.

"Please, join me." Sadar set the tray in front of her and filled three goblets.

Arella sat next to Falcon. She was so close their knees touched, which gave her the confidence she needed right now. They both stared across the fire at their uninvited guest.

"You two are quite the pair." Sadar waved her arms in the air then pointed both hands straight toward the couple. "I should cast a spell over 'ya both!"

Sadar cackled and Arella cringed. So far the woman was a good example of why witches were disliked. She glanced out the corner of her eye at the expression on Falcon's face. The man had the audacity to smile at the old witch.

"Now you, my delicious looking morsel of a man, have potential, but that one," Sadar pointed at Arella, "doesn't have what it takes."

"Of all the. . ." Arella started to rise to her feet, but Falcon grabbed her arm and pulled her back down. She glared at him. How dare he sit there, all full of himself, flirting with an ugly witch! "Think what you want." She crossed her arms over her chest and sighed as loudly as she could.

"Please, share your wisdom with us. We," Falcon glared at Arella, "would not want to inconvenience you too long. I'm sure you have better things to do."

Sadar laughed. "I can't think of anything I'd rather do than look at you across the firelight, my young warrior. You look like you can handle yourself, but that one, well. . ."

A cold chill ran down Arella's spine. She was so blatantly throwing herself at Falcon. Did she really think a man like Falcon could be tempted by an old, haggard woman?

"I know what 'yer thinkin' missy."

"Do you?" Arella watched in shock while the witch jumped to her feet as quick as a child and twirled in circles. Dust and smoke hovered around the woman in such a thick cloud she could no longer be seen. It took several seconds for the cloud to settle, but when it did she gasped and covered her open mouth with her hand.

Before her stood an erotic looking woman, about her age, very sultry, with dark hair and a body any man would kill to possess. Sadar now wore a long, flowing blue gown, cut low in front to expose her new attributes to their best advantage, with a gold cord tied around her waist to emphasize every curve. What in the universe had just happened?

"I can see by the expression on your face that I've finally made an impression."

"I uhhhh. . .aaauhh. . ." Arella was truly speechless. She hated to admit she'd judged the woman by her appearance. A quick glance at Falcon told her nothing. The man sat stoic, reveling nothing of his feelings or thoughts. How could he resist Sadar now? Between that voluptuous body and purring voice, any man would become a victim of her every whim.

"I believe," Falcon looked at Arella, "what the Councilor meant to say is we're both impressed with your magic, Sadar."

"Thank you, Falcon." Sadar stepped closer to Falcon and knelt beside him. "And I'm quite impressed with you. Do you like the way I look now?"

"What man wouldn't?" Falcon stood and took a step back. "However, I learned a long time ago that things are not always what they seem. There's usually more than we comprehend."

"Well said." Sadar stood and faced Falcon. "I think you and I should talk in private."

Anger coursed with lightning speed through every vein in Arella's body. She stood and faced the new, beautiful woman, hands fisted at her side. "I think not." Falcon smiled and now she wanted to hit them both. Did he know she was jealous? Did he suspect how inadequate as a woman this new witch made her feel?

Falcon slipped his arm around Arella's shoulders and gave her a hug. "We're partners, so please continue."

Arella watched while Sadar spun in circles again and another cloud formed around her. This time she maintained a calm exterior even though her insides were a nervous mess. She refused to show the shock and confusion she felt. Several long seconds passed before the cloud dissipated and a new form emerged.

Arella gritted her teeth to suppress her shock. Before her stood a warrior to equal Falcon, from the top of his head all the way down his muscled body to his toes. The man stood, feet apart, dressed in a form-fitting, one-piece jumpsuit that accentuated his powerful form.

"You are lovely." Sadar stepped in front of Arella, picked up her fingers and brought them toward his lips. He placed a kiss on the back of her hand. "I did not mean to ignore you."

Falcon crossed his arms over his chest. "Tell us why you're here. We've had enough games for one night."

"Uhh, do I detect jealousy from my fellow warrior friend?"

"We're not friends."

It seemed Falcon shared her feelings of jealousy. Unfortunately, Sadar was right about them both. What was going on here? The woman obviously had a point to make, she just wished she'd hurry up and get to it.

Falcon stepped in front of Arella and faced the man. "Who are you?"

"You're both a bit short on patience." Sadar concentrated on Arella. "Maybe I should talk privately with the beautiful, young woman." He turned his attention back to Falcon. "She is one of the most beautiful women in the galaxy, is she not?"

"Step back and state your business, before I lose what little patience I have left."

"My, my. Can't have that, can we?" Sadar stepped back from the couple, then spun in circles.

Arella watched the now familiar cloud form around Sadar. Who would appear next? She grabbed Falcon's arm. He turned, put his arms around her and pulled her close. He did not have to say it, she knew he was telling her he'd protect her with his life.

She lifted her head and looked into his deep, dark blue eyes where she found honesty, concern, passion, and so much more. Yes, she also saw secrets and demons, but not the kind that would harm her, only the kind that needed retribution and final justice. Both she and Falcon turned their gazes on Sadar while the dust settled.

"Well, well now. Aren't we all getting along better?"

The new Sadar was an elderly man with straight, white, shoulder-length hair and a long beard to match. He was quite short, a bit pudgy, and wore a long, black robe tied loosely at the waist with a beautiful purple satinique sash trimmed in gold. A smile lit his face and laughter danced in his pale green eyes.

"Who are we looking at now?" Falcon asked.

"I'm still Sadar."

Falcon released Arella, turned toward Sadar and widened his stance. "Which Sadar is the real one?"

"Good question." Sadar gestured toward the fire. "Let's resume our seats. We have much to discuss."

All three of them returned to their positions around the fire. Arella felt more at ease speaking to the old man than she did any of the 'other' Sadars, but having Falcon at her side offered the comfort she needed. The entire mission had become so convoluted she no longer had a plan. The wisest thing she could do was let Falcon take the lead.

"I've changed forms to demonstrate how easily deception and treachery are accomplished. Jealousy is a tool. Love can conquer, but it's also a weapon that will be used against you." Sadar took a drink of wine. "Now, you were both fairly accepting of the old witch woman. Arella, you became jealous and lost confidence in the company of the seductress. Falcon, you became jealous and your protective instincts kicked into high gear in the presence of the fit, young warrior."

"You've made your point. Which is really you?" Falcon put another log on the fire.

"Which do you want me to be? You see, I can be anyone at any time. Witch, warlock, wizard, man, woman, call me what you like. I'm all of them, and none of them. What I am is someone who can help you achieve your mission."

Arella shifted on the hard ground. Her training taught her politics, party manners, weapons and plenty of instructions on taking charge of men and situations, but nothing about how to deal with morphing witches. "Does this ability serve you well?"

"Changing my appearance has indeed been an advantage at key times in my life.

However, I used that ability tonight as a test. Before I could reveal certain things to you I had to be sure you could handle it, and that you would continue."

"You doubted us?" Falcon asked.

"Well, maybe a little. I had to be sure, but I do I believe you're both up to the task. There is one thing though, you must guard against your emotions. Every decision you make is critical, and both of your lives will depend upon even the simplest choices."

"Are you saying this will be simple?" Arella straightened her back. She was used to men making her feel inferior and incompetent, but this stranger questioned her decision-making abilities. "Think you I cannot make a decision?"

"Easy, child. I meant no such thing."

"Arella, just. . ."

She glared at Falcon because she knew what he was going to say, and he wisely stopped in the middle of his sentence. "Go on, Sadar. Listening I am."

"Don't be nervous, Arella, just cautious. And Falcon, do not let revenge rule you. Everything in its time. Patience truly is a virtue in this case. Now, for some details." Sadar leaned back against the rock behind him. "Zotar is evil, and evil is darkness. That's important—remember that well. Evil is darkness. The best way to fight evil is with light."

Falcon leaned forward slightly. "I'm not sure I follow."

"There is so much more to the universe than you know, but you need to understand that honesty, love, and all the qualities that comprise a good person work together to create light. Your thoughts are things, and they also create light, or darkness."

"Thoughts are things?" Arella asked.

"Very much so. We all create our own reality, so if you don't like the reality you're in –create a new one."

Falcon smiled. "Is that warlock humor?"

"In a small way, but it's also truth. As a warrior, you must believe you can win the battle, because if you don't, you'll surely meet defeat. Is that not correct?"

"Yes."

Sadar turned his attention to Arella. "And you my dear, if you do not have complete confidence in your abilities as a councilor, no one else will either."

"True enough."

"Then you understand how your thoughts create things, events to happen, outcomes that please you. Therefore your thoughts become reality."

"What does this have to do with finding Zotar?"

"You can find him easily enough, capturing him is another matter. And Falcon, you of all people, knows what this has to do with Zotar."

"I know what the man deserves."

"So does everyone who knows his name."

Arella wanted to scream an objection. Zotar could not possibly be as bad as everyone thought. "Sadar, I really expected a bit more compassion from you."

"Arella, you have my sympathy. I know your sister loves the man, but she loves someone who does not exist. Zotar is a very convincing actor. He can convince anyone of anything. That's the secret of his success."

"And greed," Falcon added.

"Yes, and greed will be his downfall."

This was all too much. She hated listening to her brother-in-law being drug through the mud as if he were less than human. She'd been around him enough to know he was not completely evil. After all, he loved her sister, and was a good father to his son. No, he could not possibly be the man everyone thought him to be.

"I will stop him, Sadar."

"I know, Falcon, that's why I'm here." Sadar glanced behind him when the bushes rustled. Falcon started to get up, but Sadar shook his head. "That's Soho, he's with me. You'll meet him in a moment. First," Sadar pulled a paper from a pocket in his robe, "I want to give you this map. It shows the *Pyramid of Power*. Zotar is there. He's been there off and on for two annual-cycles. He's dug an underground tunnel to access the pyramid. He's looking for the treasure, and will not leave until he finds it."

"How many men does he have?" Falcon took the map from Sadar's outstretched hand.

"I don't know. He has trouble keeping help. They either die, or run for their lives. He's tried to keep this a low-profile operation by hiring a minimum amount of workers. He thinks that will work, except the way he treats his workers is what gives him away. They talk and say things all over town. No low profile there. Plus it's no secret that it's a death sentence for those foolish enough to work for him. He saves credits since you don't have to pay dead people. If the pyramid doesn't destroy them, Zotar does."

"Zotar is true to form." Falcon glanced at Arella. "Of course, Arella does not share our opinion of her brother-in-law."

"Time will remedy her thoughts. Truth can be cruel. Truth plays no favorites—it is what it is. Truth can be viewed many ways, but it can never be denied, and always shines through in the end." Sadar concentrated on Arella. "No one means to cause you pain, my dear. It's easier to believe what is convenient, what makes us happy, but the truth is there, whether you recognize it or not. Life could be so simple if everyone lived in truth."

Falcon cleared his throat. "That may be, but my mission is to find Zotar and carry out the death sentence he was given by the Protectorate's Court."

"And if the Powers That Be are willing, you'll do so. I'm aware of Dacton and Talina's quest. They're legendary. You and Arella must finish what they began. It will not be easy, and you will be tested as they were. I offer no magic. You both have all the tools you'll need. Love and light conquers all."

"That's it?" Falcon tucked the small, folded map in his back pants' pocket.

"More or less. It goes without saying you no longer need to go to Karatk, instead proceed to Waylent. You can rest there and purchase supplies for your trip up the mountain."

"Then what?"

Arella caught the smirk on the old wizard's face while he talked to Falcon, who may have met his match. Falcon looked as confused as she felt. They both stared at the now witch-man while he cackled a bit and smiled at them in a knowing way.

"You want all the answers, warrior, but some things are up to fate, and fate is up to you."

"You do talk in circles, Sadar, and the last thing I need right now is more esoteric mumbo jumbo from a. . .a wizard-witch who can't decide whether to be male or female."

"Be patient mighty warrior, greater tests than mine are coming your way."

"More cryptic messages, wizard?"

Sadar stood, raised his arms into the air, spun into a blur and returned as the witch woman that arrived. "I'm afraid so." She turned when the bushes beside her rustled. "Except for one thing."

Arella gasped when a small ball of deep red fur rolled into the clearing from the foliage behind them. The little creature stood and stretched to its full two-foot height. The short animal made his way to Sadar in three little hops.

"This is Soho. He's a Wallato. In some respects they make the perfect pet because they understand what you tell them, but they can't talk back." Soho squeaked then groaned. "Not in words anyway. I beg a favor of you."

Falcon tipped his head. "And?"

"Take Soho with you and deliver him to my brother who lives on the other side of the *Pyramid of Power*. I didn't think you'd mind since you're going there anyway."

"I'm not sure that's. . ."

Before Falcon could finish his statement, Soho jumped the fire in one controlled leap and landed in his lap, wrapped his stubby little arms around his arm and squeaked pathetically. She wanted to laugh, but this was not the time.

"I'd be a fool to say yes."

Sadar grinned in a knowing manner while Falcon squinted his eyes and pursed his lips in defiance. She wondered why Falcon would object to such a cute little animal. Of course he'd view Soho as another complication, but she liked the little guy.

"And you'd be a fool to say no, and Falcon, you're no fool."

"You know nothing about me."

"You're a tough one. How can I get you to believe? Let's see, I could turn you into a Cremora, then you might not have the audacity to insult me." Sadar laughed. "Do you want to be a male or a female Cremora?" She raised her arm and pointed at Falcon.

"Fine." Falcon held up both hands, Soho clinging to one arm. "You win."

"You're too much the warrior. This isn't about us, in fact what you're about to do goes so far beyond comprehension. The evil you'll prevent by stopping Zotar is difficult to measure, but suffice it to say, countless lives will be saved, and countless others will be able to live the way they were intended to live, and all because of you."

"I've seen Zotar in action, and the aftermath he's left for others to clean up. The sorrow, the blood, the destruction. So, yes, that I understand. But I'm only one man."

"With one dynamic woman at your side, who will prove her worth before this mission is over."

"Thank you, Sadar, I've been trying to tell him that ever since we left Nacrem." Arella smiled. "And we'll be happy to take Soho to your brother." Falcon scowled at her when she took Soho from Sadar, but she smiled at him then cradled the fuzzy little guy in her arms. He immediately closed his eyes and contentedly purred like a cat.

"He's adorable." Arella stroked the long hair on Soho's head away from his eyes.

Sadar chuckled. "You may not think so after you've had him for a while."

"We'll be fine." Arella smiled. "Falcon loves animals, don't you, Falcon?"

"Doesn't everyone?" Falcon groaned. "How will we find this brother of yours?"

"He's a wizard so he'll find you when the time is right, just as I did."

"I should have guessed." Falcon glanced at Arella and shook his head.

Sadar picked up her scarf. "I must leave you to your mission. Remember my words. You'll need them in the future. You must succeed." Sadar turned and took a few steps then stopped. She looked over her shoulder. "Oh, by the way, Wallatos are very sensitive—easily insulted, so be careful."

Sadar's image glimmered and sparkled, turned into a translucent glow then dissipated into the night air as if he, or she, had never existed. "I must admit, I'm impressed." Arella stroked the animal's fur. "I've never witnessed anything like that before."

"Nor have I. That even beats my brother's stories." Falcon stood and walked over to check on the Bemothras.

Falcon seemed bothered. He was a man who dealt in facts, and Sadar had presented puzzles that made no sense. She'd heard truth mixed with esoteric philosophy. If she had to explain herself to the High Council right now, they'd never believe a word she said. To tell them she conversed with a witch who told her secrets about the Pyramid of Power would end the conversation right there. This assignment seemed to become stranger by the sun-cycle.

She may not have to stop Falcon. The Pyramid of Power might do it for her. Now there was a thought to hold close to her heart. She still had to stop Falcon and protect Zotar at all costs.

CHAPTER TWENTY-SEVEN

Did you believe Dacton when he first told you what happened to him and Talina?"

Falcon shook his head without looking her way. "I wanted to believe him, but it all sounded too incredible to be true."

"What finally convinced you?" She watched him compassionately stroke the Bemothras. Soho stirred in her arms and she smiled when his cute little whiskers moved up and down.

Falcon turned and faced Arella. "It's hard for me to accept what I can't see, touch or feel, but my brother and Talina don't lie."

"Sadar said there is far more to life and our worlds than we know. I believe her."

Falcon walked back to Arella, sat and slid his arm around her waist. "Do you believe that love conquers all?"

Arella's insides did back-flips. Every time the man touched her she melted into a pool of mush, and felt like an inexperienced schoolgirl. Inexperienced she may be, but she was certainly not as naive as she once was. She may not have actually made love to a man before, but she'd come close a couple of times, before they decided her body was not what they wanted. Memories flooded back with a vengeance and she pushed away from Falcon.

"What's wrong, Arella? I thought you wanted me to touch you, and hold you. Did I misread your signals?" Falcon stood. "I'm sorry, Councilor. I'll not touch you again."

A smile tugged at the corners of her mouth. "That doesn't sound like the Falcon I've heard about, or the Falcon I know. The one I know never gives up if he thinks he's right." She gave him her best seductive smile and hoped it worked since she had no real practice enticing men.

"In case you didn't notice, I'm holding Soho." She stood and walked over to the flat, stacked rocks and gently set the fur-ball down. Before she could turn around Falcon was there. He reached out and pulled her to him. Her heart raced and her breath quickened.

"I must admit this little game you're playing is interesting." He bent his head and placed a kiss on her forehead. "I've never worked this hard to get a woman, in fact, they simply. . ."

"Fall all over you?" Arella tilted her head back and looked him in the eye. "I'm not like other women."

"I'm glad." He lowered his mouth to hers. "Would you like me to show you why women fall all over me?"

She nodded, even though his suggestive words sent shivers through her. He knew exactly what to say to make her quiver and ache with desire. She ran her hands up his muscled arms and memorized the feel of his skin while her fingers made their way to his neck, and then his hair.

The moment she touched his earlobe his mouth closed over hers and his tongue traced the outline of her lips several times before pushing inside. She wanted to let herself go, to give herself to this man—to stay with him forever.

Forever was not in their future. When she stopped him from killing Zotar he'd never forgive her. He may suspect she was sent for that purpose, but he was confident she'd never succeed. He'd never trust her again and there could be no relationship without trust.

His hands roamed her back then found her waist and slowly moved lower to cup over her backside. Damn, he was smooth, but did he want her as a woman, or was he using her? They were quite a pair. Was sex always a part of the spy game?

His kiss was heaven, his touch tender and caring. Her hands roamed up and down his shoulders and arms. Every rock hard muscle in his body pulsed with power. He could crush her with his bare hands, yet she knew he'd never hurt her. His mouth moved with a gentle urgency that made her want him even more. Where was the line between duty and desire? She wanted him. If she gave in to her desire would it be duplicity? Seduction was easy, betrayal was not.

She ended the kiss and pulled her head back. Falcon stared at her with sexy blue eyes and her entire body ached for his touch. She took a couple of steps back from him to break the spell.

If she'd needed proof of why women lusted for him she just received it in a most convincing demonstration. She started to walk away, but his hands grasped her shoulders and she stopped. When she turned to face him she lost all will to fight.

"Arella, I'll never hurt you, nor will I do anything you don't want me to do."

She met his gaze. If the eyes were a reflection of the soul, she found reassuring truth in the cool blue depths. "You wouldn't hurt me on purpose, but there are many ways to cause pain."

He released his hold. "Yes, Councilor, you're correct."

Her heart sank when he turned his back on her and walked away. He'd never know how much she wanted him for the man he was. Damn them! Here she was, alone with the first man who'd ever truly wanted her as a woman, and she was duty bound to betray him. Was there no justice in the Universe?

~ ~ ~ ~

Falcon sat in the entrance of the tent and cursed. Damn the woman. First she'd given him the come-on, then she'd pushed him away. He wished she'd make up her mind. Before his next thought formed, Soho came out of nowhere and in one leap plastered his furry body against his chest. Short, hairy little arms tickled his neck and toyed with his hair. "What are you doing?"

Soho answered in some kind of squeaky chatter that no human would ever understand. "You're something else, little fellow. Now, go back to Arella." With one jump to the ground he bounced over to her and it sounded like he was giggling. Animals did not giggle.

"Listen, Falcon, he's laughing!"

"I'm not." He walked over to Arella and sat next to her on the flat rock.

"You look worried. Why?" Arella scratched Soho behind his

short, perky ears.

"You heard Sadar. The mountain is steep and dangerous, not to mention the perils inside the pyramid." He looked into her eyes. "And you must remember the warning from Father Weston. Many have entered, but none have left."

"I didn't forget."

Falcon shook his head. "I'm glad you're not worried. I have to find and kill the most wanted criminal in the galaxy, keep you safe in the process and convince you to recommend Nacrem join The Protectorate. And if that isn't enough, we have a fur-ball to care for."

Soho let out a loud screech, jumped off Arella's lap and one leap later was out of sight in the dark vegetation. "Looks like our witchy-wizard was right."

Arella crossed her arms over her chest. "Did you have to insult Soho?"

"A bit overprotective, aren't you?"

"A bit insensitive, aren't you?"

Falcon ran his hands through his hair. Arella stared at him with daggers in her eyes. "I didn't mean to insult Soho." He walked toward the one tree that rustled in the dark. What he was about to do went against his training. "Sorry Soho. Please come down."

Leaves rained down on his head and the rustling sounds grew closer. A branch snapped and the squawking fur-ball fell into his arms. He rubbed Soho's head and carried him back to where Arella sat on the rock with a scowl on her face. He handed the wiggling creature to her. "Here's your new baby."

"Thanks." Arella pulled Soho close to her chest and stroked his fur. "What's really wrong, Falcon? I may not know you well, but I've spent enough time with you to know this isn't like you."

"You're right. I don't usually show my frustrations."

"Your men might contradict that statement."

"They wouldn't dare."

"That's what I thought. Now, are you going to tell me what's eating you?"

"I don't think you want me to do that."

"Try me."

"Fine." Falcon sat on the rock next to Arella. She was beautiful with firelight dancing off golden strands of hair that framed her face and flames reflecting in her extraordinary lavender eyes. Once he told her what had been bothering him she'd hate him with a passion. "I know what you're up to, Councilor. It's my job to know."

"Think you know me, do you?"

"You've been ordered to stop me." Her inability to meet his gaze was positive confirmation. "What you don't realize is that your fellow council members have thrown you away. They don't expect you to survive."

"Kidding, you are."

"Kidding, I'm not." He took her hand in his. "I'm not telling you this to make you mad, or because I don't care. It's the truth, Arella. I'm not sure why they want to sacrifice you, but from what you've said, it's because you're a woman and they don't want you on the council. It also has something to do with your connection to Zotar."

"Criminal I'm not!"

Soho let out a loud screech, jumped from her lap and fled back up a tree in the darkness. Falcon pulled her closer. "I know. Zotar is the criminal, and your High Council is protecting him. They're working against us for a reason, and I suspect it's about credits."

"Lying you are."

"I won't lie to you. We may not live through this, but I will kill Zotar." Arella's gaze found his and tears clouded her eyes.

"You know what that means, don't you?"

"Can you accept me killing him?"

"Don't know."

Falcon smiled. "At least that's honest. That's all I ask." He wiped a lone tear that ran down her cheek. "You're a pawn in a bigger game."

"Mean what, do you?"

"Your High Council has sacrificed you for power and wealth, which means more to them than human life." He slipped a hand behind her neck and pulled her head toward his. When their lips met he took a deep breath, inhaling the feminine scent that was hers alone, sweet, innocent and loving. He traced her lips with his tongue then gently sucked on her bottom lip. She tasted wonderful and he doubted he'd ever get enough of her.

Arella touched something deep in his soul. Why now? His

timing had never been the best, but this was insanity. The thought of having feelings for Zotar's sister-in-law was total lunacy.

When she pressed her firm breasts against his chest he moaned. How he wanted to undress her and show her what it was like to be a woman, and teach her how sweet surrender could be. His body ached for her and he lost himself in her essence.

His fingers threaded through her silky hair, gently grasping her head, guiding her responsive movements. Her inexperience excited him. Would he be her first? He wanted her no matter what. Judging a woman by purity, or lack of, never appealed to him. His need to bond with Arella came from a soul level, where sharing and melding mind, body and soul became a spiritual experience. Until this moment he'd never considered being with a woman in those terms.

He freed his fingers from her hair and ran his hands over her shoulders then down her back. Her well-toned muscles intrigued him in the most feminine way. Her entire body was perfect. His hands slid lower and he grasped her derrière, so round, so soft, so tempting.

This was the moment he'd longed for, the perfect opportunity to make her his. There may not be a logical explanation for the burning need that consumed him, but he certainly knew how to put out the fire.

CHAPTER TWENTY-EIGHT

Arella struggled to breathe. Falcon pulled her tight against him and his hands roamed her every curve. She had no idea how he managed the moves he did, but she had no complaint. His efforts set her entire body on fire. He explored her mouth in ways she never knew possible. The number of men she'd kissed in her lifetime could be counted on one hand, but Falcon made their romantic gestures seem like inexperienced boys.

Falcon is who she wanted, who she'd hoped for, who she'd been ordered to seduce and stop, but she wanted him so badly all orders flew out of her mind. Orders be damned, she did this for herself, no one else. The High Council could all go to Diabolus. Tonight was for her.

Falcon somehow managed to pick her up off the ground and hold her to him without breaking the kiss he so expertly continued to pursue. She wrapped her arms around his neck and held on while he walked toward the tent with long strides.

Arella's whole body sang with need. She could not believe a man wanted her as badly as she wanted him. His rapid breathing kept pace with hers and he held her so tight she felt his heartbeat keep time with her own. Somehow Falcon managed to enter the small tent and lay her down so gently she barely realized what he'd done. His strength amazed her.

She approached the point where most men ran and she fought

the panic that rose inside. How could she live with herself if he rejected her at the last moment? After the last rejection by a man she vowed never to be vulnerable again, yet she was on the judgment block. At this point she had nothing to lose except her last scrap of pride. At least she could then tell the council what they believed anyway—she was a failure.

With ease Falcon pulled up the bottom of her tunic. He ended his kiss so he could pull the garment over her head. The tent was mostly dark except for a faint green glow coming from some kind of stone in the corner. Maybe it was too dark for him to see her flaws. With practiced movements he slipped off her boots then peeled her pants from her body. She lay before him wearing nothing but two thin undergarments.

Falcon's hands explored her exposed flesh. He traced the outline of her legs from her ankles up her calves, past her thighs and finally coming to rest on her waist. She held her breath, waiting for him to back away, to be repulsed.

"You're beautiful. Perfect." Falcon lowered his head and kissed her stomach. He raised his head and stared into her eyes. "What's wrong, Arella?"

How on the face of the planet could he know something was wrong? Her eyes welled with tears. She knew he'd bedded the most gorgeous women in the galaxy and she could not believe for one moment that he found her beautiful, and certainly not perfect. "I can't believe you said that." She wanted to run as far away as she could get. He wiped a tear from her cheek, which further wounded her pride.

"What did I do to upset you?" Falcon eased himself down to lay next to her. "Tell me, please."

"I can't." She grabbed her tunic and held it over her camisole to protect herself from his probing gaze. She turned her head away from him and stared at the side of the tent. If it were possible to melt into an invisible puddle that is exactly what she'd do. His fingers gently found her chin and coaxed her to face him. She closed her eyes, partly to avoid his stare and partly to hold back the flood of tears that threatened to spill.

"Arella, open your eyes. Look at me."

He waited to speak until he saw her eyes focus on him. Falcon looked totally confused and she felt sorry for him. He really had no idea what he'd done, or why she reacted the way she had.

"All I said was that you're beautiful." He tilted her head up with his finger. "That's it, isn't it?" She tried to turn her head but he stopped her. "I'd never lie to you. You're the most beautiful woman I've ever had the pleasure to meet. I don't understand why you don't believe that."

"You have no idea."

"And I never will if you don't tell me."

She eased away from him and quickly pulled on her tunic and pants. He did not stop her, he simply stared with a lost, questioning look on his face. She sat up and hugged her knees.

"I was given away as a baby, so I have no memory of my parents. They put me out of their life because I was not petite enough, or pretty enough to be their perfect little girl. I learned my parents belonged to high echelon society and felt I was an embarrassment. It was easier for them not to have a child."

"That's pretty cold." He shook his head. "What about your sister?"

"She was raised by my parents and lived with them until she life-mated Zotar. Shortly after she life-mated, our parents died in a transport crash."

"Why did your parents keep Nodia?"

"She was tiny, acceptable, and by then they'd decided they needed a child for propriety's sake. All their friends had a child by then, and they had to compete, so Nodia was their show daughter."

"How did you find each other?"

"After our parent's death, Nodia went through their personal papers and found the paperwork that put me in the orphanage, and where it was. She tracked me down and came for me." She looked into Falcon's eyes. "She's two years my junior." She looked into Falcon's eyes. "She's the only one who's ever cared enough to look for me. We've only had three annual-cycles together, but we've become closer than most who have spent a lifetime together."

"That's a sad scenario, but it seems you have a happy ending."

"I had a good education and was well-prepared for life. Of course I always wondered who my parents were. I was sent away before my first birthday so I never had that love and closeness that comes with parents, especially from a mother."

"What kind of parents could do such a thing?"

"Self-absorbed people who valued money and social standing over family and responsibility." She ran her fingers through her hair. "Nodia didn't have any more love than I did. She may have been raised in my parents' home, but she was always with a nanny or tutor. They had no time for her. She suffered too. The only difference was she knew what they looked like."

She saw the disbelieving look on Falcon's face while he tried to absorb what she'd just told him, which indicated his life had been vastly different. If what she'd heard about him were true, he'd been raised by doting parents and had two inseparable brothers. It appeared she'd rendered him speechless. "It's okay, Falcon. I don't blame those who have good families, so don't feel guilty."

"It's hard not to. I can't relate to the way you were raised, and I can't condone such behavior. What your parents did was despicable. You must hate them."

"That's a warrior speaking." She patted him on the shoulder, aware he'd slipped into his protective mode. "I won't deny having those feelings when I was younger, but now, I realize some people shouldn't have children. They actually did me a favor. I didn't have to look at them and wonder why they wouldn't hug me, or talk to me like Nodia did. At least I knew the people who taught me were there to do a job and had no emotional connection."

"You're an amazing woman. I admire you."

She inhaled deeply. "How can you say that?"

He reached out and took Arella's hand in his. "I say that because it's true. You could have turned out to be resentful and cold, instead you're warm, understanding and forgiving, and that, I admire."

Heat burned her cheeks. "Thank you, I do."

"Believe me, you don't." He laughed. She swung her hand at his face, but he caught her wrist before impact. "No one has ever teased you, have they?"

She stared at him trying to understand what he meant. "Understand, I don't."

"You know, joking. Making fun in a kind, yet funny way because they care about you."

"No." Arella stared at her bedroll. "I don't know anyone who jokes."

He tilted her chin up with his finger. "Now you do. *DeJorell Kari*, you do not have to be so serious all the time. It's okay to laugh and smile."

Arella sighed. "Sorry I am, sorry. Fun person, I'm not." He stared at her with genuine concern and understanding, so different from others in her life. She wanted to cry, which was an emotion she rarely experienced.

"Let me teach you."

"I'm afraid that may be an impossible task."

"Nothing is impossible if you allow it to happen."

"I wish I had your philosophy about things." He picked up her hand and brought her fingers to his lips and kissed each knuckle then ended with one in the middle of the back of her hand. An erotic tingle coursed through her.

"Now, my sweet warrior, I have one question. Why do you constantly pull away from me?"

She blinked back tears, but could not stop one from rolling down her cheek.

"Who hurt you?"

More tears escaped. "Don't you see?"

With the back of his hand, Falcon wiped her cheek. "Please explain. I truly don't understand, because I find you absolutely perfect."

"Then you're the only person, male or female, on the face of Nacrem who does." She stared down. "I've tried to be with men. They thought they could get past my size and shape, but once they saw my body they became sickened and ran from my chamber. There, now you know. Now you can leave me alone. I'll not fault you."

"By the stars! Tell me why everyone finds fault with your body."

"Haven't you seen that I'm taller than all the other women? That I have muscles and they do not? That I have scars? I'm not feminine. I simply don't fit the mold of a Nacrem woman."

"Is that all? Then you're in luck, I'm not a Nacrem man."

"How dare you! I've just bared my soul to you, and mock me, you do." Falcon pulled her into his arms and held her tight, tighter than he ever had before.

"I do not mock you, I'm joking. I'm sorry if you misunderstood.

I'm trying to tell you I find you perfect, beautiful beyond measure, and very tempting. I want you Arella. Like no other woman before."

"How can I believe you?" He pulled her to him and held her close. Her tears dampened his shirt, but for once she let them fall.

"When have I lied to you?" Falcon tilted her chin up and looked into her eyes. "I've never lied to you. I have no need. I don't know who's hurt you in the past, but if I find him, I'll kill him. Just don't blame *me* for their mistakes."

"I'm sorry." Falcon tilted her chin up with his finger.

"Don't judge yourself so harshly, and don't believe what others say about you. That is only their perception of what they want to see. What they want you to believe."

"Your words are wise. They're not helping much at this moment, but they're very wise."

"My words come from hard-learned lessons."

Arella smiled. "I must admit, I. . ."Before she could finish her sentence Soho bounded into the small tent, somersaulted into her lap and settled down with a purr. "I guess he's back." The little creature looked at Falcon for a moment, then burrowed his head into the crook of her arm.

"It appears he's succeeded where I've failed." Falcon scooted to the opening of the tent. "I'll leave the two of you alone." He pulled his bedroll with him.

"Falcon." He turned and looked at her. "I'm sorry. You're nothing like the others."

"I'm glad." He reached out and tucked stray hairs behind her ear. "I won't pressure you. When you're ready, I'll be there."

He stood, gave her a devilish wink then settled down on his bedroll by the fire. Her heart sank. To date, her success with men totaled zero. She might as well devote her life to one of the Holy Orders, but even they would not want her.

She scooted back, pulled her pack closer to use as a pillow and laid down. It was time to rethink everything. This might be her only chance to experience the willing sexual attentions of a man. She wanted to enjoy mutual satisfaction at least once in her lifetime.

If she lived through this mission she could be ordered to life-mate some ugly, mean old man who would turn her stomach. Her mind settled on a course of action. She'd seduce Falcon at the next opportunity, and would savor every moment with him.

CHAPTER TWENTY-NINE

Judging from the number of insects in the air a water supply was close. The Bemothras needed to drink and rest since they'd been pushed hard all day. Arella and Soho had not complained, but they too looked tired. It was a very warm sun-cycle even though much of the way had been shaded by trees.

In the distance to his left he watched the foliage move. Someone had been following them all day, and it was not his people. If it were they would have made contact before now, plus they knew how not to be detected, so this person was not as well trained as his men, or the watchers.

They crested the hill and there it was, a large lagoon, complete with waterfall, palmus trees, and some of the most beautiful flowers he'd ever seen. The open area of lush, green grass offered a perfect rest area, and an opportunity to learn who the clumsy shadow might be.

He maneuvered the large Bemothra down the hill, between rocks, trees and more vegetation than there should be on any slope. Thick, sharp branches slapped his face and grabbed at his clothes. When he ducked a low limb he looked back and saw Soho with his arms wrapped around Arella's neck, hanging on for dear life. She kept her head low, but when a leaf brushed her hair he heard her moan. then noticed several strands of long, blonde hair hanging from the greenery.

The damned jungle kept getting thicker by the sun-cycle, and he prayed they would not have to battle this kind of vegetation all the way to the *Pyramid of Power*. Finally thick green trees and foliage yielded to the wide, grassy bank around the inviting water. He made it to the edge of the deep blue pool and pulled his Bemothra to a stop. He dismounted and allowed the animal take a well-deserved drink. He walked to where Arella waited a few feet away and helped her down. The worried look on Soho's furry face looked comical, especially since he still clung to her neck for protection.

Both Bemothras' heads were on the water and they slurped as they drank, which he knew from experience would take a while. Arella stood in front of him, leaves in her hair, a couple of scratches on her cheek, and Soho wrapped around her neck like a fur muffler. He reached out, smoothed back a few strands of hair while she brushed leaves from the top of her head.

Soho finally released his hold and mimicked them both, brushing the last few green remnants that clung to her shiny, gold hair. She looked beautiful with the sun glimmering on her hair and skin, a princess to be cherished. He hoped she'd ask him to love her soon.

Arella took Soho's hands and helped him down to the ground. "You'd better get a drink." Soho scampered off toward the waterfall. "That was a fun ride."

"I wouldn't go that far." She smiled at him and his heart melted. For the first time her lavender eyes looked relaxed, and spoke with a playful quality he was not used to. Maybe she was learning how to joke and laugh.

"Are we staying long?"

"That depends." The way she looked at him right now could lead to an extended stay. She reached out and put her hand on his cheek, then slowly trailed her fingers down his neck until her hand came to a stop in the middle of his chest. He took a deep breath. What was she up to now? Had she come to a decision, or was he reading more into her actions? He was good at wishful thinking.

She leaned toward him until her lips were as close to his as her slight frame allowed. "You have my attention, Councilor."

"Good. Now, kiss me."

Falcon leaned closer and brushed her nose with his. "Are you sure?"

"I asked, didn't I?"

Her lips parted in anticipation and he threw caution to the wind. Without further hesitation his mouth found hers with a consuming urgency. He wrapped his arms around her, his hands exploring her back until they came to rest on her derriere. He cupped her shapely behind and pulled her tighter against him. He wanted her to feel how much he wanted her.

She tasted as sweet as the aroma of the surrounding flowers, and felt even better. If he had his way, he'd never let her go. She moaned softly. He deepened the kiss and reveled in the feel of her firm breasts against his chest.

Flames of desire consumed him. Her well-toned body was soft in all the right places. The perfect combination. How the other men made her feel was a crime and he'd like nothing better than to deliver appropriate punishment. A moan deep in her throat nearly sent him over the edge of no return. As much as he hated to, he had to end this little frolic. Too many were watching. It was too easy to forget his people watched around the clock, but the stranger that lurked close by occupied his senses.

Ever so slowly he moved his hands to her cheeks. He ended the kiss and eased her back. A slight breeze blew strands of hair into her eyes so he smoothed them back behind her ears. Her gaze bore into him as if asking what she'd done wrong. "*DeJorelle Kari*, I would like nothing better than to continue this, however, this is not the time or place."

"I see. Well, uhh. . ."

He leaned into her and kissed her cheek. "No you don't, but you will when we find lodging for the night. Then we will not stop." Her eyebrows raised and her eyes got big and round. "But only if that is what you want."

She managed a little nod that made him smile. It had been a long time since he'd rendered any woman speechless. She turned and walked toward Soho who jumped off a rock and disappeared behind the waterfall. Arella followed Soho so he decided it was a good time to put the Bemothras up for a while since they had finished drinking. He led them to a couple of nearby trees and tied them to low branches, then untied his backpack from behind the saddle then carried it to a nearby rock and sat.

He pulled one of his shirts out to create a makeshift carrier for Soho. Arella needed both hands available at all times, just in case they were attacked, or the Bemothras spooked. He tied the arms of the shirt together, tied off the shirttails and secured the fasteners down the front. It would have to do.

When he glanced up he detected a slight movement in the distant foliage in front of him. He pretended to be engrossed in his project, but his trained eye remained focused on the stalker. Arella's distant laugh announced she was fine. He could not see her or Soho behind the cascading water, so it was time for a closer inspection. He stood, hung his makeshift animal pouch over her saddle horn, then proceeded toward his destination. The entity in the jungle stayed hidden, but paced his movement.

The fine cool spray felt good on his face when he ducked behind the curtain of water and found Arella and Soho playing. He was almost jealous of the hairy little creature, but he'd have his chance this moon-cycle. "Ready to go?"

"Actually, I could use a few moments alone to wash up a bit, if you wouldn't mind?"

It was possible she needed some personal time, yet his gut told him she was up to something. "Fine. I'll wait for you on the trail above the falls."

"Would you take Soho for me?" She picked Soho up and held him out toward Falcon. "Just until I catch up."

"Don't be long." He took Soho from her, tucked him under his arm and briskly returned to the Bemothras. He grabbed the pouch from her saddle, stuffed a screeching Soho into it and hooked it over his saddle horn. He mounted, then nudged his mount into a quick trot. He headed in the direction he told Arella he would, but as soon as the jungle hid him from view he circled back around to where he had a perfect, concealed view of the lagoon. It did not take long to put his suspicions to rest.

~ ~ ~ ~

Arella quickly took care of her immediate needs because she certainly did not want Falcon coming back for her. A woman sometimes needed private time, and he was far too attentive to give it to her without her asking. She secured the waist fastener of her pants and started to duck under the overhanging rock to leave. Before she could straighten someone shoved her backwards and she fell to the moist, mossy ground.

When she looked up her worst nightmare had returned in the flesh, looking meaner and more determined than she remembered. "Jorken, what are. . ." He grabbed her arm and jerked her to her feet, inflicting as much pain as possible.

"I ask the questions here," he released her arm, "and you'd better have the right answers."

"What do you want to know?" Jorken stepped closer to her and she gritted her teeth in anticipation. She knew well his capabilities and did not want to further experience his cruelty.

"Where are you headed?"

"I don't know." He scowled at her and her skin crawled. "He doesn't talk much." Jorken quickly thrust his fist into her stomach and she doubled over in pain.

"Have you slept with him yet?"

"No." He grabbed her neck and forced her upright.

"At least that wasn't a lie. So, what's 'yer excuse, bitch?" He shoved her backwards.

Her back slammed against the tall rocky wall behind her and she coughed several times in an effort to catch her breath. With her right hand she tried to rub his fingerprints off, but he made her feel dirty and violated. "I can't very well rape the man."

"Oh yes you can, and you'd better. If you don't, your sister and her dear son won't live to see the next sun-cycle."

"What do you know about my sister?" Jorken gave her an evil laugh that said it all. He was obviously up to something and she knew he would not reveal details.

"I told the High Council they picked the wrong woman for this job. You're not capable of seduction. They were stupid to think Falcon Rovarn, playboy of the galaxy, would bed the likes of you. I damn sure wouldn't."

He cackled at her, but she refused to let him provoke her. She doubted she could take him in a fight. It would be difficult enough to explain the new bruises on her neck and arm without adding more. "I'll do my job."

"Your sister's life depends on it, not to mention yours." He chuckled.

His laugh was short, but packed with complete malevolence. She'd love to pick up a rock and smash it into his head, but none were close.

"Remember, I'm watching, and it's up to me if you live or die."

"Well if you're watching so closely, you must have seen us kissing by the water."

"I saw. You weren't trying very hard, bitch. That looked more like a brother to sister kiss. Didn't impress me as anything more. If it were, he'd have you on the ground in a flash. Instead, he walked away like all the men in your life have done."

She opened her mouth to reply, but he disappeared as quickly as he'd appeared. The man was a slimy lizorodous, who had no conscience or moral convictions. If anyone deserved to die it was Jorken. Every rumor about the deceitful man rang true; torture, threats, blackmail and murder, all with the High Council's blessing. She knew the man was serious about his order of *sleep with Falcon or die.*

Just when she thought she'd made a willing choice, she realized she'd only lied to herself. She'd convinced herself sleeping with Falcon was for love. The mind could justify anything if it wanted to, but could it escape truth? At the moment she didn't even know what truth was.

After several deep breaths she ducked the rocks and cascading water to emerge outside. It was a wonder Falcon had not come looking for her by now. Soho had probably kept him busy. She hurried to where her Bemothra waited by a bush, untied him, led him to a large rock and mounted. Once in the saddle she nudged him up the hill and headed to where Falcon said he'd wait.

A short distance away she saw him sitting on the ground, his back against a palmus tree. She heard Soho screeching, but couldn't see him. "Where's Soho?" She pulled her Bemothra to a stop behind his.

He stood, took something off his saddle, carried it to hers and hung it on her saddle horn. Soho's head popped out the top of a sack that looked like Falcon's shirt.

"He's all yours."

"Thanks for watching him." He simply nodded, walked to his Bemothra, mounted, and spurred the animal into a fast walk. Falcon's mood had certainly changed, which made her believe he'd seen Jorken. She could not change what happened, all she could do was plan her next move. Should she tell him the truth, or play stupid? Another situation where she was damned if she did and damned if she didn't.

They climbed higher and the jungle vegetation slowly gave way to trees, grass and rocks. This mountain was the steepest yet and she hoped they were near the top because she hated going uphill on the large beast. The bemothra's gait was rougher when he climbed and she had to lean forward to stay in the saddle, which shoved the saddle horn into her stomach, and after Jorken's punch it was still rather tender.

Time passed slowly since Falcon maintained the silent treatment. Not that he was usually chatty, but his silence grated on her nerves. She liked hearing his deep voice, especially when he called her DeJorelle Kari, whatever that meant, it sounded wonderful coming from his sexy lips. Or was it his deep voice? Falcon had more masculine appeal than any man in the galaxy.

His silence was for the best since she did not yet have a plan. How could she lie to an intelligent, experienced warrior? She wanted to trust him, but if she did, everything she'd ever worked for would be lost.

Her life had always revolved around Nacrem. It had been a long road to Councilor, and she still struggled to win acceptance from her peers. All of that would be erased if she failed. If they did not kill her, she'd be banished from Nacrem. What a choice. How had she ended up in this position? She rescued a dying man in the desert, took him to the High Council, now her life lay in the balance.

If she were a man, a prostitute would be hired to ply Falcon. That still could have been done, but they chose to force her? Why? Maybe they just wanted to degrade her until she resigned her position. They would inevitably dispose of her permanently one way or another.

What motivated a government? The possibilities were endless, but knowing the answer would not change her predicament. Credits were behind everything, or so it seemed. Too bad she could not buy her way out of this mess. Of course, it would change nothing. Even millions of credits could not make the High Council respect her or treat her as an equal.

The ache in her backside screamed for relief. It seemed like they'd been in the saddle for several sun-cycles without rest. If these big hairy animals were not so wide it would be considerably easier. She hoped Falcon stopped soon because she desperately needed to keep her knees together for a while. She was considered tall, but when it came to straddling this monster, she came up short.

Soho had fallen asleep long ago in the cozy pouch Falcon made. The little guy was cute and cuddly, but he could be a nuisance. He made a great pet, but as a traveling companion, there was room for improvement.

Falcon looked back over his shoulder for about the hundredth time. Was he worried about her, or did he think she was meeting with the enemy at every turn? His constant glances and self-imposed silence verified he'd seen Jorken. She'd be a fool to think otherwise. Nothing escaped the Chief Protector. There were times his diligent abilities were a blessing, but his prudence to duty did not help her cause one bit.

It didn't matter what she or Falcon thought, lives were at risk as well as politics. The High Council hid covert activities well, but their hands were dirty. A select few Council members were honest, but the majority were corrupt to the core.

The Council's operating funds had increased greatly since Zotar arrived. She'd been a fool not to make that connection sooner. Zotar, or Modark, arrived with untold wealth. Since almost everyone on the High Council had an agenda, honesty was scarce, so Zotar had no problem buying his asylum.

Until Falcon's involvement she'd never questioned Zotar's wealth. For Nodia's sake she ignored signs of duplicity and corruption. Secretly she wondered where he'd gotten all his credits, but since he was her brother-in-law, she ignored that nagging feeling of doom every time she was around him.

Thinking about Zotar helped pass the time, but her legs and muscles screamed for a rest. The lush, open expanse of green grass they were crossing looked peaceful enough, in fact it was beautiful. She opened her mouth to ask Falcon if they could stop, but before she got a word out her Bemothra let out a loud screech and reared up, his front legs thrashing at thin air. She wrapped her arms around the animal's neck in an effort to stay in the saddle, but she felt herself falling backward, unable to stop herself.

Her teeth jarred together when she hit the hard ground, landing on her backside with a hard bounce. She fell on her back and her head hit something concealed in the grass. With her arms she pushed herself to a sitting position.

"Don't move a muscle."

Falcon's restrained voice held a serious warning, she'd heard it before. She knew him well enough not to question. She obeyed in silence because whatever spooked her Bemothra could not be good. Falcon unsheathed his sword and slowly walked toward her, carefully parting the tall grass in front of him with his weapon so he could examine his every step.

Then she saw what he searched for and her breath caught in her throat. She was not sure what it was, but it resembled some kind of sardnake. It wove back and forth in the pasture until it rose high enough to look Falcon in the eye. It had long fangs that dripped brown slimy venom, and its' body was as big around as Falcon's upper thigh.

The long, round creature followed Falcon's every move with its head. It made a rattle-like sound with its tail then thrust its head toward Falcon's neck, but he managed to dodge each lunging strike. Falcon challenged the animal with amazing speed and grace. The mutant reptile was strong, swift, and vicious, but Falcon's calculated defense was amazing.

A rattle behind her signaled the angry sardnake had a mate. "There's two!" Unfortunately the second reptile turned its attention on her. She remembered Falcon's words and did not move a muscle, hoping it would lose interest in her. Beady dark eyes with bright red centers focused intently on her. She did not dare move her arm to pull the cutter from its holder on the inside of her boot, nor could she out-run it. Every move Falcon made toward her was thwarted by the first creature. Then she saw his sword slice through the skin and the creature let out an excruciating hissing noise. The sardnake behind her flew by her to join the life and death battle.

"Look out!" She knew he heard her, but maintained his concentration. The two sardnakes banded together, side by side, weaving back and forth, thrusting their fangs at Falcon. She watched him raise his sword over his head and wave it in circles.

In the blink of an eye he swung. Two heads flew through the air, then landed with loud thumps in the grass while two long, scaly, bodies fell lifeless to the ground.

Falcon ran to her side, knelt and scooped her up into his arms. "Are you okay?"

"A little bruised, but nothing broken." She smiled, relieved that Falcon would think all the bruises Jorken inflicted were sustained in the fall. He carried her over the grassy plane in the same direction the Bemothras had fled.

Her left arm wrapped around his neck and she reached up with her right hand and clasped her fingers together to hold on. He carried her with ease and she enjoyed the ride for a while, but decided she'd taken advantage long enough. "Falcon, I can walk." He glared down at her. "Really, you can put me down, I'm fine."

He stopped, lowered her feet to the ground, but his arms lingered at her waist longer than necessary. "Thank you. You saved my life." She looked into his eyes. "Again." She truly was not used to anyone being concerned about her. Nodia cared, but she was the only living person who had knowledge of anything other than her name and position. It was safer to keep to herself and not risk being hurt.

Warmth from Falcon's arm sunk into her skin in the cool breeze of the waning sun-cycle. He studied her intently, but his deep blue gaze sent a mixed message. She was not sure whether to interpret that look as desire or distrust. Her heart voted for desire. She stepped back and took a deep breath. "How far did they run?"

"I'd say they're in the valley at the bottom of this mountain. They were spooked. All snaketors are their natural enemies."

"Mine too. I hate anything that doesn't have legs, and even legs don't help some creatures." She started walking in the direction he pointed, but heard a subdued chuckle behind her.

Without a mirror she had no idea how bad she looked. Her hair needed washing, she felt dirty all over, and not just from travel grime, but from the worst human filth possible. No mistake about it, Jorken represented the most despicable entity any planet had to offer, and more dangerous than animals –animals played fair.

CHAPTER THIRTY

Falcon glanced over his shoulder in the waning light to be sure Arella still followed. The sound of hooves stomping against dirt and rock told him she was near, yet he wanted to see her face and read her enticing lavender eyes. Granted, she lied to him, again, but he knew the man had threatened her in some manner.

Without a doubt her government had sent him. If it were Zotar's man she'd be dead. Zotar never gave warnings. Her new *shadow* just bullied and punched women. He wondered how brave the low-life would be if he faced a man? The low-life should be more careful than to leave telltale bruises. He'd seen fresh marks on her neck and he was sure there were others he hadn't seen. Thank the stars they weren't under the waterfall any longer than they were.

The Nacrem government had a plan and somehow Arella was a key player. She did not seem aware of her true purpose, only the assignment. Why they chose her would answer the question. The outcome was all they were concerned with, and based on his experience, Arella was expendable. She appeared genuinely naïve and had no conception of the evil Zotar possessed, nor did she suspect herself a pawn in some perverted government game.

If his calculations were accurate, they'd soon be in Waylent where they could rest and regroup. This trip had taken a toll on them both. Why they had to travel so primitively he'd never understand. It was especially exhausting for Arella. Thank the Gods this primal planet had three bright moons so they could maneuver the steep hills. He refused to stop and spend another moon-cycle under the stars, no matter how beautiful they were. They needed a good meal and facilities where they could bathe, rest, and enjoy the finer comforts of life for at least one moon-cycle. Neither of them were used to the primitive lifestyle for an extended period of time.

They both had their priorities which literally put them worlds apart. Mingling their duties would spell disaster. For any relationship to grow there had to be common ground, and sex did not qualify. They were definitely attracted to each other and would be good together in bed. Her eyes clearly said yes, even if her mind said no. He wished he could be the man to show her the ways of love, and undo the damage others had done to her feminine self-esteem.

For the first time in his life he'd found a woman who made him want more than sex, but sleeping with the enemy never ended well. Secrets were learned and passed, but only one usually lived to spy another day. At heart, Arella was not capable of such capers, nor did he want to involve her in anything so dangerous. He cared about her too much to let sex rule over his better judgment. As it was, he feared they'd have to fight each other to fulfill their respective missions.

He crested the hill and stopped. A valley of twinkling lights below promised well-deserved relief from life on the trail. Arella rode up and stopped beside him. Her eyes widened and her lips parted slightly which caused his imagination to wander. For every reason he had to stay away from her there were a hundred more to want her. She was a woman who could tempt the Gods.

"Thank the Gods." Arella sighed deeply and shifted in her saddle.

Indeed. She'd never say that if she could read minds. "You thank the Gods when I'm the one who led you here?" She gave him a puzzled look. He quietly chuckled while she shook her head, pretending disgust at his arrogance. She was predictable, and he liked that about her.

"Silly me." Arella's Bemothra stomped his foot and swished his tail. "How long?"

"Less than an hour." She wrinkled her nose and he smiled. "We'll rest a couple of sun-cycles in Waylent. We have much to learn and prepare for. But first we've got to get our stories straight."

"I don't understand."

He lifted his left leg over the bemothra's neck and turned sideways in the saddle to face Arella. "We'll pose as a happy, newly life-mated couple on the run."

"From what?"

"What crime would you like to commit?"

"Theft?"

"Fine. We stole the crown jewels from the King of Rateland, and we killed several of his personal guards in the process."

"I never heard of such a king."

"There actually is one in a remote galaxy, but that's the point, we don't want to make it easy for anyone to check up on us. The Zapartulla Galaxy is so little known that even if someone wanted to check we'd be gone before they could obtain results."

"Why do we have to be life-mated?"

"I don't believe you even asked that question, especially after the Bartose Inn. I know you think you can protect yourself, but that job is mine, at least for now. I can't protect you if you're not with me."

"I could call you arrogant, but I've already done that." She forced a smile. "I understand."

"Do you? There's only two of us against an entire planet full of fugitives and criminals. We must stay united to survive. We have to watch each other's back."

"I rather like watching your back, Commander. It's by far the nicest back I've ever watched."

"I'd rather watch the other side of you, it's far more interesting than your back, however, your backside is quite nice."

"There's a difference between back and backside."

"You're right. You watch what you like and I'll do the same." He swung his leg over the animal's neck and slipped his foot into the stirrup. "Let's go. I'm hungry." He nudged his Bemothra into a walk and started down the last, steep hill. "One more thing. Let me do the talking, and stay close."

"If I weren't so tired, hungry, and in need of a bath, I'd argue with you."

"I knew you'd see it my way." A few choice words crossed her perfectly shaped lips and he laughed to himself. She'd actually flirted and joked with him. He hoped she'd continue to explore that playful side because he liked it a lot.

While hooves scraped against rocks, his thoughts wandered, and he was helpless to stop the intimate visions his mind conjured. It might take more self-restraint than he possessed not to submit to his overwhelming lust for Arella. Falcon Rovarn, avoiding a woman? That was a joke. His brother would certainly have a warrior's day teasing him when he found out, and considering he was heading up surveillance, he already knew.

Then again, there were no official rules against sex, and often sex with the enemy was recommended. His main concern was hurting her emotionally. She was the perfect prey; too honest and vulnerable. He knew her orders, so why should he hesitate? When had he become a gentlemen with scruples beyond reproach? He needed a rest more than he thought if he couldn't answer those questions.

The mountain was now behind them and city lights illuminated the way, but he felt no relief. Danger lurked everywhere. Traveling with a beautiful woman was a major handicap. No man could miss Arella. She needed a disguise. Next sun-cycle he'd attend to that matter, this moon-cycle he'd try to keep her hidden.

It was crucial for Arella to maintain silent, and that alone would be a challenge for them both. She'd never been on an undercover mission in her life, and he was afraid it might cost her dearly. Her devotion to duty was admirable which made him wonder even more why her superiors wanted to throw her away. Her High Council expected them to fail and he knew why. Zotar bought them all.

The Nacrem council did not understand that he still had the backing of The Protectorate. There was enough fire power close at hand to annihilate the entire planet. His every move was documented. He'd tracked numerous missions from the main ship himself so he was well aware of what they knew.

They chose him to finish this vendetta with Zotar, and he was grateful, because when Zotar drew his last breath he wanted to watch. For every innocent victim, for every destroyed family, he would inflict justice, and for his beloved brother, Baleko.

Arella rode silently beside him, chin up, long, golden hair blowing in the breeze, her lavender eyes focused toward their destination. She was a sight to behold, and hold her was exactly what he'd like to do this moon-cycle and every moon-cycle. Her brown leather traveling garments were not feminine, yet they clung in all the right places, and did little to hide her full breasts and luscious curves.

He pulled his Bemothra to a stop and she did the same. "We're almost there. I need to be sure I can count on you to follow my lead." She averted her gaze. "Look at me, Arella." He waited for her attention before he continued. "It's important you understand."

"I'm not stupid, Commander. I know how to follow orders. And this is an order, is it not?"

"It is designed to keep you safe and alive."

"Fine."

"If you go off like you did last time, I cannot protect you. You'd be violated before you turned the first corner."

"I'm not weak and helpless."

Falcon reached over, tilted her chin up with his index finger and groaned. "I know you're not, and I count on that." He shook his head. "I suspect your head hurts where the blood is in your hair."

"A little." Her hand moved to the cut in her scalp.

He nodded. "You need rest. We'll both feel better soon." He nudged his mount forward and headed toward the closest lodging facility. Even warriors got tired and enjoyed a bit of luxury. He glanced skyward, not surprised to see air traffic. Hopefully Waylent was not as primitive as Usted, and offered better lodging. So far, nothing on this planet suited him.

Air traffic meant more people, and that worked to his advantage when he did not want to be noticed. His Bemothra also seemed in a hurry and broke into a canter. Arella kept pace and even lurched ahead of him at times. Soho peeked out the top of his pouch, his hands clinging tightly to the fabric below his chin. At least the little creature had behaved better.

Lights flashed along the road they were on.

"This is one strange place," Arella said, riding up next to Falcon. "there's air traffic, surface vehicles, and us." She laughed. "We must be quite the sight on these monsters."

"No worse than those cameoras you provided."

"Those darling animals got us where we wanted to go, didn't they?"

"And so did these. Or should I say your 'baby' did."

"You're just jealous mine is cuter than yours. His hair is much nicer."

He loved the way her smile lit her face in the moonlight. "Why Counselor, I do believe you jest."

"You're right. It is more fun not to be so serious."

"I like this side of you." Her laughter was musical and he hoped to hear more. The Bemothras began to dance and sidestep. Soho let out a screech loud enough to wake the dead. Overhead several different types of air-transports traveled low and buzzed in different directions. Their noisy engines made their mounts extremely nervous.

Two loud hovercraft approached from behind then whizzed by at breakneck speed. He cursed under his breath. There seemed no safe place for man or beast on this God forsaken planet. At least they were still in the saddle heading in the right direction.

Cautiously he led the way down the right side of the road with a silent prayer there would be no more speeding vehicles. There were times he enjoyed riding in the country on esroths, but only to relieve stress and commune with nature. He was spoiled since he commanded the fastest and most technologically advanced ships in the galaxy.

This slow, animal-dependent method of travel might be necessary, but it left much to be desired. Arella's Bemothra trotted slightly ahead of him. The only plus was watching her cute little behind in the saddle. Soho popped his head out of the pouch and glared at him as if he knew where his thoughts had strayed. His thoughts had traveled to those questionable areas too many times lately. Would he ever physically experience his mind's daydreams? The tougher question was should he?

More traffic cluttered the highway and sky the closer they came to the heart of the city. When they passed a tavern he heard several whistles from the parking lot, and they were not meant for him. It was dark and Arella was barely visible, so he could imagine how much attention she'd draw in the sun-cycle. The Bemothras still acted spooky from all the commotion, but they trudged on, both of them working hard to keep the animals calm and on track.

Several large buildings lay just ahead, some nice, some not so nice. Lights flashed on tall signs illuminating the way to eateries, lodging, lounges, and of course prostitution establishments. People were everywhere, walking, driving, flying, and even riding Bemothras and Cameoras. This planet was indeed a contradictory mixture of old and new, good and bad, rich and poor, and a little of everything in between.

A tall, upscale lodge caught his attention. The area they were in now suited him perfectly since it was primarily new and well-kept. Large numbers of people made it easier to remain in the background. Waylent might just be a pleasant surprise, but he'd reserve judgment until he was sure.

The fancy lodge straight ahead where the road turned looked acceptable so he headed straight for the corral on the left side of the building. They entered the fenced area and halted in front of a small office. A man, dressed in some kind of uniform, stepped out the door.

"Good evening sir, madam. May I stable your mounts?"

Falcon dismounted. "Yes, please." He walked over to Arella, helped her down then removed the pouch. He leaned close to Arella, handed Soho to her and put his mouth to her ear. "Try to keep him quiet."

"Will you require your mounts to be ready in the morning?" the man asked as he took both sets of reigns and tied the animals to the rail in front of his office.

"No. We'll be staying a couple of sun-cycles." He reached in his pocket for credits then handed the young man a one-hundred credit bill. That raised a smile and several nods.

"Thank you. Thank you, sir. I'll take good care of them. You can count on that."

"I'm sure you will." The young man looked honest and hard-working. "Do you have any accommodations for smaller animals?"

"Actually, we do, over there."

Falcon looked to the small outbuilding the young man pointed to. "Is it secure?"

"Yes. Each animal has a caged area."

"Good. I'd like to leave our little Soho with you." Falcon took the pouch from Arella. "Please show us the cages." They both followed the man into the small shack-like building. It was adequate. Soho was trouble, and this was the only solution. The boy opened a large cage on the bottom row. He pulled a squeaking Soho from the bag.

Arella kissed the little critter on top of his head. "You'll be fine here. Be good little guy. I'll be back soon."

Soho hugged her then hopped down and scampered to the back of the cage and pouted. "Let me know immediately if there's any problem."

"You can count on me, sir. Yes, sir. Of course, sir."

"Very good." All three of them returned to where the Bemothras were tied. "I'll just get our bags." He untied the backpacks from the his saddle and slung them over his shoulder. He took Arella's hand and turned to leave.

"Have a good moon-cycle, sir. Enjoy your stay."

"Thanks." They walked hand and hand toward the gate. He glanced over his shoulder and saw the rear-ends of their Bemothras as they were led away.

"That's one overzealous stable boy." Arella looked up at Falcon and smiled. "Then again, you're quite an imposing figure, especially since you're twice his size, and throwing around credits as if you're loaded."

"He'll grow into himself. As for the credits, they're necessary."

"Really?"

"Everyone respects credits. Even if they don't, they respect the man who owns them."

Arella shrugged her shoulders. "Can't argue with that."

They arrived at the front door of the upscale lodge where a uniformed man opened the tinted glass door for them to enter. Inside only a few guests lounged on the opulent gold and burgundy furnishings. They walked through the huge lobby, past tall, gold columns, overstuffed chairs and settees to the rare, highly polished, burlwood counter. Another uniformed man smiled and gave a friendly nod.

"Good moon-cycle sir, madam. Welcome to the Stargazer. How may I assist you?"

"We'd like a room with a view."

"Do you prefer the countryside or the city?"

"City." They were now playing the part of new life-mates,

deeply in love, and on the run, so he gazed at Arella as if he wanted to devour her on the spot.

"I have a lovely room with that particular view." He stroked his moustache. "It's our premier love suite on the corner with a view of the entire city. However, it's quite expensive."

Falcon gave the man his most nonchalant hand wave. "Fine."

"How long will you be staying, sir?"

"Two moon-cycles, maybe three."

"Very good, sir. That will be twelve-thousand credits for two nights."

Falcon struggled to keep his eyebrows from rising at the outrageous price. He'd paid similar rates before, but on planets known for expensive life-styles.

"Is there a problem, sir?"

"Of course not." He reached into a zippered pocket, pulled out his special credit tab. He handed it to the man who touched it to the reader then returned it to him. He glanced at Arella while they waited for screen clearance, and just for show kissed her long and passionately. He could have continued kissing her all night, but he heard the clerk clear his throat.

"Very good, Trader Marcon. Welcome to Waylent."

"Thank you." He handed two hundred credits to the man. "You'll let me know if anyone asks about me, won't you?" He leaned closer to the clerk. "It's just that we're newly life-mated," he glanced at Arella and gave her a suggestive wink, "and we need our privacy."

"Of course, sir. I understand completely."

"Good." Another young man dressed in the lodge uniform walked up to the counter, stopped and awaited further instructions.

"If you'll both step closer and press your left eye to the viewer I will set your door locks."

Falcon pressed his eye to the viewer then Arella did the same. At least they'd be reasonably secure while they slept, and they needed sleep.

"Take them to forty-fifteen." The man looked down and made electronic entries. "Rest well, Trader Marcon. Madam."

"Thanks." They walked toward the glass lift and stepped inside, the porter right behind them. "What's the best restaurant in the city?" The clear lift door slid closed from above and they began to move upward.

"That would be Vigilintees, sir." He held out his hand. "May I take your bags, sir?"

Falcon shook his head then pulled another hundred credits from his pocket and held it until the door opened onto the fourth floor. Once the lift stopped and the door slid open he and Arella followed the young man to the door of their room.

"You have to open it, sir. Simply look into the eye-scanner."

He did as requested and the door slid to the side and all three of them entered into the large parlor. It was impressive to say the least. Lush white carpet, luxurious furnishings covered with fabrics in every shade of blue known to man, yet it was done with style and extreme luxury with all the touches of gold. Arella opened the double doors on the right that led to a separate bedroom with a huge bed adorned in gold metallic and purple silk. The entire set-up looked fit for a king, and he had to admit, it was a welcome surprise.

The young man turned all the lights on then patiently waited for further instructions, or was it the tip? Credits always spoke loudly. He approached the man slowly, released Arella's hand, and then dropped the bags he'd refused to let the man carry. "I have a couple of requests."

"Gladly, sir."

Falcon handed him the large credit bill. "My new life-mate and I would like to dine in tonight. Please send up two complete seven course meals with the appropriate wines."

"What do you want to eat?"

"The best Vigilintees has to offer. I'm sure the chef will know. We'd like that dinner served as soon as it can be arranged. It's been a long sun-cycle."

"Right away, sir." He turned and quickly departed.

He chuckled at the grin he'd seen on the young man's face, who appeared barely older than a boy. His generous tip would insure excellent service, and hopefully, tight lips. This could be the night he showed Arella what it was like to surrender innocence and become a woman. Right now he did not care if he should make love to her, or leave her alone for the mission's sake. He wanted her. He wanted to be her first and her last.

If he didn't know better, he'd swear he was falling in love.

Chief Protector Falcon Rovarn could not fall in love. He should give her distance and privacy, leave her alone, as in untouched and in the same virginal state as when they met.

Who was he fooling? She was ordered to be with him, which meant he needed to concentrate on maintaining control of the situation. He really was not as bad as his reputation. Everyone knew reputations could become greatly exaggerated. There had been plenty of situations that started the rumors that he was the best and most popular lover in the galaxy, some of which he'd like to forget.

To be honest, Arella brought out the domestic side of him he never knew existed. She managed to incite thoughts he never dreamed he'd have. What was it about Nacrem's only woman Councilor that he found so irresistible? There was not one thing, it was the entire package. The way she looked at him, her walk, the little twitch in her nose when she was mad, and the huskiness in her voice when he made her blush.

By the tone of those musings he had it bad. He was beginning to realize what happened to Dacton when he was forced into his journey with Talina. They'd fallen so deeply in love it was as if they were one person. Sure they had their rocky times, but he pitied anyone who tried to come between them. Dacton and Talina shared a mutual love and friendship he hoped to have with a life-mate someday.

For now, he'd concentrate on finding Zotar and exacting final justice to the most heinous criminal in this, or any other galaxy. The universe would be a better place without Zotar, and he needed all his wits if he wanted to fulfill this mission successfully and return Arella to Nacrem.

CHAPTER THIRTY-ONE

Z otar paced the confines of his newly finished quarters inside the *Pyramid of Power*. One thing he insisted on was a bit of luxury even in the worst circumstances. Once he realized he'd be here longer than he'd planned looking for the treasure, he had to build his own private refuge. His men slept outside on the rocky floor or in the dust and dirt, exactly where they belonged. They were no better than animals, but they served their purpose. Soon he'd own palaces on every planet in the galaxy and his name would be spoken in every household with respect, as it should be for a leader of his superiority.

A knock on the door halted his steps. It had better be important. He turned, opened the wooden door and stared at his stupid helper. The man could barely dress himself. "What?"

"Excuse me, sir, but I just received word that the man and woman you wanted followed just checked into the Stargazer Inn. Our contact said he paid for two nights."

"I want to know his every move." The man gazed at the floor, afraid to look into his eyes. It was always a good sign when your men knew who was in charge. "Trydon! Do you hear me?"

"Yes, sir. Yes, sir." Trydon fixed his gaze on Zotar's face.

"Don't stare at me like that. Damn it man. Act like you have a brain! Do I have to tell you everything?" Of course he did. Even if the idiot could think for himself he'd never allow it. "Fine.

Maintain surveillance and keep me posted. We're about to have company, and I have a party to plan."

"Ya want me to get some ale, boss?"

"Not that kind of party you imbecile. Get out of my sight!" Trydon left and slammed the door behind him. How had he hired such a moron? And to think he was about the smartest of the bunch. Stupid actually served his purposes quite well. If they were too smart they'd realize his plan. Besides, they made him look like an even greater genius than he was, and that he enjoyed.

He was pleased Arella was with Falcon. She was a far more delectable morsel than her sister, and he'd always wanted to bed the wench and take her virginity. There was nothing like a virgin. No matter how many he took, they were always a treat. He married that bitch, Nodia, for political gain and to insure safe asylum. It was the most expensive safe haven he'd ever bought, but it had worked well. . .so far.

The Nacrem High Council was in his pocket, and he had them convinced The Protectorate was evil and would destroy Nacrem. It was so easy to buy people. Everyone had a price, some just demanded more credits than others. Greed was a wonderful tool, almost as effective as fear. He much preferred feeding fear since it was a never-ending source of entertainment, and it had saved him millions in credits.

At least Ducard was now safe on Millia and being looked after by far better people than his slut of a wife. Nodia could not raise a maggot so he damned sure did not want her with his son another sun-cycle. The bitch would arrive before the moon rose and he certainly had a few surprises for her, none she'd like, but all of them would be amusing for him.

Dacton had made his life miserable and almost got him killed. He still didn't know how he lost that fight on Ora and ended up in Protectorate custody, but it would certainly never happen again. Luckily his more intelligent crew from Millia managed the rescue and even left Falcon alive as he'd ordered. Now Falcon would soon knock on his door, and he was ready.

Putting Falcon through a living hell with his special drug had been pleasurable; but as he planned, Arella found him and nursed him to health. He hoped she'd enjoy watching Falcon die as much as he'd enjoy killing him. There was nothing more fulfilling than the taking of a life.

The decision now was if he should take Arella in front of Falcon, or kill him so he could take his time and relax. He was not sure yet which way would be most satisfying. Time would tell. Either way, he'd enjoy himself immensely. Rape, torture and murder were all entertaining pastimes.

For now, he had plans to make. Falcon was no fool, so he must be prepared. It would be fun to watch Falcon bravely protect Arella, and that would be his downfall. Watching the Chief Protector squirm and beg for his life will be so fulfilling. All his effort would pay off. Whatever he decided to do with Falcon would involve lots of pain and blood. Yes. Lots of blood. His true pleasure would be taking Falcon's life. So far he'd only been able to kill one brother. One down, two to go.

~ ~ ~ ~

Arella leaned her head back against the gold inlaid tiles that formed the top edge of the sumptuous sunken tub. Hot water swirled around her body and it felt so good she never wanted to get out. It was amazing how therapy baths eased soreness. Simply heaven. Once she saw the luxurious bathroom she could not help herself. She left Falcon chatting with that young hotel worker without a word.

Scented foaming bath salts filled the air with light, exotic perfume, quite a relief from moldy, mildewed, bug-infested jungles and smelly, slimy reptiles. She never thought her life in Mardin, the desert outpost where no one else wanted to be, could be considered lavish, but next to some of the places they'd just traveled, that is exactly what it was.

Her recent experiences actually made her miss the outpost she reluctantly called home, the same place she considered primitive now seemed rather advanced. Although nothing in Mardin compared to the Stargazer. She inhaled deeply and tried to identify the sweet, intoxicating fragrance softly wafting around her. It must be from a flower found only on this planet because it was not familiar.

Right now she wanted to enjoy the luxury of this place and not worry about tomorrow. This moon-cycle she'd give herself to

Falcon because she wanted to, because she had deep feelings for him. What she felt might be love, but without prior experience how could she know? Her assignment remained complicated, but this moon-cycle was for her and no one else.

The High Council would be satisfied that she'd done her duty, and for all appearances she would have. There was no way she could, or would, explain her feelings for Falcon, or why she wanted to make love to him. May the Gods forgive her, she wanted him desperately, all for herself.

A knock at the door pulled her back to reality. "Yes?"

"Are you okay?"

"I'm fine. I. . ." The door opened and Falcon stepped inside. He stood tall, handsome, all muscle and brawn with his gaze focused on her, and this time she did not mind. In fact, she wanted him to see her, and to want her the same as she wanted him. If the fire in his deep blue eyes was any indication, she had her answer.

For the first time she felt a woman's power. She, Arella DeSillian, the woman scorned by men, was now the object of one man's desire, and Falcon Rovarn was no ordinary man. She had managed to attract one of the biggest playboys in the galaxy. His reputation preceded him and she was anxious to learn how he acquired that dubious title.

Falcon cleared his throat. "In order to protect you, I must know where you are at all times."

"I'm sorry. I just saw this tub and couldn't help myself. It's not like I left the lodge." His facial expression remained intent, and every muscle in his body tensed. "You need to relax, Commander." He stepped closer to the tub and she smiled.

"That's not easy around you."

"Why not?" She loved the grin he gave her. It made him seem very sexy. Just looking at him sent tingles throughout her entire body.

"I think you know the answer to that question, Councilor." He sat on a small stool by the edge of the tub and took off his boots and socks.

"Do I?" She was glad the water was hot and steaming, causing moisture to cling to her heated face, that way he might think the bath caused her blush instead of him. His boots hit the floor with loud thuds. He stood and walked to some kind of panel on the wall and before she could ask what he was doing, the lights dimmed, while soft music filled the room and mingled with the sounds of bubbling water.

He returned to the tub, knelt down, leaned over and placed a kiss on her lips. His mouth worked magic and she wanted to melt into the marbelus tile. His tongue searched and teased, yet he taught her how to give in return. She wanted to please him. Every woman's first time should be memorable, and Falcon was the man to fulfill her dreams.

His hands found her shoulders, then roamed down her arms and back up again. His touch was pure magic. She felt like a princess, and he was the man sent to honor her. A moan came from deep within her and she barely recognized her own voice. She reached up, slid her arms around his neck and pulled him to her. He was not the only one who could make advances. This time a moan came from him, rumbling long and low within his chest.

Her fingers threaded themselves through his dark, shaggy hair that gently curled on top of his shoulders. On some men his hair would look long and out of place, yet on him it was perfect, handsome, and oh so male. Everything about Falcon reeked feral masculinity.

She moved her hands to the top of his shirt and unfastened it down the front. When she freed the last closer, her fingers inched their way up his chest, threading through the sprinkling of hair in the center. He was not overly hairy like some men. He had just the right amount of chest hair to tickle the senses and entice the eye. She explored every well-honed muscled plane she'd admired from afar.

When his hands found her breasts she inhaled sharply. Butterflies danced in her stomach and her entire body tingled. He toyed with her left nipple using one finger to softly circle the tip until she wanted to scream. He was like a master artist with a blank canvas and knew exactly what he was doing.

She eased the shirt back over his shoulders and down his arms. He moved his hands from her breasts so he could shrug off the garment. He broke the kiss, leaned back and tried to shrug off his shirt, but had a hard time since the long sleeves were soaked from the elbow down. It only took him a moment longer to get it off and toss it aside.

He simply stared deeply into her eyes as if he were looking at her very soul. His usual hard-line manner had been replaced with a softness he'd never shown before. Would she learn Falcon Rovarn's secrets? One step at a time. This moon-cycle she would steal his heart.

"Are you sure you know what you're doing?"

His deep, mellow voice had a tinge of apprehension, like a humble request for affirmation. "I think so."

He reached out and cupped her jaw with his hand. "*DeJorelle Kari*, you must be sure. I told you before, I'll not do anything you don't want me to do." He tucked several strands of hair behind her ear. "You need only to ask for what you want."

"I want you to make love to me, Falcon Rovarn. I want you to show me what it's like to be a woman. You know I've never been with a man before. I couldn't fool you if I tried, you've been with too many women to think me experienced. But at the same time, I don't want to disappoint you." She lowered her head and stared at the swirling water. Right now she wanted to slide under the surface and never be seen again. She'd never been more embarrassed in her life.

"My sweet Arella." He reached out and tilted her chin up with his finger. "Look at me."

It took a moment before she dared meet his gaze. The moment of truth had arrived and she prayed she was ready.

"That's better. First, you have absolutely nothing to be ashamed of, or embarrassed about. You're perfect exactly as you are. And you need not apologize for being a virgin."

"Do you prefer virgins?"

"It's you I prefer, not what state you're in. Besides, after tonight, you'll no longer be a virgin. Do you think that will make me not want you again?" Falcon shook his head. "My sweet, sweet Arella. You know me not."

She smiled. "I have the distinct impression I'm about to know you much better than I ever have." She laughed. "Am I right?"

"You've never been more right." He rose from his knees to stand in front of her.

He had a devilish grin on his face, one that told her she'd read him perfectly. Slowly he reached down with both hands, freed his belt buckle, then pulled it off along with all the weapons attached to it and laid it on the floor. His hand hovered over the fastener that secured his pants. She held her breath in anticipation. His movements were slow and precise while he undid the fasteners along the front of his pants until the fabric hung open.

He pushed down, slightly exposing his belly button. She let out the breath she'd been holding then gulped in another and held it as if it would calm her nerves. Oh, he was good, and very deliberate with every tempting movement he made. He knew how to entice. Without further hesitation he pushed off his pants and underwear in one swift movement and stood before her as naked as a babe.

What a sight. She'd imagined this moment many times, but the reality defied words. Perfection could only describe his body. Every bulge, ripple and smooth spot were toned to combat readiness. She'd worked out with many warriors, but none ever attained Falcon's extraordinary level of physical fitness.

Her gaze wandered below his abdomen to his ready state of maleness. Her experience may be limited, but she knew he was better endowed than any average man dared brag about. She let out the breath she'd been holding and swallowed hard. He stepped into the large oval tub and settled down into the water facing her.

She stared at him knowing good and well her lack of experience was blatantly showing, and he knew it. The satisfied grin on his face said he liked her looking at him. She had no words at the moment, only extraordinary feelings and sensations. If she wanted to stay chaste she would ignore everything in her mind right now, but this was the time to be bad—really bad. Customs and traditions be damned, she was about to have her love match.

His foot found hers under the water. When she originally sat in the tub, alone, it felt like a swimming pool, now the space seemed far too small and intimate. His foot rubbed her ankle, then eased up her leg. His exploration crept higher, inch by inch, past her knee, up her inner thigh, finally coming to rest at her most private apex. His toes tickled the feminine hair between her legs. Somehow he started a movement with the pad of his foot that felt absolutely delicious and sinful. He managed a little circular movement, and all she could do was breathe deeply and enjoy each new sensation.

After a few minutes she decided this was too one-sided, so she slid down a bit, found his leg with her foot and worked her way up his lower leg, over his knee, up his thigh and stopped when she reached something soft between his legs. She ventured a bit higher and found something hard, and when she did, he moaned.

He sat up, leaned toward her and pulled her onto his lap. She straddled him, and when she opened her mouth to gasp for air, he pressed his lips to hers and started a kiss she'd never forget. The core of her womanhood throbbed with a need only Falcon could satisfy. His tongue traced the outline of her lips, then darted into her mouth to explore and tease.

She closed her eyes and concentrated on the feel of his strong arms around her waist. He pulled her closer so her breasts pressed against his chest and his manhood teased and begged for entry. He kissed her as if he were trying to consume her, and she loved every moment of it.

Her hands moved up his arms to his shoulders, then down his back, every muscled inch of him rock hard to her touch. The more she explored, the harder he grew. His arousal moved and throbbed against her exposed womanhood. She wanted him inside her with a desperation so new and overwhelming she could not think past this moment with this man.

Bravely she pulled her right arm from his back and moved it to his manhood. She could no longer resist feeling him, and he was amazing, every luscious inch, and there were many. It was a silly thought, but she wondered how all of him would fit in her, but she knew he would.She released her hold, raised up higher on her knees and lifted herself over the top of him. Just when she was ready to settle down over him his hands found her waist and he broke the kiss abruptly.

"Are you sure, my sweet?" He looked into the depths of her eyes. "This is a gift you can only give one man, once. I want you to be sure."

"I couldn't be more sure. I want you in me. Now." She tried to press down on him, but he held her firm."

"It may hurt a bit at first, my love. But trust me, it will pass." He kissed her softly. "Are you ready?"

All she could manage was a nod, but he needed no further confirmation. He guided her down gently at first, then in one long, rapid thrust it was over. He was completely inside her, and she did not know whether to cry out in pain or ecstasy. He remained still and she wondered what he was waiting for. He kissed her and started to move. She glimpsed heaven.

She joined him in the mating dance, committing every thrust, every movement to memory. Tonight would live forever in her mind. There may not be a next time. This moment, this man, this experience had to last a lifetime. It felt so right to be in his arms, to have him inside her. To be truly loved and wanted was an all-consuming emotion, so new, so precious, and ever so fragile.

Water sloshed with their movements, so he rolled her over so he was now on top. He put one hand behind her head and held on to the edge of the tub with the other. With every stroke something deep within her began to build. Faint moans escaped her lips, deep groans rattled his chest, and she knew something in him was nearing a fevered pitch.

Every precise movement he made was aimed to please and pleasure. She knew he was taking care to make her first experience extraordinary. The bubbling water obstructed her full view of him, but what was above the surface was the best visual treat a woman could ever want. His rippled abdomen reminded her of the form-fitting armor her men wore.

He orchestrated his movements like a professional dancer on stage, yet he loved with tenderness. He had a soft side he'd never admit to and she loved that part of him. Love? Is that what she felt? It was possible, but she had nothing to compare this new emotion with.

He ended the kiss and stopped his delicious movements to look at her. With his hand he stroked her cheek, then trailed his fingers down her neck and chest to rest over her breast. She inhaled sharply, not sure what he was doing.

"*DeJorelle Kari.*" His hand moved to her waist. "Not here. I want you to enjoy this."

"But I. . ." His fingers silenced her words. She noted a twinkle in his eye and a sexy smile on his lips.

"You'll see." Falcon rose, stepped out of the tub, grabbed a towel and tucked it around his waist. He grabbed another large towel and held it out for her.

She rose to her knees then stood and stepped out of the tub. When she leaned into the soft, blue fluffy warmth he closed his arms around her then picked her up in his arms and carried her into the bed chamber. Ever so gently he laid her in the center of the bed. She was glad to have the towel over her because his hungry gaze devoured her like an animal devoured his prey.

He reached down and in one smooth motion pulled the towel from her body and tossed it on the floor behind him. Natural instinct told her to cover herself, yet she knew it was time to be brave and allow him to see all of her. If he were going to run as all the others had, it might as well be now.

"My sweet warrior princess, you're so beautiful."

He lowered himself down on the bed beside her. He wasted no time in exploring her flesh. His hands roamed her body from head to foot and back up again. When he caressed her skin she felt calluses on his hands, but it only added to the erotic sensations coursing through her.

She gasped when his lips and tongue found her breasts. He traced circles around her nipple ever so lightly then moved to the center of his attention. Oh, the sensations he created. She wanted to cry out, to tell him how she liked what he was doing, and beg him never to stop. If there was such a place as heaven, it had to be right here with this man. He moved to her other breast then lavished every bare inch of her, leaving no area un-kissed.

Then she caught her breath when he kissed his way in a slow descent lower, down her stomach, then lower yet, closer to her very core. She heard some men did this type of thing, but she never could picture it, especially not Falcon, but here he was, exploring her with his tongue. He left no place untouched. When he found the most sensitive spot on her body he concentrated all his efforts on that one spot until she moaned out loud.

That building sensation she'd experienced in the tub returned with a vengeance, and if he did not stop she'd come apart, she was sure of it. Then she felt a tightening and throbbing from deep inside push to the surface in one exquisite explosion that made her quiver and pulse. She let out the breath she'd been holding and sighed with a satisfaction she never dreamed possible.

Falcon kissed his way back up her abdomen, slowly, erotically, leaving his mark on every inch of her skin. When he reached her mouth he took possession with a passion so great it scared her. He groaned deep and long, then pressed his manhood against her, as if asking for permission to enter. She ended the kiss and looked into his eyes. "Make love to me, Falcon. Please, love me."

"It will be my pleasure, sweet lady."

With one hard, fast stroke he entered, but there was no pain this time, only sweet sensations of him filling her so completely and totally. They were one. At this moment, nothing existed except them. He began a slow rhythm with his hips, while his strong arm muscles flexed and fine beads of sweat broke out on his brow. She closed her eyes and savored this passionate man who found her desirable.

Her hands roamed his arms, his shoulders and back. He felt so good, too good. How could she ever let him go? For the moment she pushed that thought from her mind. Tonight was for selfish pleasure. Tomorrow was soon enough for reality.

Gradually his pace quickened until his thrusts became frenzied. Then she felt it again, and knew she was about to experience a second completion with this man. He shuddered beneath her touch, a low feral growl sounded from deep within his chest. She joined him in ultimate release.

His movements slowed, then stopped. He lowered his head and kissed her, hard at first, then tenderly. After one last kiss he rolled off her and collapsed on the bed next to her. He deserved a rest after the performance he just gave. All she heard was ragged breathing which made her feel awkward since she did not know what to do.

This was the moment the High Council told her secrets were shared. As much as she hated to think about it, she did. She gave herself to him out of need and pure desire, but that nasty responsibility still lay between them. Since she had him where she wanted him, she might as well take advantage of the situation, no matter how cold and calculating it seemed.

She rolled toward him, put her head on his shoulder and her arm over his chest. He slid his arm behind her neck and shoulder and pulled her close. She let out a long, satisfied sigh. If only this perfect tranquil moment in time could last.

His breathing slowly returned to normal and he seemed more relaxed than she'd ever seen him. They'd shared passion, and so much more. Every delicious sensation that had coursed through her body faded to peace and tranquility. So this was afterglow, that mysterious state of being she'd heard about. She had to admit it was a pretty fabulous state to be in.

With his free hand he cupped her cheek and turned her face toward him, then lifted his head and gently kissed her lips. Tears burned her lids. This man was her dream and she'd love nothing better than to spend the rest of her life in his arms. Reality would tear them apart, so this moment could well be all they had.

"Falcon, I. . ."

"My sweet lady warrior." He slid his arm out from under her and propped himself up using one elbow. He looked into her eyes. "I pray you have no regrets. I. . ."

She silenced him with one fingertip. "You were wonderful. I have no regrets." Relief flooded his masculine features. "Thank you, Falcon."

"For what?"

"For being you." He'd never understand if she told him what was in her heart and mind. She barely understood the relentless mixed feelings herself. "I do have one request though."

"And that would be?"

"Feed me, please." He laughed long and hard then slid out of bed. She loved the sight of him walking away, bare as the day he was born. He had a backside she could not resist. No man had a right to look that good wearing nothing.

CHAPTER THIRTY-TWO

Falcon laid his fork down and pushed back from the small table for two. Breakfast never looked this beautiful before, but he'd never had Arella seated across from him with morning light dancing on her golden hair. One dainty hand held a fork, the other a muffin. "You certainly have an appetite this morning."

"I never thought I'd eat again after that fantastic dinner last night. But we used a lot of energy when we. . .auhh. . ."

"Made love all night?" Her cheeks turned a bright shade of red while she sheepishly nodded. "You're definitely a fast learner, but I wanted to give you enough practice so you wouldn't forget any of the lessons."

She smiled. "I shall never forget your lessons, Commander."

"If you do, I don't mind teaching you again." She lowered her head to avoid his gaze. She could be shy at times, and he was not certain she was as comfortable about the night they shared as she pretended. They'd loved with a true and honest passion. He'd know if she pretended. Hell, he'd seen it enough times. He may be known as a ladies' man, but he'd also been bedded for information and privileges, and he'd done the same.

Those women had been good, and he'd been young and inexperienced, however he silently thanked them all for teaching him the sensual arts. The other lesson they taught was betrayal and they'd all taken lying to new levels.

Arella's job may be to betray him, but it was simply not part of her nature. He doubted she had a mean bone in her body. Warrior indeed. Oh, for a woman she was tough, she'd proven herself worthy, and she had a well-toned, athletic body, but she was not capable of the underhanded duplicity her High Council demanded.

"So tell me, Commander, what do you have planned for today?"

"Securing supplies for our trek to the *Pyramid of Power*."

"What do we need?"

"All the basics, and more."

"More? You have my attention."

He smiled at her mischievous grin and sexy manner. He may have created a monster, but one he'd enjoy. She had no idea how many feminine powers she possessed, which was good for him because if she decided to wield those powers he was not sure he could resist her. "You'll have to wait to see the more, but if you're really good, I'll get a surprise for you."

"So you think I'm a little girl that needs a reward for being good?"

He stood, walked around the table and kissed her on the lips, long and hard. "Absolutely, but I need you to wait here while I take care of business and take the temperature of the place before I let them see you."

"I don't embarrass you, do I?"

He cupped her chin with his hand. "Quite the contrary, my sweet. I'm trying to keep you safe, and that seems to be my greatest challenge." He leaned closer and gave her a kiss. "And I want to be sure I am the only one to touch you."

"I hope that's true." She stood and placed her hands on his chest. "Go, do your snooping. I'll just take a nap. I'm a bit tired this morning." She blinked several times.

"Don't give me that look. I have to go, but I'll be back soon enough." He kissed her cheek, turned and left the room, making sure the door locked securely behind him. This time he prayed he could trust her, but if she snuck out he would not be surprised, just disappointed.

Arella frustrated him more than any woman ever had. He'd never allowed a woman to get this close and it seemed strange. One huge issue stood between them—trust. In reality he knew very little about her, only the standard background info, but his heart felt a connection that defied explanation. Once their confrontation with Zotar was over, they might have time to pursue a future.

He took the lift down to the main floor, walked across the richly appointed lobby and out onto the pedestrian walk in front. Bright sunlight caused him to squint when he looked up then down the street to get his bearings. It was an odd place with fancy buildings next to primitive ones, fine clothing stores next to pubs. He walked north until a gown in the window of a ladies fashion store caught his eye.

Without a doubt Arella needed that, and he found himself pushing open the glass door and entering the establishment. A curvy dark-haired woman smiled at him as she approached.

"Well, hello there. What can I find for you today?"

She patted her bushy, long, dyed locks and gave him the "come on" look he was all too familiar with. The woman held appeal, but he only wanted the lavender-eyed vixen back at the hotel. "I'd like that gown in the window."

"The high-necked one, or the low-cut one?"

"I'll give you one guess." That brought a smile to her overly-painted red lips.

"It's quite expensive."

He smiled. "Wrap it up."

"What size and color?"

"The black one in the window will be the right size."

"I can see you're one determined man."

The clerk walked to the window, opened the partition, stepped up on the platform and removed the gown from the mannequin. While she procured the garment he glanced around the place and found another gift. He picked up a thin, red sleeping garment and examined it thoroughly. There was not much to it, and it would not keep her warm, but it would be a treat for him. He took it to the counter where the woman was busy boxing the gown. "Wrap this as well."

"My, my, my. She must be some woman. That's the most expensive negligee in the store. Most men don't like to spend much on something they're planning to take off." She giggled.

"I'm not most men."

"I knew that the moment I saw you. Mind if I ask where you're from?"

"Does it make a difference?"

She chuckled. "Suppose not." She looked him up and down. "And I don't suppose you're gonna tell me what your business here is."

"You're one smart lady."

"Thanks." She concentrated on the tab. "That will be three-thousand, four-hundred credits, please."

He pulled his credit tab from his pocket, touched it to the scanner then pulled a hundred credits from his pocket and handed the bill to her. "For your help." Her eyebrows raised high causing her round-shaped eyes to look huge.

"Thank you so much, sir." She slipped the bill into her pocket then set the two packages on the top of the high counter.

"Please have them delivered to the desk attendant at the Stargazer and tell them Trader Marcon will pick them up."

"As you wish."

"Thank you." He turned and left the shop before the woman asked another question. The weather was pleasant enough to enjoy the walk, but he picked up the pace, anxious to return so he could see a certain someone in a red sleeping garment.

He stepped inside Galaxy Outfitters and found it contained everything he needed for the upcoming journey. The place was busy with several male shoppers looking at heavy jackets, tents, tools, clothing, packs, weapons, food packs, climbing equipment, everything he'd need. This place was better than a resort, full of high quality, high-tec supplies.

It did not take long to collect the items he came for, but it was hard to concentrate when his mind wandered to Arella in her new garments. Better yet, how she'd look without them. His shopping suddenly took on a desperate urgency.

~ ~ ~ ~

Arella paced the width of their room. It felt strange to miss someone, but she'd grown used to having Falcon close to her and she was impatient for his return. He'd made her feel secure, wanted, and loved. It may be dangerous to allow such emotions, but how could she feel any different? She enjoyed his company, and his touch, neither of which she'd ever get enough of.

Since she had no idea how long he'd be gone she didn't dare go out like last time. She glanced around the room and decided to watch galaxy news on the vid-screen. It was past time she found out what was going on back home. She announced her choice and the Nacrem channel appeared.

There was the usual political report, the weather, reports on the upcoming Founders Holiday, and how the High Council would be in recess for their annual vacation. Just her luck to be working with no choice in the matter.

Then she heard the news commentator say, "There have been no new developments in the kidnapping of Nodia and Ducard Connin, life-mate and son of Modark Connin, Nacrem's biggest financial magnate and advisor to the High Council. Master Connin has offered a ten-million credit reward for information leading to their return. Mr. Connin is off-planet, desperately searching for his family and is unavailable for comment. We will keep you updated on this story. In other news. . ."

"Off!" She sank to her knees in the middle of the room and tears flooded her eyes then flowed down her cheeks. How in the universe could this have happened, and why? Credits? Politics? Damnation! Here she was on another planet stuck on assignment unable to search for them, yet she had to do something.

It was a kidnapping, which meant Nodia was still alive. She wiped her tears with the sleeve of her robe, but it was useless when she sobbed uncontrollably. Her sister and nephew were in danger. Nothing was going as planned. She was a failure as a spy and could do nothing for her only family. How much worse could it get?

She heard the door swoosh open and looked up to see Falcon step inside carrying two gold wrapped packages. He immediately dropped them on the floor and ran to her side. He knelt on the floor beside her and pulled her into his arms.

"What's wrong? Are you hurt?"

She sucked in a deep breath in an effort to control her tears. "Just hold me, Falcon. Hold me tight." Several long moments passed and he simply held her against his chest. She allowed his comfort to sink into her, and hoped his courage would also penetrate into her. Finally, he eased her back and looked at her with genuine concern.

"If anyone has harmed you, I'll kill them."

"That's reassuring, but no one harmed me. It's my sister, Nodia and her son, they've been kidnapped!"

"Who told you this?"

"Galaxy News." She wiped a stray tear from her cheek. "I have to find her. I have to leave. Now." She stood and he rose with her. When she tried to run to the door he held her firmly in place.

"Arella, we need to discuss this rationally."

"I'm rational. I'm their family and they need me!"

"You're a Councilor, on a mission, and you can't return alone, and I can't go with you. We must finish this assignment. We have no choice."

"Are you telling me that killing my brother-in-law is more important than finding my sister?" She stared deeply into the depths of his eyes. "They're all I have, I can't lose them."

"You won't. We'll find her when we find Zotar. Trust me, he's responsible."

"How in the universe could you possibly know that?"

"I know Zotar. She's part of his plan somehow."

She wiggled free of his hold and went back to pacing the width of the room. What Falcon said made some sense, even if it was difficult to comprehend. Would Falcon lie to her? How far would he go for the mission? "I'm supposed to believe you on blind faith?"

"I thought I'd earned your trust, but it seems I was mistaken."

There was genuine disappointment in his voice. He turned and walked to the in-wall refreshment center and poured a drink. "I'm sorry, Falcon. I'm upset and I. . .well, I. . .uhh.. . ."

"Trying to say you were wrong, and you're sorry for the insult?"

He turned and the full force of his warrior's gaze bore down on her. She stepped toward him, and he took a defensive stance. How could she blame him? She reached out and took his free hand in hers. "I'm sorry, Falcon. I do trust you, you know that. I'm just so worried about Nodia, the same as you'd be about Dacton if he were missing."

He set his drink down on the bar then placed his hands on her shoulders. "I've been in your shoes, and I've faced worse."

"What do you mean worse?"

"Zotar murdered my brother, Baleko, in cold blood. He made a vid of it and sent it to my family so we could watch him die a horrific death after numerous sun-cycles of torture."

Her hand moved to cover her mouth. She was speechless. His eyes misted and she felt his pain. "I'm so sorry. I had no idea." She slid her arms around his waist and rested her head against his chest, the steady beat of his heart a firm reminder that this tough, capable warrior was still a vulnerable man.

"We'll find her. I'm sure it's all connected. Zotar controls all the people in his life and he. . . She's his life-mate, maybe he missed her?"

"I don't believe I heard you correctly. That would mean he had a heart, and according to you, he does not possess such an organ."

He chuckled. "You're learning. Let me rephrase. Zotar has need of Nodia, so he had her brought to him and he didn't want anyone to know where she went, because he's trying to keep his whereabouts a secret."

"You don't mean he needs her as a life-mate, do you?"

"I wish I could say yes, but I won't lie to you. Nodia has something to do with the pyramid and what he's doing there."

"I hope you're right, because that means she's close. But what about Ducard?"

"I doubt Zotar brought him here, but I'm sure he's safe."

"You said that? We're back to the no heart issue again."

"Ducard comes under vanity. I have it on good authority that Zotar values his son. It may not be love, but he'll not physically hurt him. The Protectorate will return Ducard to you when this is all over. I'll see to it."

"You'd better be right, and I'll hold you to your words.

"We'll both get what we want." He kissed her lightly on the cheek. "Are you feeling better now?"

"A little. Why?"

"I have a present for you." Falcon walked back to the entry area and picked up both boxes. He walked back to Arella and handed them to her. "I don't usually shop for a woman, so I hope you like these."

She took the boxes from him, walked to the velvet-covered bench and sat. The gifts brought tears to her eyes. She studied the elaborate boxes. "I've never received a gift from a man before." She glanced up and caught him staring at her.

"If you cry I'll take them back." He moved closer to her. "Are all Nacrem men blind and stupid?"

"Believe it." She ran her hands over the fine gold paper and lightly touched the shiny metallic gold bow. "It's beautiful."

Falcon shook his head. "You haven't even seen it yet."

"The package is beautiful."

He sat on the bench next to Arella. "Don't people give gifts on your planet?"

"Of course, it's just, well, there isn't anyone to give me presents, except Nodia. Before she met Modark, I mean Zotar, she had limited credits, and after they life-mated, we didn't see each other much." Arella bent her head down and fought back tears. Family was not her best subject.

Falcon stood. "Are you going to open those or look at them all day?"

"I think you're more anxious than I am." She smiled at his childlike demeanor. "Thank you."

"You haven't even opened it yet."

"Thank you for making me smile. That means more than the gift."

"If I'd have known that I could have saved a lot of credits."

She picked up the largest box. It didn't take long to destroy the beautiful wrapping, and when she pulled off the top and peeled back the thin paper she gasped, and her hand moved to cover her gaping mouth. She pulled the silky black gown out of the box then stood and held it against her. "It's beautiful." She turned her gaze to Falcon and laughed at his pleased, arrogant expression. "You did good, warrior." She smiled. "It may be a bit more revealing that I'm used to, but. . .."

"You'll look stunning. Now open the other one."

She picked up the smaller box, removed the wrappings, and pulled something red from the box. Her eyes widened when she held up the short, translucent fabric. It took a moment before she realized it was a negligee. Heat rushed to her cheeks. When she met Falcon's gaze she recognized that look of sexual longing, the same look she'd seen numerous times last moon-cycle.

He cleared his throat. "Well?"

KATHLEEN GARNSEY

"It's. . .it's very. . .uhh. . .lovely." Disappointment took over his masculine features. "What I meant to say was that I can't wait to wear this for you."

He pulled her into his arms and gave her a short, tender kiss on the lips. "I was hoping you'd say that. You'll look great in red."

She could not help the small laugh that escaped without warning. "There really isn't much red, now is there?"

"And there won't be any when I take it off you. But what fun we'll have in the process." He bent his head and kissed her.

How she loved his lips on hers, especially when he deepened the kiss and pulled her tighter like he was doing now. If he could hold her like this forever life would be perfect. Ever so slowly he eased his hold and ended the kiss so sensually that when he pulled away she still sat with her lips pursed. She took a deep breath to ground herself back in reality.

"*DeJorelle Kari*, you taste so good."

"Are you ever going to tell me what that means?"

"My sweet warrior."

She smiled. "I like it."

"Then I shall call you that all the time." He smiled. "In private. It wouldn't seem right to call a warrior sweet while she was working."

"I'm glad we got that straight." He grinned from ear to ear and he'd never looked more irresistible. "When will I wear that fantastic gown? Camping doesn't require formal wear."

"I've made a dinner reservation at an elite club. You deserve a night out."

"We can't, we need to find Nodia."

"Not until our equipment is ready, and that's not until tomorrow. Do you really think Zotar will harm your sister?"

Would he? At this point she did not know what to believe. They had to be prepared. Rushing into anything was usually a bad idea. "You're right, Commander Rovarn. One moon-cycle won't change anything." She gazed into his unbelieving eyes. "What's the matter, warrior? Didn't think I could change my mind?"

"How about changing into that little red number?"

"You're not very subtle, Commander." She moved close to him and put her arms around his neck and gave him a short kiss on his lips. "I assume you have an ulterior motive for going out?"

Falcon rubbed his chin with his hand. "You're quick." He smiled. "You might make a spy yet."

"I'm sure you can teach me what I don't know." His amused look turned dark and way too sensual for this time of sun-cycle. She immediately knew what he was thinking and rather liked the idea. "Maybe you should give me a lesson right now."

Before she had time to take another breath his mouth consumed hers. He picked her up in his arms and held her tightly against his hard, muscled body, exactly where she wanted to stay.

CHAPTER THIRTY-THREE

Zotar threw the silver chalice against the wall, it fell and bounced several times on the floor. The loud clanging of the chalice on the stone floor was a sound he liked to hear, especially when it echoed throughout the chamber. He turned and faced his men who waited for him. Their posture was very stiff and they anxiously fidgeted like the idiots they were. "I told you to bring the bitch to me! Now go get her, you fools!"

Such incompetence was impossible to deal with, especially since their usefulness was nearly at an end. It would not be long before he located the hidden wealth in this miserable pyramid. Then the universe would be his. No one could stop him!

Once he had his hands on all that treasure he could begin all the projects he had planned. First he'd take over that small planet next to Millia, buy an army and train them to destroy everything in their path and ask no questions. Then, after taking a few more planets, he'd finally be ready to turn his forces loose on The Protectorate and end their lofty reign.

Words could never express how sick he was of The Protectorate! Especially since the damned Rovarns had taken over the top positions. Granted, the High Council gave the ultimate orders, but they'd given far too much power to Falcon and Dacton. No two men deserved to die more than those arrogant brothers. He only killed Baleko to piss them off, and he accomplished his goal.

It was really Dacton he wanted, and once he cut Falcon's throat Dacton would be sure to follow. It was time to draw blood and send another Rovarn to his maker.

Falcon would soon knock on his door. He hated the wait, but patience would bring him exactly what he wanted. Of course the bastard would survive his traps, how else would he have the satisfaction of killing him with his own hands?

Falcon would arrive with Arella, his beautiful sister-in-law. He hated to kill Arella. She was more comely than Nodia, smarter too. The only problem with her was she hated men and did not want anything to do with them. He'd fix that, whether she was willing or not. How fun it would be to teach her about all the pleasures of the flesh. Too bad she was too much trouble to keep alive for long, but her brief stay would be memorable.

Avenging his sister's death would feel so good. Dacton's interference had ruined everything all those years ago. Just because the arrogant Rovarn found him cheating on the Protectorate's final exam and turned him in to the officials. The Chancellor had been unforgiving! In fact he chastised him and threw him out of the academy, refusing him his rightful Protectorate Accrediation!

If Dacton had left well enough alone his sister would be alive today instead of crashing into that mountain. It was Dacton's fault he missed Jana's pick-up as planned. Instead, Jana left and flew in an overly emotional state and her craft crashed into the side of the mountain. All because of Dacton! Falcon may pay first, but Dacton would still pay the ultimate price. One brother at a time.

A knock on the door made him turn. Finally. "Enter!" Four of his men opened the door and rushed inside with Nodia between them. They pushed her forward.

"As you requested, sir."

"Leave us." He waited for the door to close behind his men. "So my wayward life-mate, what do you have to say for yourself?" He loved it when she cowered in front of him, shaking in fear.

Her head remained bent and that infuriated him. "Look at me, bitch!" Still she refused, so he reached out and slapped her without mercy across the left side of her face. "Well?" Finally she turned her scared doe eyes on him. He took a satisfied breath when tears rolled down her cheeks. She was pathetic, worse than a scared animal.

"I don't know what you want me to say."

"You've never had anything to say."

Nodia wiped tears from her face with her sleeve. "That's because you've never allowed me to speak."

He grabbed her shoulders, pulled her to him and gave her a hard, quick kiss on the lips. "That's because you're only good for one thing, and you're not even very good at that."

Nodia lowered her head and stared at the ground. "No woman could please you."

He took a step back then jammed his fist into her right cheek as hard as he could. She staggered back but refused to fall. He'd give her credit for being tougher than in the past. At least now both her cheeks would look black and blue, his favorite color next to blood red. "You're no match for me, Nodia."

"Little did I know what a bad match we were."

Zotar laughed. "It's about time you grew a bit of a backbone, but be warned not to go too far. I won't think twice about killing you."

"I believe you." She raised her head. "What have you done with our son?"

"He's been taken to a safe location. I'll not hurt him. I have plans for the boy."

"Why did you take him from me? What have I done wrong?"

"You're weak. You can't teach him to be a man, a leader, a warrior. Only I can do that."

"Will I ever see him again? Please, tell me, I. . ."

"Stop begging!" She sank to her knees in a blubbering heap. "You're pitiful!"

"Why did you life-mate me?" she managed between sobs.

He laughed long and hard, crossed his arms over his chest and stared down at her. "I needed a safe haven and I had a high society contact on Nacrem who put me in touch with your father. I needed to look like a solid citizen so I bought you from him, Nodia. Your own father sold you for credits."

She gasped at his statement and he was satisfied he'd made his point. "You know that terrible accident your parents had?" He laughed. "It was no accident. You see, I agreed to pay him only after we were officially life-mated, and he did not deserve the credits, nor were you worth what he wanted. So, killing them

solved all that, and silenced the only two people who knew about
the arrangement. Two love birds with one explosion."

"What about Ducard?"

"He was an unfortunate accident. However, I decided that
having a son could have its advantages."

"You'll turn him into a monster just like you!"

He raised his foot and spin kicked her in the thigh with his
heavy boot, satisfied when she fell hard and fast to the floor. "Of
course, he's my heir! Now get up, bitch, and get out of my sight
before Ducard has no mother." He crossed his arms over his chest
and watched her drag herself to her feet then limp to the door.
"Obey my men. They have orders to kill you if you don't." She
stood speechless. "One more thing." He held out his hand. "I'll
have that crystal pendant I gave you."

"I don't have it."

"I told you never to take it off! Ever!" Zotar rushed to her,
grabbed her shoulders and shook her so hard her head snapped
back and hit the thick, wooden door behind her. "Where is it,
bitch!"

She groaned. "Wouldn't you like to know."

"I'll kill you right here!"

"Then you'll never know what I did with it. Go ahead. Kill me.
You've taken everything that matters, you might as well take my
life too."

He opened the door and shoved her out. "Not yet. Especially
since you asked me to. I'd hate to make you happy. Now, get out
of my sight!"

Nodia turned and looked back at him. For a once pretty woman
she looked terrible. Her filthy hair framed a gaunt, bluish
complexion, but bruises had that effect. Her clothes were torn, she
wore no make-up, or jewelry, or anything else to make herself
feminine. "You've been warned. If you behave, I may not have to
kill you. At least she wisely kept her mouth shut and went with his
men back to her cage. She'd never been very bright. Part of him
did not want to kill her, yet she'd give him no choice in the end.

Right now he'd concentrate on Falcon's arrival. There was
nothing better than a good fight, and Falcon would provide that,
and more. He hated to admit Falcon was capable, but he had one
flaw that would be his downfall.

A caring man was a dead man. That's where Nodia would play her part. Oh, this would be sweet. Tasting Falcon's blood would be an incredible experience, one he'd waited for all too long.

Soon. Very soon it would all be his.

~ ~ ~ ~

Falcon smoothed a few stray hairs from Arella's forehead. It was hard to believe they'd made love most of the afternoon. Had lust consumed his better judgment? Lust certainly played a part, but he'd listened to his heart which was worse. He knew well that sleeping with the enemy was dangerous and complicated.

Now he had to feed her false information. Before they left Waylent her contact was bound to demand further information, so this was for her own safety. After finding her bruised and unconscious in that Usted alley he knew they'd stoop to torture to force her to do her job.

She was merely a pawn in her government's plan. Most governments proved to be ruthless employers by owning you, your family, and everything in your life. The Protectorate and the participating planets in their galaxy system were exceptions. The Protectorate upheld individual freedoms, and respected those in their employment. They actually stood behind families in crisis, and fought for equal treatment for all people under their protection.

Each planet had their own government, The Protectorate was the overseer that insured the basic principles of freedom and democracy were upheld. They keep out evil tyrants like Zotar, who took over, raped and pillaged then left ruins in his wake.

He hated lies, but the mission must succeed. "*DeJorelle Kari*, the things I want to show you, places I want to take you. But first we must finish this assignment, and to do that, I have several errands to attend to."

She stroked the side of his face with the palm of her hand. "And what might those errands be?"

This was his perfect opportunity. He'd lied many times to many agents and spies, but it never felt wrong before. Caring too much about anyone was a weakness his enemy would use against him. Zotar's evil, demented mind thrived on physical and mental torture. The man was a master at punishment, and emotions were one of his prime weapons, especially when his victim was already bleeding.

"What's wrong Falcon?"

"Why do you ask?"

"You seemed so happy and relaxed, now you're worried, and that worries me as well."

"Sorry, my sweet, but I must tell you what I learned earlier." This lie had to be good. "You know the map Sadar gave me?" He watched her nod. "Several pyramids were built in this section of the planet, and the one Sadar directed us to is the wrong one. Waylent is the jumping off point for all the pyramids, but the map directs us due south when we actually need to go west."

"Why would Sadar do that?"

"Why indeed." From the questioning expression on her face he knew she believed the deception. "Because of this, I must delay our departure until I can confirm which pyramid we need to go to. It is not as simple as Sadar claimed it was. It may not even be the *Pyramid of Power,* but I plan to find out for sure."

"How long do you think it will take? My sister is out there somewhere, fighting for her life. We have to leave as soon as possible."

"I'll work as fast as I can, but my concern is safety. We can't help your sister if we're dead, and we can't find her if we're going in the wrong direction."

Arella's gaze dropped and her hand stroked the blanket. "You're right, of course, it's just that, I. . ."

He kissed her long and hard, then pulled back and gazed into clear, lavender eyes that focused on him with trust and admiration.

"Falcon, there's something I need to tell you."

"Go on." Arella was worried about her sister, but he suspected there was more on her mind.

"When we were in Usted, I took something from your bag. I'm not sure what you call it, but it's some kind of communication device. Anyway, I want to give it back to you." She stared deep into his eyes. "I want you to know I trust you, and that I. . .I. . ."

"Stole it to stop me?"

Her mouth dropped open. "I hoped you didn't know."

"It's my job, and I'm good at what I do."

"I never doubted your abilities. I overestimated mine."

He could see she was about to cry. "*DeJorelle Kari*," he tucked a few long hairs behind her ear, "I could have taken my palm-com back whenever I needed it, but I wanted you to willingly give it to me, and you did not disappoint me." He sat so he could look her in the eye. "I had faith in you."

"I'm honored."

"As you should be, my sweet. I don't trust many people." He scooted to the edge of the bed and headed to the lav. His back might be to her, yet he felt her hot gaze on him as he walked to the door. He wanted her to want him as a man, not because she thought she could gain better information between the sheets. They were both in the same predicament, together, but on different sides. The irony was how it paralleled Dacton and Talina's experience.

He closed the door behind him and got in the shower. So many thoughts floated in his mind, but the one he could not dispel was the irony of how this mission paralleled his brother's experience. If history repeated itself, that meant he'd find Zotar and finish his quest. But would he spend the rest of his lifetime with Arella like his brother was with Talina? Part of him hoped so, the other part feared the ending.

The shower stopped with the simple request of *off*. He did appreciate technology. He quickly dressed in the last of the clean clothes from his backpack then opened the door and walked into the bedroom where Arella lay on the large bed, stretched out on her stomach, the blanket barely covering her backside.

"That was fast."

Falcon noticed she appeared too tired to open her eyes. "I must have worn you out."

"No argument."

"Take a nap, and then get ready for our evening out. I'll be gone for a while taking care of business."

"Do me a favor?"

"What?"

"Check on Soho. I'm sure he's miserable and scared caged up like that all by himself."

"I'll take him some treats." He heard her groan of approval and took that as his cue to leave before he was tempted to wear her out even more.

"Wait." She slipped out of bed, pulled the sheet around her and walked to where her backpack sat. She dug toward the bottom, unzipped a hidden pocket and pulled out his com device. She stood, turned to face him and held her hand out. "Here."

He walked to her and accepted her gift of trust. "Thanks." With a grin he flipped open the circular object, nodded, then closed it and slipped it into his pocket. "I do appreciate the gesture, Arella. I know it was a difficult decision."

"Just find my sister and get us all back in one piece."

"I promise." He leaned toward her and lightly kissed her lips. "Rest, my sweet. I'll see you soon."

CHAPTER THIRTY-FOUR

By the Gods, what had she done? When this was over so was her political career. If the council knew she just gave Falcon an advantage they'd execute her for stupidity. How could she give him back his communication device? She needed her head examined. Her motive was her sister's welfare, but the Nacrem High Council did not accept excuses.

Well, they could all go to Diabolus as far as she was concerned. She knew what her priorities were and the price she'd have to pay. If her sister lived, she'd gladly give up her Councilor's position, she'd even give up her home planet if it came to that. There was not much in life she cared about, but her sister and Ducard were at the top of her list.

She pulled herself out of bed and headed for the bathroom. This time she'd take a quick shower, disobey Falcon once again, and do some checking around Waylent herself. She might be able to salvage a little dignity if she could provide some kind of information to the High Council.

Jorken had to be lurking close by, and she could tell him what direction they'd be going. She never read the map Sadar gave Falcon, she had no reason to since she went wherever he went. Hopefully, this new information would be valuable enough to satisfy Jorken and the High Council for a while.

Falcon's face flashed through her mind when she turned on the shower and stepped under the spray. She lathered her body in cleansing lotion and hoped her relationship would not wash away as fast. It pained her to deceive him, but he knew what she was sent to do, and it did not seem to bother him. She really had not had a choice from the beginning. Now there was no question, she had to help him to save Nodia.

Duty before anything was the creed of all Councilors.

Enough. She turned off the water, grabbed a towel, dried herself, then walked into the bedroom and quickly dressed in a clean tunic and a pair of pants. How boring. She was tired of looking like the same, mannish warrior she pretended to be. After being with Falcon she realized she'd never be a real warrior. Next to many of the men on her planet she could ably compete physically. Against Falcon, never.

At least she fell in love with a real man. Her hand flew to her mouth as if she'd said the words out loud. When had that happened? If she were honest, from the moment she first laid eyes on him. Reality arrived last night while he made love to her so tenderly. He was amazing in bed and out. There seemed to be nothing that could stop him. He was always in total control of his mind and body. The perfect warrior, lover and loyal friend. Did the man not have a shortcoming? Everyone had at least one weak spot. Everyone except Falcon.

She ran the brush through her hair then tossed it into her bag and headed to the door. She put her eye to the identifier, but nothing happened. Damn. She pushed the com button to ring the desk.

"Control desk, may I help you Mrs. Marcon?"

"I need to go out for a few moments. Can you please set the lock for me?"

"Certainly."

"Thank you." No sooner were the words out of her mouth when the door slid open and she stepped out into the hall. The lift door at the end opened. She ran into the empty transporter, the door closed and her descent from the top floor amazed her once again. The lift was entirely made of high-density, clear material and moved along the outside of the building. It gave the rider a sense of floating through thin air, but it reminded her too much of flying, especially when all she could focus on was the ground rising up toward her.

They could have made the floor solid instead of transparent. She wondered how many people got sick in this thing?

The view astounded her. In the distance she noticed the tip of a pyramid and wondered if that was their destination. Of course not, that would be too simple. Nothing about this mission was simple. Nothing in life was ever simple.

The lift door opened and commotion in the busy lobby greeted her. As soon as her feet touched the carpet someone grabbed her arm and guided her to the front door. She knew that hurtful grip, not surprised Jorken had found her. Good. This way she'd be back in the room before Falcon returned.

Once outside, he pushed her around the corner and forced her into a fast pace to the far end of the main parking area and stopped beside the back privacy wall.

Jorken stepped in front of Arella. "Tell me something I can use."

"A man named Sadar told Falcon that Zotar is at the *Pyramid of Power* and gave him a map to the location. The map indicated a southern route, but Falcon said it was wrong, it's really to the west."

"You're absolutely sure of this?"

"Positive. Falcon trusts me now."

"And how did you manage that?" Jorken laughed. "Don't tell me you actually slept with the man?"

"Why is that so funny?"

"He has my sympathy, that's for sure." Jorken stared into Arella's eyes. "What else?"

"There's nothing else to tell." The nasty looking man pulled his arm back then punched her in the stomach with his fist. She doubled over in pain. She coughed in an effort to breathe. If she had Falcon's strength and ability, she'd lay him out cold. Jorken looked at her as if she were concealing national secrets. "You think I'm holding back?"

"I don't think you're smart enough."

The urge to draw blood roiled in her stomach until she doubled her fist and swung at his nose. He grabbed her hand and pushed her against the rough, stone wall. If she had a fazer weapon she'd simply shoot him and be done with the slime-snake forever.

"Exactly as I thought." Jorken rubbed his chin for a moment.

"You'd better get back to your lover before he misses you, and before I draw blood." He snickered. "Remember, I'm watching you."

"I have nothing to hide."

"You'd better not, because your sister will pay."

He turned on his heel and marched out of the parking area, turned north and disappeared up the street. At least that was over and she doubted her stomach would bruise. Tonight would be special and she did not want anything to spoil the magic. Once they left Waylent the mission would shred the tenuous bond they'd built. Tonight might be the last with the one man she could love.

Falcon did not realize she'd opened her heart to him. Yet what good would it do if they were doomed? She'd always been a realist, and she knew a love like theirs could never survive. Why worry about the test of time when their respective governments would tear them apart. Falcon could not love a dead woman, and that is what she'd be if she did not stop him.

With a deep sigh she made her way into the hotel, then stepped on the lift and tried to enjoy the view on her ride to their floor. The door opened and she began to walk down the hall, thoughts swimming in her mind. She'd told Jorken their plans and what Falcon told her. She'd betrayed her one love, and that was unforgivable. Guilt ripped through her because of what she'd done, yet what was her choice? Damn duty!

She'd never been one for pity parties, or "what if" games. She relied on facts, did her job and moved on. That meant she had one viable choice; enjoy tonight and commit every moment to memory so she'd have something to fondly look back on when she was old, grey, and alone. Not a happy thought. Her life had been far from a fairytale, and this was simply another chapter.

~ ~ ~ ~

"Brother, it's good to hear your voice at last. I should beat you for taking so long."

Falcon cleared his throat and gave a quick check to be sure he was alone. "Sorry. It's good to hear your voice, Dacton." He leaned against the exterior wall of the tavern. "You know well how it is dealing with women."

"One woman, and I fully understand. That sword collection is going to look great on my wall."

"Don't count your swords until they've been won, brother. Just bring me up to date."

"I'm sure you've heard Zotar has Nodia. She's with him at the pyramid. Rescuing her should not be a problem. Ducard has been taken to Illkaram, a planet out of our jurisdiction. Our sources say Ducard is fine and he's in the care of Zotar's people there, and very well-protected on a private compound. We believe he's fine. Surveillance is limited. Zotar has too many detection devices and The Protectorate is not welcome in that quadrant."

"Understood. What can you tell me about the man who's been following us?"

"Very seedy character. His name is Jorken Hewlist and he's the sweeper for the Nacrem High Council. Of course they'd never admit they know him. And before you ask, he's the one who beat Arella. His current assignment is to be Arella's watch-animal."

"I assumed as much. Have they met here yet?"

"Briefly. He only hit her once in the stomach. She stood up to him, you should be proud."

"This is a man I need to kill."

"Easy there, Chief Protector. Duty dictates. . ."

"To Diabolus with duty!"

"She's fine. She's back in your room waiting for you, so simmer down. You can't afford to upset the Nacrem Council just yet. You know the plan."

"Sorry."

Dacton chuckled. "I do know how you feel." He cleared his throat. "How are things going with the lady, little brother?"

"Just doing my duty."

"Knowing you, your job duties have expanded."

"Easy, brother."

"Where's your sense of humor, Falcon?"

"I have none where women are concerned."

Dacton groaned. "Oh, I see. You've finally met your match! I knew it the moment I laid eyes on Arella. Congratulations! It's about time you settled down and. . ."

"Hold it right there before I take your head off!"

"That might be difficult since we're orbiting and you're

standing there in that little alley all by yourself."

"I'll see you again, and when I do . . .." Falcon heard laughter and almost joined in. He knew he'd sounded overly sensitive about Arella, but he could not help himself where she was concerned.

"Anything else?"

"What about Zotar? And do we have to ride those miserable animals up the mountain, or can we fly?"

"Flying is out of the question. You're stuck riding."

"Great."

"Is that a complaint, Chief Protector?"

"Of course not, Mr. Ambassador."

"Good. Command out."

Falcon closed his palm-com and slipped it into the front pocket of his pants. Dacton had his number to be sure. What had Dacton seen in Arella to make him think she was his match? He could not possibly know how much she unnerved him, or how he worried about her. Dacton was doing far too many comparisons between their adventures. Not every strange assignment ended with a life-mating.

So, Jorken met with Arella. He felt confident she fed him the planted information, and that should delay the man long enough for them to make a clean getaway. The games people played, all in the name of duty, power and greed, with greed the biggest motivator.

Arella's face formed in his mind. She was predictable, feisty, and so damned beautiful she drove him crazy! She'd ingrained herself in his life. It had to be that special spark everyone talked about, but could never explain. Until now he'd never understood the concept. He pushed off the wall he'd been leaning on and walked up the street toward a clothier shop.

His last errand today was to find evening attire to wear out with Arella tonight. He could barely wait to see her in the black dress, the least he could do is look appropriate next to her. It should not take him long, it never did. So many high level government dinners and diplomatic missions, yet this was different, very, very different.

~ ~ ~ ~

Arella stared out the corner window of their suite and watched the sun set. Lights came on along the street and in one building after another. Some signs flashed messages, others simply glowed brightly in the rapidly approaching darkness. Where was he? She'd taken her time bathing, primping and dressing. Now she stood like a schoolgirl waiting for her date. She really hated waiting.

Falcon was a man worth waiting for. In fact, she'd waited her entire life for him, so why not a little longer? It seemed like an eternity when their time was so limited.

If Falcon were successful, Zotar would be dead, and her failure would be obvious. Jorken would not let her live long enough to return to Nacrem and plead her case to the High Council. If she could not continue to see Falcon, or return to her Council position, then she really had no wish to continue living. Everything would be lost, and that she could not face.

In all her sun-cycles of life she'd never once thought of giving up, or committing suicide, not even when faced with rejection and ridicule. Never. However, this was different. She'd given her heart and body to a man who appreciated her for the woman she was, not for the woman she was expected to be.

Falcon would hold a special place in her heart forever. He was the kind of man every woman wanted; handsome, smart, highly accomplished, loyal, and a fantastic lover with a body built by the gods. His deep voice never failed to touch her soul. He sounded so tough, yet under that professional demeanor and behind the emotional wall he'd so carefully erected, he was tender and caring. There may not be such a thing as a perfect man, but to her, Falcon fit the description.

Had she really lost her mind, body and soul to The Protectorate's best? No one would believe her, but the answer was yes. She was told to sleep with him to fulfill a mission, but she was not wired to be cold and calculating. This was the final proof the High Council needed to prove women incapable of being Councilors, and she was about to hand it to them on a platinum platter.

It was not enough she failed herself, she failed every woman on Nacrem. She represented hope for women's recognition and future positions of power. Now that hope was gone. How could she live with that? She'd worked so hard over the annual-cycles to help women gain independence and respect, and in one assignment erased every trace of progress. Tears welled in her eyes. Failure was hard to swallow. She could handle the blame, the finger-pointing, even banishment, but if Falcon hated her for betraying him that would be hard to swallow –if she ever could.

Behind her the entry door swished open and her heart began to race. She cursed under her breath for not having more control where Falcon was concerned. She'd not even looked at him yet and he had an overpowering effect on her entire body. Slowly she turned to face him and her jaw nearly dropped to the floor.

"Greetings, *DeJorelle Kari*."

"Hello, Commander Rovarn." The huskiness of her own voice surprised her, however the sight of Falcon dressed in formal wear was the real surprise. No man had the right to look that good in anything. "I'm glad to see you."

Falcon walked to her, picked up her hand in his, raised her fingers to his lips and kissed them. "You're the most beautiful woman I've ever laid eyes on." He lowered her hand then released her.

If her pulse were any faster she'd be on the floor in complete cardiac arrest. He certainly took her breath away. "I truly doubt that."

"I'm not a liar, Councilor."

"I never thought you were, I just. . ."

"Thought I was saying that to make you feel good?" He watched her nod. "You could not be more wrong."

"I must say, Commander, you're a tempting sight."

"I hope so." He laughed. "I'd hate to think I spent so many credits for nothing." He stepped closer. "And I do mean to tempt you." He slid his arm around her waist and pulled her against his chest.

When she opened her mouth to answer him he pressed his lips to hers and gave her a deep, satisfying kiss she felt all the way to her toes. He tasted, teased and tempted, yet when he finally pulled back all she could think of was how she wanted more.

"If we continue this we'll never get to dinner, and I have a reservation at the finest dining establishment Waylent has to offer." Falcon backed up several steps. "You are. . .exquisite."

Arella fingered her crystal pendant and the gold chain that held it. "Thank you." Her eyes took in his perfectly fitted black suit and the crisp white shirt he wore under the jacket and vesteel. At the top fastener of his shirt he wore a chatelaine, the newest, most popular men's accessory. His was made of silver in a freeform shape covered in beautiful, deep verdant stones that glistened bright green when light danced off their finely cut surface.

"Is something wrong, Arella?"

"Quite the opposite." She closed the gap between them and slid her arm through his. "Let's keep that reservation, Trader Marcon."

"Very well. I could think of nothing better than spending a night on the town with my new life-mate."

"I knew we mated, but I didn't know it was for life." She loved the sound of Falcon's laughter and joined him. It was a bittersweet joke to be sure, but funny none the less. He guided her to the door and the moment it opened escorted her out. They were halfway down the hall before she heard the door secure itself behind them.

The view out of the clear lift walls on the way down was a virtual wonderland of lights. Dazzling white, stunning colors, some constant, some blinking, but all shining brightly in the moon-cycle. "This town is amazing after dark."

"It certainly is."

She glanced up at Falcon and he was not looking at the view through the glass, he was staring at her. "You are the sweet talker of legend, aren't you?"

"I wouldn't want to disappoint you."

"There are several questions I'd like answered. First. . ." He placed two fingers on her lips and gave her a sexy grin.

"I never kiss and tell." He kissed her cheek and removed his fingers from her mouth.

"I should hope not. However, it might be best for your actions this evening to answer the questions I have."

"Then I hope you get the answers you want."

He was about to kiss her when the lift doors opened and several people stood staring at them, waiting for them to exit, so they complied. Falcon simply flashed them his unforgettable, amiable smile, gave them a nod of acquiescence and escorted her past the group as if they had all come to pay homage to them.

That arrogance of his usually irritated her, but tonight it smoothed the awkward moment. She might even learn to appreciate that egotistical quality. Maybe he could teach her how to pull it off because she could use a stiff dose of confidence, no matter how contrived.

He whisked her through the lobby, out the door and into a waiting sky transport. She swallowed her fear of flying, leaned back and tried to relax.

"Pinnacle Club, my friend." Falcon handed the driver several large bills then settled back in the seat.

"That seems like an exorbitant amount of credits for a short ride." He nonchalantly put his arm around her shoulders.

"Uhh, my beautiful life-mate. Do not trouble yourself over credits, you know well we have more than enough to share." He leaned closer to her hear. "Credits are no object."

Arella noticed how intently the driver listened to their every word while he whisked them away from the hotel, into the air, and headed up an invisible route. "Of course, you're right." She smiled. "This is all still new to me, darling."

"I know, princess." He gave her a hug. "You'll never want for anything again."

"I do love you, Trader Marcon." Falcon grinned at her as if the words were real. Were they? She could not afford to travel that mental road right now, she was too busy acting.

"Have you spoken to our contact?"

She had no idea where this was going, but it would be interesting. "No, have you?"

"Earlier this sun-cycle. He's to meet us at the designated location about one hour's flight west of here."

"Will he bring what we need?"

Falcon nodded. "Without it we can't succeed."

"When are we leaving?"

"Three sun-cycles from now, no sooner or we'll miss him."

Arella ran her hand over the front of Falcon's incredible jacket, taking her time to reach the top and move her hand to his freshly-shaven cheek. "We can't afford a mistake."

"That's why I choose you as a partner, we think alike." He tilted his head to hers and covered her mouth with his.

Arella knew this kiss was for show, but it still held too much passion for backseat entertainment. Falcon made it easy to comply with this act when he awakened her desires so easily. He pulled her close and tightened his embrace. The rapid beat of his heart kept pace with hers.

"Sir, we're here."

Falcon pulled back and sighed. "Very well." He slid to the side of the seat, opened the hatch and exited the vehicle.

Arella took the hand he offered and he pulled her to her feet. She was thankful to be free of the confining aircraft. She no sooner took a few steps toward the building when the craft sped off, and a man came running at them from the front door.

"This way, Trader Marcon."

The out-of-breath man rushed to open the restaurant's entry door for them and ushered them inside. He escorted them to the lift then stood like a statue while they stepped inside the conveyance. Falcon placed too many credits in the man's hand just an instant before the door slid closed.

"I'm so glad credits are no object, darling."

"Oh my sweet, you're very astute."

"You may not say that when I go shopping in the morning." She loved the sheepish look he gave her.

"I doubt you'll have time for shopping, my dear."

"Of course I will, we're not leaving for three sun-cycles, so that means. . ."

"You have more time to spend in the bedchamber with your new life-mate."

Heat flooded her cheeks and she was sure they'd turned bright red. "We shall see about that."

"Yes, we shall."

"You're bad."

"And you love it."

Before she could answer the lift door opened and Falcon offered her his arm and together they walked into the subdued lighting of the top floor. The room was almost like the lift with clear walls and ceiling. It was like being outside, but with perfect climate control. Soft, warm amber lights highlighted indoor plants and three separate waterfalls. A well-appointed man marched up to them and bowed.

"Your accommodation for the evening is ready, Trader Marcon."

Falcon placed five-hundred credits in the man's hand. "Have all my requests been carried out?"

"Per your instructions, sir."

Chapter Thirty-Five

Falcon watched Arella finish the last bite of her dessert then lean back in her chair. He'd not been able to take his eyes off her the entire evening. Through all seven courses he'd watched her smile, eat, laugh, relax, and for the first time actually enjoy herself. It made him feel wonderful to know he'd succeeded in bringing a little joy to their otherwise miserable assignment.

Her sparkling lavender eyes mesmerized him. No woman had ever looked at him the way she did, nor had any woman breached his defenses, but Arella had succeeded where many others failed. He suspected these new strange feelings came under the heading of love. Love. The simple word that struck terror in his heart.

The server entered their private area, removed the last of the plates, poured another glass of wine for each of them, then quietly left. He'd reserved a private dining room, they'd neglected to tell him the walls were transparent, and they were definitely being watched. At least their conversation could not be overheard. Arella looked at him with a sudden sadness. "Is something wrong?"

"It's been a wonderful evening, and I thank you."

"But what?"

"I feel guilty enjoying myself when Nodia is missing, and possibly being tortured and abused." She lowered her head and stared at her wine.

He reached across the table and tilted her chin up with his

finger. "Look at me, Arella. You have nothing to feel guilty about. It's Zotar's fault, not yours." Her eyes blurred with tears she tried to blink back. "I'll find Nodia and make Zotar pay."He grasped her trembling hands in his. He knew all too well who caused her pain. The same man who had caused pain for his family and thousands of others.

"Arella, shed your tears this moon-cycle, but then I want you to put on your armor and be ready for battle. Do you trust me?"

"With my life, and my sister's life."

"No matter what happens, never doubt that trust. I'd never do anything to hurt you."

"I know, it's just that. . .I. . .."

"You're confused, and I understand that. You've been told The Protectorate is your enemy, that you're nothing but a woman, and what you think and do is of no consequence. Well, neither of those statements are true. You know I'm here to help you, yet something inside you fights against me."

"You're right, but I can't apologize for doing my duty any more than you can."

"And I respect that." He saw skepticism in her eyes. "But right now we're on the same side, fighting for the same goal. Forget the differences between Nacrem and The Protectorate. You're fighting for your sister's life, and I'm at your side. Concentrate on that. Others will decide political formalities. It's not up to us."

"I hate it when you make perfect sense. And I hate it when you're always right."

"But do you hate me?"

"How can you even ask?"

She leaned toward him across the small, intimate table and pressed her lips to his. All he wanted to do was take her in his arms and make love to her right here, right now, but he had to behave himself. He broke the kiss and leaned back.

"Is something wrong?"

"You little vixen, you know what's wrong." Her face lit up in a triumphant smile. He took a deep breath. "So, you like games?"

"Depends on the game and whose rules we're playing by."

"I see." Arella laughed and it made his heart sing. She'd come a long way in the short time they'd been together. "I think I like this new you."

"Really?"

"It may take some getting used to, but yes, very much. A confident warrior makes the best warrior, and a sense of humor comes in handy at times." He lifted her fingers to his lips and nibbled at her fingers. "I need a warrior with me. I'm counting on you."

"I won't let you down. I promise."

"I'll hold you to your word."

"Just hold me and I'll be happy."

"I never knew being newly life-mated could be so. . ."

"Challenging?" Arella laughed.

"That's one word for it." Falcon glanced around and noted several men who might be possible spies. He'd expected Jorken, but as yet he had not showed himself. He still held Arella's hand and was surprised when she suddenly tensed and tried to pull away. He held tight. "What's wrong, my sweet?"

"Nothing. I think we should go now. I couldn't eat or drink anything more."

"We've not had our glass of Kotron. Every fine meal must end in that deliciously sweet liquor."

"If you wish."

"I do." He nodded at the server who awaited instructions outside the glassed-in room. A man and a woman were being seated at the table closest to them, facing their door. Jorken. Of course, why else would Arella suddenly panic and nearly freeze?

This was the perfect opportunity to plant information, which is what the man came for, and he did not want to let the miserable spy down. He turned his attention on Arella and smiled broadly to distract her attention away from Jorken.

"Will you be ready to leave in three sun-cycles?" She nodded. "Good, because the plans I've made cannot be changed. I've hired a guide who will meet us on route just west of the city with our supplies."

"More riding?"

"Beats walking." Out the corner of his eye he caught Jorken rolling his beady eyes. He'd looked better in the picture Dacton sent than in person. His short, curly blond hair looked dirty, and he was too wiry to fill out his cheap, wrinkled, out-of-date evening wear. The man obviously detested Arella, and he wanted to take some revenge out on the man for all the injuries he'd given her. Unfortunately that was not possible without tipping his hand. All he could hope for was one opportunity before the mission ended.

Their drinks arrived in the customary tall, silver-stemmed goblets and were placed in front of them. The server bowed, tray in hand and gave him the questioning look all waiters acquired. "Thank you for your excellent service this moon-cycle." He placed an envelope on the tray.

"Thank you sir. Will there be anything else?"

"No." The man left smiling, as he should since he'd been very well paid for his efforts. There were times he enjoyed spending The Protectorate's credits. He held up his glass. "I'd like to make a toast." Arella picked up her goblet and held it up against his. "To our mutual success on this mission, and to a very intimate moon-cycle to come."

They tapped glasses and a slight, humming ring blended with the soft background music, then they took a long sip. As if planned, they both set their glasses back down on the gold brocade table covering. She was so beautiful he had no words. The dress he'd bought her showed off her assets so well she'd turned every male head when they walked through the dining room to their table.

The low cut neckline had kept his attention most of the evening, yet it was still her eyes that held him captive. They just stared at each other as if they'd never met. Maybe this was their first true meeting. Enough, he'd given Jorken more of a show than he deserved.

She picked up her glass and held it up. "I'd like to toast the most capable warrior I've ever met, and the best lover I've ever had."

He touched her glass with his. "I'll certainly drink to that." He wanted to add that he was her only lover, and if he had his way he'd always be her only. They both took another sip then set their goblets back on the table.

"If you'll excuse me, I need to visit the facilities."

He rose from his chair, walked to her side and helped her to her feet. "Shall I escort you?"

Arella laughed. "I'll be fine."

"Very well." He returned to his seat without taking his eyes off her for a moment. Sure enough, the moment she was out of sight down the hall Jorken headed toward her. He wanted to follow, yet he could not let the slime-snake know he was on to him or the information plant would be for naught. He swore if the despicable man laid one finger on her this moon-cycle he'd kill him in his sleep. He'd had enough hiding in the background, but a warrior always waited for the right opportunity.

~ ~ ~ ~

"Glad you've made progress."

Arella wanted to strangle Jorken with the ridiculous looking string tie he wore around his neck. "Too bad you didn't dress properly. You might have fit in better. And that prostitute you brought, well. . ." Jorken reached for her throat but paused in midair when a man entered the hall and walked past them to the men's facility.

"Watch your mouth bitch. I can still kill you."

"You could, but you'd have to answer to the High Council, and I can't complete the mission if I'm dead. And they do want me to succeed. Such a dilemma."

"I had no idea sex would loosen your tongue." He touched her hair with his fingers. "Maybe I should sample your wares now that you're experienced."

Arella shoved his arm away and cringed at the suggestive smile on his ugly face. "Not until this is over. One arrogant man to service is enough."

"What's your next move?"

"We travel west in three sun-cycles, no sooner."

"Why not sooner?"

"Falcon hired a guide who is bringing supplies and will meet us at the prescribed time, and that cannot be changed.

"You wouldn't lie to me, would you?"

"I'd think you'd know if I lied since you've followed us every step of the way."

"Just remember, missy, I'm watching, and I'll be there to pick up the pieces. You won't have to look over your shoulder to know I'm there." He chuckled.

"Laugh while you can, little man. I have a feeling you won't have much to amuse you later. Falcon is very jealous, and when he loses his temper it can be ugly." She gave him the sweetest, most innocent smile she could. "And he's bigger than you." His hands fisted at his sides. Apparently her words started a silent rage he was loathe to control. The man deserved her contempt and more, but her newfound feeling of power over him exhilarated her.

"The bigger they are, the easier they fall." He showed her his teeth. "Or haven't you heard?"

"Winner takes all, so we'll see. Won't we?" She laughed while his anger grew. "I really must go before Falcon comes looking for me. You wouldn't want him to see you." With that said, she turned away from him and walked the few steps to the women's facility, pushed open the door, thankful when it closed behind her and she was alone in the room.

Actually she was surprised Falcon hadn't come after her, but he may have seen them in the hall. It would be like him to spy on her. With haste she took care of business then hurried back to the table. She found Falcon sitting with his legs crossed, impatiently tapping his fingers in succession on the table.

"Sorry that took so long, it was crowded." He gave her a skeptical look that made her wonder if she were capable of telling a convincing lie. For everyone's sake, she hoped so. This was not the time or place for a confrontation.

"I just missed your company, my sweet." He stood and took her hand before she had time to sit. "Let us be on our way. I have more surprises for you."

She smiled in an effort to lighten his mood. He seemed depressed compared to a few moments ago. If he'd seen her with Jorken he'd be angry. She preferred Falcon happy and playful, the way he'd been the past couple of days since they made love.

He whisked her to the lift and they rode down. Before she knew it they were outside in the perfect night air. A man approached Falcon, bowed and handed him a controller.

"The vehicle you requested, sir."

"Thank you. Pick it up tomorrow night at the Stargazer." Falcon tipped the man then turned to Arella and waited until they were alone. He opened the side hatch and held her hand while she slipped into the aircraft. "You're going to love this."

Arella smiled when he closed the hatch. The happy fervor was back in his voice and step while he hurried around the craft to enter from his side.

"Buckle up, my sweet, and hang on."

Arella pulled down the locking harness and wrapped her fingers around the thin bars that secured her to the seat. They slowly made their way out of the vehicle area and Falcon eased his way up into the overhead air traffic. Then he pulled back on the controls and she gasped. They went up so fast her heart was in her throat.

"Falcon, please. . ."

"Trust me. You're perfectly safe."

"My body may be, but the rest of me is terrified." She closed her eyes tightly.

"You've never had fun flying before, have you?"

"No, and I don't want to." They leveled out and it seemed like they slowed. She finally summoned the courage to open her eyes and look out the front shield. "That's magnificent! You can see every light in Waylent from here."

"I told you you'd like it. Relax and enjoy. Sorry about the climb, but I didn't want to be tracked. A climb like that in a small craft throws off most tracking devices long enough for me to disappear undetected."

"I've never been in this small of a craft. I guess I've always traveled commercial, or the hard way, like Cameora." She laughed. "I know how much you loved Hateu."

"She did steal my heart. Enough of that. Don't you want to know where we're going?"

"You said it was a surprise and to trust you. I'm trying to do that." She looked him in the eye. "It's not easy."

Falcon laughed loudly. "I know. We're almost there. Prepare to land."

Arella's white knuckles released their hold. Falcon's vertical landing was so smooth she did not know they were on the ground until he shut the engine down.

The hatch opened and Falcon exited, walked to her side and held out his hand. She willingly let him pull her to her feet. He kissed her passionately. Her heartbeat quickened and butterflies danced in her stomach. She wrapped her arms around his neck and held on as if her life depended on it.

Slowly he pulled back and she heard a deep moan, but he held her tightly, as if he never wanted to let her go. If that were true she'd be the happiest woman in the universe. Falcon may have had many women in his past, and soon she'd take her place in that long line, but until this dream ended she planned to enjoy every moment.

"Come, I have something to show you."

He took her hand and led her a few feet away from the craft toward what looked like the edge of a cliff. "Oh Falcon, this is so beautiful." She glanced at him standing next to her looking quite pleased with himself. "Waylent didn't look this good when we were there."

"Cities always look better from a distance."

"Thank you for bringing me here to see this."

"This is not why we're here." He took her hand and led her back toward the craft, but instead of going to it he veered to the left into a heavily forested area. Just when she thought she'd be unable to walk in the heels she wore, they stepped onto a paved walk that led to a long staircase. She took her first step up, but stumbled because of the long dress.

Without hesitation he swept her up in his arms and climbed the steep flight of stairs. She felt his muscles work and his heartbeat quicken. Admiration for this incredible man grew deeper, which amused her, because before Falcon she considered no man incredible, or desirable.

They reached the top of the stairs and he eased her feet to the ground. She looked at the sight before her and shook her head in disbelief. "Where. . .how. . ."

"I'm well connected."

"So I see."

"It may appear like we're totally on our own, but I assure you, we're closely monitored."

Did he know about her implanted tracking device, or was this about him? Playing stupid would be best. "How closely?"

"When we're outside they can see us, but not hear us. They know what buildings we're in, but they can't hear or see us, unless the building is rigged with monitoring devices."

"I hope you're right."

"Our private activities are still private. Of course, we can't stop suppositions being made because we've been traveling alone all this time."

"I can handle suppositions. Now, tell me," she said, pointing to the large, beautiful cabin built into the side of the mountain which looked like the mountain itself, "who owns this place?"

"A very rich diplomat who wishes to remain incognito for obvious reasons. He's a friend of The Protectorate, and offered the use of his residence."

Falcon touched the lock-pad with his finger and the large, rough sawn wood door swung open and interior lights came on when their feet touched the floor inside. "This is wonderful." She turned in a circle. "Are we going to stay here?"

"Tonight. In the morning we leave for the pyramid."

"I thought we had to ride our Bemothras, and what about Soho?" The moment she said his name she heard a familiar squeaky-squeal come from the corner of the room. She looked at Falcon and he nodded. She ran toward the noisy sound and found Soho sitting in an ample cage with food, water, and a little bed.

"As you can see, he's been well cared for. But if you wish to have a peaceful night's rest, I suggest you leave him in that carrier."

Arella walked back to Falcon and put her arms around his neck. "And where should I put you if I want a peaceful night's rest? Hmmmm?"

"Your wish is my command. If it's peaceful you want, say the word, and you shall not be bothered."

He smiled down at her, his gorgeous blue eyes dancing with mischief. "I think you should stay by my side at all times. I may need a Protector."

Falcon scooped her up in his arms and carried her to a lift hidden in the back wall of the main entertaining room. Once inside a clear door slid closed and they were whisked up three stories so fast it made her head spin.

He carried her to a large circular bed that faced an entire wall of tinted glass. Gently he laid her in the center then sat next to her. He leaned down and kissed her softly, then deepened the kiss, driving her straight into a burning need for him. His tongue explored, tempted and tasted. The duel went on and on while her desire reached new heights.

He untied the halter top of her dress then pulled it down. His hands found her breasts and explored every peak and valley with expert finesse. She eased his jacket off his shoulders and he moved his arms back to free himself of the garment. She unfastened his chatelaine, opened the front of his shirt and pushed it back until he managed to shrug it off and drop it on the floor.

His warm, taut skin beneath her fingers felt oh so sexy. She ran her hands up and down his arms, relishing the feel of firm muscles. He was all man, and when he lay on top of her she knew he was more than ready by the feel of his erection against her leg.

Falcon ended the kiss and rolled to the side. He reached for her gown and slowly eased it toward her hips. Instinctively she stayed his hands. His deep blue eyes questioned her move.

"What's wrong?"

"I. . .I'm not comfortable being naked. I uhh. . ."

"To me you're perfection, you must believe that." Falcon smiled. "I know you're aware I've been with many women, and you, my sweet, truly are the most gorgeous creature I've ever seen."

"That's not possible. I have eyes, Falcon. I've seen women far more beautiful than me, and I know you're attracted to those women."

Falcon sighed. "I've been known to attract lots of women, some more beautiful that others, but I'd never lie to you."

"Then it's clear you're from another planet." She pulled the top of her dress up to cover herself.

"That's no secret."

"True." She wanted to laugh at his attempt at humor, but under the circumstances she could not.

"Tell me who hurt you. What did he do?" He leaned closer to her. "I'll kill him for you if you like."

"Great. You'd have to kill at least four men, could be more by now, I really don't know for sure. I'm sure they spread the word."

"Tell me, my sweet. This must end here, tonight. For your sake."

Tears welled in her eyes while hidden memories pushed to the surface of her mind. "I never wanted to think about them, or what they did again. I worked hard to bury those incidents, and I don't want to talk about it." Repressed tears flowed like a swift river, which only made her more embarrassed.

Falcon cupped her chin with the palm of his hand and made her look at him. "*DeJorelle Kari*, this will not end until you acknowledge your pain."

"Damn you! Why do you always have to be right."

"It's a habit of mine, and I rather like being right." He cupped her check with the palm of his hand. "Please. Talk to me."

She pulled the top of her dress up and quickly tied it behind her neck. "I was fifteen annual-cycles, it was my best friend's birthday party and we were playing typical kissing games popular at that age. I was chosen by the cutest boy there. I felt honored and went with him out back for the kiss he'd won. It excited me, I wanted to kiss him very much. When we got out back he had three friends waiting. They held me down, stripped off my clothes and. . ." She sobbed for a long moment.

"You were raped?"

She shook her head violently. How could she explain total humiliation? "They stood there and laughed at my naked body. They called me skinny, bony. They said I was flat and called me a boy. Then the names got worse. I rolled over in a futile effort to hide myself, but their laughter continued."

"Arella, you were all children. It's time to let it go."

"If only that were true. Those same four boys caught me alone one afternoon in the gym working out. I was twenty-one annual-cycles and they did exactly the same thing. This time they touched me, laughed, then touched me some more. They called me the worst female on the planet of Nacrem. They said boys had bigger breasts, and that no man would ever want me. They took pictures this time and posted them on the info-net for everyone to see. I received hate correspondence, was threatened in more ways than I can count, and humiliated beyond human endurance. Now, are you happy?"

Falcon pulled her into his arms and held her tight. He rubbed her back gently with a reassuring hand she needed so badly. He remained silent which was a relief. This was the first time she'd actually told anyone about her experience. She'd not even told her sister and they shared everything. "I'd planned to take that experience to my grave."

"*DeJorelle Kari*, I'm sorry for your pain. They were cruel, and if it were possible, I'd torture them before I killed them—slowly.

And never think I don't mean that. You know me well enough by now."

"I do, warrior, I do. Thank you. And if I knew where they were I'd tell you." She wiped her eyes with the back of her hand. "They're best forgotten."

"I have a very long memory."

"Is that your only flaw?"

"That is not a flaw my sweet." He kissed her on the forehead.

She stared at him and wondered what she'd done to have such a fantastic man in her life. Could the fates be so cruel as to give him to her then take him away? It seemed that way, but this moon-cycle she'd not question the fates, she'd simply enjoy.

When he pulled her into his arms again she untied the top of her dress and let it fall. She enjoyed the feeling of her naked beasts against his bare chest. He felt so good. When his lips met hers she greeted him with all the passion she had to give. Losing her soul was a small price to pay for a love.

He tasted and explored, stimulated and reassured. His magic touch erased their differences and made time stand still. They only needed each other.

Nothing felt better than being held and loved by someone who looked past the physical and appreciated her for the woman she is today. With Falcon at her side she might finally be able to put the past behind her. He was honest to a fault, and she knew in her heart, he'd never do anything to hurt her.

The dress was off and his hands were everywhere, caressing and exploring. He made every man she'd ever known seem like a bumbling fool. Not because of all the women he'd bedded, but because he showed sensitive and genuine concern.

Her hands found his belt and she freed the clasp then pulled it from his waist. She opened the front closure of his pants, then pushed the fabric down until he was able to shrug off the garments. He was naked as the day he was born, and even more beautiful. His perfect body begged her exploration, and she was determined to do just that.

With her fingertips she traced every contour carefully, permanently relegating every curve to memory, because once he returned to The Protectorate, it would be all she had when she closed her eyes, alone in her bed. No warm body lying on top of hers, no large hands exploring her skin, and no deep blue eyes looking into her soul. She'd miss him terribly, and no man could ever replace Falcon.

He made quick work of removing her stockings and panties, then lowered his naked body to hers. He entered with commanding ease and she gasped with delight. Every calculated movement he made brought pleasure to them both. Their connection went far deeper than the physical. They bonded in that magical realm where words could not do justice to the mystifying melding between them.

Time and place disappeared. The only thing that existed was love. He consumed her. He completed her. Tears escaped her closed eyes. Rampant emotions erased her tears. Maybe love could cure everything.

While Falcon's movements increased so did her delicious sensations. She held her breath in anticipation of the fulfillment only Falcon could provide.

CHAPTER THIRTY-SIX

Falcon slipped away from Arella's warm, sexy body and made his way into the bedroom down the hall. He opened the back sliding door and stepped out onto the balcony for privacy. He opened his palm-com, waited for the fourteen planets and crossed swords to appear. "Egnever". His password was immediately accepted so he punched in the code to contact his brother.

"Falcon! It's about time I heard from you. You gave me all those instructions then disappeared."

"I've been busy."

"I'll bet, but I won't go there."

"Good." Falcon listened to his brother's 'I told you so' chuckle. They were too close to fool each other. "Is everything set?."

"You've already found Soho, I'm sure. Your Bemothras are saddled and waiting in the stable out back. You also have a pack mulus loaded with the gear you purchased, and the gear you asked us for. That was quite a list."

"I have no idea what we'll find in that pyramid, or what traps Zotar has set."

"I *can* warn you about your worst fear."

"Snakes?"

"Yeah, and lots of them. We followed his men and they've secured hundreds, if not thousands of them."

"Great." If there was one thing he hated, it was those damned snakes. Dacton knew well why he had a phobia about them. "How many of Zotar's men do you think I'll run into?"

"From what we know right now he has eight men stationed between you and the pyramid."

"The terrain here is conductive to surprise attacks. What about that jerk that's following Arella?"

"You mean the sweeper, Jorken. So far he believes what Arella told him at the restaurant. If she fails her assignment, he'll kill her."

Dacton's words froze his heart and mind. He took a deep breath. "That will never happen."

"I thought not. Protecting women is our specialty. Right Brother?"

"Absolutely." More parallels between him and his brother. They were close and their jobs brought them even closer. "Has anyone caught on to our departure plans?"

"No. We sent the best doubles we could find to stay in your hotel room. They'll fool everyone for the next couple of days, then they'll head west. Jorken's no fool, but he's also not the brightest we've had to deal with. He may already have guessed what you're up to, but he's in Waylent as we speak."

"Did you take care of that little stable boy at the hotel?"

"Yeah." Dacton laughed. "What did you do to that kid? He thinks you're some kind of hero. He'd do anything for you."

"Credits speak loudly."

"It's more than that. Anyway, he'll have a couple of Bemothras to sell which will make everything well worth his trouble. We told him if you did not come to pick up your mounts in four sun-cycles, they would be his."

"Good. Anything else?"

"Arella's implant must return with the air-transport. Do you have it?"

"It'll be there." He heard Dacton groan. "I know my duty."

"Sorry, little brother, but this is Arella we're talking about, and I know how you feel about. . ."

"No you don't. So if that's all I'm. . ."

"Just remember, we can aid you any time before you enter the pyramid. Once you're inside, you're on your own. So far no communication devices work from inside, or even a large perimeter outside."

"Understood."

"Falcon, watch yourself. I cannot lose another brother."

"I plan to avenge our brother's death, and the deaths of all the innocent people he slaughtered. I will survive. You can't get rid of me that easily."

"That's a relief, I think."

It felt good to hear Dacton's voice. He missed working closely with him, and seeing him whenever he wanted. "I'd better go. It's a long ride and I'm determined to make it in one day."

"Good luck. May the Gods be with you."

"Falcon out." He sighed. This mission was nearly over, yet the most difficult tests were yet to come. So far everything had been relatively easy. Zotar had left them alone, but that was about to change.

He went back inside the bedroom, shut the door and returned to Arella's gorgeous, sleeping body. In the faint light of pre-dawn she looked perfect and he longed to love her over and over.

Pure magic transpired last moon-cycle. Arella now completely owned his heart and soul. It would be difficult for them to work out their differences, but he had faith that when this mission was behind them, they'd find a way to be together.

If he looked at her any longer he'd be back in bed and they had to leave. He walked to the closet, opened the door and pulled out a small bag. Inside he found a complete soft leather outfit for him, and one for her. His was black, as usual, and hers was a medium brown. He quickly dressed then returned to the closet for his boots.

Dacton was good. The clothes fit perfectly and so did the boots. He carried Arella's clothes and boots to the bed and set them next to her. "Arella?" He gently rubbed her exposed shoulder. He tucked some loose hair behind her right ear. "It's time to get up, my sweet."

She moaned softly and he smiled. In one quick movement he pulled the covers down, exposing her lovely, and oh so naked body. It took every ounce of resolve he possessed not to make love to her one more time. A tempting thought to be sure.

"Arella." She rolled over on her back and opened her eyes. "Hey, sleepy, it's time to go."

"Where?" She grabbed the corner of the blanket and pulled it up to cover herself.

He wanted to take the blanket from her, instead he simply smiled. "There's your clothes." He patted the pile beside her that was now under the covers. He walked to the closet, picked up the empty bag. "We weren't very neat last moon-cycle." He followed the path of strewn clothes from last night and put them all in the bag.

"You looked fantastic last night." He put her dress in the bag. "But I think you look even better without it." She squinted at him with a frown on her face. Too bad she had so much trouble believing she was beautiful.

Arella put on her undergarments and pants. "Why do we have to get up so early when we're just going back to the hotel?"

"We're leaving immediately for the pyramid."

"But I thought. . ."

"Do you want Jorken on your heels?" At his question her cheeks turned a bright shade of red and her eyes became wider than he'd ever seen them. She pulled her tunic down over her head, then stood facing him with shock written on her face.

"You know about Jorken?" She stepped closer to Falcon.

"How could I not? He's not careful, he's left his mark on you more than once, and he's quite obvious when he's following us."

"You saw him at the waterfall?"

"Of course. He all but waved a flag." He put his hands on her shoulders. "I'm Chief Protector. Do you understand what that means?"

"I'm beginning to."

"Arella." She stared down and he waited for her to look him in the eye. "We're about to fight for our lives. The time for honesty is now. If we don't trust each other completely we'll fail. Do you understand?" She nodded. "I know your assignment, and I know Jorken's. You've known mine all along." She pushed away and turned her back to him. "It's okay, Arella. I understand."

"Do you?" She spun to face him. "I think not."

"Then tell me what I need to know. Please."

"Fine. If I don't stop you they'll kill me. They'll kill Nodia. I can't let that happen."

"Do you really believe you'll both be safe if you stop me?"

Falcon shook his head. He did not want to hurt her, but it was time for her to face reality. "You're naïve, Arella. Nodia's life is in Zotar's hands. If you want to save her you need to help me, and that means destroying Zotar."

"I'm not even sure Zotar has her. For all I know The Protectorate took her to control me!"

"I don't mean to burst your little warrior's bubble here, but controlling you is not even on The Protectorate's list of things to do. You're no threat." Tears rolled down her cheeks and he wanted to wipe them away, but this was not the time for tenderness. "You want to be a warrior. Think like one."

"I thought I was."

"You made one fatal mistake. You trusted everyone, now you don't know who deserves it and who doesn't." He watched her wipe tears with the back of her hand. She was confused and worried, but she had to work this out for herself. "You need to decide right here, right now, if I'm your enemy. Your life and Nodia's life depends on your choice."

"I thought that. . ."

"Choose." He took her hand in his. "I know this is the most difficult decision of your life. Your career could well be over, but lives are in jeopardy. This is your decision." She closed her eyes in silent contemplation. In his heart he knew she'd do the right thing.

"Zotar is my enemy. I trust you."

"You're positive? There's no going back."

"I'm positive."

"You'd better be. Zotar will test you in every way possible. Before this is over you'll question your own name."

"I won't pretend to be as experienced as you. Yeah, I thought I was a tough warrior. I am next to other women, and I rank well with the men. I don't compare to you, but I'm loyal, and my word is as good as titanium."

"I like titanium. Very useful." She pushed her body against his and wrapped her arms around his neck.

"I'm useful too. Or haven't you noticed?"

"Oh, I've noticed, but right now, we must leave." She was precious to him, and he'd give his life to save her. He could only pray the outcome would be positive for them both.

He stepped back. She reached for her socks, but paused. Ever so slowly she turned her head toward him with a concerned look on her face.

"You must promise me to keep Nodia safe. If you can't. . ." She sat on the edge of the bed and put her socks on, then reached for her boots.

"You have my word that your life, and Nodia's life are my main concern. Killing Zotar is the only way to keep you both alive. I will kill him. Make no mistake about it."

"What if he kills you first? What will happen to Nodia? Or haven't you thought about that, Commander Rovarn?"

"So you're mad at me?" She stared at him with a strange intensity that bordered on hatred. She'd used his title in a serious manner, a signal he was in trouble. "If I perish, The Protectorate will know immediately and send someone to rescue you. Their stake in this is far greater than yours. I'm not belittling your sister, but thousands of lives depend on the successful execution of Zotar."

"How will they know what happens if you're underground in that stupid pyramid? I haven't seen anyone from The Protectorate here. For all I know they don't even exist."

"How do you think we got here, in this beautiful, hidden house? How is it we have mounts waiting for us in the stable out back? How did travel clothing appear that fits you perfectly?"

He watched her eyes widen in surprise. "We've been under surveillance the entire time we've been together. They can't see us in detail in buildings, only heat impressions, but they have perfect visual outside. You disbelieve, and I understand."

"How is that possible?"

"I have an implant that gives my location and physical readout at all times." She hung her head and sighed as if she knew exactly what he was talking about. "You know my words are true."

Arella slipped her boots on then stood to face Falcon. "I do." She hung her head. "I'm just worried, and a bit scared."

"I'll excuse you for being human. I'd worry about you if you weren't. Zotar is to be feared and respected. He's very good at what he does, but so am I."

She signed. "I know. Let's end this. I want my sister back, and I have a few bones to pick with Zotar myself."

"Before or after I kill him?"

"I can't question him if he's dead, now can I? But if you kill him first, I suppose I can live with that."

"Are you up to riding this morning?"

"Before Coffa?"

"We'll take some with us." She nodded and brushed past him into the hall.

"Are you coming?"

"You leave me no choice, my sweet." She had no idea what he meant by not having a choice. He told her this was the time for complete honesty, but she failed the test. The Nacrem High Council was to blame, but he had given her the opportunity to admit she too had an implant. Now he'd have to remove it without her knowledge.

He followed her to the lift and they rode down together. The door opened and they stepped out. She headed to the galley and he slipped the small canister of somna from his pocket. He clicked it once and came up behind her.

"Arella." She turned at the sound of his voice and he sprayed her face. Instantly she melted into his arms. He picked her up, carried her to the dining table and laid her on top of it. From his pocket he removed a retractable scalpel, and three small, sealed packets.

It was a good thing she'd have no memory of this because she'd hate him for the deception. He lifted her left arm and took it out of her tunic then laid her arm back down by her side. He'd felt the implant in her left arm long ago. Over time implants became undetectable to the touch, but hers was too new. He opened one packet, removed the contents. It still amazed him to watch next to nothing turn into a sterilized cloth.

He wiped her arm then made a tiny vertical cut. He held his wrist-piece over the opening and within seconds a tiny piece of metal popped out and attached itself to the metal by the band. That magnet had performed many tasks, ID removal was but one. He readied the second packet, patted away the blood, then applied the wound-bond. He opened the third packet and covered the sealed wound with OTS-heal. Then he carefully put her arm back in her tunic.

While Arella lay on the table he returned to the air-transport and placed her implant inside the vehicle, hiding it up under her seat.

Dacton had a man who would return the transport, but not until the sun was high. He hurried back into the house, gathered all their belongings, including Soho, and carried them to the stable out back.

It was time for his last, but most important pick-up. He returned to the galley and found Arella still unconscious on the table. He gently slid his arms under her then picked her up. Once out of the building, he climbed the steps to the stable above.

Inside the shelter he laid her down on the soft hay. He secured everything to the pack mulus, then tied the animal's lead-rope to the back of his saddle. He opened Soho's cage and Soho jumped into his arms and squeaked several times.

"Easy there. You're fine." Soho's short, hairy arms wrapped as far around him as they could and he did not want to let go. He patted his head and stroked the hair on Soho's back. "You must ride by yourself until Arella wakes up." The little guy tilted his head back and stared at him with his big, round eyes. "I know you don't like being by yourself, but it's only for a little while."

Soho reluctantly cooperated by letting go of him and helped to settle himself in the leather pouch. "Looks like you're getting spoiled." He could swear Soho laughed while he settled into the soft fabric lining and enjoyed the new, larger space. "It's time, little guy."

Falcon left Soho and walked to Arella's Bemothra. He untied the tall, hairy creature, brought him close to his then secured the animal's reigns to the opposite side. He led all the animals out of the shelter then pulled his reigns over the animal's head and wrapped them around the saddle horn.

One last detail. He walked over to Arella, picked her up from the hay and carried her to his Bemothra. She seemed heavier when she was unable to help herself, but he managed to place her in a reasonable sitting position toward the front of the saddle. She fell forward onto the animal's thick neck. He steadied her with his left hand on her waist while he put his left foot in the stirrup.

When he swung his right leg up he bumped the reigns of Arella's Bemothra causing both mounts to dance a bit. Finally his leg cleared the obstacles and he settled himself before pulling Arella up to rest against his chest. With a nudge of his heels the tall, sturdy-legged animal began to trudge up the hill.

The early sun barely lit the path into the forest ahead. At least mild weather allowed easier travel and fewer supplies. He could not take all the provisions into the pyramid, but he'd brought enough to be prepared for any eventuality. From the entrance on it would be all about weapons.

A face off with Zotar required as much wit as weapons. Remaining patient and calm was a must. Zotar had a way of unnerving his opponent to gain the advantage. He would not fall for Zotar's demeaning rants designed to weaken the best of minds, but he was not sure about Arella.

The sun barely peaked over distant hills making the trail easier to follow. Visibility was crucial because he expected traps, one of Zotar's trademarks. The brush grew thicker under the tall tree branches offering the perfect cover for some kind of ambush. He reduced the pace so he could better watch the path.

Time passed about as slowly as the Bemothra's progress in the hilly terrain. Arella stirred in his arms and he knew the effects of the somna had worn off and she'd be awake soon. He'd have his hands full explaining the situation to her. For some reason she was even cuter when she was mad—harder to handle, but cute. Her intense mood swings were part of who she was, and he loved everything about her. There was that word again, love. Was it possible? Would it last? Did she feel the same?

It was possible, he wanted it to last, and judging from Arella's reactions when she was in his arms, she shared his feelings. She may not realize yet how important she was to him, but he planned to spend a lifetime showing her. He'd watched Dacton and Talina over the annual-cycles and envied the bond they shared. Now he understood what it was all about.

Arella stirred in his arms and moaned softly. It was time to prepare everything for her return. He could easily stage the area, lying to her would be more difficult. Training would guide him through it, but he'd never had to deal with his heart where professional matters were concerned.

CHAPTER THIRTY-SEVEN

Arella finished the drink Falcon had given her, still trying to understand what had happened. One minute she'd been in the galley, reaching for a cup of coffa on the counter, the next thing she knew she was sitting in the wilderness under a tree with no memory of how she got here.

Falcon's explanation made sense, but she'd never passed out from hunger before. Since time was of the essence she was not surprised he'd started the journey. She rubbed her left arm with her right hand. The implant still bothered her. It itched like never before. A twinge of guilt gave her one big shiver.

He'd given her a chance to admit to her implant, but she'd kept that detail to herself. For some reason she suspected Falcon already knew. Obviously it was of no big concern. To her it meant Jorken was close by. Falcon may have fooled him temporarily, but her worst nightmare was good at his job.

"Ready?"

Falcon stood in front of her looking quite tempting in his black leather pants and tunic. No warrior on her planet looked that good in leather. If they had she might have been tempted long ago. Then again, no man on Nacrem had found her worthy of bedding.

"Arella, are you okay?"

She rose to her feet and handed him the canteen. "Fine. I'm ready." He followed her to her Bemothra and helped her mount.

By the time she settled in the saddle and turned toward the trail he was waiting with the pack mulus in tow.

Up the trail they went. She hoped the mountainous terrain would stop. She hated the forward position that was necessary in order to remain seated. It would be even better if they did not have to ride these big creatures. Esroths were far sleeker and faster.

Bottom line, she wanted all this to be over. Nodia belonged with Ducard at their home on Nacrem. Although her duties in Mardin were not really to her liking, it was a better option than this. Falcon was the only good thing at the moment. She would miss him terribly when he left. Some things in life left you with no choice. This mission verified that in so many ways she'd lost count.

Falcon raised his hand so she halted. He drew his weapon, slid off his Bemothra and crouched low. Every muscle in his body tensed when he moved forward. He turned and motioned for her to dismount and stay put. She did as he wanted, her gaze fixed on his every move.

It did not take long before Falcon stood erect and motioned for her to join him. She rushed to his side. When she looked down her hand flew to her mouth and her stomach turned upside-down. Two dead bodies, covered in blood lay in a twisted heap in the tall grass. They had the look of a heinous death still visible on their faces, both with their eyes and mouths wide open.

"Zotar's work."

"We have to bury them." She started toward the mulus, but he grabbed her arm.

"Touch nothing. We were never here."

"You can't just. . ."

"I can, and I will. These are Zotar's men. I recognize them from the tavern in Waylent. It could very well be a trap."

"I don't care who they are, or what's going on, they deserve a burial."

"If we bury them, Zotar will know we were here. Or worse, we're attacked while digging a grave. We do nothing. Now, get on your Bemothra and ride."

She wiggled free of his grasp and stared at the men. Their throats were cut, same as the men at the mission. It was hard to deny Falcon's accusations about Zotar, but these men deserved better than being left on a hillside like dead animal carcasses.

She turned to see where Falcon had gone. He stood by her Bemothra, feet slightly apart and his arms crossed over his chest. His impatient look only served to spur her anger. As a warrior she knew he was right, but she did not have to like it.

"Fine." It took only a moment to reach her mount and allow Falcon to help her into the saddle, but it would take a lifetime to erase what she just saw. Further proof that life was not fair—never was and never would be.

In her mind she could hear him say, "Arella, if you want to succeed, and live to tell the story, you'd better get tough, and stay tough." No better advice existed, she just wasn't sure if she were capable.

Falcon picked up the pace to a fast walk. Damn the man! Until he arrived her life had a logical plan. Now she found herself disobeying all the rules and finding pleasure in the arms of the enemy.

How could she possibly comprehend the mind and actions of a diabolical monster? How had she not known what kind of a man her brother-in-law was? Even worse, how had Nodia fallen in love with him? There were far more questions surrounding Zotar than answers.

She was not sure why she felt so mad at Falcon. Anger did provide determination. Love did this to people, it made them crazy and illogical. Falcon had not done anything wrong, yet she was taking her frustrations out on him. Guilt flooded her once again. If they had another moon-cycle together, she'd make it up to him in a way he'd never forget.

The sun-cycle was nearly over and they'd ridden so long and hard every bone in her body ached. It was a small price to pay to save Nodia, but a short rest would be appreciated.

Falcon must have read her thoughts because he pulled to a stop in front of her. When she halted next to him she gasped out loud. From this vantage point she saw a glow coming from a glass pyramid-like structure. "It's magnificent."

Falcon nodded. "I wasn't sure what to expect, but that's not what I pictured."

"It seems to be alive, like it's calling to us."

He turned to face Arella. "Be prepared for anything. I have a feeling there are things in that pyramid that will defy logic and explanation."

"That, my son, is an excellent deduction."

Arella and Falcon both turned abruptly toward the sound of the voice she recognized. When she looked up she found Sadar standing on a rock to their left behind them, his long purple robe blowing gently in the breeze. His white hair and beard gave him a wise, wizardly appearance.

"I wondered if we'd ever see you again." Falcon dismounted and walked toward Sadar.

"Thought I'd wish you luck, and offer some last minute advice."

Falcon crossed his arms over his chest and widened his stance. "And that would be?"

"No need to bristle up, my boy."

Arella hopped down to the ground and walked over to the men. "He wasn't bristling just for you, he always acts like that." Sadar laughed and she wanted to join him, but knew better.

"It seems you've come to know this man quite well. Good. That's good, because I came to give one word of advice, *trust*."

"I'm in no mood for riddles." Falcon stepped to the side and leaned against a tree.

"No riddle involved. Simply trust each other. It's your only hope."

"You traveled out here, to the middle of nowhere to tell us something we already know?" Falcon shook his head. "I was hoping you had new information."

"New? I like that word, probably because I'm so far removed from new." Sadar chuckled and watched Arella walk away. "I wanted to check on Soho and tell you he must go inside the pyramid with you. You cannot leave him alone." Arella returned to her Bemothra, pulled a sleeping Soho from his pouch and carried him back to Sadar. He cuddled against her while she walked, and he began to purr. "As you can see, he's fine." She lay Soho down on a patch of grass.

"It's imperative he stay with you."

Falcon rubbed his chin. "What's this really about, Sadar?"

Arella pulled the crystal pendant to the outside of her tunic so she could feel the stone in her hand. It reminded her of Nodia and helped keep her calm. Between Sadar and Falcon she could use a pendant in each hand.

"It's about you and Arella, it's about thousands and thousands of people you've never met, on planets you've never heard of."

Falcon nodded. "That I understand."

Arella stared at Sadar, wondering exactly who, or what he was. "Why is this of such concern to you?" She thought she detected a frown, but with all that facial hair she could not be sure. She let go of the crystal and shoved her hands in her pockets.

"It concerns us all. We're all connected. The universe is smaller than you realize." Sadar climbed down from the rock to stand in front of Falcon and Arella. "When evil is left to fester we all pay the price. This is more difficult for you, Arella, since you have a sheltered view of Zotar. Falcon, on the other hand, has witnessed the aftermath of Zotar's destruction many times. It's personal for him as well."

"It's become personal for me too."

"True." Sadar reached out and palmed the cut crystal Arella wore. "This is an interesting piece."

Arella waited for Sadar's reaction, relieved when he had none. "My sister gave it to me. To protect me."

Sadar released the stone. "Then never take it off."

"I won't." Arella took a deep breath. "Sadar, if killing Zotar is so important, why send only two of us? Falcon is a great warrior, that I understand, by why me? Why not take the place by storm with hundreds of professional warriors. That way everyone would be assured of success."

"It's been tried before and failed miserably. The most successful mission was Dacton and Talina's. They captured him and returned him to The Protectorate for trial. Now it's your turn."

"I may never understand the logic, but I'll do my part." She exhaled loudly when she really wanted to scream at the top of her lungs. "You still didn't give me an answer." Sadar tilted his head back and chuckled. She wanted to slap him silly. It irritated her to the core to be laughed at.

"My dear, I'm not laughing at you. Far from it. I'm amused because you do not see your own value. Without you Falcon will fail. That's how important you are. Now, do you see?"

"Actually, no. I've yet to find anything I can do better than Falcon. He's smarter, stronger, he's. . ."

Sadar held up his hand. "Stop right there. Never demean yourself. Strength and intelligence come in all forms. You are his equal, whether you believe it or not. Truth remains truth. Your success hinges on whether you believe yourself capable."

Falcon cleared his throat. "I've been trying to tell her the same thing."

She glared at Falcon knowing her disdain showed, but she didn't care. "Oh, really? In which one of your arrogant speeches was that tidbit of wisdom buried?"

"Children, children. When this is over you may fight all you like, but until then, please, play well together." Sadar shook his head. "Don't make me cast a spell on both of you."

"Sadar, we've had enough of this nonsense." Falcon stepped closer to the man. "Is there something specific you want to tell us, or do you simply enjoy harassment?"

"I'm crushed by your insinuation. I came because I care, and I wanted to wish you luck. But I know when I'm not welcome."

Arella gasped when Sadar vanished in a puff of smoke. She expected that, but belief in the supernatural was not her strong suit. "That was fun."

"Sadar is always entertaining."

"You could have been nicer to him."

"Why? He shows up out of nowhere with nothing to say and I'm supposed to be nice?"

"Why don't you admit you have a problem with nice?" Her heart raced when he rushed toward her. He wrapped his arms around her and kissed her with so much passion she felt her toes curl. His lips covered hers, and his tongue explored her mouth with demanding urgency. His hands roamed her back, then dropped lower and cupped her derriere, pulling her tighter so she felt his need against her.

Strong emotions brought tears to her eyes. She wanted to hate him, but that was impossible. He made her heart and her body sing. He deepened the kiss and her only remaining thought was how good it felt to be loved by Falcon. Her world was upside-down, yet while he held her there was hope for the future, and problems dissolved. Or did they? Damn him. She pulled her head back, raised her hands to his chest and pushed him away. "Where did that come from?"

"Didn't you like it?"

"You know I did. That's the problem." She shook her head. "Falcon, you can't solve everything with a kiss."

"It beats other methods I've employed."

She had to laugh at that comment. "I do love your sense of humor, but right now I'm not in the mood." He looked at her with an amused grin on his face and a fiery twinkle in his blue eyes. "I'm angry, okay?"

"You can be angry if you like, but please, be angry at the right thing, for the right reason."

"Is that a 'don't blame me' lecture?" She stepped back and crossed her arms over her chest. "It's never your fault."

Falcon reached out and put his hands on Arella's shoulders. "*DeJorelle Kari*, I don't like to see you like this. There's enough for us to fight without fighting each other."

"Damn you!" A few of the tears that burned at her lids escaped without permission. What difference did it make if she had a weak moment? With one finger he wiped her cheek. There was compassion and understanding in his touch, which only brought more tears.

"I'll save your sister. You have my word."

She wrapped her arms around his waist and hugged him, her head against his chest, and his heartbeat in her ear. After a few deep breaths she regained her composure and pulled back. "Thank you."

"Thank me when it's over."

"I'm thanking you for being here, with me, at this moment." He looked so deeply into her eyes it seemed like he'd literally gone inside her. "It's okay to take a compliment, you know. It doesn't make you weak, or less of a warrior."

"I'm not used to compliments. I just do what's expected and move on to the next job. Thanks are not required, and are usually not given."

"It's a lot like that on Nacrem too, but it shouldn't be. I mean, the least we can do is be nice to each other. How hard is that?"

"For some it's impossible."

Arella sighed. "I believe there's still hope for you."

"I'm relieved you think so, but I was referring to Zotar for the impossible part."

"It scares me to say this, but I agree with you."

Falcon chuckled. "We've come a long way, and I don't mean distance."

"You're right, Chief Protector Rovarn." She looked deeply into his enticing blue eyes. "Now what?"

Falcon pointed toward the Pyramid. "We finish what we came for." He put his arm around her shoulders. "We'll rest here." He glanced down at Arella's face. "We're both tired, and the sun-cycle is soon enough to begin our fight."

Arella nodded. Falcon let go of her and returned to the pack mulus and removed camping gear. He set up camp like the professional he was. Before she knew it the tent was up and he beckoned for her to join him. One more night in his arms was an offer she could not refuse. She owed him a night he would never forget.

~ ~ ~ ~

The overly-bright sun beat down on his back with unduly hot intensity considering the early hour. They'd reach the base of the mountain soon and would face the entrance to *The Pyramid of Power*. An odd feeling swept through him like a rapidly moving storm. Once they entered the pyramid their lives would never again be the same.

He glanced back at Arella. She was busy patting Soho's head and telling the little creature he was safe and would not fall down the steep slope. She'd certainly bonded with the fur-ball, and from the looks of it, overly bonded. He'd wanted to ask Sadar why he saddled them with Soho, but he doubted he'd get the truth out of the strange old man.

Larger animals, like the Bemothra he rode, suited him better. Although Soho was more than capable of walking, hopping, running, jumping, or whatever kind of movement he wanted, Arella seemed to think he needed to be babied and Soho ate up her attention. She might even shed a tear when she had to let him go.

The trail leveled out and he lost sight of the pyramid in the midst of all the vegetation that surrounded them. Birds sang and squawked at each other, which meant they were alone, so far. Jorken should be at least one full sun-cycle behind. It was Zotar's men he watched for since they meant business.

Rich, green foliage nearly covered the trodden path they followed toward their destination. The pathway widened, but the palmus leaves lying across the middle indicated a trap. He held up his hand and halted his mount.

"What's wrong?"

"Not sure. Stay where you are." He carefully walked toward the leaves, reigns in hand. His right foot found a deep hole hidden beneath the large leaves. He pulled them back and straightened quickly. Snaketors filled the bottom, poisonous snaketors.

"Well?"

"A pit of snaketors big enough for both of us and our Bemothras. Follow me around. You can stay mounted, I'll walk." He turned and started forging a path around the trail. Potential dangers lurked in dense foliage and under plant debris, and if Zotar's men were good, they'd anticipate the detour route and lay another trap.

Luckily there were no more creatures, especially of the snaketor variety. Ever so slowly he led the way around the trap. Then he heard the sweet sound of water falling and headed straight for it. The animals were thirsty and he wanted to fill all canteens before they entered the pyramid.

Memories of dehydration and lying near death on the scorching sands of Nacrem's Crystal Desert were still too fresh. Thank the Gods for Arella. He owed her his life and he'd never forget it. The jungle opened a bit and he saw a large lagoon ahead. The area looked safe enough, so he continued to the natural pool, surveyed the surroundings, then gave the okay to Arella. When she pulled to a halt next to him he helped her dismount.

"This is beautiful." She knelt down and felt the water with her fingers. "It's warm enough for a swim."

She stood and stepped closer to him. "It's a wonderful idea if we had time." She nodded her compliance, but he detected disappointment in her expression. He wanted to kiss her, strip off her clothes, and take her in the water. It would not serve either of them to give his men an eyeful. Forgetting about surveillance was an often made mistake.

Instead he stepped past her and led their mounts and the mulus to the water's edge so they could drink. He removed the canteens and filled them for the last leg of this strange journey. It was time to be the warrior he was instead of the lover he wanted to be.

Life was not fair, a lesson he learned long ago. A man had to do what was required, no matter the sacrifice. The price was often high, but as long as the outcome was correct it was all worth it. Or so he'd been told.

He could only hope Zotar's death would not affect Arella in a negative manner. He had to secure Nodia and keep both women safe while he finished off Zotar. No easy task. Zotar was a worthy opponent and would not succumb easily. He felt Arella's hand on his back. Her touch warmed his soul and made him love her more each sun-cycle.

"Falcon, is something wrong?"

He stood and secured the tops of the water containers. "I'd be lying if I said no." She stared at him with a thousand questions written on her face, questions he had no answers for. "We can't afford mistakes. We'll be tested." He looked deeply into her beautiful lavender eyes. "Are you ready, my sweet?"

"I'm scared. I know I shouldn't be. I'm supposed to be a tough. . ."

"You *are* a tough warrior." He pulled her to him. "There's no shame in being scared. We tough guys don't admit it, but we have those feelings too."

"You? Falcon Rovarn, scared?"

"For you and Nodia. Not for myself." He stroked her hair. "DeJorelle Kari, I want to make slow, passionate love to you. I want to take away your fear. I want to give you pleasure."

Arella wiped her eyes. "You just want to make me cry."

He kissed her thoroughly, but ended it before he wanted to. He'd given his men enough of a show. "Feel better now?"

"I'm not sure about better, but I'm as ready as I'll ever be."

He hung the canteens on the pack mulus then walked to Arella's Bemothra and waited. She came to him, kissed him on the cheek, then quietly mounted with a little push from his hand on her bottom. Damn the woman for being so feminine and tempting.

With a groan he mounted and nudged his Bemothra forward. The tip of the pyramid towered above the distant trees like a giant monument to civilizations past. He traveled parallel to the path to avoid further traps.

No information about the interior layout was available, and that would impede progress. Since Syramis did not belong to The Protectorate, only a few trips had been made here to apprehend extremely dangerous, rogue criminals, so the charts were crude compared to all the others.

The foliage began to thin, and shards of bright light shone through the tree tops leaving rainbows on the broad leaves. It was beautiful and he smiled when he heard Arella's words of appreciation and Soho's squeaks behind him.

The terrain turned flat and the foliage gave way to sumptuous grass. The lawn lay in bright green contrast to the immense glass structure that stood sentinel in the center of the plateau.

"Falcon, it's absolutely fantastic!" She pulled to a stop next to him.

They both stared in awe in front of the breath-taking structure. "That it is."

"The lawn is perfectly manicured and the glass shines like it was just cleaned. That seems strange based on what we've heard."

"I agree." It was a mystery and he had no theory as to how everything looked perfectly tended.

"I expected the jungle to have overtaken it."

"I've heard a lot of things about pyramid power. Maybe the stories are true." He loved when she smiled at him the way she was at this moment. Without words her expression said she enjoyed his company, and he hoped it meant there would never be another man in her life except him. She was perfect. If they survived this mission he'd never be able to let go of his Nacrem Goddess. He smiled at her with all the love he felt. "But I'll hold judgment on pyramids and legends until we're safely back outside."

Arella laughed. "You're a born skeptic."

"After listening to Dacton and Talina's stories, I'm not a complete skeptic, but I require proof to become a believer."

"Don't be surprised when you experience strange things. Pyramid power can be all consuming whether you believe it or not."

Falcon dismounted, helped Arella down, then pulled Soho from his pouch and handed him to her. "You sound like Sadar." He stepped closer to the mulus and removed several packs. The requests he'd made to Dacton were stuffed into three packs. He handed the smallest one to Arella to put on, and set two on the ground.

"Wait here." To keep their arrival secret, he walked the animals into the nearby foliage and secured them. He removed the gear from the pack mulus and hid the supplies on the ground close by, covering them with large, dead leaves. He strapped on his sword and weapons belt, slipped a pack over each shoulder then hurried back to Arella.

"What about the other stuff?"

"We won't need camping gear." Out of habit he patted every one of his numerous pants, shirt and vest pockets. He double-checked for high priority small weapons and first aid supplies. Dacton had provided all the standard Protector's items for his belt, boots, and pockets, the rest he strapped to his arms and legs.

Arella put Soho down then took his outstretched hand. He gave a reassuring squeeze then pulled her toward him and kissed her on the forehead. "We'll be fine." He let go of her hand and tilted her chin up with his finger. "Your sister is alive, you'll see."

"I believe you." Arella adjusted her pack and secured the clasp across her chest. "Falcon, I just wanted to say. . .I'm sorry."

"For what?"

"For getting angry with you. It's scared, angry and frustrated I am."

He pulled her tightly against him and held her head to his chest, his other arm around her back. "I understand. You don't need to apologize."

She looked up at Falcon. "I do. You've been nothing but helpful and kind. Then I go off on you, get an attitude. . ."

"Arella, my sweet." He silenced her rant with his fingers. "This is your first real test and it's natural to be afraid of failure." He tucked several stray hairs behind her ear. "I'd be worried about you if your weren't, but remember to believe in yourself, and in me. Together we'll get through this."

"Promise me you'll save Nodia, even if it means sacrificing my life. Do it. Give me your word."

Her eyes welled with tears. He had to lie to swear to that, but she left him no choice. "I promise I'll do everything in my power to reunite you and your sister." He prayed he never had to make the choice between her and her sister, and he knew, as an experienced warrior, that decision may not be his to make.

She stared at him deep in thought and he knew she needed time to sort it out in her mind. Love versus duty was the most difficult decision anyone could make. Arella was practical and logical. He had confidence she'd understand what he'd said, and forgive him if he could not fulfill her request.

"Come on, warrior. Let's do this."

Arella walked quickly toward the entrance and he followed behind, a position he'd learned to favor. His gaze should be on the pyramid, but when her hips swayed so seductively he could not resist the sight.

Soho jumped around the entire area like an over-wound spring, but he kept his gaze on Arella. She stopped in front of an engraved stone close to the pyramid's wall, her expression fixed on the words. He looked over her shoulder, but it was not written in Universal. "What language is that?"

"It's Kartram, which is very close to Nacrem. It says we're forbidden to enter." She turned and looked into Falcon's eyes.

"I've yet to meet the man who can forbid me anything." He smiled, but his charm had no effect. "Read it to me, please Councilor."

Arella cleared her throat. "Those who enter must live in truth and integrity, all others will perish. The pyramid is alive and knows betrayal. Enter at your own peril. Survival rests solely on you."

She took a step back and fell into his arms. He gently turned her around and hugged her. Her heart raced and her breathing was rapid. "I'll take care of you, *DeJorelle Kari*, you know that."

"But it said. . .we'll die."

"Not if we live in truth and integrity. I have no problem with that, do you?" She shook her head, but he'd heard the fear in her voice. He'd run out of ways to convince her that everything would be fine. It was easy to deal with men, but working with a woman he cared deeply for was an entirely new experience. Uncharted territory always provided unexpected problems. With one finger he tilted her chin up and stared into her intriguing lavender eyes. "We will not die. We will find your sister. Do you trust me?"

"Do I have a choice?"

She smiled and his lips covered hers. If this kiss could talk it would tell her she was his heart's desire and that he'd never allow anything to hurt her ever again. She stirred him to the depth of his being, something he never dreamed would happen, not in this lifetime. Slowly he pulled back, knowing the end of this mission could not come fast enough. It was their future he wanted to concentrate on.

Soho jumped up between them, forcing them both to catch him together. "You're a real. . .."

"Remember Falcon, he understands you."

The word he wanted to use was pain. "A real cute, cuddly little guy." Soho squeaked and Arella smiled knowingly, but at least they were both happy.

"Let's finish this, warrior."

CHAPTER THIRTY-EIGHT

rella watched Falcon run his hands over the glass, looking for a way in. There was no visible door or seams in the glass. Considering the thickness she doubted they had anything strong enough to penetrate the structure.

"Maybe we should go in through the tunnel we saw on the other side."

"We can't, Zotar would instantly know we were here."

"You said it was his tunnel, but you can't be sure."

He gave her the look that said, 'think'. "I forget your people are watching." Damn him! Did he always have to be right? This did little for her confidence level. She stepped closer and placed her hands on the glass. Their hands touched and he slid his on top of hers. When he did that the glass began to vibrate and shake, then the entire side of the pyramid turned as if there were an invisible hinge at the top.

They stepped inside hand in hand, both of them in total awe of the structure, and the way they opened it to enter. Their boots echoed on the shiny black marbelus floor. Soho slid in, the slick floor carrying him to the far side before he spun to a stop. "Wow. I'm at a loss for words. It seems even bigger now that we're inside. And those statues are magnificent."

Falcon walked behind the art works. "I don't see a fuel source for this flame."

Arella stepped close to the eternal flame that burned between the male and female figures. The fire-bowl was glass, supported by a thin, glass rod with no visible fuel flowing through it. "Guess it's the beginning of all the weird stuff Sadar warned us about." He gave her his non-believer squint.

"Considering how long ago this was constructed, it's truly an engineering accomplishment. There are no visible supports, hinges, devices or anything to operate the wall that opened."

Falcon walked back around to Arella and stood by her side. She pointed to inlaid words in the floor. "Look. Queen Phedra was not happy with her life-mate."

"Father Weston said she turned Thoran and his lover to stone, and here they are." Falcon gestured toward the statues, then looked down. "What does it say?"

"Love is built on trust and exists on truth. Sacred vows of integrity and love are spoken. When truth and love no longer live in the heart, the sacred vows are broken. Punishment will reign down with vengeance. The innocent will be avenged. The guilty will pay for eternity."

"That's a long punishment."

"It appears cheating on Phedra was the last thing Thoran ever did." She pointed at the male statue and heard Falcon's deep groan.

"Do you really believe that's Thoran?"

Arella sighed loudly. "You're obviously not a romantic. But the good news is we don't have to believe anything. We just need to save Nodia and kill Zotar. So, now what?"

"We figure out how to go down into the pyramid. The only possible way is through the floor somehow."

She watched Falcon walk the perimeter of the room and joined him on his second lap. "The Marbelus tiles are solid, nothing is moving." Falcon kept walking, intently focusing on every step and square beneath his feet. This could take forever. She went back to the letters in the floor and knelt down.

With outstretched arms she traced the recessed letters with her fingers, feeling each one completely before moving to the next. When her right index finger completed the letter "T" in trust she heard a grinding sound. The floor began to move and she scooted back, half rolling away to keep from falling when four, large Marbelus slabs dropped down as one, then slid back under the others.

Strong arms slipped around her waist and she was lifted to her feet. "Thanks." They both leaned over to peer into the opening in the floor. Falcon flashed his light down the opening and moved in front of her. He paused and slipped a device over her finger that seemed like a ring, but it exuded light.

"Follow me."

When she took her first step down she was surprised to find an actual staircase with hand carved wooden rails on both sides. It sure beat the shaky ladder she expected. The surprise was the amount of steps and the vastness of the space in every direction.

One after another they continued down until she lost count of how many steps she'd taken. A strange flapping sounded behind her and approached at a rapid pace. Something brushed her head as it flew by. Then more creatures came directly at her and several hit her shoulders and back. She panicked and screamed. Falcon grabbed her and pulled her low on the steps.

"Stay down."

He stood, took something from his pocket, pulled a pin from the top of the object then tossed it into the air. Whatever it was slowly floated downward, leaving a smoky trail behind. "What is that?"

"A chemical deterrent for batwallers. There are two kinds, batwallers, and mega batwallers." He turned to face her. "Do I need to tell you which kind you don't want to run into?"

"They have beady eyes, sharp claws and strange webbed wings."

"They're ugly, but they shouldn't bother us for a while."

She felt a tickle behind her neck. When her hand reached back she found Soho nuzzling her. She patted his head then stood. "Let's go."

Falcon nodded, turned and took the lead. Their lights did not reflect off the solid stone walls, in fact they absorbed light. Her skin crawled with a feeling of foreboding. Was she afraid for Nodia? No, the source of her fear was Falcon. If anything happened to him she'd never find her sister.

This mission paralleled her relationship with Falcon, each step brought them closer. They depended on each other to complete the assignment, but her dependence went far deeper. Her biggest, unattainable goal had been met in Falcon. She'd found a man who respected her opinions and goals and loved her for who she was. A man like that she could not lose.

They finally reached the bottom of the staircase and now stood in the center of a main area with at least six tunnels leading in different directions. "Which way?"

Falcon scratched the back of his head. "I'm not sure."

Soho scampered from one opening to the next, running short distances in some, and not taking steps into others. Arella watched the comical animal until he started the procedure all over again. "Maybe he knows something we don't."

"It's possible. There're no maps of this place, so we're on our own."

"Soho." Arella braced herself when he ran toward her. Soho jumped into her arms as she predicted. "Okay, little guy. Which way should we go?" Soho hopped down and sprang into action. He carefully considered three tunnels, then sat down in the entrance of one. "I'll go with it. What do you think?"

"Why not." Falcon walked over to Soho, patted him on the head then entered the large opening.

She was surprised Falcon actually went with Soho's choice considering the way he felt about him. She followed the male pair for a few hundred feet then found herself on her knees, crawling through the tunnel. "I hope we don't have to do this very long."

"I wish you were in front of me."

"Why?"

Before Falcon could answer her question they emerged into a large, open space and were able to stand. The chamber had two tunnels leading out and one set of double doors. "What do you think?" Soho hopped over to the wooden doors and jumped up and down.

Falcon pushed the doors open and Arella gasped at the sight of glistening silver. Crates, boxes, shelves, stacks and piles of silver. "I'd say we found the treasure."

"At least some of it." Falcon walked into the separate section.

"It's strange that everything is silver. You'd think there would be different kinds of treasure."

"There's probably a separate room for every metal. Seems Queen Phedra was organized and particular."

Falcon held up a skimpy silver halter type top that most likely exposed more than it covered. He wiggled it with that *come on* look on his face. "Get serious." Soho joined the game by putting several heavy silver chains around his neck. She had to laugh when a chain got hung up on one of his floppy ears and it ended up across his nose and one eye.

After removing all the jewelry from Soho, she watched Falcon run his hands over the walls as if looking for a secret passage. She walked closer and stood beside him. "What are you looking for?"

"Wish I knew. Best I can tell these walls are solid black otonix."

Arella reached out and touched the dark structure. "We have very little otonix on Nacrem, but I agree." She looked him in the eye. "This has to be the most expensive room in the galaxy. It's a double find, the room and what's in it. No wonder every criminal wants to pillage this pyramid."

"It's hard to believe they haven't. Everything so far has been intact."

Soho bounced up to her, put a necklace over her head and it settled nicely over the top of her tunic. "You're bad."

"I'd say he's smart." Falcon reached out and fingered the circlet. "Leave it on, it makes your eyes sparkle."

"That would be stealing."

"I'm sure Phedra wouldn't mind. "Look at all this." Falcon waved his arm. "She'd never notice."

He stepped closer, pulled her to him and kissed her deep and hard. His love flowed into her, she felt his need, and craved his touch. She committed the feel of him to memory. He pulled back and took her face between his hands.

"I don't have the words to tell you how you look, but trust me, I like it."

"You've been using the word 'trust' a lot."

"True. But it's necessary."

A crashing noise behind them made them both turn abruptly. They both laughed at the sight of Soho sliding down a huge pile of silver coins and trinkets. The little guy landed on his rear when he hit the floor. He stood, ran over to her and jumped up into her arms. "We'd better go before he hurts himself." She removed the circlet and laid it on top of a pile to her left.

She put Soho down and followed Falcon back into the main

area. He secured the doors to the silver room then headed to the tunnel on the left. Soho ran to the opening on the right. Falcon looked at her and they both shrugged their shoulders and followed Soho.

They walked and walked. The corridor zigzagged down a steep passageway that never seemed to end. She had no idea how much time had passed, but her leg muscles were not used to the downhill stress and were starting to cramp. She was about to ask Falcon for a short rest when they reached a crossroads. Another high-ceilinged open area with closed doors and open tunnels. "I feel like we just walked in a circle and now we're back where we started."

Falcon opened the door closest to them. She followed close behind when he stepped inside the room. Her jaw dropped when she saw more gold than her eyes could comprehend. Soho jumped all over the place and ventured into another play adventure with the precious metal find.

"At least rumors about hidden treasure have proved true."

"Let's hope all the rumors aren't true. I'd really like to get out of this place." When she glanced at Falcon he gave her a disapproving frown. "You know what I mean."

He nodded. "Let's find Zotar and Nodia so we can finish this game."

"What do you think my sister has to do with his plans?" She'd pondered that question many times, but no answers ever surfaced.

"Whatever part she plays you can bet it has to do with credits. Which means Zotar hasn't found the treasure yet. Why is beyond me. It was easy enough for us. However, we came in through the top, and Zotar is entering blind through an underground tunnel." Falcon wiped his forehead with the sleeve over his forearm. "Architectural diagrams don't exist, so Zotar had to guess where to enter. At least we're following a path." Falcon took her hand in his. "I have a good idea where we are."

"I hope your idea says we're down as far as we can go because I'm tired of this downhill trek." He bent his head and kissed her gently on the forehead, his touch tender and caring.

"Remember, if we jump to conclusions we'll be wrong."

He let go of her hand just in time for her to catch Soho when he jumped up into her arms. Falcon rescued her and grabbed the little guy. He took something from Soho's hand and held it out for her to see. A wave of shock vibrated through her and she shivered. "By the Gods!"

"I'd guess it's from one of those 'rumored' entrants who never left."

"Where did Soho find a human bone?" She watched Falcon take Soho from her arms and set him on the floor. He followed the little guy to the back of the room and around a tall pile of gold blocks and platters. She hurried to catch up, and when she did a loud gasp escaped her lips. There was a large mound of skulls and bones of all types spread before them. Not at all what she had expected.

Falcon squatted to examine the bones. He pushed them around until the floor became visible. She had no idea what he thought he'd find, but he appeared serious and deep in thought. Soho scampered past them and headed toward the front. She knelt next to Falcon. "Have a theory?"

"If I had to guess, I'd say these bones are several hundreds of annual-cycles old." He stood. "Not much help I know. None of it makes a lot of sense. I wish we could find better clues. Although treasure will not reveal where your sister is."

He stared at her. "Everything is so esoteric. Hints here and there. But I agree with you, all this gold has nothing to do with Nodia. Our," She paused and put her hands on his shoulders, "my mission is to find my sister, and you must find Zotar. Hopefully we'll find them together. "Let's go see what else we can find."

They walked back into the large open area and Falcon closed the big doors behind them. The gold room turned dark and foreboding, hiding mounds wealth that could do so much good for so many.

"Look." Falcon pointed to Soho. "Shall we follow him?"

"He's been right so far. I lost my sense of direction long ago in one of those zigzag tunnels."

"We're approximately three-thousand UMLs down, heading," he pulled a small device from his pocket, "northeast."

She wracked her brain to equate universal measurement lengths to what Nacrem used. The largest athletic field was approximately one hundred UML's which gave her a pretty good idea how deep underground they were. "Excellent, warrior. How far do we have to go?"

"I'm good, Councilor, but not that good." He dropped her hand

and adjusted his backpacks. "I'll let you know when we get there."

She loved the smile he gave her. He made her feel so loved and appreciated. For the first time in her life she felt truly important. He respected her, and she'd worked her entire life to achieve male respect.

Falcon headed for the opening Soho had taken. She reached for the strap to tighten her pack and a pain shot through her left shoulder area. She rubbed her arm and wondered why the implant would still hurt. Would Jorken be able to follow the signal down here? Falcon said most technology proved useless around the pyramid. She'd enjoy her reprieve and not give the slime-snake another thought.

Why did her arm hurt so much? She rubbed it for a few seconds then noticed that Falcon watched her every move. "Is something wrong?"

"Your arm pains you?"

She nodded. "I don't know why." She watched him step closer then stop directly in front of her. He had a strange look on his face, but she was not sure what the expression meant.

"We're supposed to operate in truth down here." He cupped her cheek with his hand. "I have a confession to make."

"So do I." She looked directly into his beautiful blue eyes. "I have a tracking device in my arm."

"Not anymore."

"What?"

"I removed it."

"Without telling me?"

"I gave you a chance to confide in me, but you did not, so I had to remedy the situation before that jerk killed you."

She exhaled. "Jerk is actually a nice description of Jorken."

"I wanted to kill him for hurting you."

"You're not angry at me for not telling you about the implant?"

"It would have been easier if you had, but no. I used your implant to lead Jorken astray." Falcon smiled. "He has no idea where we went."

"I wish I'd thought of that." She took his hand in hers. "I'm sorry. I should have trusted you all along. I was ordered to get that implant, and. . ." He put a finger to her lips.

"It's behind us. We should have total truth between us now. I think we both know each other's intentions."

"We do, and I trust you in a way I've never trusted anyone before."

"I'll take that as a compliment." He bent his head and pressed his lips to hers.

She melted into his kiss. He tasted good and felt even better. Her hand wandered up his arm and she marveled at the tight feel of his muscles. His strength was beyond any man she'd ever seen, yet he was so gentle. Her heart sang and she fought back tears of joy. Finally she'd found a man to love, a man who loved her.

Soho's distant cry echoed through the tunnel and Falcon pulled away from her. He literally ran toward the distress call and she followed close on his heels. He stopped abruptly and she ran into his back. "What's wrong?"

"Stay here. I'll take care of it."

From her vantage point she surveyed the entire area in front of them. In the vast open area a monolith rose nearly to the four-story tall ceiling which was located in the center of a small platform completely surrounded by a very deep and wide moat. Soho clung to the corner of the tall, four-sided structure, his entire body shaking in fear. He squealed again, his eyes wide with terror.

From the backside of the monolith a giant arachnid appeared and crawled over the top. The hairy, eight-legged creature was so big she actually saw teeth. She watched Falcon slip both packs from his back and pull out a fazer pistol. Before he could turn to fire the arachnid swung from the structure attached by a web cord.

The black, hairy thing landed on Falcon, wrapped its legs around him until she could no longer see him. Her heart raced so fast she thought she'd explode. She pulled the faze pistol Falcon gave her from her pack, aimed and fired. The black, hairy creature fell off of him and tried to wobble away, but its' hair was on fire and it floundered and fell into the moat. She rushed to the edge and watched a glowing ball grow faint as it fell deeper and deeper into the bottomless pit.

"Falcon." She rushed to his side. "Are you alright?"

"Pain. . .poison. . .in my pack. . ."

She knelt down, slipped an arm under his neck and lifted his head up. "What are you trying to say?" He winced and she knew it was bad. "What should I do?"

"Get it out."

His head rolled to the side and his eyes closed. He was barely breathing. It was up to her. She laid his head back down, her hands shaking badly. She opened his back pack, removed the silver blanket, spread it as best she could then pulled him onto it.

She rolled him over and gasped when she saw two large holes ripped in his tunic in the middle of his back. It dawned on her what he'd been trying to say before he passed out. The damned arachnid bit him and the poison had to be drained immediately or he'd die within hours.

She emptied Falcon's pack onto part of the silver cloth, picked up the first-aid pouch and removed disinfectant and a cutter. She grabbed the small scissors and cut out the back of his tunic because she did not dare allow him to move any more than necessary. The puncture wounds were extremely red and swollen. The veins around the area had begun to enlarge and turn red, which meant the poison was on the move.

She'd once heard Lara talk about this exact type of bite and knew what was necessary. In the kit she grabbed the sterile wipes and cleansed the area. With great concentration to keep her hand steady and her nerves under control, she made a vertical incision across both punctures. She laid a wipe over the area, put pressure on both sides of one wound and pushed. Poison erupted against the wipe. She did the same to the other wound, satisfied with the results.

Lara warned not to suck poison out by mouth because even the smallest amount ingested orally meant instant death. Inside Falcon's pack she found another first-aid kit. She sprayed the wounds, satisfied she'd done all she could. Even the swollen, red veins looked close to normal when she placed gauze over each open wound.

She wanted to roll him over, but he was better off not moving. His thick muscular frame, usually so full of life and strength was now heavy and lifeless. Tears fell and splashed on his back, but he did not move a muscle, which caused more tears to flow. She'd stayed strong when she had to, now she was falling apart.

Then she remembered the poison had to drain. He was heavy in his unconscious state, but she finally managed to roll him to his back. All she could do now was wait. Falcon's life hung in the balance. Was this a part of the battle between light and dark? She knew in her heart that was yet to come, but it did not lessen her fear of losing the one man she loved. She felt so alone and scared. What would she do if Falcon never woke up? That thought was too horrible to consider.

Soho. She turned to see him sitting a few feet behind her. "How did you get back over here?" The furry little guy hopped over to her and jumped into her arms. She settled down next to Falcon while Soho made himself at home on her lap.

"Well, my little friend, don't tell Falcon, but he was right again. I should have watched that vid." Soho looked up at her with his shiny, brown eyes. She stroked his hair, silently praying Falcon would recover.

She had no idea where she was or how to get out. As usual her body shook, but at least she'd been able to help Falcon before it set in. She reached into the backpack, pulled out another silver blanket and unfolded it. With one arm around Soho, she pulled the cover over Falcon then lay next to him.

Falcon was incapacitated, but she'd done all she could. She should get some sleep, yet that was the last thing on her mind. She took her ring-light off and set it next to her. No way did she want one of those arachnids sneaking up in the dark. Just in case, she set her fazer beside her. Soho stirred, then started to purr. She wished she could be that relaxed, but it was impossible with Falcon fighting for his life.

After several long, deep breaths, she whispered one last prayer. "Please, don't let my worst nightmare come true."

CHAPTER THIRTY-NINE

Falcon fought the stabbing pain in his back. He felt hot and weak. What happened? His eyes were closed, but he was afraid to open them. He'd dreamt Zotar was doing terrible things to Arella, and he was afraid if he opened his eyes it may not be a dream.

Hands pressed against his chest. Cool, soft skin gently caressed his, and he felt love seep into him. "Arella, I'm glad you're here." He wanted to say he was glad his dream woman was alive and well beside him. When he opened his eyes she looked confused. When he reached out to touch her pain shot through him. "What happened?"

"You don't remember being attacked by that hairy arachnid?"

"How long have I been out?" She placed a reassuring hand on each of his cheeks.

"Seems like an annual-cycle. But in reality it's been about," she dropped her hands and checked her left wrist, "one and a half sun-cycles."

"Damn." He sighed. "I can't believe I've wasted so much time." How could this have happened? He was aware of the possible dangers, yet he'd failed to see it coming.

"I know that look. Just be glad you're alive, warrior." She scooted around him and looked at his back. "I think it's safe to stop the bleeding now."

He pulled two cylinders out of the small bag right beside him and handed her the first one. "Spray this on the wound and hold it together for a couple of seconds." The spray felt cold and he jerked a little.

"Sorry. I didn't mean to hurt you."

"You didn't." He handed her the second vile. "Now use this." Even though he prepared for the frigid blast it still startled him.

"I'll get the bandages."

"No need. By the time we pack up, the wounds will be healed."

"That must be some good stuff."

"You know it is."

"Falcon, don't you think it's time to tell me what other dangers are lurking in the dark, waiting to annihilate us?"

He laughed at her exasperated expression. "You're the one who turned her back on the vid." He looked her in the eye. "Now you change your mind?"

"I've changed my mind about a lot of things."

With one finger he traced the outline of her jaw, then her lips. "Am I one of those things?" She kissed his finger then moved her lips to his.

"You know you are," she whispered.

Nothing could stop him from kissing her. His hands found her breasts and he savored the feel of her. Slowly he reached down, pulled up the bottom of her tunic then did the same with her undergarment. He broke the kiss long enough to free her from the unneeded garments. "This is how I like to see you."

This time, it was Arella who took his mouth and explored him with the same urgency he felt. He let her have her fill then started an assault of his own. She tasted good and he never wanted to let her go. If he could stop time it would be at this moment, holding her tight.

Arella pulled back and screamed.

"What?" He looked down and saw the agitating fur-ball. "That figures."

"He rubbed against me and his fur against my bare skin startled me." She looked down, grabbed her clothes and dressed.

"I suppose Soho's right. We need to get moving." Falcon pulled his only spare tunic from his pack and put it on. He stood, picked up both packs and slipped the straps over his shoulders. When he looked for Arella he saw her struggling with the covers. He walked to her, picked up the opposite end and helped her fold.

Arella stepped closer to Falcon with her ends of the silver blanket. "What do you call this?"

"Therma-cover. It's scientifically designed to adjust to your body temperature no matter what the weather."

"They're great, and light."

She took the blanket from him, finished the final folds and put it in the pack. Together they packed away the second even quicker. "*DeJorelle Kari.*" He reached out, took her hands in his and pulled her to him. "We make a great team."

Her beautiful lavender eyes filled with tears while she nodded. "What did I say to upset you?" She pulled away from him and slipped on her pack. Her tears still bothered him, but he had no idea what he'd said to upset her.

"Don't those packs hurt your back?"

"The pain is gone and in a few more hours it will be completely healed."

"I've heard about the new healing aids, but I've never actually used them before." She looked Falcon in the eye. "Is that spray why you don't have any scars?"

"Amazing, isn't it?" She shrugged her shoulders at him then led the way into the next tunnel.

"Are you sure?"

She glanced over her shoulder. "While you were out, I explored the other rooms and exits. This appears to be our best option."

He gladly followed her shapely form. The path wound back and forth several times, still in a downward direction. He couldn't help but wonder how far down this structure went, and where was Zotar? They had yet to see one sign of the man, which seemed impossible. Had they gone the wrong way?

The path widened, the ceiling elevated and it seemed like they were walking in a large room that never ended. There were stalactites and stalagmites in an array of colors that set the whole area aglow in a pink haze. Up ahead, water trickled down the cavern wall and fed a large pool. He thought he saw movement in the shadows close to the pond. It was possible they were getting close and Zotar had lookouts.

He put a hand on Arella's shoulder to stop her, then bent his head close to her ear. "Pull your fazer and be ready. I sense a trap. A human trap." She nodded and he took the lead. After a few more steps his suspicions were confirmed. He counted three men waiting behind the rocks at a narrower portion of the path.

Arella grabbed Falcon's arm and stopped him. "I see two men."

"There's one on the left and two on the right. When I point to the ground, I want you and Soho to run to the left and come up behind the man. Keep your fazer drawn and don't hesitate to use it. These are Zotar's men."

"I understand."

"What about your little buddy there?" He pointed to Soho who stood as tall as his short, little legs allowed. Falcon squatted to get as close to the fur-ball as possible. "Protect Arella for me." He patted him on the head then stood. "Let's go."

They walked forward a short distance then he pointed down and took off running to his right. He ducked behind a large rock and slipped off his packs. Both men on his side were leaning against a rock talking and had not noticed their presence. He circled behind them and came up close enough to hear their words.

"If I don't get my pay this sun-cycle, I'm outta here."

"Zotar's crazy, he is. Never seen a man who'd cut his own man's throat like that. I don't care what he does, I'm leaving."

"He'll kill us, ya know?"

"Maybe, but I'll take that chance."

The man pushed off the rock and stretched. "First we gotta find that man and his bitch."

The other man stepped forward. "I won't mind killing him right off, but I'm gonna enjoy 'er first."

Falcon cringed while both men grunted and laughed, each trying to outdo the other in a crude mating movement. That was more incentive than he needed. There were no more rocks between him and the men so he rushed toward them. They both aimed fazers at him so he dropped to the ground and rolled. Three shots missed him and sparked off the surrounding rocks. He aimed and fired. One man fell. Another bolt hit the ground beside him. He pulled the trigger on the second man and it was over. He walked closer to be sure they were dead and recognized them both from the Bartose Inn. Two more victims of Zotar.

From the other side of the cavern he heard a battle in progress.

Without another thought he ran toward the sounds coming from behind the distant rocks. He closed the distance in record time and when he turned the corner he was relieved to see Arella standing over the man she just shot, her finger still on the trigger, the weapon in her shaking hand.

He pulled her into his arms and took the weapon from her cold hand. Experience told him she'd never killed anyone before and was going into shock. "Are you all right?"

"Fine, I am. Dead he is."

She was upset. He usually found her nervous speech pattern cute and amusing, but not this time. Her entire body shook and she felt cold. A screeching sound caught his attention and he looked up to see Soho jumping up and down. The silly little fur-ball seemed to know his way around the place like he'd been inside before. He took her hand and headed in Soho's direction.

Arella walked as if she were dead. She had no emotion, and that was the worst thing for her. It was easier to recover when the deed was expressed rather than repressed.

~ ~ ~ ~

Zotar stopped pacing when he heard a knock on his door. "Enter."

"Sir, I uhh. . .uhh. . ."

"Spit it out you fool!"

"Saw it myself. That man we've been watching fer killed Trydon and Doyle, and the woman with him killed the new guy!"

"And how did you get away?" Zotar casually reached behind his back and wrapped his hand around the hilt of his cutter which he kept tucked in his belt for just such occasions.

"He never saw me, so I hurried back here to tell ya'bout it."

"Good work." He walked to his man and gave him a friendly slap on the back, then guided him to the door. "Good work." When the man turned toward him he placed his cutter under the left side of the man's jaw, pressed hard and followed the curve of his neck to the other side with the blade. At one point he pressed too hard and ran into bone, something he hated to do because it dulled his blade.

The man slumped to the ground and he kicked him with his foot to be sure. He'd have to drag the body himself since he had no one else to drop him down the ravine in the adjacent room. That little bottomless pit came in very convenient for getting rid of corpses, and he'd managed to create quite a few.

Every man he'd hired had turned out to be a complete idiot. If they didn't die for their stupidity they died because they demanded pay. The fools all thought he owed them something. They should be grateful to serve him. At least he'd reached the last of his incompetent employees. He was beginning to get bored killing them since they were all too easy—they didn't even put up a fight. Cowards, all of them!

Finally he had no more need for help, good reason to kill the last worker. He'd dug his last tunnel, and he certainly did not need anyone to protect him. He'd planned a very private murder party, and he knew exactly how it would go. Falcon would stroll into his sanctuary thinking he was in control, but the fool would be wrong. The same as he'd been his entire career! How the fool made Chief Protector he'd never know. Then again, The Protectorate was not known for making good decisions.

The remaining battle would be long and enjoyable, because he'd finally have the satisfaction of killing the youngest Rovarn. Once he took Falcon's life he'd move on to Dacton. Both bastards would pay for taking his sister from him. As for that bitch of a sister-in-law, he'd relish raping her. If Arella was as good as he anticipated, he might let her live so she could serve him. At least until he tired of her.

As for Nodia, well, he'd gladly cut her throat once he had his hands on Arella. Her only function here was to insure Arella's cooperation. Nodia had been nothing but a bore since the life-mating ceremony. She cried and complained and she was too stupid to talk with. He'd sacrificed a lot to get an upper hand with the government, and closer to Arella. It was always Arella he wanted, but he knew she'd turn him down. Forcing a woman never bothered him, in fact it added excitement to the entire situation.

The only constructive thing Nodia had done to date was produce Ducard. He'd never thought about having a child, but he rather liked the thought of training his son to take over his work. At least his son would appreciate everything he'd done to attain power and wealth.

It was time to make final preparations to welcome Falcon and Arella. Revenge was always sweet, and the more blood he drew, the more satisfaction he would have.

CHAPTER FORTY

Arella shivered even though she was wrapped in the magic silver blankets and Falcon held her close. How could she have killed a man? She'd been trained for it, but never believed herself capable. Yet when the man aimed and fired his weapon at her, she did not hesitate, she just shot him.

Falcon said nothing. He simply held her and allowed her to think without interference. To say he was perfect probably went too far, but he was close. He was the only man she'd ever met who gave her any emotional support. After having parents that were condescending and cold, it was easy to put Falcon on a pedestal. She and Nodia used to hide from their parents to avoid the ugly words that would be hurled at them, even when they'd done nothing.

To say her parents had a loveless life together would be an understatement. Their joining was political and economic, a recipe for perfect robots. Androids had more emotions than her parents, which still hurt down to her soul. It was sad that most life-matings were for political or economic reasons, when a love match seemed to be so much better. Everyone said love matches never lasted, which was why politics and credits determined everyone's life course.

She had not one memory of being held or cuddled as a child, neither did Nodia and she was raised by parents, yet not one word of encouragement or love was spoken in their home. She never wanted to pass that legacy to a child, which was the main reason she never wanted to life-mate or bring a child into the world.

Children deserved love, and on Nacrem that commodity was so scarce it was close to an extinct emotion. Whenever anything was forbidden long enough, it ceased to exist. She hated that she'd been raised that way, hated that was the mainstay of her government and a way of life for nearly everyone on Nacrem.

At the moment, she was not sure if there was anything about Nacrem that made her want to go back. That might be good since they'd probably kill her for not completing her mission. There was no way she could, or wanted to stop Falcon from ending Zotar's miserable life. Plus, the more she thought about it, the more she realized Zotar deserved Falcon's wrath.

For too long she'd believed Zotar was the façade he'd created for the Nacrem council. Deep inside she'd never trusted him, but she'd always thought that was because of the way men had treated her. Yet she instinctively knew there was something fundamentally wrong with the man, but for Nodia's sake, she'd ignored all the warning signs, and there were plenty.

It seemed to her that any nice things Zotar did for Nodia were forced, that he did not mean them, that it was against his very lifestyle. That man was the best at fake feelings, he was better than androids she'd seen once. As far as she knew Nodia loved the fantastic fake, but she'd seen some signs of disbelief, and when her sister looked at her husband there was a blank look where love used to be.

Falcon stroked her hair and rubbed her back. She should tell him she was fine now, but his attention was way too nice to stop. He may be Chief Protector and a Commander, but learning about his softer side was way too much fun to want to stop. His soft spots and tenderness would remain her secrets –forever.

"Arella." Falcon tilted her chin up. "Are you all right?"

"I've been better, but I'm not sure when that was." She rubbed her shoulder. "Thanks for understanding. Most men wouldn't."

"Men aren't as bad as you believe them to be."

"Don't be so sure, warrior."

"Do me a favor, Councilor. Don't judge me by all men."

"I couldn't if I tried. It wouldn't be fair." He looked at her strangely, as if she insulted him. "That's a compliment." He tried not to smile, but she saw the little muscles at the corner of his lips tugging. "You're no competition for Nacrem men and probably not for men from your planet either."

"I don't know what I've done to deserve such high praise, but I rather like it."

"You've given me what no other man ever has. And for that, I'll be forever grateful." She could not help laughing at his bewilderment. It was fun to tip him off balance. "You don't have to understand. I just wanted you to know I'm grateful."

"I thought you were upset for killing a man, yet you're giving me a compliment. You're right, I don't understand."

She cupped his cheek with the palm of her hand. "You need a puzzle to solve once in a while." Soho squeaked from the top of a distant rock then scampered away. He'd done that same thing before when he sensed she and Falcon wanted to be alone.

"As long as you're the prize, I'll be happy to solve it. Where should I start?"

"Right here." She pointed to her lips and he needed no further coaxing. His lips caressed hers, then he kissed her with more passion than ever before. It was as if he understood her needs because they were also his own. His arms wrapped around her and he held her so tightly it was hard to breathe, yet his sexual hunger was exactly what she needed.

Falcon eased his hold and his hands wandered to the bottom of her tunic. She found the bottom of his tunic and they both ended the kiss. She finished removing his shirt and he made quick work of her tunic and undergarment in one practiced motion. The sight of him caught her breath. It was impossible not to stare at his muscled chest and arms. His well-honed physique excited her beyond reasonable temptation and sent her straight into animal lust.

His gorgeous blue eyes focused straight on her breasts, and for the first time, she was comfortable letting him look. Her hands found the band of her pants and she slowly pushed them down, taking pleasure watching Falcon's eyes widen when she shed her remaining garments.

"You are so beautiful."

She leaned toward him and ran her hands up and down his bare chest, the curves and bulges tightening beneath her touch. "You're beautiful too, my handsome warrior." He grabbed her around the waist and pulled her to him. She loved the feel of her skin against his. It felt naughty and oh so nice. His tongue teased and explored until she wanted to scream for mercy.

He laid her down on the thin blanket, but she didn't care how hard the ground was, as long as he made love to her here and now. She tried to push his pants down but he moved away, his mouth first kissing her neck and working his way to her breasts, down her stomach, not stopping until he reached her most private place. He gently nudged her legs apart and continued his assault. Start here

Never had she thought such intimacy would be enjoyable, but it was far better than she ever imagined and she found more pleasure each time. He moaned while he explored, and she knew as a woman she pleased him. Then his tongue found its mark and it was her voice she heard. The sensations he caused were too good for words.

Her fingers threaded through his hair and wanted to pull him up so she could kiss him. She wanted him inside her, now. He continued to pleasure her, brining her to the brink of fulfillment. Sensations built until she could no longer wait for him. Her stomach tingled and her muscles shuddered in ecstasy.

"I need you now, Falcon." The huskiness of her voice surprised her almost as much as the speed at which he managed to shed his boots and remaining clothes. He was over her in a flash, teasing to enter, building her anticipation to an almost painful need. Then he entered slowly, deliberately, showing her the finer arts of a master lover.

When he began to move her excitement soared to new heights. His breathing grew ragged and his movements quickened. She held on to him to stay grounded, and cherished every moment with the man she never wanted to let go. . .the man she loved.

~ ~ ~ ~

The long hike through the never-ending cave had taken its toll on Arella. She looked tired and pale so he slowed his pace and looked for a resting place. He was so close to confronting Zotar he felt it in every muscle of his body. The bastard would die this sun-cycle. Every innocent life taken would be avenged. Somehow Zotar's one miserable life could never atone for the thousands he destroyed, but it was the only insurance to keep more souls from dying by his hand.

Whether killing one man would be enough was not for him to judge. It was his sworn duty, and it might help mend the ache in his heart for Baleko, the brother he missed every sun-cycle. Zotar's death would do nothing to ease that pain. Time was the only antidote and even that was not enough.

Love, duty, heartache. Emotions had a way of intertwining, becoming inseparable. His life had been one battle after another, each with its own reward, but none compared to what was about to happen. This was personal. Winner takes all.

Out the corner of his eye he saw Soho hop from one rock to another until he was in the lead. The fur-ball now stood in the center of yet another large, open area at the foot of an obelisk, the likes of which he'd never seen.

Arella stopped next to Falcon. "What is that?"

"Another marker of some sort." He surveyed the area and saw no signs of life, human or otherwise. "It appears to have writing on it." He took Arella's hand and together they stepped up to the tall, monolithic pillar.

Arella took a deep breath. "Only the worthy have access, only the honorable have egress. The Honor Crystal destroys greed and rewards integrity. To venture deeper you must know your own soul, for one step past this stone and there is no turning back. Go with the Gods, for your life depends on their guidance and your judgment. Listen to your inner voice for it is "Them". If you do not hear "Them" you will be lost."

"Those are powerful words."

Arella wrapped her hands around his arm. He liked the feel of her hands on him and wished he had more time to show her his feelings.

"It's a dire warning." Arella looked into Falcon's eyes. "Do you think we're worthy?"

He stared into the depths of her lavender gaze. "*DeJorelle Kari*, we're most worthy. Believe it. Trust it."

"I trust you. I believe in you."

Falcon slipped his arm around her waist and pulled her to him and kissed her lips, savoring the taste and feel of her. She quivered in his arms. He deepened the kiss, never wanting to let her go. Here she was safe and loved.

A loud squeal made him pull back. Soho was throwing one of his impatient tantrums. "It seems your little friend has an urgency to move on."

"My little friend?" Arella laughed. "Our little friend. Sadar put both of us in charge, but I'm still not sure why."

"Right now, it doesn't matter." Falcon glanced in the direction Soho had gone, then back at Arella. "We need to keep track of him, so let's go."

Arella smiled while she headed toward the path Soho had taken. "Why does he seem to know what we don't?"

"Wish I knew." Falcon followed, silently amused by her correct observation of the silly fur-ball. Soho innately sensed where to go, as if he'd been in the pyramid before, which was highly unlikely, but considering Sadar, nothing was impossible. They followed the path around several large rocks and stalagmites. With each step the footing area grew smaller. There was a huge, empty pit in the center that forced them to hug the rock walls in a circular direction. The farther down they went the more an eerie feeling of impending doom crept through him.

Up ahead it appeared the path disappeared. The closer they got the more his suspicions were confirmed. Arella stopped and turned toward him.

"Now what? We know what's behind us, and there's nothing beside us but a giant hole with a tiny little center island barely big enough for one person to stand on."

"I don't know. Even Soho doesn't have an idea." The furry guy was sitting in front of a thick steel door with the biggest lock on it he'd ever seen. He removed his weapons pack and dug through it, looking for something to cut metal. "This might do it." He held up a powerful laser he'd used in similar situations.

"Take Soho back a bit, just in case." He waited for them to move a safe distance away before he fired at the thick metal lock. The heat of the blue-white beam sparked off the lock and the door. The weapon functioned normally, but had no effect. He fired again, concentrating on the thinnest part, waiting for the metal to melt away. Nothing. He pulled the trigger again and held it even longer this time, still nothing.

"What's wrong?"

He reached out and touched the metal and could not believe what he felt. "I should have burnt my fingers. The lock should have melted off, but it's ice cold."

Arella put Soho down and touched the lock. "You're right. Have anything else in your bag of tricks?"

Falcon held up the circular tube tool. "This has never failed me before." He reached out with his other hand and touched her hair, trailing his fingers down the length to where it lay on her shoulder. "It's the best weapon for the job." Squeaks from the ground beside them drew their attention.

Soho jumped up and down, squawking loudly and waving his short, little arms. "What?" Falcon squatted down next to the animal and focused his gaze and light where Soho was pointing. It looked like something was in the dirt close to one of the rocks on top of the small flat island area in the center of the deep, circular pit.

"Falcon, look!" Arella grabbed Falcon's arm. "It's a key!"

He pulled an eyepiece from his backpack and looked through it. The device magnified anything it was aimed at to perfect viewing size. "You're right." He let Arella look and her smile warmed his heart. She released his arm and he returned to his pack to locate his slide-line gun.

"What's that?"

"You'll see." He aimed at the center of the island and fired. In the air, the end of the small tube opened and a sharp, anchoring spike popped out and landed as it should. When he pulled the line tight it slipped off the rock it caught on and fell into the void below.

"What was supposed to happen?"

"The spike should have penetrated deep into the rock, anchoring the line so I could slide over using a grip, but it didn't hold."

"Let me guess, it never failed you before?"

He groaned, hating to admit to the irony of her words. The device held two shots so he tried again with the same result. Slowly he pulled the thin line back. This pyramid thing was annoying. He was used to real rules in real worlds. Dacton's stories about magical amulets and crystal links suddenly seemed all too familiar.

Soho started jumping then ran up and down the trail several times. "What is he doing?"

Arella shook her head. "I don't know."

Before he finished wrapping the line, Soho grabbed the end of it and ran. Falcon dropped the coiled line and held tight in case the crazy animal fell into the abyss. Soho took three huge hops up the trail, then leaped up the side wall and sprang off into the air. The fur-ball soared over the deep circular canyon, arms and legs flailing in a strange type of air-dance. If it was not happening in front of him he'd never believe a Wallato could fly.

His prayer was answered when Soho landed, fighting for balance on the edge of the tiny island. The little guy picked up the key and held it in the air. Arella clapped excitedly and he held tight to the line, anticipating Soho's next move. As expected, Soho jumped off, the key in one hand, the line in the other.

Falcon pulled the line as tight as he could before Soho hit the side of the crevasse in front of them. Soho used his legs as springboards several times, and with each bounce he was able to shorten the line and bring Soho closer to the top. Soho pushed off a final time and he was able to pull him to the path where Soho landed on his rear on top of Arella's foot.

Arella bent down and picked the animal up. "You're such a good boy." Soho handed the key to Falcon. "Has he earned his keep yet?"

"I believe he has." He patted the fur on top of Soho's head. "You really are incredible. Good job." Soho squeaked some kind of an answer then started purring. "I suppose Wallatos do make interesting pets."

"Useful pets." Arella put Soho down. "Now, let's see if that key opens the lock."

"Gladly." He slipped the key in the lock, relieved to hear the click of release. The mechanism sprung open in his hand and he removed it. When he pushed open the door, the sight before him made his jaw drop.

The chamber was well-lit and an immense alter toward the back of the large open area was highlighted. A wide, ornate staircase led to the top center area of the large, raised dais. Soho hopped in front of him and ran all the way up the staircase. The silly fur-ball sat in a throne-like seat and stared up at the centerpiece no one could miss.

"I don't believe my eyes." Arella walked to the steps and paused. "Is it safe?"

Falcon looked the room over. They appeared to be alone, and everything seemed as normal as it could this deep under an ancient pyramid, yet his gut warned something was amiss. "Be careful." He caught up with Arella and climbed the steps by her side. They both stopped at the top and stared in awe at the giant golden outstretched hand with an enormous crystal ball balanced in the center of the palm.

Arella reached out and touched the tip of one gold finger. "This is. . ."

"I agree." Words escaped him while he stood by Arella's side and stared at the testament to a lost civilization from Syramis' past. She looked at him intently and he felt as if they were silently sharing their deepest thoughts. "It does leave one speechless." He pulled her to him and kissed her gently on her forehead.

"You do have a way of explaining things, warrior."

Soho tugged on his pant leg. The silly fur-ball had the worst timing. He tried to shake him off, but he clung and tugged harder. It was then he realized they were no longer alone.

Falcon turned. Across the room in the center of the main floor stood the focus of his life, the purpose of his mission, the ultimate villain of the galaxy. He slipped the backpacks off his shoulders and mentally prepared himself.

"I've waited a long time for this, Falcon Rovarn." Zotar chuckled. "Do come closer. I want to see the look in your eyes when I kill you."

CHAPTER FORTY-ONE

Modark!" Arella's hand flew to her mouth. She could not believe her brother-in-law stood before her, dressed as eloquently as always in a fancy white shirt intricately embroidered in black around the neck and front opening, black pants and boots. The main difference now was the large sword in his right hand and a sharp, glistening cutter tucked in his belt.

"My dearest Arella. You may call me Zotar. I do believe the secret is out."

Evil laughter echoed off the cavern walls and her stomach turned at his insidious tone. "Where's Nodia?"

"Everything in it's time, my dear. Or should I call you whore? Surely you've slept with Falcon. His reputation does precede him. Or haven't you heard?" Zotar chuckled. "Personally, I never could see why any woman found him attractive, unless they just like his title of Chief Protector. Talina liked the title well enough." He glared at Arella. "How about you?"

"What have you done with Nodia?"

"Anything I like. She's my life-mate. But I'm thinking of trading her for you. How about it, Falcon? Want to trade for a while? I'm sure you're bored with this one. Not even her own countrymen find her appealing."

"You never tire of hearing yourself talk." Falcon pulled his sword and started down the steps.

"Going to challenge me for insulting the bitch?"

"I'm going to do more than challenge you."

Zotar stood his ground. "Think you can do what Dacton failed to do?"

"I don't think, I know."

"Of course. You're Mr. Chief Protector since Dacton lost that position."

"Say what you will, we both know the truth." Falcon slowly approached Zotar, sword in hand.

"Plan to kill me without rescuing Nodia first? Not very heroic of you." Zotar wrinkled his nose. "Exactly why you're overrated. Killing you will be an even greater pleasure than Baleko. I only tortured him for twelve sun-cycles. I think I'll take more time with you."

Arella's body began to shake and she struggled to maintain control. How could she have known Modark for three annual-cycles and never saw his true, evil Zotar persona? "Enough! I want my sister. Now!"

"Still the bossy little bitch you've always been." Zotar walked in a circle toward Falcon.

"Leave the women out of this, Zotar. It's me you want."

"Not even you are that damned important. This is about power and wealth, something you'll never understand. You've always lived a life of privilege. If it wasn't for your daddy, you and your brothers would never have reached such rank in The Protectorate."

"You've always thought cheating would get you ahead."

"Hasn't been too bad of a plan." Zotar waved his sword in circles over his head. "And once I get the treasure out of here, I'll have everything I need."

"You'll have everything except what really matters. But you're not smart enough to figure that out, are you?"

Arella watched Falcon descend the stairs and join Zotar in his circular pace. Both men held their swords tightly in hand, nearly touching, every muscle taut, their facial expressions intent and focused. She was about to fail her moment of truth. She could not stop Falcon as ordered, nor could she betray the man she'd come to love.

Every emotion she'd ever felt for both men battled in her mind. She pulled a fazer pistol from Falcon's backpack and started down the stairs. Damnation! Her professional conscience still yelled for her to shoot Falcon, but her decision had become simple. Nodia came first, then Falcon, and Zotar had created his own fate.

The loud clashing of metal made her heart race and beat heavily in her chest. Her fingers clasped the faze-pistol and her legs shook so bad she barely made it to the bottom of the staircase without falling. Metal struck metal and sparks flew, both men intent on drawing blood. She loved Falcon and could not bear it if anything happened to him. She needed to help Falcon so they could find her sister.

She raised the pistol and aimed toward the dueling men, placing the sight-dot on Zotar's chest. When she pulled the trigger both men lunged left and her shot missed its target. Zotar jumped back and Falcon's intense gaze bore into her.

The tip of Zotar's sword slashed through the fabric of Falcon's shirt and she saw blood on his left forearm. It was her fault for drawing his attention away from the fight. Falcon raised his sword and lunged toward Zotar, but instead of continuing the fight he froze then fell unconscious to the rock floor. Or was he dead?

Before she could raise her weapon Zotar rushed toward her and she landed hard on the rock floor. She fought with all her might, but he was too strong. He gained control of one arm, then the other and pain shot through her. He pulled a rope from his pocket and tied her hands

together behind her back.

"So, you thought you'd kill me? I've got news for you, you little whore. You're not woman enough, but I'll be the final judge of that soon enough." Zotar jerked Arella to her feet.

The rough rope dug into her skin and the burn radiated up her arm. He'd taken pleasure in tying it tighter than necessary. Zotar grabbed her upper arm and pulled her toward the staircase, then proceeded to go behind the tall podium. He pressed a gold medallion in the center of the rock wall and a panel slid to the side. He shoved her through the opening.

A scream escaped her lips and her heart lurched into her throat when she tumbled down several stairs. She rolled to a stop against a cold, stone wall then pushed to a sitting position. She squinted in an effort to focus in the dim light. Her jaw dropped when she saw Nodia, lying naked and unmoving on a bed across the room.

Nodia's hair appeared dirty and disheveled, and her face was badly bruised, scratched and pale.

Arella rocked to her knees, stood and rushed to her sister's side. A blanket lay in a heap on the floor at the foot of the bed. She stooped, groped behind her for a corner of the blanket. Finally she felt the blanket and managed to pull it up over her sister. While she fumbled to arrange the blanket better her hands brushed Nodia's cold leg. She turned toward her sister and tears rolled down her cheeks. Nodia looked so pale, and her breathing was so shallow she feared for her life. What had that bastard done to her? Damn him to Diabolus!

She sank to the floor beside the bed, unable to stop the flow of tears. Her sister lay close to death, and the love of her life lay unconscious because she stupidly thought she could save him. The High Council would be happy because she'd stopped Falcon. How could she have made such a mistake?

"Arella?"

She rose to her knees and faced her sister. "Nodia. Oh, Nodia."

"Modark is. . .evil. He wants to. . .to. . ."

"I know. What can I do to help you?" Arella leaned closer so she could hear her sister's bare whisper.

"Ducard. I don't know where he is. My precious little boy. He took him from me. How will I ever get him back?"

Arella wanted to smooth the hair away from Nodia's eyes, but she could only wiggle her fingers behind her back. "Falcon will get him back for you. I know he will."

"Who's Falcon?"

Nodia's bare whisper said she'd never comprehend anything in her present state. "Falcon is from The Protectorate. He'll stop Modark and find Ducard. I promise."

Nodia blinked heavily. "Why would he help me? He's. . .an enemy."

"Modark is our enemy." This was not the time to tell Nodia she'd actually life-mated the most heinous and wanted criminal in the galaxy.

"I hate him, he. . .."

Nodia fell unconscious. It was probably for the best. She needed to conserve her energy if she were to survive. Arella hung her head. She'd failed yet again. She'd failed her sister, her orders, and

Falcon.

Tears rolled down her cheeks. Nodia had to survive, but would Falcon live to forgive her?

~ ~ ~ ~

Falcon opened his eyes. He found himself tied to a chair in some type of bedroom. It did not seem possible, but there was expensive furniture, including a large fancy bed, complete with eloquent linens. He wiggled his fingers, at least with his mind, but there was no physical response.

May Zotar burn in Diabolus! Once again he found himself the victim of Zotar's paralyzing drug. This time it would be different. Doctor Dryko said his previous near lethal dose would cause his body to manufacture antibodies, and if he were ever dosed again it would not be as effective.

Where was Arella? With that thought the door flew open and Arella stumbled in as if she'd been pushed. Behind her was Zotar, a satisfied grin on his face. He tried to speak, but the drug was still too strong.

"Well, well, Mr. Chief Protector. What's the matter, frustrated because you're not in charge right now?"

Falcon cringed while Zotar chuckled in his triumphant, 'I-told-you-so' voice. All he wanted to do was silence the man forever. Instead he could only watch like a helpless child. Dacton had an experience just like this, and he prayed his would go better.

Zotar grabbed Arella around the waist and tossed her on the bed. "I believe it's time I showed this woman what it's like to have a real man." He looked at Falcon. "I'm sure you tried, but it appears your efforts were futile."

The evil man stared at him as if waiting for a replay, knowing good and well he could not speak.

"I think I may keep this one and get rid of her sister."

Zotar grabbed the neckline of Arella's tunic and jerked it down. The leather seams pulled apart and the top fell open, exposing her brief undergarment. Every muscle in his body screamed to move, but all he could do was watch Zotar trace the outline of Arella's cleavage with his finger while his rage grew. His stomach turned. Arella needed his protection, yet he was helpless. He would not stand for failure.

Zotar stopped his repulsive touching and stared at Arella's neck. He wrapped his hand around the crystal pendant, jerked the chain and pulled back. He triumphantly held it up in the air. The evil glint in his eyes said it all, he'd found something he desperately wanted.

"Give that back! Nodia gave it to me."

Arella lunged toward Zotar in an effort to grab the chain. Zotar backhanded her across the face so hard her head hit the heavy wood headboard before she slumped lifeless on the bed. Falcon strained to move his fingers and was encouraged by a slight movement. Soon he'd save Arella from Zotar's heinous intent.

"Now I will have it all!"

Falcon worked on the ties around his wrists, but stopped when Zotar walked over to him. The man held the pendant by the chain right in front of his face and slowly swung it back and forth. He wanted to curse Zotar, but he'd lose the element of surprise if Zotar became aware the drug was wearing off.

"This key will give me riches untold."

Arella stirred on the bed and managed to pull herself to a sitting position. "Leave him alone!"

Zotar turned his gaze to Arella. "You're more attractive unconscious." He turned his gaze back to Falcon. "And I might consider sharing it with your whore over there, if she treats me right."

"I'll never let you touch me! And to think I believed you loved my sister!"

Zotar chuckled. "I think I did. . .at least for one moon-cycle."

"You *are* a bastard."

"Oh, my dear sister-in-law. You're finally beginning to know me." Zotar returned to the bed, shoved Arella down flat, and then laid on top of her. "I plan to know you intimately."

Falcon's fingers worked faster, and he silently swore to kill the bastard here and now. For Arella, Nodia, Baleko, and every person who had the misfortune to suffer the wrath of his sinister, vile, heartless actions. His nails dug deeper into the rope while Zotar forced Arella to kiss him. She fought like a warrior, but was no match against his strength.

Zotar's physical condition matched his. They'd always been

formidable opponents, especially during training in the early days at the academy, before he was expelled for cheating. The galaxy could have benefited from Zotar's driving energy if he'd only used it for good.

The rope around his wrist fell to the floor. While Zotar continued his assault on Arella, he untied the ropes around his ankles then stood. Still a bit shaky, he managed one giant lunge at the bed. His hands found Zotar's throat. He squeezed hard and pulled him off Arella.

Zotar fought back as he knew he would. He wrestled Zotar to the floor and maintained his chokehold. His opponent applied pressure to all the prescribed pressure points, and he made every defensive move. Out of the corner of his eye he saw Arella slide off the bed and head toward the door. Once she went behind his head he lost sight of her, but at least she was out of the room and safe for the moment.

Cold steel grazed his neck and the warmth of his blood trickled over his skin. He freed his right arm and used the palm of his hand to shove Zotar's chin back far enough that he could roll him over and gain the advantage. He wrestled Zotar's cutter away from him, then Zotar scrambled to his feet and ran out the open doorway.

He'd thought about this battle many times, but this was not what he'd anticipated. He followed Zotar into the main area, but saw no one. Where had Arella gone? Zotar knew and he had to find them.

After a few steps, Zotar, Arella and Nodia appeared from behind the tall podium. Zotar held Arella on his right and Nodia on his left, his fingers digging into their forearms. He suspected Nodia would fall if Zotar let go. Arella looked scared, but Nodia appeared close to death. All warriors knew that look, the one a man had before he drew his last breath.

"So, Falcon. You want these women?" Zotar shoved Nodia in front of him and drew his sword. She staggered then fell to the floor. "This one is useless, and this one," he jerked Arella against his side, "still has a little life left in her. But, you may not want her after I'm finished with her."

Falcon spotted his sword a few feet away to his left. Since Zotar did not have a visible faze-pistol, he took the chance and rushed to grab his weapon. The moment the hilt was in his hand he spun around, ready for Zotar's attack.

"Now we're even, warrior. I've killed unarmed men, but with you it's different."

"You're no match for any Rovarn." His comment made Zotar push Arella away so he could swing his sword. They'd fought each other before, but only in training exercises.

Zotar waved his weapon in small circles over his head. "I proved one of the Rovarn brothers was no match for me. I so enjoyed my little game with Baleko. Too bad he only lasted twelve sun-cycles."

Falcon lunged at Zotar and sliced the shirt that covered his belly. "You're such a coward."

"Am I?" Zotar parried. "Dacton is the coward. He killed my sister, Julya, and he deserves to die for it."

"How many people do you plan to kill to make up for your own stupidity?" Falcon used his sword aggressively, but Zotar was a worthy opponent and deflected his moves.

"I had nothing to do with Julya's death!"

"Neither did Dacton. He reported your cheating to the Imperial Academy Headmaster, but Julya crashed her transport-craft into that mountain all on her own." Zotar thrust his sword at his chest several times, one strike made contact with his shoulder.

"It was because of Dacton she was upset. It's his fault she died that night."

Falcon jumped to the side to avoid a close swing of Zotar's blade. "Believe what you will. It's you who will pay this moon-cycle." Zotar came at him with renewed passion. It took all his expertise to ward off the attack. Sweat rolled down his forehead into his eyes and made them burn.

Swords clashed over and over. Zotar was unrelenting in his efforts, but the man would not win. Not this time. He had two women counting on his protection, and he would not let them down. The woman he loved, and her sister, would remain free from Zotar's wrath. Their safety was in his hands. With renewed energy he charged his nemesis, his purpose clear.

~ ~ ~ ~

Arella stroked Nodia's hair. Since her earlier words, Nodia had remained silent, and she had not opened her eyes. She was far too thin, and her skin was completely devoid of color. She checked Nodia's barely perceivable pulse again and knew it would not be much longer. How could she stop her sister from dying? Her medical training was limited, and so were their supplies.

The clanging of metal became more intense and she turned toward the dueling men. Her heart raced in her chest and she could not stop her body from shaking. She wanted to save Falcon, but the last time she tried she'd made matters worse. She eased Nodia's head off her lap then stood. There had to be something she could do.

Blood soaked Falcon's shirt. She saw a wound across his left forearm, but could only assume the other holes in his shirt were also serious wounds. Falcon's sword penetrated Zotar's right thigh and blood immediately covered his pants' leg. Zotar stumbled, but still managed a vicious attack that inflicted a nasty cut to Falcon's left calf.

Both men grabbed each other and struggled for supremacy. First one, then the other sword clanged against the stone floor moments before the two warriors fell as one, embroiled in the heat of battle. This was a fight to the death. She gasped when light flashed off the razor-sharp metal cutter in Zotar's hand while he pushed it closer and closer to Falcon's throat.

It was impossible to tell who had the upper hand when both men rolled over and over across the floor. Her heart raced out of control. She'd seen Falcon fight monsters in the wild and worried he'd get hurt, but this time she feared for Falcon's life. He'd always been bigger, stronger, smarter, but he'd met his match with Zotar.

Grunts and groans echoed in the high-ceilinged subterranean chamber. The eerie sounds sent cold shivers down her spine. Falcon's fist made swift contact with Zotar's jaw. They rolled away from her, their bodies entwined in vicious combat. She looked back toward the foot of the staircase and noticed a discarded faze-pistol. She rushed to it, picked it up and aimed. This time she would not fail.

Zotar was on top of Falcon. By the time the laser sight found the back of Zotar's head, he moved and it was now on Falcon's forehead. She stepped closer. The second the men rolled again she fired, the high pitch of the pistol resounded off the walls and made her ears ring. Both men fell limp and motionless.

Zotar fell to the side. Falcon rose to his knees, and Arella let out the breath she'd held. She rushed to Falcon's side. "Are you all right?" He smiled at her and her heart skipped a beat.

"I've been better."

She threw herself at him and kissed him so hard her own lips burned from the contact. He put his arms around her and held on as if their lives depended on his hold. He'd never tasted so good. Slowly he leaned back and ended the kiss. Gently he eased her aside then reached down to feel for Zotar's pulse.

"Well?"

"He's barely alive, and judging by that hole in his side, it shouldn't be long." Falcon rolled him over.

"Your cutter is imbedded in his stomach." She should feel remorse at the sight of her bloody brother-in-law, instead she felt relief.

"So it is." Falcon pulled his blood-soaked cutter free and slipped it into the sheath on his belt.

"Help my sister, Falcon. Please." She rushed back to Nodia's unmoving body and knelt beside her. Falcon raced up the podium steps, picked up the three back-packs and hurried back to her. He dropped the packs between them and rifled through the bags, removing certain items from each.

She watched intently while he pulled out a syringe, filled it with something from a vial, then injected it into Nodia's chest. He looked at her with an expression she'd never seen before, and doubted she wanted to see again. "What did you give her?"

"We call it IC." Falcon stroked the side of her cheek with his hand. "It stands for instant cure."

"Does it work every time? Or are you saying she'll either wake up or die?" Repressed tears spilled when Falcon nodded. She stared at her still, ashen sister. Why did she have the

feeling that Falcon just killed her sister? She'd never heard of instant cure, and Nacrem had always been a leader in technology.

Falcon picked up Nodia's hand and pressed his fingers to the inside of her wrist. He stared at her as if she were dead, and he was offering condolences. He removed his fingers and reached for her, but she brushed him away. "Will she make it?"

"She should have opened her eyes by now." Falcon stood. With the back of her hand she wiped her eyes. "Is she dead?"

"Not yet."

"Well do something!" Panic held her frozen in place. "Don't let her die, Falcon. Don't let her die!"

CHAPTER FORTY-TWO

Falcon leaned against the cavern wall behind Arella and slid down to a sitting position. From here he could not see Zotar, but the man was mortally wounded and could not escape. His own wounds needed attention, but he did not have the energy to tend to them.

Damn Zotar to Diabolus! Even in death the bastard managed to ruin lives. If Nodia died Arella would blame him. She'd come to her senses, but by the time she did, it might be too late for them. He loved Arella, without question, so he'd wait.

A scuffling noise behind the tall podium drew his attention. Before his mind could decipher the cause, Soho scurried toward him and did not stop until he was on his lap. He patted Soho's head and the little fur-ball reached out and hugged him as much as his short arms allowed. "Thanks little guy. I'm glad you're okay." He stroked his back a couple of times, then Soho scurried over to Arella and sat by her side.

He closed his eyes. Arella's tear-stained face filled his thoughts. She was so distraught she was nearly hysterical. The love she had for her sister was so deep she did not want to see the truth that lay before her. Nodia would die. He'd done all he could. The IC vaccine had saved untold numbers of Protectors, but he feared Nodia would not recover.

The only thing he could do now was offer Arella his

understanding and patience, both issues were his weakness. He opened his eyes to check on Arella, who still sobbed over her sister's lifeless body, but more quietly than before. She held Nodia's hand and Soho clung to her other arm.

At least Zotar was dead by now; however, to complete the mission he had to verify the fact. He pushed to his feet and his body screamed from so many places he could not tell which injury was the worst. He walked around the side of the dais that blocked his view.

When his gaze swept the open area his worst fear stabbed him in the gut. Zotar was gone. Damn the man! Then he saw the fool heading up the podium stairs in a pathetic struggle to reach the top platform where the giant gold hand with the huge crystal ball sat in wait.

"Zotar!" The bastard's insidious laughter echoed throughout the chamber and made his skin crawl.

Zotar reached the top, then turned slowly and straightened. "What's the matter, Falcon, shocked I'm still alive?"

"Nothing about you shocks me." Falcon pulled the faze-pistol he'd tucked in his belt. "No more games. It's over."

"Not until I see the treasure." Zotar stared down at Falcon. "I'll share it with you."

"You can't share what's not yours." Falcon turned when he heard Arella's gasp behind him. "Stay back. I can't afford you to get hurt."

"What are you going to do?"

"Finish this." Arella stared at him with so many emotions written on her face he could not guess how she felt at this moment. Did she have compassion for her brother-in-law? Or did those daggers in her eyes mean she wanted to do the job herself?

"You're right Falcon, he's a monster, and deserves to die."

"Now isn't that sweet? Even my dear, sister-in-law wants me dead." Zotar started to laugh, then coughed and spit blood on the floor. "I'm truly touched, my dear, that you care so deeply." He wiped his mouth with his sleeve. "Of course, the way you're bickering only proves you've slept with him. I can't wait for us to bicker."

Zotar wove back and forth, barely able to remain upright. Falcon watched him stagger away from the top of the stairs to the far side of the golden hand. He grabbed one of the fingers to keep himself from falling. Zotar was a walking dead man.

Arella rushed past him up the stairs. He followed on her heels. What was the crazy woman up to now? She stopped and stared at Zotar, then looked at him with a questioning gaze. A strange energy permeated the chamber and he felt it invade his body. It was not a bad feeling, it made him feel energized and powerful. He looked at Zotar and Arella and knew they were experiencing the same effect.

Then a soft mellow hum filled the air and he glanced at Arella, then Zotar. He visually searched the room for the source of the musical sound, unable to admit it came from the large crystal ball perched in the enormous gold hand.

Zotar reached into his pocket and Falcon pointed his pistol so the red dot from his laser-sight marked his enemy's forehead just above his nose and between his demonic, soulless eyes. He could drop Zotar for eternity with little effort, but curiosity stopped him.

"This," Zotar raised his arm and held Arella's crystal pendant in the air, "is the key to untold riches." He stepped closer to Falcon. "There's enough to keep both of us happy forever." Blood dripped from his abdomen and puddled on the ground. "Come on, Falcon. You know you want to be rich." Zotar grabbed his stomach with his hand.

Falcon watched blood ooze through Zotar's fingers. This moment had played out in his mind for more sun-cycles than he cared to count, but he never once thought he'd see the man look pathetic. The truly pitiful part was that Zotar would never find what was missing in his life.

"Do you really think I need untold credits to be rich?"

"What else is there?"

"You're the biggest fool I've ever met!" Arella reached out and slapped Zotar across the face, nearly knocking the man off his feet.

Falcon grabbed Arella and pulled her back. He bent his head and pressed his lips to her ear. "Just go with it. Follow my lead." She turned her head and looked deeply into his eyes. He knew the hatred and anger that burned within her because he'd spent a good part of his life in the same state of emotion.

The pendant in Zotar's right hand responded to the melodic hum of the giant round ball that grew louder and louder. Zotar lifted the necklace again, and when it was the same height as the ball, both crystals glowed so brightly he had to turn his gaze away the same as Arella and Zotar.

Arella grabbed Falcon's arm. "What's happening?"

"I don't know." Falcon looked behind them and found Soho jumping up and down, his hands covering his ears. "It's okay. You're fine." The fur-ball stopped his movement and stared at something behind their heads. He lifted his short, little arm and pointed.

"By the Gods!" Arella tightened her hold on Falcon.

"Well said." The huge crystal ball in the enormous golden hand hummed so loud it hurt his ears, and the intense light prevented him from looking in that direction. "You know all that mystical mumbo-jumbo Sadar babbled about?" Arella nodded, her mouth agape. "I think this is it." Arella's body shook against his, but he did not have time to calm her.

"I'm scared."

"Remember what Sadar said?"

"Not exactly."

"He said Evil is darkness, and you fight evil with light. The pyramid's warnings said evil would be destroyed; only truth would survive. Look at him, Arella. He's evil personified and hasn't spoken a word of truth in so long he can't remember."

"I can hear you both!" Zotar coughed and spit blood. "You can't believe all the insipid mumblings of priests, and the bitch that built this death trap."

"I'm sure those esoteric warnings don't apply to you, Zotar, the man most feared by the galaxy, the man who's above the law." Zotar snickered at his words and Arella's grip on him tightened.

"This," Zotar raised the crystal pendant, "is the key. *I* will unlock the riches." He staggered closer to the center of the four-foot high crystal in front of him. "It's mine, all mine. All I have to do is put this missing piece in its proper place and its mine!" Zotar turned and stared at Falcon. "You can't stop me, *Chief Protector*. You and your self-righteous brother can burn in Diabolus!"

Zotar's eyes were crazed, as if he'd completely lost his mind. Pain could push a man on the edge over the precipice of no return. He had the feeling Zotar's next move would prove to be suicidal. Zotar stared at him as if waiting for a reply. "I won't stop you."

The humming grew even louder, and the color of the large, round crystal turned a pale lavender color, and so did the pendant in Zotar's hand. Arella still held his arm as if her life depended on it, and she trembled so badly it was a wonder she remained on her feet.

They watched Zotar reach out slowly and place the diamond-shaped crystal pendant in a perfectly carved depression on the top of the sphere. When the two stones merged as one the room electrified. Sparks flew in all directions, bouncing off the otonix walls. A blinding explosion of light preceded even louder harmonious tones until all conscious thought was erased and all he could think about was this moment of truth. That feeling built in intensity and he felt peace and love course through his veins as if that were all that existed.

The podium began to shake and Arella lost her grip on his arm and fell to her knees. An electrifying current ripped through his body and it took every ounce of his remaining strength to stay on his feet. He squinted, and through the blinding light he saw Zotar turn into a glowing silhouette. He was literally on fire from the inside out, with a translucent appearance that made him look ethereal. The brilliance of the room mixed with the music and he watched the giant crystal turn dark purple. After a few moments, the purple globe slowly lightened and the musical tones softened.

Falcon helped Arella to her feet and held her close to him. She still trembled, but he also felt her strength. He tilted her chin up with his finger. "I believe it's over." She nodded. He took her hand and walked closer to Zotar's lifeless form.

Zotar's charred remains were a truly ugly sight. All of Zotar's skin had burned off, along with his clothes. What was left was so badly charred and melted that nothing was recognizable. Arella hid her face in his chest. If he had not just witnessed Zotar's death he'd never be able to identify the remains.

"Zotar's victims can finally rest in peace." He'd said the words, yet the whole situation felt surreal and anti-climactic. This was not the way he'd pictured Zotar's demise, yet it was fitting that the man's greed finally ended his miserable life.

Arella stared at Falcon. "What just happened?"

"Somewhere between Father Weston's words, Sadar's cryptic messages, and Phedra's warnings, we've just seen the ultimate battle of light."

She stepped back and turned toward Zotar's remains. "He deserved this. Too bad he can only die once."

"He died twice. The only thing that saved him was a dose of IC."

"How could it work for him and not for Nodia?" Arella shook her head. "I need to get back to her."

He watched her descend the stairs and return to her sister's side. All that was left was documentation. He pulled his palm-com from his pocket and shot an all-encompassing vid that would tell the story. He kept shooting while he backed down the stairs. When he reached the bottom he finished with shots of the lower level then slipped the device back in his pocket. Their trek inside the pyramid had been recorded by the snap-cam on his uniform, but he wanted insurance.

The ground beneath his feet began to shake and the entire cavern rumbled so loudly his ears rang. Rocks fell from the ceiling and tumbled from their resting places on the walls when cracks appeared. They were about to be buried alive.

The shaking continued, but he managed to get down the steps and back to Arella who held Soho in one arm and stroked her sister's forehead with her other hand. He knelt next to her and felt Nodia's neck for a pulse. If she had one it was unperceivable. The tall podium creaked and groaned and he feared the worst.

"Pick her up, Falcon. I know where we'll be safe."

They had to leave, but he could not carry Nodia out of the pyramid with all the shaking, but he could get her to a safer resting place. He picked up the unconscious woman and followed Arella behind the dais. She opened a door and went down some steep stairs and he descended behind her. When he reached the bottom he saw a bed and laid Nodia on it. Arella covered her sister then sat next to her.

Soho started screeching and jumping the way he always did when he was excited or scared. "Arella, we have to get out of here."

"I'm not leaving my sister."

Falcon pulled her to her feet. "I'm afraid you have to."

She jerked away from Falcon. "I will not leave her!"

Tears rolled down her cheeks. She looked at him, her eyes

glazed and unfocused. She was experiencing post traumatic shock, common for warriors, especially when they suffered a loss. She was oblivious to everything except her sister. "We must leave, now."

"My sister needs me." Arella wiped Nodia's forehead with her hand. She looked up at Falcon. "Why is she so cold?" Arella pulled the blanket over Nodia. "See if you can find me another blanket."

Arella was lost in grief. This was still a mission and he had a job to do. He picked her up, tossed her over his shoulder and headed up the stairs. She beat on his back with her fists and screamed at the top of her lungs. The pyramid continued to shake and groan and took on a life of its own.

At the top of the stairs, he dashed around the podium and headed for the door they came through when they entered. Pieces of black otonix stone rained down on them, each hit leaving its mark. He tried to protect Arella, but she was so preoccupied trying to stop him she did not notice the rocks hitting her.

Bolts of light bounced around the room. The giant crystal globe once again threw bright, white, blinding light everywhere. He was only steps from the door when a giant slab of stone fell on the path in front of him, completely blocking the only way out. A storm of smaller stones followed and he quickly turned and ran back toward Zotar's quarters.

Once inside he dropped Arella on the bed. She stayed where he put her, wiped tears from her eyes and gasped for breaths. He wanted to comfort her, instead he forced himself to ignore her and search for a way out. He ran his hands over the walls, and hoped against all odds there was a secret panel that led to a tunnel. Zotar always had an emergency exit and he was determined to find it.

Nothing. There were no hidden panels or doors. It made no sense. He pushed aside a storage chest along the far wall and flipped up a hand-woven carpet, but still found no way out. He glanced at the bed then stepped toward the foot-posts. With both his hands around the carved wooden foot-posts he pulled. It had to be the heaviest bed he'd ever encountered. He leaned back and gave it his all.

Four wood legs scraped loudly against the rock floor. It took immeasurable strength in his current condition to pull the bed several feet from where it originally sat. Arella sat up, her eyes wide, but she remained silent. He walked to the area behind the head of the bed and thanked the powers that be. There it was; a wood door in the rock floor. He reached down, grasped the handle and removed the cover. Below was a tunnel that could save their lives.

"Arella, get up." The shaking increased and he was afraid the tunnel might collapse before they got out.

"Not without Nodia and Soho."

He walked around the bed, went back into the main chamber and fought his way through the rubble to the room below the podium. The stairs had nearly disappeared, but he managed to make his way to Nodia. Even in the dull light she looked dead. He checked for signs of life but found none. He had a strange feeling about Nodia's condition.

Arella would never accept the news that her sister was dead. He wished he did not have to be the one to tell her, but he rose to his feet and climbed back up to the main room. When he stepped around what was left of the podium he found Soho limping toward him.

The little guy had blood on his forehead and wobbled instead of walked. He grabbed Soho and pulled him into his arms an instant before a crack appeared in the floor that was big enough to swallow the Wallato. He managed to get back inside the reinforced security of Zotar's quarters.

Arella sat on the bed with a vacant look on her face, her eyes blank and emotionless. In all the time they'd been together, never had she looked so defeated and empty. He thought she'd try to get back to her sister, but she had not moved a muscle.

He set Soho on the bed next to her and the little guy crawled onto her lap and hugged her, but she did not respond and that scared him to the bone. He'd witnessed warriors on the battlefield behave exactly like this. Only time could ease the emotional and mental strain of shock. She'd always shown compassion and concern for Soho, yet she did not even try to touch him or tend his wound.

"Arella." Soho squeaked and he could swear the little guy shed a tear. "Arella. We have to go. Now." He reached for her hand and took it into his. "Get up." She did not react to his words or his touch. He let go of her and picked up Soho. "I need you to stay up with me. I'm going to have to carry Arella, so I can't carry you. Okay?"

Soho gave him a nod. He put the little guy down on the floor and pulled Arella to the side of the bed. He leaned down, situated her over his left shoulder, then straightened. The room shook more violently and Zotar's private domain began to crumble.

Falcon eased down the stairs, paused while Soho scooted by and jumped to the floor, then he pulled the door closed behind him in hopes it might help. Luckily the tunnel was lit and the space was high enough for him to comfortably stand and carry Arella. Rocks littered the path and the smell of earth filled the air with fine dust that continued to fall with each rumble of the mountain.

Arella was awake, but hung like a lifeless doll. She lost her will in that chamber and he feared he'd lost her. She'd made him promise to choose Nodia over her, but there'd been no choice. He feared she'd never forgive him for leaving Nodia behind because he knew how he'd feel if it were Dacton.

Arella had stolen a part of him that would be hers for eternity. Losing his heart to a woman was something he claimed would never happen. Now he had to hope that she'd forgive him and understand the choice he made. At least Nodia would be the last life Zotar would ever take.

Forgiveness was difficult, he knew the struggle well. Could he convince Arella that he loved her with all his heart? She could be stubborn, a trait that was a blessing and a curse. He cherished her, and that included every aspect of her. He had to reach her and convince her he'd made the right choice because he refused to spend his life without her.

The straight path continued uphill. Soho squawked while he walked ahead, constantly looking back. "Lead the way. We're coming." The furry little guy seemed reassured and hopped ahead even faster than before. He glanced down at his leg, glad the bleeding had slowed, but he pushed through his pain by employing techniques all warriors used when they needed to continue despite their physical wounds.

If this were indeed the way out, was he headed for freedom or a new kind of torture? Life without the woman he loved would be the worst future he could imagine.

~ ~ ~ ~

Arella opened her eyes and immediately squinted at the bright light. Her head felt like it was splitting open and her heart hurt so bad she thought she'd die, but it was Nodia who was dead. Her life would never be the same. She closed her eyes. How could she face the future without her sister?

"Arella?"

She heard a man's voice, but it was not Falcon.

"Arella? I saw you open your eyes. Open them again, please."

She remembered the voice. "Dr. Dryko. Where am I?" She opened her eyes and found the doctor smiling at her.

"Glad to see you back, my dear. You're in the med-unit on Falcon's command ship. From what I hear, you've had a rough time. But you and Falcon are alive and Zotar is dead. The mission was completed. You're both to be congratulated."

"I'm sorry doctor, but it does not feel like a success."

The doctor pushed the exam light away from Arella. "Please accept my condolences on the loss of your sister."

Tears welled in her eyes and memories flooded her consciousness. "Thank you. I assume Falcon told you what happened."

"He did, and he feels terrible about your loss."

"I'm sure he does." He probably did, but at the moment it brought no consolation. Her sister was alone, deep underground, abandoned with no one to even say a prayer over her passing.

"You don't sound convinced."

The doctor read her too well. "Where are we headed?"

"We're taking you home. We should be docking soon."

"Has the High Council been informed?"

"Yes, and they're anxious to welcome you."

Kill her would be closer to the truth. She'd failed miserably and there was no way to deny it. Jorken was sure to be there to add his version of events. Finally Nacrem would be rid of their first woman Counselor, and this mission would prove, without a doubt, that a woman could not handle the job. They knew they'd asked the impossible, and they knew she'd fail.

"Are you in any pain?"

"No." She looked into the doctor's eyes. "How is Falcon?"

"He sustained four serious and several minor wounds. He's lost a lot of blood and he's very weak and dehydrated. Carrying you the distance he did took a lot out of him. I've put him in a HSC chamber."

"A what?"

"A hyper-sleep chamber. It's a pressure-sealed tube that speeds recovery through induced sleep and medication."

A twinge of guilt coursed through her. She'd been so concerned over Nodia that she'd not even thought about Falcon's injuries. He'd been covered in blood, but she'd thought most of it was Zotar's. Her heart nearly stopped when Zotar's sword drew Falcon's blood. She loved Falcon beyond words.

As much as she loved him, he'd betrayed her. She'd begged him to choose Nodia over her, yet he carried *her* to safety, not Nodia, and that was unforgivable. It mattered not because soon she'd be back on Nacrem and Falcon would return to The Protectorate, never to be seen again.

"How long will he remain like that?"

"Based on his condition, at least four sun-cycles."

"May I see him?"

"Of course. Whenever you're up to it."

"Now is fine." She sat up, swung her legs off the exam table and stood. Everything felt okay, except for the dark hole in her heart.

"Follow me."

The doctor led the way out of the room, down three separate halls then into a sort of storage chamber for humans. He walked up to a glass wall, behind which were several empty clear tubes and one occupied. Falcon lay flat on his back, arms at his sides, his face straight up. She studied his profile and he looked amazing. His masculine features were perfect, from his gorgeous hair down to his toes. His magnificent body was visible, except for a covering over his abdomen and upper thigh area. She yearned to touch him, to love him, to hold him close. The hole in her heart stabbed her with renewed pain.

"Arella?"

She remembered that voice well. "Dacton." She turned and watched him walk toward her. "It's good to see you."

Dacton hugged Arella then held her at arms length. "It is I who am glad to see you. You'll never know the worry you and Falcon put us through."

"I know how you care for your brother." She looked deeply into Dacton's eyes, eyes that looked like Falcon's. Intense, tough and determined, yet filled with compassion that neither of them would acknowledge.

"I'm so sorry about Nodia." Dacton tilted Arella's chin up with his finger. "I mean that."

His gesture reminded her of the numerous times Falcon had done the same thing. She'd miss him more than she could bear to think about. "Thank you. I know you understand the bond between siblings."

"That I do. And I understand my little brother too." Dacton released Arella and took a step back. "He cares deeply for you, Arella. Before he was put in this chamber he made me swear to ask you something."

Dacton hesitated. He looked back and forth between her and Falcon several times. She liked Dacton and knew his relationship with Falcon was even closer than she was to Nodia since they'd been raised together. Tears burned her eyes, but she blinked them back. "I'm waiting, Dacton." He sighed deeply and she silently questioned his reluctance.

"The doctor had to sedate Falcon to get him into that tube. He refused to go in there until he spoke to you and knew you were safe. . .and well. At the time, we didn't know how long it would be before you came out of your. . .uhh. . ."

"Psychotic break?"

"I wouldn't have put it that way."

"It's the truth. And I'm not sure I'm 'out' of it, but I'm able to hold a conversation."

"Fair enough." Dacton scratched his head and leaned against the glass. "I debriefed Falcon before he went under, and it wasn't easy when his only concern was you. I've never seen him like that."

"Don't flatter me."

"It's not flattery, it's fact. Every man must find the one and only love of his life. I found Talina, and now Falcon has found you."

"We're not the same as you and Talina."

"I believe you are."

"It's not possible."

"Why not?"

"Falcon has his responsibilities and I have mine. We're from different worlds." Dacton smiled, then chuckled softly. She wanted to wipe that smirk off his face, but he was every bit the warrior and she was not stupid.

"He wanted me to ask you to go with him to his home instead of returning to Nacrem. He desperately wanted to ask you himself, but the doctor and I forced him into that tube before he lost the use of his left arm and leg."

That was the one request she'd not anticipated. Her heart was broken in half, and her sister's half was in control. She looked at Dacton who impatiently waited for a reply. "This is awkward." She knew he desperately wanted to plead Falcon's case, but he maintained silence. "I came to care deeply for your brother, but I begged him for a favor before we entered the pyramid." She looked Dacton in the eye. "He broke his promise to me, and I cannot forgive him."

"Come to The Protectorate with us. Discuss this with Falcon when your mind clears."

Arella shook her head. "It's my heart that's broken, not my mind." She looked away from Dacton's pleading gaze. "Tell Falcon I'm sorry."

"You need to tell him yourself, but I'll respect your decision."

Three soft consecutive chimes filled the chamber. "What's that?"

"We've reached the Nacrem docking port." Dacton walked to the door and stopped. "I wish you'd change your mind."

"I've enjoyed seeing you again. Please, tell Falcon good-by for me." Dacton looked so distressed it made her stomach sick. The man truly loved his brother, and so did she, but there could be no future for them. Falcon sealed his fate when he chose the wrong woman to save. She'd never trust him again.

~ ~ ~ ~

Arella sat outside the High Council Chambers. It had not taken long for her to reach her quarters, bathe, dress and answer the summons to appear before the council. This may be her last suncycle on Nacrem, or on any planet. She had no idea how deep the corruption went. Before she'd gone with Falcon she'd only suspected some members had been bought, now she knew.

A lot had changed the sun-cycle Zotar arrived, and nothing would ever be the same, including her. She left these chambers as a physical and emotional virgin. She'd surrendered her heart and soul to Falcon. There was nothing left. Whatever the High Council decided to do with her was fine, because she no longer cared. If she could not have Nodia and Falcon in her life it was not worth living.

Suicide was not an option. She'd never take the easy way out, but all the joy in life was gone. She'd wanted to be successful as the first woman Councilor, now she'd go down in shame, and she'd single-handedly ruined the chance for another woman to serve. She could not be a bigger failure if she tried. Even from the grave Zotar's destructive hand was wrapped tightly around her throat.

When Falcon first tried to convince her Zotar was evil she'd laughed at him, thinking him the biggest liar in the galaxy. Now she had no idea who was honest. There was no one she could turn to and no one to care about her, or the loss of Nodia. She did not even know where Ducard was, but assumed Zotar had moved him to another location. Her Nacrem sources said Ducard had been summoned by his father, but no one knew where he'd been taken.

If she survived, she could locate Ducard and raise him. At least she could teach him who his mother was and she protected him from his father's evil. She knew the little boy well enough to know he was a good child who had not yet been ruined by Zotar. Maybe her life would be spared so she could be useful to someone.

As for Falcon, he would always own her heart and soul. She wanted to blame him for Nodia's death, but deep down she knew Zotar had destroyed her. Nodia had no pulse or heartbeat, but she'd refused to believe her sister was gone. Falcon did what he had to do, but the thought of her sister's body, alone in that cavern would never give her peace. A man cleared his voice and she glanced up.

"Councilor Arella, the High Council is ready to receive you. Follow me."

She walked behind the page through the large, open doorway, a guard on each side. The page stopped in front of her and loudly announced her arrival. She took her place in the dreaded railed box in the center of the room. She'd often felt sympathy for those unlucky enough to be requested to 'report' to the High Council. Now it was her rear in the hot seat. She stepped up onto the small platform and gave the customary bow of respect to the High Council.

"Counselor Arella DeSillian. Was your mission successful?" Councilor Whitten asked.

"It was not. Zotar Alucard is dead." A collective gasp rang terror in her heart, but she held her head high. Now was not the time to show fear.

The doyen rubbed his chin. "Are you sure of this?"

"Without a doubt. He is dead. The same man known to all of you as Modark, is dead."

"How did he die?"

Arella swallowed hard. This would not be easy. "He was the victim of his own evil."

"You lie! He was murdered by Falcon Rovarn."

She took a deep breath and searched deep inside for the courage to do the right thing. They would not believe the truth, but she was about to let them have it. She'd lost her sister and the love of her life; she had nothing more to lose since her life was of no useful value.

"Our source has made his report, so be careful what you say."

"No disrespect to The Council, but neither you nor your source was there, so I don't know where your source got his information. And if your source is the lying woman-beater,

Jorken, I highly suggest no one believe a word he has to say."

The doyen opened his mouth to speak, but she held up her hand. "Please, if you allow me to finish, I'll answer all your questions."

"Continue."

"I have sacrificed much for this mission. My beloved sister, Nodia is Dead. Falcon Rovarn is returning to The Protectorate as we speak. According to the instructions from this High Council, I have failed my mission." Arella took a deep breath.

Before the mumblings grew louder she continued. "I don't know what the Council's plans are, or were, but joining forces with Zotar and protecting him was wrong. I realize

agreements were made for credits and power, however, no agreement with Zotar could ever be good for the population, which *is* why we're here."

Several council members nodded their heads and looked at their neighbor as she spoke. She could only hope some of them would be on her side and understand. "I was instructed to stop Falcon Rovarn from killing Zotar Alucard, also known as my brother-in-law, Modark. Falcon did not kill Zotar. Zotar died from his own greed, and I don't expect you to understand, but it was not Falcon's sword, knife, or fazer. When Zotar placed a special key into a unique security lock that protected the hidden wealth of Syramis, he was electrocuted."

Arella straightened her shoulders and tilted her head up a bit higher. "There was a warning from Queen Phedra that the Pyramid would destroy evil, and so it did. Zotar was a man determined to attain ultimate wealth and power, and he did not care what the cost to human life was as long as he attained his goal." Her nails dug deeper into the smooth wooden rail in front of her.

"As the first woman Councilor I'm well aware my presence here is not welcome. I know many of you hoped I would not return from my assignment. I'm quite sure, if honesty could be found, I was never meant to live through this ordeal, which offered all of you a simple solution." She fought back a wave of panic that coursed through her. It was time to settle this once and for all.

"As a Counselor I took an oath to do what is right for my planet and my people. I did that, whether any of you agree or not. Greed is ugly. It has no place on this Council's agenda. This Council has no right hiring assassins like Jorken." Arella looked around the room, happy to see many shocked faces. At least some of the council members still maintained integrity.

"Jorken also failed his assignment." Arella noted the faces that stared with anger. "I know Jorken was hired to 'keep me in line', and I knew he'd kill me if I did not cooperate." She took a long, deep breath.

"If this High Council wants to banish me from Nacrem, so be it. If it's my life you want, so be it. But I will _not_ apologize for my failure. Zotar was a murderer of the worst kind. He's killed far too many people in the name of greed and pure evil. And if this Council supports enemies like that, then I refuse to be a member." She tipped her head down and remained silent. There was not much more she could say. She'd already sealed her fate.

Whitten stood. "Councilor, please explain why you removed the tracking implant from your arm."

She felt all the blood drain from her face and tried not to show any feelings to the Councilors who watched her every move. Her mind whirled. No matter what she told the council it would not sound right. Whether Falcon took it out, or whether she did, the result was the same and she did not want them blaming Falcon. "I sustained a large cut on my arm during a fall. I must have lost it then."

"That will be investigated further." Whitten shook his head. "We will not take your life. You will be banished from Nacrem for the rest of your natural life."

"Wait!"

Whitten turned his head to address the objection. "How dare you interrupt me!"

Arella's mouth dropped open when several Counselors stood with Counselor Paropen, the man who dared gainsay Whitten. A few more men rose to their feet. Soon over three-fourths of the members were standing. Then Paropen walked from his seat to the center dais where Whitten remained.

"The leadership of this Council has failed, and I, Senior Counselor Paropen, am assuming the role of doyen until an investigation can be made and a special election held." He turned toward Arella. "Counselor Arella, you have done your planet proud. You did not fail." Paropen looked Whitten in the eye. "You were sent to fail, but let me be the first to congratulate you on having more courage than any member here. You stood up to the corruption we all just watched."

Paropen walked around the table and stepped off the dais. He stood in front of Arella. "Let me welcome you back to Nacrem, and I insist you take your seat on this council as an honored member who holds duty and honesty close to her heart." He glanced at the guards. "Arrest Whitten and the council members with him. Now."

Arella watched while Whitten and several councilmen were escorted from the room. She then took Paropen's outstretched hand and he led her to her seat. She'd anticipated several different responses, but this blessing seemed like it came from another galaxy. The remaining members stood and gave her an ovation that lasted long enough for her face to burn in embarrassment.

Councilman Paropen motioned for everyone to be seated. "I call this meeting to order and we shall discuss pending business. First, we shall vote on the offer from The Protectorate."

CHAPTER FORTY-THREE

Falcon paced in front of his brother's desk and glanced at the hour display for the twentieth time. The wait had his nerves on end. He'd not seen Arella since he carried her aboard the surveillance ship. He still cursed his brother and Dr. Dryko for drugging him to get him in "the tube".

Thank the Gods two other Protectorate ships were standing by so a rescue crew could be launched immediately to retrieve Nodia. At first he thought it was his hand-drawn map that enabled them to locate Nodia, but he'd sent Soho with his men, and they said he led them directly to her without missing a beat. The little fur-ball even warned them of every pitfall along the path. Soho had turned out to be a blessing in disguise, and thankfully, Nodia would not go down in history as Zotar's last victim.

At least Zotar had been predictable in his perversions. Next to swords and cutters, drugs were his weapon of choice. He still wondered if he should have voiced his suspicions to Arella, but it would have been worse to give her false hope. Nodia was pronounced fit last moon-cycle after her time in "the tube", and that's all that mattered.

Arella and her entourage were due to arrive any moment, but he did not know if she'd agree to see him. She was furious with him, and even when he presented her with Nodia he doubted she'd forgive him. Maybe there was not enough trust in their relationship to move forward. His heart felt heavy, and. . ."

"Falcon! Sit down. You're wearing out my carpet with all that pacing."

"You don't understand."

"Oh, but I do." Dacton stood and walked around the desk. "Have you forgotten my story?" He grabbed Falcon's shoulders, guided him to a soft leather chair and pushed him down, then sat in the chair next to him. "When you do see her, don't forget humility."

"What?"

Dacton crossed his legs and took a deep breath. "I know you well, and humility is not your strong point."

Falcon frowned.

"Okay, maybe all the Rovarns have the same problem." Dacton shook his head. "I know you love her. Don't blow this. You'll never get another chance."

Falcon nodded and looked his brother in the eye. "It's up to her."

"True, but she's a woman."

"What's that supposed to mean?"

"You're used to bedding them and leaving them. Arella is different. You've never had a long-term relationship." Dacton held up his hand. "I know what you're thinking, but in this, I do have more experience than you."

Falcon waited for Dacton to continue his lecture, but he just stared. "Well?"

"When it comes to women, no man is an expert; but remember, no matter how tough you think they are, their hearts are fragile and their emotions run deep. Tread softly. Show compassion. Tell her you love her."

"That's not bad, brother." Falcon laughed and Dacton joined him. He'd learned a lot about relationships from watching Dacton and Talina, enough to know he spoke truth.

"You were able to save her sister. That should mean something." Dacton scratched his head. "How did you know Nodia had been drugged?"

"Need you ask?"

"I suppose not. It's hard to believe someone as careful and diabolical as Zotar would be so predictable."

"He was a coward and a sadist, so the only way he could easily torture his victims and prolong their agony was to paralyze them. He'd tormented Nodia before we arrived, and unfortunately her fragile state became enhanced by the drugs and made her life signs impossible to detect."

"But you also had a personal wizard waiting outside for you, and you had Soho."

"You still have your Atew, and you had some wizard-like help of your own." The intercom announced the arrival of the Nacrem Delegation and he rose from his chair and rushed out of the office. He ran all the way to the port reception area so he could see Arella step off the ship. He would at least be able to see her even if she wanted nothing to do with him.

The moment he reached the platform the ramp was lowered from the Nacrem ship and the delegation began to disembark. Arella walked front and center, her gaze straight ahead and unwavering. She sensed his presence because her hand shook slightly when she offered it in greeting to the executive Protectorate officer.

He stayed in the back, but followed the group to their lodgings and watched one member at a time enter their assigned quarters. Arella was the last to be shown a room. When her door opened she paused, but still looked straight ahead.

"Falcon, I need to speak with you."

He entered her room right behind her and the escort group went on their way. He inhaled deeply of the sweet scent that belonged only to her and aroused all his senses to full alert. She set her info-pack on the floor beside a chair, then took a seat. Finally her gaze found him and she'd never looked more beautiful. Her usually flowing hair was tied up with a fancy gold clip and all he could think of was freeing those sun-kissed locks and running his fingers through the silky strands. Her piercing lavender eyes looked inviting, but he could be reading something that was not there.

"Please, have a seat."

Her voice was music to his ears, but he did not want to sit, he wanted to pull her into his arms and kiss her senseless. Instead of following his heart's desire, he sat on the chair closest to hers, silently cursing the small table that separated them. Her body trembled and he knew this was difficult for her. She crossed her legs; unfortunately, they were well hidden behind the long pink skirt of her gown.

"I'm sure you know why I'm here."

Falcon nodded.

"I've been given the honor of heading negotiations between Nacrem and The Protectorate."

"May I ask what changed their minds?"

"When I returned, Zotar's actions were examined, as well as the Councilors and officials who dealt with him. That investigation resulted in the arrest of nine high-ranking Councilors, including Whitten." Arella tapped her nails on the arm of the chair. "Nacrem is essentially under new control."

"Speaking for myself and The Protectorate, congratulations. It will be our pleasure to welcome Nacrem to our league of planets."

"Thank you, however, I want to clarify any misunderstanding between us."

"I want the same thing, Arella." Her beautiful eyes misted with a sadness that broke his heart. He sensed her negativity rather than her exuberant, sexually charged energy that was so contagious.

"From here on, we are business associates. Nothing more."

"Is that what you truly want?" Her words struck more terror in his heart than any enemy he'd ever faced. He moved from his chair, knelt on the floor in front of her and took her hands in his. Slowly he lifted her fingers to his mouth and kissed them lightly. "I want you in my life. I *will* fight for you, Arella."

"I've seen you fight, warrior, but this is one battle you've already lost."

"Don't be too sure, Councilor."

Arella scooted to the edge of her seat. "Falcon, you betrayed my trust. I thought you were a man of honor." She pulled her hands from his.

"You're telling me I'm not a man of honor because I saved your life?"

"You left Nodia when you promised not to. Ducard will never know his mother. He's too young to remember her."

He reached up and with one finger wiped a tear from her cheek. "You're wrong,

DeJarelle Kari. I'd never betray you." Falcon's heart ached. He now realized if he were to have a future with Arella, she had to choose him of her own free will, not because Nodia was alive.

"How can you say that when you already have?"

Arella stood, stepped around him and walked to the window. She stared through the glass at the courtyard in an obvious effort to ignore him. He rose, walked up behind her and placed his hands on her shoulders. She stiffened under his touch. "I did not make that difficult choice lightly." He turned her around to face him. "I'd do anything for you, my sweet, you know that. I'd raise the dead if I could."

She looked at him with conflicted emotions painted on her face. He wanted to tell her Nodia was alive and well, but he needed her decision to be of pure intent, based on love, not gratitude. "Tell me you don't love me."

"You know I can't." Arella turned her back to Falcon and faced the window again. "I suppose I'll always have feelings for you, Falcon. But we have no future."

She might as well have run a sword through his heart. Pain gripped him deeply and he struggled for a breath. He'd thought he could reach her, that their love could overcome any obstacle. She'd made it clear he was wrong, because without trust they had nothing. "If that is your wish, Councilor, I'll respect your decision." He walked to the door, paused and looked back at her. "I have a gift I wanted to give you in person, but considering the circumstances, I'll send it to you."

"I do not want any gifts from you."

"You have no choice in this matter." He pressed the wall button and the door slid open. "Just so you know, I'd make the same decision again." Before she could say another word he left, the whoosh of the sliding door behind him made it final. She was too stubborn for her own good, one of the endearing traits that made him fall in love with her. It was over.

He should have maintained his reputation as the 'love them and leave them' rogue of legend. Instead, he'd given his heart and soul to the one and only woman he'd ever love, but could not have. Above all, he wanted her happiness, and she'd soon have it. His misery had just begun.

~ ~ ~ ~

Tears rolled unchecked down her cheeks. She'd hurt Falcon badly. "Damn!" She stood frozen in place while her only love walked out of sight, and her life. Losing Nodia had been the most intense emotional pain she'd ever suffered, but losing Falcon felt just as devastating. Her heart was truly empty.

Falcon made the only decision possible. He was a warrior, a leader, trained to take care of the living first, and if she'd been in her right mind, she'd have done the same. It was easier to blame him out of anger and grief than to admit that Nodia life-mated Zotar of her own free will and fell prey to his evil.

Truth be told, she could not blame Falcon for anything. All he'd done was love her like no one else ever had. He'd proven his loyalty countless times, yet she pushed him away. Why was it so hard to let go and be with him?

She wanted him, wanted his arms around her, wanted to make love to him, and most of all, she just wanted to be with him. He made her feel like a woman, gave her confidence and completed her in so many ways she never dreamed possible.

Surely he'd accept her apology, he had to. Her heart raced just thinking about all the ways they could make up for lost time. She could no more stop loving him than she could stop breathing. He was her life, and her future. He taught her that without love, life meant nothing.

Falcon was a good man, who deserved to be happy. Could she be the one woman in the universe who could accomplish that task? It was a tall order, but she wanted to spend the rest of her sun-cycles trying. She was a fool to doubt him, and an even bigger fool for letting him leave. She still could not believe that Falcon Rovarn loved her, Arella DeSillian, the woman no Nacrem man found attractive—but he did.

Her moment of weakness was over. She was a warrior and it was time to fight for the most important thing in her life. No matter what the future held for them, she owed him honesty. It was past time she thanked him for saving her life in more ways than one, and he deserved to know how much she appreciated him, needed him, and desired him. She'd throw herself on his mercy and. . .

The door chime sounded and she jumped. It was probably the gift Falcon insisted she accept. The chimes sounded repeatedly. Whoever was there seemed quite insistent. Since the door could work on verbal command she saw no reason to personally greet a delivery person. "Enter."

Arella heard someone enter, but continued to stare out the window. A sense of a familiar presence washed over her. Had Falcon changed his mind and come back? She turned slowly then gasped and her hand flew to cover her mouth. "By the gods! Nodia!"

She ran to her sister, threw her arms around her and held her close. She'd never let her go again. Tears of joy escaped her closed eyes while her heart sang with unleashed joy. Finally she eased back. She put her hands on Nodia's cheeks. Warm skin greeted her fingers. Nodia was real. "Am I dreaming?"

"No, my dear sister, I'm alive." She hugged Arella again then held her at arms length. "It's true. I've come back from the dead, so to speak."

Arella took Nodia's hand and led her to the couch where they both sat side-by side. "Tell me! How, who, when?"

Nodia chuckled. "Slow down so I can."

"I can't remember the last time I heard you laugh."

"I think it was my wedding day, right after the ceremony. Then my life-mate took everything from me. Slowly, sun-cycle by sun-cycle he robbed me of my life." Nodia bowed her head. "The only exception is Ducard."

"If I'd known I would have. . ."

"What? Killed him? I wanted to."

"We can discuss his evil for the rest of our lives, what I want to know is how did you manage to show up here, alive?"

"Falcon Rovarn is the most remarkable man I've ever met, and he talks about you constantly."

"What did he say?"

"Only how he loves you, how wonderful you are, how beautiful you are, and on and on. The man is a besotted fool. I hope you appreciate him. I know you'll find happiness together."

"I wish that were true."

Nodia leaned closer. "What do you mean?"

"I sent him away."

"He told me what you made him agree to, and I've never heard anything so ridiculous in my entire life! Sister! What were you thinking?"

"I was thinking about you."

Nodia turned Arella's hand palm up and traced a line. "If I were a fortune teller, I'd say, you have a long life, and you have found the perfect man to share it with." She let go. "But only if you come to your senses and throw yourself on his mercy."

"We'll discuss mercy as soon as you explain how you got here."

"There's a lot I don't remember. I woke up on a ship with your adorable furry little friend watching over me." Nodia smiled. "I love Soho, he's so cute and cuddly."

"Tell me how you got on a ship."

"Falcon had a hunch I was still alive, and before he went into 'the tube' he ordered a

rescue party to the *Pyramid of Power.*" Nodia shook her head. "I didn't even realize any time had passed. I had a vague memory of you sitting on my bed, then several men appeared and put me on a stretcher. Next thing I knew I found myself being released from 'the tube'.

"I woke up and saw the most handsome man on any planet, only to learn he was in love with you. He told me we met in the pyramid, but I don't remember, so he introduced himself and told me the unbelievable story of your mission together. He also knew what he promised you. It killed him to leave me behind, but I suspect it took everything he had to save your life considering the injuries he was treated for."

"How long were you awake down there, all alone?"

"According to my memory no time at all. But I was told it was less than half a sun-cycle. I was too weak and injured to stay conscious, even after they gave me that injection."

"Why wasn't I notified?"

"Falcon took full responsibility for that." Nodia squeezed Arella's hand. "No one knew if I'd live until I came out of 'the tube'. He was afraid that if you were told I was alive, and I didn't make it, you'd suffer losing me again. And I think that was wise. Besides, it was only late last moon-cycle that I was let out of that thing."

"That wasn't his decision to make. I should have been told. How could he let me think you were dead all that time!"

"Whoa. Don't be so judgmental. Falcon didn't want you to have false hope. They weren't sure I'd live, and he didn't want to put you through losing me twice. Hence the surprise."

"But still, he could have. . ."

"Stop and listen to yourself. You're being self-absorbed and ungrateful. What more could the man have done?"

Repressed tears of relief and regret mingled and poured from her eyes. Her sister hugged her and allowed her to release her frustration until she recovered her composure.

"That's better. Now, tell me, would knowing I was alive a few hours sooner made any difference?" Nodia leaned back and held Arella's shoulders at arms' length. "Arella, the doctor told me my chance of survival was close to zero. It's a true miracle I recovered, and I'm glad Falcon handled it the way he did."

"I've been out of my mind from the moment I thought I'd lost you. To say I've acted like a fool is putting it mildly. I'm thrilled that you've come back to me, but I've lost the one man I could ever love."

Nodia smiled. "Now we're getting somewhere." She patted Arella on the back. "I must say, Falcon is a very special man who possesses qualities any woman would fall for."

"Really? He's stubborn, arrogant, possessive, domineering, obnoxious, handsome. . .and the best lover on any planet."

"My, my. That's quite a list, and for your information, it matched his list about you very closely."

"I suppose I'm glad to hear that. But before I get sidetracked, you must tell me where Ducard is. I've been worried about him. Is he okay?"

"Everyone believes he's fine. He's being held at Zotar's stronghold on Illkaram. Falcon sent a ship to retrieve him before I even woke up." Nodia smiled. "I'm telling you, he's amazing, and if you weren't my sister, I'd be jealous."

"How did they learn he was there?"

"They're The Protectorate, that's what they do, Arella." Nodia shook her head. "You really do have trust issues."

Arella sighed loudly. "How do I fix this?"

"Go to him. Tell him how you feel. He loves you, I know he does. He'll forgive you."

"But will that be enough?"

Nodia stood. "Love is always enough. Come on, let's go find him."

"Are you up to it?" Arella stood and grabbed her sister's hand. Nodia chuckled. "I'm fine."

Arella rushed to the door, pulling her sister with her. "Then let's go!"

~ ~ ~ ~

Falcon sat on the sofa in his office, Soho in his lap purring while he petted his head. He'd become attached to the little guy more than he wanted to admit, but he held him now because it reminded him of Arella. He could not get the woman off his mind. Sadar had laughed at him when he tried to give Soho back to him before he left Syramis. Sadar insisted he needed the Wallato more than he did, and he'd been right.

Soon he'd leave on another assignment, and with luck he'd be gone a long time. Without a family at home, there was no limit on time away. He used to enjoy his freedom, now it felt lonely. How a man could go from being an avid bachelor to being dependent on one woman in such a short time amazed him. Everyone, including himself, assumed he'd be the last Protector to ever commit to a long-term relationship.

Maybe now that would be true. It would be Arella or he'd remain single. He set Soho on the cushion next to him, stood and began to pace. His assignment could not come fast enough. Space always calmed him. The voice com sounded and he listened to his assistant's voice announce a visitor. "Send him in." He'd expected his orders in a few sun-cycles and was pleased they may have arrived early.

Falcon froze in his steps when the door slid open and Arella's beautiful, tear-stained face greeted him. She rushed toward him, threw her arms around his waist and hugged him. He accepted her willingly and hugged her back. They stood silently and he relished the feel of her body next to his. He was hesitant to ask, but he had to know. Gently he eased her back, his hands on her shoulders. "Arella, why are you here?"

"Apologize, I am."

He wanted to laugh at her language slip, but knew it would be a mistake. It would be best if he remained silent and let her speak.

"Falcon, so sorry, am I." She lowered her gaze. "Trust you I did not. Blame you, I did." She looked up into his eyes. "Forgive me?"

"That depends." She stared at him, questions dancing in her eyes. He had to know what was in her heart. He wanted to believe her visit was out of love and not gratitude. Then again, how would he ever know for sure?

"On what?"

"On why you suddenly feel a need to talk to me." He took a step back. "You shut me out before. Tell me, why the change of heart?"

"My heart?" Arella shook her head. "I have been to Diabolus and back. I doubt I could have felt any worse than I have, but now, well. . ."

"You have your sister back, so you can go on with your life." He took a page from her book and turned his back on her. It was hard to look into her lavender eyes when he wanted her so badly. Restraint only went so far.

"You think I'm here only because you brought Nodia back to me?" She stepped around him to face him. "You're wrong, warrior."

"Am I?" She placed her hands on his forearms and gripped him tight, the heat of her skin against his felt like a mixture of sorrow and joy.

"You think you're always right, and I must admit you usually are, however, this time you're wrong. I came because I love you, and for no other reason."

"You came out of gratitude. I brought Nodia to you, and I understand how grateful you are." He pulled his arms back and she lost her grip on him. If he could not have her as his forever love, he did not want her attentions at all. "I accept your thanks. You can go back to Nacrem now and enjoy your life with your sister."

"Oh no you don't, you stubborn man." She stepped closer. "Tell me you don't love me."

"Using my own words against me?"

"Not against you. To make you think. To make you realize." She reached her hand out and cupped his cheek. "I love you, Falcon Rovarn. I not only gave you my body back in Waylent, I gave you my heart and soul."

He pulled her against his chest and held her tight. "I want to believe you. I really do, but. . ." Her fingertips silenced his lips.

"Trust." One word with so much meaning. His lips found hers

and he kissed her with all the passion he had. He'd missed her more that he thought possible. He deepened the kiss and enjoyed her softness, her taste, her perfume. Everything about her sent his senses reeling, and made every part of his body ready for her.

She pulled back and inhaled deeply. "If I'd have known how excited the word *trust* made you I'd have said it a long time ago."

"*DeJorelle Kari*. I do trust you."

"And I trust you." She smiled. "We now share a hard-earned trust that I'll never question again."

"Nor will I."

Soho jumped up and down on the sofa making his little screeching noise. The fur-ball even clapped his hands. The door whooshed open and Nodia stared at them with a huge grin on her face. Nodia rushed toward them and put her arms around them both.

"Can I assume we're all playing nice now?"

Arella laughed. "You can." she looked up at Falcon. "Right, warrior?"

"I always play nice."

"Well, I don't know how you two play, but you've both had me worried." Nodia looked at Falcon. "First I had to listen to you, then," she moved her gaze to Arella, "you. So I'm hoping you've made up?" She cleared her throat and stepped back. "Sorry I barged in; I couldn't wait any longer, the suspense was too much."

Falcon let go of Arella, guided her to the sofa, and gestured for Nodia to sit next to her sister. Falcon knelt on the floor in front of Arella. He took her hand in his. "I love you Arella. We've gone through much to be here, and I never want to be separated from you again. Arella DeSillian, I want you to be my life-mate."

"Did I hear you correctly? You, the playboy of the galaxy, ready to life-mate?" Arella laughed.

"What's so funny about that?"

"I've spent my entire life feeling unattractive to men, and you, above all, find me so appealing you wish to life-mate me." She slid forward and kissed him.

Falcon relished the taste of her, the feel of her. He treasured her. Arella was the woman he wanted in his bed for eternity, the woman who would challenge him and love him for the rest of his life.

Arella pulled back and looked into Falcon's eyes. "Forgive you, I do. Love you, I do. Life-mate you, I will."

ABOUT THE AUTHOR

Born in Michigan and raised in California, Kathleen moved to the beautiful Missouri Ozarks with her husband to raise cattle. She joined Ozark's Romance Authors to keep her sister-in-law company, never dreaming romance writing would become her passion. Once she found sci-fi romance she was hooked.

She lost her husband last year but still has her son and three fantastic grandchildren who keep her busy in Ozark, Missouri. She also has her dog, a Boxer named Ginger who keeps her on her toes. She loves to hear from her fans. You can reach her at: kgarnz@yahoo.com Kathleen Garnsey's other books are all available on Amazon.

OTHER PUBLICATIONS BY KATHLEEN

Available at amazon.com, barnesandnoble.com, booksamillion.com and other online retailers.

Warrior's Link
The Alluring Traveler
Hawk's Redemption
Secret of the Kiah

www.ingramcontent.com/pod-product-compliance
Lightning Source LLC
Chambersburg PA
CBHW061924170626
46813CB00006B/2293